I0819017

Take Me with You

ALSO BY STEVEN ROWLEY

The Dogs of Venice

The Guncle Abroad

The Celebrants

The Guncle

The Editor

Lily and the Octopus

Take Me with You

A Novel

STEVEN ROWLEY

G. P. PUTNAM'S SONS
NEW YORK

PUTNAM
— EST. 1838 —

G. P. Putnam's Sons
Publishers Since 1838
An imprint of Penguin Random House LLC
1745 Broadway, New York, NY 10019
penguinrandomhouse.com

Book design by Daniel Brount

Library of Congress Cataloging-in-Publication Data has been applied for.

Hardcover ISBN: 9780593851494
Ebook ISBN: 9780593851517

Printed in the United States of America
1st Printing

The authorized representative in the EU for product safety and compliance is Penguin Random House Ireland, Morrison Chambers, 32 Nassau Street, Dublin D02 YH68, Ireland, https://eu-contact.penguin.ie.

For Byron

I never thought I could act this way
And I've got to say that I just don't get it
I don't know where we went wrong
But the feeling's gone and I just can't get it back

—GORDON LIGHTFOOT, "IF YOU COULD READ MY MIND"

There are as many atoms in a single molecule of your DNA as there are stars in the typical galaxy. We are, each of us, a little universe.

—NEIL DEGRASSE TYSON

Take Me with You

Two men sit in the shade of a blue lifeguard tower staring out at the Pacific. They met only moments ago when they collided on the beach's bike path. They're under strict orders from the lifeguard to sit. Within the hour they will have sex.

The younger of the two, boyish, twenty-two maybe, sand stuck to his skin, smelling of sandalwood and sweat. He is tall, noticeably so, even sitting, and is just growing into his good looks; he wears athletic socks but no shoes. The older one, nearing thirty, sports bent sunglasses that sit below prominent eyebrows. There is sand in his hair (and some premature salt), which, thanks to the ocean breeze, is handsomely mussed. The taller man leans in and rests his head on the older man's shoulder. The older rests his cheek against the taller man's head.

"My aunt and uncle had a small cottage in Maine, and I would spend the summers with them near Blue Hill," the taller man says.

"Maine." The older man is impressed. "What's that like?"

Laughter. "Like this. There's an ocean, except over there." He points behind them. "My aunt would make us this soup called Chicken & Stars."

"Us?"

"My cousins and me," the taller man clarifies. "I forget how the soup was made, from a dry mix or a can. But the noodles were shaped like stars." He nervously fiddles with a discarded straw wrapper he finds in the sand, twisting it tightly around a finger that is long like his legs. "This is stupid," he groans, growing self-conscious. Newly out, he hasn't had much experience with men.

"No, no. This is good!" The older man sits up and removes his sunglasses; his dark eyes are kind.

The taller one continues reluctantly, his gaze focused on the paper wrapper in his hands. "After lunch, whatever soup we didn't eat would get poured down the drain because it wasn't much worth reheating. Only, the pipes under the sink were not connected to anything. It was an old cabin—we were lucky there was a proper toilet. Anyhow, the pipes, they just ran twenty or so feet from the house before emptying in a ditch filled with pine needles. My cousins and I, we would burst through the door and race alongside that pipe to see if we could beat the stars, racing faster and faster each time. And sure enough, one summer my legs had grown long enough, I got fast enough, and I reached the end of the pipe just as the last of the soup reappeared."

The older man is enthralled. He could only imagine how gangly the taller man, at least six foot five, must have been as a child.

"I would watch as star-shaped noodles made constellations in the mud and give them names I already knew, like Hercules and Orion. And one I called Billy for some reason. I don't know, I think I had a boyhood crush or some—" He cuts himself off and turns a deep shade of red. "*Oh god*," he moans before burying his face in his hands, the straw wrapper brushing his forehead. "I just now realized when you asked if I saw stars, you wanted to see if I had a concussion."

The older man reaches for the taller one's hands, taking them in his own and holding them until they each feel the perfect warmth of the other. The young man is uneasy at first, he's never held hands with a man so publicly. But only at first, as the lifeguard tower, then the gulls, then the kids flying a kite, then the entire beach falls away and they become the only two people on earth.

"This is much better," the older one says, genuinely impressed. "You raced the stars." The connection between them, a small atom when they collided, is now ignited by an unknowable heat, millions and billions of degrees, causing an explosion that will grow and expand the rest of their lives.

"I raced the stars and I *won*."

The lifeguard interrupts, his shorts red, the hair on his tanned legs blond, his build like a college water polo player. An hour ago both men would have stared agog, but now he doesn't exist. The lifeguard shields his eyes to examine the taller one's pupils. "I think we're good here. Just be careful out there on the bike path. And maybe invest in some helmets." He hands them each a bottle of ice-cold water and then he is gone, yelling at some kids with an inflatable raft.

The older man stands and extends his arm for the taking. He nods toward his bike and the tall stranger's Rollerblades, which lie abandoned nearby in the sand. "Are you coming?" he asks.

The taller one needs only a split second to answer. "Where you go, I go," he says as he grabs his new friend's arm and pulls himself up to full height, blocking the sun.

"Where you go, I go," the older man repeats with a devilish grin. "C'mon. I promise it will be an adventure."

JOSHUA TREE

Their eyes met in the mirror as they stood at their new bathroom sinks. This happened often when they were young, when there was only one sink to huddle over, and they would break into the kind of stupid grins you could have for a person before you were intimately acquainted, before you shared a mortgage account and multivitamins for men over fifty, a login for a finance tracking app for couples called Honeydue, and a crush on the same local waiter. Now, thirty years on, Norman was openly scraping his tongue with some kind of repellent tool their new dentist had given him.

"What?" Norman asked, and Jesse, towering over his husband, quickly replied it was nothing, even though every muscle in his face said that it was very much something.

To cover, Jesse scrambled for something to say that was not on the topic of oral hygiene. "The nighthawks haven't been around in a while." The nighthawks used to come in pairs to hunt insects that had been drawn by the landscaping lights. You could set your clock by their arrival, promptly at eight forty-five. "Sorry. That sounded like the opening line to a play. You know, by Tennessee Williams or William Inge." Jesse could picture it so clearly. A woman steps out onto her veranda at sunset and says, *The nighthawks haven't been around in a while.* And then she looks mournfully over the prairie, which of course is a set. One of those homesteader windmills, perhaps, and papier-mâché corn, a scrim lit to make the sky look just so.

Norman, however, was confused. "William Inge?"

Jesse grabbed two Advil from a large bottle. "Don't even."

Norman shrugged, perhaps assuming it was just one of those things Jesse was reading as he was preparing for his return to teaching. "Mating season is over," he said of the nighthawks.

Jesse laughed and pointed at his husband's dental tool. "You said a mouthful there."

Norman rinsed the tongue scraper under the faucet and traded it for his toothbrush. "It's supposed to improve my taste."

"Well, I think you have excellent taste," Jesse said, leaning over to give his husband a peck on the cheek. "But we should rethink these mirrors."

A flickering of the bathroom lights, then a jolt. Jesse grabbed the double vanity to steady himself. Norman, toothbrush in one hand, phone in the other, glanced up at his husband. Earthquakes were a way of life in the California desert; usually they were more often the rolling variety, not the kind that gave you a lurch.

"You okay?" Norman asked, and Jesse swayed his hips like he was standing on a surfboard. Norman flipped the light switch off and on again, and the flickering stopped. He mumbled something about calling their electrician. The wiring was new; they had only recently completed a total renovation. "They don't make things like they used to," he griped.

Jesse didn't make much of it. "Our wiring is old, and we still flicker."

"We bicker," Norman corrected. "I don't know about flicker."

Their Joshua Tree home, built in 1974 by two renowned architects, a husband and wife whose names Norman knew but Jesse could never remember, had been redesigned by Norman before they moved in. The real estate agent who sold them the house heralded the property as the perfect marriage of high design and ecotopian living; Jesse and Norman chuckled at the time, convinced that that perfectly described them as a couple even if, with a gun to their heads, neither could tell you what *ecotopian* meant. The house was cutting-edge when it was built, then dated, now somehow modern again with Norman's expansions and upgrades, as if the future that was being written had somewhere, somehow taken a turn.

Jesse stood upright and stared at his reflection over the sink. "Yeah, I definitely hate these mirrors."

"No you don't."

"Yes, I do. We need different ones. These look too much like church windows." Indeed, the mirrors were tall and arched at the top; there were two of them, one over each sink. They had settled on them as a compromise pick—Jesse was six five and wanted to see his reflection without bending. But maybe crouching was good for him, it could keep aging joints limber. He squatted to see if they might make do with another choice, something more classically shaped. His knees responded with a horrid crunch, like someone crumpling a plastic water bottle for recycling.

Norman just shook his head and went back to his phone.

"Toothpaste," Jesse said, and without glancing up Norman handed the tube over, like they were surgeons passing a scalpel, unable to tear their eyes from a patient's open viscera; Jesse's Sonicare toothbrush, which needed replacing, was loud like a bone saw. Forty-five seconds in, it died. "Gweat," Jesse managed, opening a drawer to look for a free toothbrush from the dentist before remembering that he could still use the Sonicare manually. He did so slowly at first, like it might bite, then elbowed Norman to see what held his attention. He seemed to be growing increasingly agitated.

Norman held up his phone. "Look at this email."

Jesse squinted. It seemed like run-of-the-mill spam. "I don't see anything."

Norman sighed. "Look again." The email was from *Bonk of America*.

Jesse spit in the sink, then reached for the readers Norman was wearing, carefully slipping them off of his husband's ears; he then held them up to the phone like opera glasses. "Does that say *bonk*?"

"BONK." Norman reclaimed his glasses. "Obviously it's a scam. But my father wouldn't know that. He'd be replying with his login information." He continued his rant about how the world was becoming both less just and more stupid and how there had to be a better way. Jesse agreed, having recently himself yelled at his own mother for sharing a photo on Facebook of a glowing couple celebrating their seventieth wedding anniversary because it was clearly AI.

"How do you know it's AI?" she had asked, as if *he* was the one who was artificial.

"Because the woman has fourteen fingers!"

But Jesse knew Norman well enough to know he wasn't so much concerned about his elderly father as he was about himself turning sixty, a milestone that gay men who came of age in the eighties and nineties never thought they would see. He feared that the day when he'd feel out of step with the world was not all that far off. But the truth was Norman had never been more attractive or sharp, his hair now more salt than pepper, his eyes the same warm saddle brown, and he had recently opened his own architectural firm. The house they were living in was their dream, remodeled with Norman's design. Or rather, it became their dream after other dreams had fallen apart.

Jesse tried to lighten the mood as he dabbed a cream called AGE DEFENDER, all caps, under his eyes. "Hey. A man walks into a bar."

Norman reached for the floss. "A joke? Really?"

"Gross," Jesse said when a small piece of their dinner was launched onto the mirror by Norman's aggressive flossing. "Now we *have* to get new mirrors."

"A man walks into a bar . . ." Norman prompted.

"Oh yeah. A man walks into a bar," Jesse repeated. "BONK."

The lights flickered again. At least they seemed to appreciate the punch line.

"Remind me before bed to check the generator," Norman instructed, unmoved. "If the power goes out in the night, I want to be prepared." Neither of them could sleep without the symphony of air-conditioning, their white noise machine, and a fan.

"Check the generator," Jesse said unhelpfully, screwing the lid on the jar of his eye serum.

Their eyes met again in the mirror. This time Norman glared.

"What is it you think we're doing? I'm literally going to bed right now."

They had both been drawn to the desert, but Norman's attraction had bordered on obsession. The desert was wilderness stripped bare, he would say, no pretension, no airs. Fresh water was scarce, yes, but it didn't keep life from thriving. Jesse preferred civilization. The desert, yes, but Palm Springs. "*Embalm* Springs?" Norman protested at the time, referring to its population of retirees. "We're too young to be old."

"We're too old to be young," Jesse had countered, but he gave in to Norman's prodding, and the generator, which Jesse had insisted upon, eased some of his concerns. And Joshua Tree *was* pretty cool. The first civilizations sprang from the desert sand, after all, and moving there felt like a return to basics despite the freeways and outlet malls and casinos and cell towers that blighted the once pristine landscape. But when it came right down to it, it was the stars, and indeed this far out from the most densely populated parts of the Coachella Valley you were rewarded with a breathtaking display of them smattered across the sky almost nightly. Amateur photographers from around the world drove deep into the neighboring national park to photograph the Milky Way, away from all light pollution. And despite development and sprawl, most of the desert remained intact. Perhaps that was what their agent meant by *ecotopian*.

"Come with me," Norman insisted.

"To check on the generator? What are we, conjoined twins?"

"It's dark. I need someone to hold the flashlight."

Jesse didn't want to. There were too many spiders out there.

"C'mon. It will be an adventure."

Jesse shook his head. "Oh, no. I'm not falling for *that* again," he laughed. "But hey, I want you to know something. I love you. I love you very much." To show he was being sincere, he enveloped Norman in an enormous bear hug until Norman relented and went limp. "Even if mating season is over."

Norman groaned, then pushed his husband off him. He paused in the doorway and knocked twice on the frame, which, unlike them, was solid. Jesse took that to mean *I'm annoyed, but I love you, too.*

Jesse took one last look in the mirror and frowned. Maybe it wasn't the mirrors he disliked so much as what they reflected back at him; it seemed like only yesterday their faces were young. He turned on the shower and whipped off his shirt.

I'm outta here.

It was the last thing he thought he heard Norman say as he stepped into the shower, the words muffled under the spray. Jesse assumed he meant he was going to check the generator, or that it was the latest in a long string of threats to go live off the grid, as if they weren't already doing pretty much that; he never got the chance to ask. Before Norman could return, Jesse had dried off and was asleep in their bed.

Sometime around two, maybe three, in the morning, Jesse sprang bolt upright, jarred by the rattle and hum. Another earthquake, this time with a blinding flash of light. He shielded his eyes with one arm and reached for Norman with the other; his husband, usually out cold with a book tented on his chest, was not there. The plantation shutters covering the sliding glass door to their backyard (which Norman called *louvered* so as not to sound regressive) clattered like a rickety roller-coaster car on an old wooden track, and one by one they fell open. Squinting, Jesse peeked over the crook of his elbow.

Night eerily resembled day, the feathery leaves of the tamarisk trees blowing violently in gales of hurricane-force wind. That was not right. The digital clock was impossible to read, its red numbers lifeless, drowned in mysterious white light, but he knew in his bones the sun was still several hours from rising. Cautiously he gathered courage, swung his legs out from under the covers, and placed his bare feet on the ground. *What in god's name?* An earthquake would have ended by now, giving way to an eerie still, but their mattress—advertised as having the magic ability to keep a glass of wine upright on one side while a restless partner tossed and turned on the other—belched Jesse onto the floor, where the polished concrete purred, tickling the soles of his feet. He tripped over the Williams Sonoma rolling pin he kept by the bed to work his plantar fasciitis. Norman had given him hell for this (you use it for your *feet*?)—the utensil had been a wedding gift—but honestly, when was the last time either of them had baked a pie? As a small crack appeared by the doorframe and plaster fell from a wall, he grabbed the rolling pin by one of its easy-grip handles and brandished it like a weapon. An earthquake would not emit blinding light (unless the generator blew), nor would it whip up winds that shook the roof—this was clearly something more menacing. Jesse was immediately aware of his nakedness, the strange luminescence highlighting his nightly tumescence. All six and a half feet of him cast an imposing shadow on the wall behind him.

"Norman?" he called, tentatively at first and then again with increased urgency. No reply came. Or not one he could hear over the deafening, mysterious roar.

Jesse fumbled his way down the glass hallway, rolling pin extended in front of him. The floor-to-ceiling windows, original to the house, seamlessly connected indoors with out and beautifully framed the extensive landscaping—those windows had sold them on the property, which was already near the top end of their budget. Now Jesse felt like an ant under a magnifying glass in the hands of cruel, outsized children. He raced down the hall, afraid the glass windows, which were radiating heat, might shatter. Thrown off balance, he hit the doorframe hard, even though they had enlarged it in the remodel to accommodate his height, then squinted as he made his way to the main living area rubbing his shoulder.

In the dining room, he cast around for his sunglasses, which he'd that afternoon abandoned on the long Danish table that anchored the space (it sat eight even though they were but two). Norman had assigned the lacquered box that sat on the sideboard by the front door as a place for their wallets, glasses, and keys, and they argued frequently about Jesse's inability to adhere to the organizational systems Norman carefully put in place. Clumsily, Jesse put on the sunglasses, poking one eye with a temple. Despite their premium polarized lenses, the glasses barely made a difference; about all he could make out was Norman's phone on the table and he picked it up to dial 911, forgetting momentarily how to access the keypad on a phone that wasn't his. When he pressed the emergency button, an angry screech yelled back at him, and he threw the phone in frustration.

The movable wall off the living room was partitioned all the way open—far wider than they ever opened it for themselves—as if someone had broken in (or rushed out) in a hurry, flinging it open with the same abandon one would use to spin that damn wheel on *The Price Is Right*. Jesse stumbled into the backyard. The pavers that led to the grass felt cool on the soles of his feet, but the rest of his skin felt warm from the mysterious light like he was the bubbling cheese on a sad rectangle of school cafeteria pizza. Wind whipped up a cloud of sand and debris and even with his sunglasses it took both of his arms to shield his face. The locals here called sandstorms haboobs; they would occur on occasion when the temperature dropped, in what felt like the flip of a switch. But it was too early in the season and the temperature was too warm and it was obvious this was no haboob. When he felt a small patch of grass under his toes, the winds stopped and everything fell silent and still; he'd stepped into the eye of whatever this was—suddenly all he could hear and feel was the beating of his own heart. He knew it wouldn't last, but he was grateful for the respite. Once the thick cloud cleared, Jesse spotted his husband, also naked, as if he, too, had been roused from sleep, just outside a perplexing beam of light. Norman was tickling the light with his fingertips, like he had once dipped them into a waterfall on a trip to Kauai to see if it was dry on the other side.

"NORMAN!" Jesse scolded, his husband a toddler standing too close to a hot stove. Norman responded by taking a step closer to the beam instead of back. They stood there, eyes locked, thirty years of highs and lows, laughter and grievances, passion and apathy—three decades of *life* in between them.

I'm sorry, Norman mouthed, and he walked backward until he was bathed in it, spreading his arms like Christ. By the time Jesse reached him, Norman was rising, floating above him just out of reach.

It was a strange thing to be standing underneath one's spouse. It didn't rain in the desert, the house had no gutters to clean; Jesse couldn't even recall them owning a ladder, as he was tall enough to access most things. What registered through Jesse's shock were the bottoms of Norman's feet, soft and pink, perhaps the result of a pumice stone that had mysteriously appeared in their shower several weeks prior. Alas, the light they were bathed in, blinding as it was, didn't allow Jesse to make out much else. New words would have to be invented to describe his expression; Randall Moss, the conspiracy theorist who lived in the Airstream on the property across from theirs, complaining nonstop about even the mildest inconveniences their renovation had caused him, was sure to be having a field day. But what Jesse *could* see plain as day was Norman's aura, as he was swallowed by luminescence that had once radiated from within. Norman's light used to shine so brightly it would suck everyone into his orbit, and now, about to lose him, Jesse was drawn to his husband all over again. He swung at him wildly with the rolling pin like one might at a piñata but failed to land a blow.

"Don't you dare!" It was all Jesse could think to yell, and it might have worked if Norman had indeed been a toddler testing his patience or a dog disobeying a command. But Norman was an adult, and even when they'd first met, Jesse had never been able to control him. And so Jesse dropped the rolling pin and with one ambitious jump (fueled by a lifetime of people asking, *"Do you play basketball?"*) leaped up and threw his arms around his husband's calves, holding on for dear life and finding that he, too, was now floating several feet above ground.

But Jesse was no match for the light, which seemed determined to take Norman from him. He took another deep breath and held the air in his lungs, uncertain if that would make him heavier like a rock or lighter like a balloon, and attempted to climb Norman's hairy legs as if they were the wretched ropes in junior high gym class, the bane of every closeted kid's existence. He reached Norman's knees before he started to slip, the ground a good five feet below his dangling toes. Six feet even, then maybe seven. Norman looked down, his face finally in view, his expression serene if surprised, a happy calm Jesse hadn't seen in many years. Which only enraged Jesse more. "I'll call your mother!" Norman's mother was eighty-four, had retired to Italy, and used a chairlift to get up the stairs, so Jesse wasn't sure exactly what he expected Rosemary Alfano to do, unless offering dry butter cookies from one of those circular tins could convince her son to stay. Norman smiled as if amused by the very idea, then raised his arms above his head and they began rising faster.

Jesse's grip became tenuous, and he slipped farther down Norman's bare legs. They met when Jesse was twenty-three; his entire adult life Norman had always been there. Norman—a man who said *orangutang* instead of *orangutan*, a man who maddeningly left his whiskers cemented to the side of the sink when he shaved, a man who didn't know how to reinstall Hulu on their TV when the app froze. "Do not leave me!" He clung to Norman's ankles, and then his feet, muttering, "Please, please, please," until he had no choice but to let go.

Jesse hit the ground with a thud, landing on his tailbone, the air forced out of his lungs. Pain radiated through his body in all directions. There was no part of him that wanted to go with Norman into the light, but the man was his whole life, and he had just about exhausted his other options. So he took one last deep breath, held out his right arm, and screamed, "FINE! LET'S CHECK THE GENERATOR!" Then he waited to see what his pleas might do.

Nothing, as it turned out. Norman disappeared into the sky, an Olympic diver knifing the water without so much as a ripple.

And then the light disappeared, too.

And the darkness that blotted the sky whisked away at impossible speeds as the winds both whipped up and died down, this time for good, and the tamarisk trees gave one last wave before falling still. Coyotes howled in the far distance, awakened in the night by something they couldn't explain to their pups. Jesse howled back, dazed and brokenhearted.

For a time, Jesse lay naked in the grass as if nothing had happened at all. This had to be a dream. Surely he would come to his senses. He took stock of what he knew for sure. The ground was cold. His back hurt. The sky was empty of clouds. Slowly, a smattering of stars reappeared. He sensed a faint tinge of smoke, as if there were distant wildfires. The yard was littered with leaves and palm fronds and bark and husks and the air was thick with dirt, the only real proof that something out of the ordinary had just happened. Except for the owl that sat in the tallest palm tree who gave a plaintive *hoo,* Jesse was alone.

Hoo, indeed. Who was he without Norman?

WHERE THE STREETS HAVE NO NAME

DAY NINETEEN

B*am. Bam. Bam.*

Jesse was startled awake by rapping on his car window, unaware until that moment he had dozed off. He remembered reclining the Jeep Laredo's driver's seat as far back as it would go, desperate to grab a few moments of sleep in the faculty parking lot, the iced coffee in his cupholder weakening as ice melted and temperatures rose, caffeine no longer having its desired effect. The car had been an ill fit, both for his personality and his lanky frame, but he found it of comfort lately. He had shared the vehicle with Norman, a compromise purchase a few years back when many cars were stuck in the ports and there was a shortage of chips.

"Chips?" Jesse asked at the time, first imagining potato before landing on *CHiPs*, the show about the California Highway Patrol starring Erik Estrada and Chris Pine's dad. Norman said semiconductor, modern cars had thousands of them, before instructing him not to be daft. Norman always knew stuff like that. When Jesse glanced over, he could see his husband in the passenger seat as clearly as if he were actually there. If only he were; there were many things Jesse needed explained.

Nights were traumatic. He'd lie awake, afraid to close his eyes, waiting for the inevitable blinding announcement that some unknown thing had come back, this time for him. He'd weigh the pros and cons of calling the police, or obsess over some meaningless detail, Norman's reading glasses on the bathroom counter, for instance—surely he would be missing them—and despite his anger over being abandoned he would try to imagine a way to reunite him with them. On the rare occasions Jesse felt more upbeat, when he went to bed with a full stomach (of alcohol, yes, but also a decent meal), insomnia gripped him, his heart racing with the idea that Norman might return with the same fanfare with which he had left. He was both upset and elated by this idea and wanted to be awake to give him a stern dressing-down, so he'd lie awake watching reels on his phone. (His favorites came from a woman who worked at Dairy Queen who filmed herself making every ice cream treat the restaurant had to offer, both on the menu and off.) Of course, the idea of Norman returning was Jesse's logical brain trying to make sense of something very illogical. It was just as likely if not more that Norman was gone for good, dead, vaporized, held hostage, or so far away he could never return in a human lifetime. But he tried not to focus on that.

Which is to say, more and more Jesse had only been able to sleep in public, surrounded by the safety of others, or in the light of midday, where it would be harder for anything to startle him. That meant naps on the couch with the shades fully open, or in a wooden cubicle inside the small Joshua Tree library, or during an indulgent trip to the movie theater in Palm Springs, where he'd plunk down twelve dollars for a matinee simply for the privilege of sleeping through it.

Or in the Jeep before class when traffic on the 62 was mercifully light and his hour commute was made in forty-five minutes.

"You really can sleep anywhere," Norman's phantom image said from the passenger seat, with only a hint of jealousy.

Not anywhere. Not anymore.

Jesse had been unconscious for five minutes or twenty—time had no meaning—when the rap on his window jolted him awake. He jumped, startling Luisa Flores, the English Department head, who had hired him. She had an armload of books and supplies but still managed to move her hand in a circular motion, the universal sign for rolling down a window for anyone Generation X or older. Her gray curls bounced with each swing of her arm until Jesse obliged and lowered his window to save her from dropping her thermos.

She blew her curls to one side. "It's usually students I catch sleeping before class, not teachers. I hope we're not boring you already, Mr. del Ruth."

"Transcendental Meditation," Jesse lied. It was a popular practice here in the desert, one he knew would not make her bat an eye.

Jesse had agreed to teach only one class this semester, a trial of sorts before accepting a full-time position. Two years back he'd taken a sabbatical from his steady gig at UC Irvine to finish his new novel, as he was out of both excuses and time and his publisher was threatening to ask for repayment of money that he had long ago spent on a house, for which he now carried the mortgage alone. The novel had still not materialized, so back to teaching it was. Given his current circumstances, he was grateful for the light schedule, even if it wasn't enough money to sustain him long-term. In the wake of Norman's disappearing act, it wasn't the grading of papers and the planning of lectures or the usual banality and drudgery he couldn't imagine working through, but rather showing his face in a classroom, plastering on the costume of normalcy. The idea that his one course was humor writing had, well, tickled his funny bone. Until life changed suddenly before the semester began and the only humor he recognized was the absurd.

"First-day jitters?" Luisa asked.

Jesse faked a laugh, wondering if anything would ever be truly funny again. "A little back-to-school ritual. It helps me get in the *zone*." He said *zone* with a Cockney accent for some humiliating reason, following it up with a pump of his fist, also undignified.

"The funny-bone zone," Luisa said, and Jesse forced a weak smile. He reached for his iced coffee and leather messenger bag, rolled up his window, and slowly exited his Jeep. He closed the door with an awkward thrust of his hip.

"How was the rest of your summer?" Luisa asked, balancing her enormous Stanley on a stack of binders while dropping her keys in her bag. They had not seen each other since his interview, as he had skipped the faculty orientation.

"Oh, the usual," Jesse replied. "Barbecues. Reading in the shade. Husband was abducted by aliens."

Luisa, whom Jesse guessed to be flirting with retirement, furrowed her brow, lowering her curls again over her eyes. "*Abducted?*"

"You're right. 'Abducted' may be too strong a word." Jesse paused for comedic effect. "He may have gone willingly."

Luisa stared blankly for a beat, and then two, before bursting into such a fit of laughter that her Stanley, its color an unappetizing salmon, rolled off her stack of binders, Jesse catching it just before it hit the curb. "Contradiction!" she declared, placing a finger alongside her nose.

He froze as she reclaimed her water bottle. "What?"

Luisa looked at him confused as she rebalanced her armload. "*Contradiction.*"

"What the fuck are you talking about," he muttered. As of late, he was quick to anger. Then, remembering she was his boss and he needed this job, he grinned like he'd been kidding. But Luisa cut him off by laughing again just as riotously. And then she stopped just as abruptly.

"Are you okay, Jesse?" She tilted her head with concern.

"I'm sorry, I— *What?*"

Luisa rebalanced her stack of books so that she could touch his arm with a free hand. "For a second there it looked like you might cry."

Jesse dug deep and immediately regained his composure. "Comedy, tragedy. Two sides. Same coin."

"That's right!" she said triumphantly, then gave his arm a little squeeze before letting go. "I'm so glad you showed up ready to be funny on day one! *Husband abducted by aliens.*" As she continued on to her office, she glanced back over her shoulder and hollered, "If you see them again, send them my way. I would happily give them mine!"

I can't teach anyone to be funny," Jesse warned as he walked into the classroom to find six eager students gathered near the front of a room so comically large for a class of this size he wondered if Luisa hadn't arranged it as an inaugural joke. The room had three enormous blackboards as well as two more that had been wheeled in on easels; if his current fear wasn't his inability to save important things, he could write his new novel entirely in chalk. Instead, he wrote only his name, Jesse del Ruth, for some reason underlining the *d* and the *R*. His voice echoed (he didn't think he was imagining it) and fell silent with no response. "If you're dull now, you'll still be dull at the end of the semester. I want to be up front about that so that you don't ding me on your evaluations."

"That's not what COD says." A young blond woman fished in a teal backpack for something urgent as Jesse set his bag down on the desk at the front of the room. As she leaned forward, he admired her lowlights, but she wore far too many friendship bracelets. No one should have that many friends.

"*God?*" Jesse misheard, appalled. He reached in his breast pocket for his glasses. Although he had to admit as of late, god had a pretty good sense of humor.

"COD," Backpack replied. "College of the Desert." She found what she was looking for and presented it to him. It was the course catalog, which he presumed overpromised on what any reasonable person could deliver in the way of humor instruction. She held it out for him to read, but he swatted it away with disinterest.

"Cod is a fish."

"It's a fish and an abbreviation."

"An abbreviation, yes. For cash on delivery or cause of death, depending on if you work in sales, or, you know—the morgue."

"We're college students, Mr. Doctor." A handsome kid with enormous headphones spoke loudly, making it clear he was also listening to music. He looked not unlike Jesse's old college roommate, who was Black and Japanese, and Jesse made a mental note to ask his new student his heritage, as there might be some cultural humor to mine. As it was, the kid made a show of stuffing his long legs under his small desk, which made several of his classmates laugh. In fact, he probably rivaled Jesse in height even if the kid was much leaner.

"*Call of Duty*, then," Jesse said, matching his volume and gesturing for him to lose the cans. This seemed to satisfy Headphones, who gave two enthusiastic thumbs up before sliding his headphones back until they were resting around his neck, revealing two black gauges where earrings might be. "Hold up. Did you call me Mr. Doctor?"

"You underlined the *d* and the *R* in your name."

Jesse turned around and looked at the way he had written *del Ruth* on the blackboard. He *had* underlined those letters.

"I thought it was because you were overcompensating. You know, for not having a PhD." If Headphones weren't already Headphones in Jesse's mind, he would have absolutely been Freud.

"I could have a PhD."

"*Do* you have a PhD?" Headphones asked skeptically.

"Go fish." Jesse bowed his head and chuckled, still annoyed at COD. "FYI, I have an MFA from UCLA, and I hope that will be A-OK and we can be BFFs. Otherwise, TTFN."

Headphones sat up in his chair like this new professor might just have something worthwhile to say after all; he was wearing a sleeveless Def Leppard shirt, which was either ironic or belonged to his parents, who were most likely Jesse's exact age. Jesse took inventory of his students; only one could be considered nontraditional, old enough to actually wear an eighties band tee. He was graying in his beard and carried a briefcase, looking not unlike one of the accountants they drag onstage at the Oscars.

Jesse slipped his glasses on and took a second look at his eager students, then at their names on the roster. He was never good with remembering names, so they became Backpack, Headphones, Non-Trad, Snickers, Mountain Dew, and Unicorn. Doling out nicknames was a first-day-of-class tradition, and he always picked one Unicorn, who was recognizable right up front. The student who was not only there to learn but had the talent to go all the way. Only once was he ever wrong. This year's Unicorn had a mane of blue hair coupled with a *Don't fuck with me* expression that dared anyone to joke about it, and no one, at least in this classroom, did; she sat apart from the group, leaving at least one empty desk on all sides. She (or *they*, kids today were fluid with pronouns) wore a *Once Upon a Mattress* T-shirt, and while it was from the more recent Broadway revival, the original production had been a launching pad for Carol Burnett. Not bad for a comedic pedigree.

"You all have the same books on your desk," Jesse observed. "Are you in some sort of cult?" Unicorn was the only one whose desk was clear.

"It was the suggested reading, Mr. Doctor," Non-Trad explained, and his copy looked well-thumbed. Non-trads were rule followers, always.

"Okay, you can just call me Jesse." The familiarity of nicknames, he felt, should be a one-way street. "All of you, I mean. Not just Non-Trad."

Jesse wet his thumb and tried to erase the underlining of his name on the chalkboard, then swiped a book from the desk closest to him, nearly knocking Snickers's (you guessed it) chocolate bar onto the floor. Snickers, the varsity jock in this Breakfast Club, grabbed it just in time; upon closer inspection, it may have been a protein bar. The book was *How to Be Funny in Eight Steps* by a man named—Jesse squinted and looked twice—Peter Killjoy. "Suggested reading," he scowled. "Suggested by whom?"

"Ms. Flores," Mountain Dew replied before opening a two-liter bottle of what looked like radioactive waste, which hissed when she unscrewed the cap. She poured herself a tall glass in a cup from Pizza Hut. Her hair had a similar yellow-green tint, as if PepsiCo had opened their factory to misbehaved children Willy Wonka–style and she had ingested too much of the swill (*You're turning vio-*

let, Violet!), although it was much more likely she was a swimmer who'd spent too many hours in a chlorinated pool. When she caught Jesse staring in disbelief, she inched the plastic soda bottle toward him. "I'm sorry, did you want some?"

"Do I want Mountain Dew *in the morning*?" Jesse asked incredulously.

She shrugged, unfazed. "It's ten o'clock somewhere."

"No, thank you," he declined politely, smiling. Mountain Dew might actually be funny. "I had too much Fanta at breakfast."

Focusing, Jesse flipped through the book in his hand. It fell open to Rule 6: *Contradiction*. Finally, he understood this morning's interaction with Luisa Flores. He would be having words with his department chair; there was only room for one of them to teach this class. (Technically, in this room, a veritable clown car of adjuncts could drive through the center aisle, but that was not the point.) It was all he could do not to rip chapter six out in frustration; it worked for Robin Williams in *Dead Poets Society*, after all. Up until one of his students shot himself and Williams was ultimately dismissed. Jesse didn't want to incite anything like that—he already had one person's fate to answer for. So instead, he threw the book back on Snickers's desk; it landed with a *thwap* on the wooden surface.

"Okay. Well, I suggest you *don't* read this book, unless you want to fail." Jesse guessed he could name at least half of these so-called rules as he watched his students tuck their books back in their backpacks and briefcases and, in the case of Headphones, score a three-point shot right in the trash. Say no when you mean yes. Inventing numbers (eleventy) or exaggerating them for comedic effect ("What are you, a thousand years old?"). Employing the Rule of Threes. "The problem with these books is that they are written by painfully unfunny people with no comedic pedigree but with lots of time on their hands."

"Those who can't do, teach," Headphones helpfully observed.

"Exactly," Jesse said before realizing that did not sit quite right. "Wait a minute, no. *I'm* teaching."

"But not with a PhD." Headphones crossed his arms, pleased with himself.

Jesse smirked, impressed. "Good job. In comedy, that's known as a callback." Headphones was clearly tickled. He'd stumbled into a subject where being a smartass might be an asset.

"What *is* your pedigree?" Mountain Dew asked. Jesse was going to have to institute a policy of raising hands. "I'm sorry. Was that rude? I haven't had my Mountain Dew yet this morning." She said it as if Mountain Dew were as common and acceptable as coffee and everyone had at least four gallons before lunch. (Exaggeration.)

"My pedigree? Belgian sheepdog." As a joke, it bombed. His students shifted uncomfortably in their seats. He should have backed out of the semester as soon as Norman disappeared and took Jesse's ability to be funny with him. "My pedigree is that I was hired to teach this class."

Non-Trad looked at his watch, the old-fashioned kind that didn't keep track of his steps. "He wrote a novel. He won the Mark Twain Prize."

"Thank you. It was not the Mark Twain Prize, but another prize named after a different humorist. But that's beside the point."

"What is the point?" asked Headphones, but not in a malicious way.

"The point is, I'm being serious."

"About the Bolivian—" Backpack began.

"*Belgian.*"

"Belgian dog? I thought you were joking," Backpack said.

Jessie hid his face in his hands. "I'm being serious about the types of people who write these books. I am joking about being a dog."

"I guess you really can't teach someone to be funny," Mountain Dew said under her breath before downing half her glass. It was the first real laugh from the class.

Jesse plucked Headphone's discarded book from the trash and read from the author's note on the back cover to make his point, before losing control of the class irrevocably; a lot was always riding on first days. "*I watched one thousand hours of talk show appearances and here's what makes an audience laugh.*" This, he knew, was no exaggeration, and was pretty par for the course. "These books can't tell you what makes an audience laugh; every audience is different. And anything can be funny. Someone tripping and falling can be funny. A man getting dumped can be funny." Jesse caught a lump in his throat. "But humor is not just what's funny, in this case on the page. Humor is a tool. What's important is how you employ it. What you use it to say." For the first time he held their attention. "Books like these are for weak-minded people. People who don't observe the world they are living in, they just amalgamate other people's observations. Or they're thinly disguised self-help screeds disguised as humorous insight, the type of thing you used to find in *Reader's Digest*." *Reader's Digest* was an outdated reference, and went over as such. Nowadays, this kind of dreck populated online posts people wrote behind screen names like LOLlypop, Shaquille Oatmeal, or SunnySideUp, if these users were even real and not bots engagement farming for clout or for money, or posts under subreddits like r/standup, r/socialskills, r/publicspeaking, or r/DecidingToBeBetter.

r/YouKiddingMe, Jesse always wanted to scream.

Snickers raised his meaty hand. "You wrote a book that won an award?"

"I did," Jesse sighed. And then quickly added, "For humor," staving off the inevitable follow-up questions, and sure enough—three hands in the process of being raised were lowered. His second novel had won the prestigious award in humor writing nine years back, much to both his and Norman's shock (although Norman was a little *too* shocked for Jesse's liking, if he were being honest); winning had been a double-edged sword. Before he was handed the award, Jesse would have said books that win literary prizes were bland consensus picks. True genius was always divisive, sure to alienate a judge or two. Winners did not offend. Then he won and changed his tune—cream absolutely rises to the top! The award had opened several doors, figuratively and literally, as he was newly a welcome guest at parties on the rare occasions they visited New York, hosted by literati or cartoonists from the *New Yorker.* And it had given Jesse the authority to teach others the subject, something he found wryly funny given the adage. But winning had deadened the humor in his own work, as if he'd used up his allotted jokes for this lifetime in his prizewinner and was now stuck, humorless (and therefore naked) in a world that felt increasingly, sometimes violently, unfunny. And now his husband had gone, for lack of a better term, *missing*, and he didn't feel like anything would ever be funny again.

"Well, that's cool," Snickers added, breaking his train of thought.

It *was* cool. They had flown to an award banquet in New York, where, during the cocktail reception beforehand, the other nominees kept coming up to Jesse to tell him how much they loved Norman. Norman, as it turned out, had had one too many Tanqueray martinis and was telling everyone else *they* were going to win; he had boundless optimism for everyone except, it seemed, his husband, who received no such assurance. Jesse, on the other hand, was greeted by people commenting on his tuxedo, a suit that was perhaps not his usual style, but something that made him feel quite sophisticated until the ninth or tenth person approached him to say, "I wish I could wear something like that" and he realized from a tilt of the head or a twist of the lips that it wasn't meant as a compliment. In truth, had Norman abandoned him a long time ago?

It gave him an idea.

"Your first assignment. I want you to write a short story about a time you felt abandoned."

"Abandoned?" Backpack asked, nearly knocking her bag off her desk. "That doesn't sound funny."

"I know. It doesn't sound funny at all. But that's where you come in! Look at something not funny in a humorous way. Find something absurd. Something ridiculous. Something over-the-top. Or go small. Find something funny about the tiniest detail for your character to obsess over when their world is falling apart. I don't know. I'm not here to do the hard work for you." He had sudden empathy for his students, who looked frightened to be left to their own devices. "But. I will do it *with* you. And we'll all share our stories next week and see if we can't find a laugh."

In the spirit of looking at things in a new way, Jesse tucked the textbook by Peter Killjoy into his messenger bag. He then said a silent prayer that this ragtag group he was assigned would come through. He looked at Unicorn and sent her a thought telepathically: *I'm counting on you.* He couldn't teach a class to be funny, but he hoped to god they already were.

His husband was missing. He desperately needed a laugh.

THE TIME BEFORE

Joshua Tree, which many assumed was a town in California's Mojave Desert, was actually not a town at all but rather a census-designated place, or CDP, a third-level political division akin to a barrio or township—less than a city, more than a ward—known largely for the national park of the same name (*The Monument*, locals called it) that rubbed against its outskirts. The boundaries of a CDP have no legal status; they may not correspond with a local's understanding of the area or anything that appears on a map, and so it didn't much matter that no two residents thought of Joshua Tree exactly the same. Criteria established for the most recent census required that a CDP name be "one that is recognized and used in daily communication by the residents of the community" (as opposed to a name developed solely for planning or other purposes) and recommended that a CDP's boundaries be drawn according to inhabitants' regular use. To that end, Joshua Tree shared undefined borders with both the Yucca and Coachella Valleys, and to the east, Twentynine Palms, and boasted a population of just north of seven thousand. Joshua Tree remained unincorporated, and a municipal advisory council acted as an official liaison between the community and the government of San Bernardino County.

Eight months ago, Joshua Tree's population grew by two when Jesse del Ruth and Norman Alfano completed their elaborate renovation on the home down a private drive near the southern outskirts, the one that had been for sale for nearly two years as it came down in price every ten weeks like clockwork. They liked the vague definition of Joshua Tree, how it could mean as many things as there were people in it, and had many a laugh comparing the town that wasn't a town to their marriage that by its own definition was unconventional, and was at the mercy of voters or state legislators or the Supreme Court.

The house was a bit of an architectural oddity that wasn't to everyone's taste (and sadly in need of repair), and Norman, despite his professional expertise, soon realized how difficult it was to secure the required permits. He talked about joining the advisory council to put his stamp on the community soon after they moved in.

"We need to shake up this town!" Norman would proclaim to Jesse whenever their renovation hit a bureaucratic wall.

"It's not a town so much as a CDP," Jesse would remind him.

"You're not a husband so much as a life sentence."

They would go back and forth like this, each trying to drive the other a little more mad until one of them would break and laugh, which someone always did, and then they would close the debate with a kiss. Neither of them ever joined the council, although they did go to several meetings before Jesse put two fingers to his temple and mimed blowing his brains out from boredom.

The house was little more than a listing online, a bit of a pipe dream really, when Norman first laid eyes on it. He would scroll through the photos and fantasize about retirement under the shade of the trees and evenings in the cowboy tub that sat ten feet from the deck, until a drumbeat inside him grew steadier, louder, convincing him it had to be his. As a couple, they had talked about the desert in no uncertain terms; it was a place they had escaped to often from the drudgery of L.A., first to the clothing-optional resorts for men in Palm Springs, then to private rental homes in Rancho Mirage, but in terms of uprooting their lives and moving there? It was Norman leading the charge. And it was Norman who was most excited when their move-in day finally came.

"We have four foam rollers?" Noman asked as they unpacked in their new space. "Why do we need *four*?"

Jesse thought the time for that question was when they were packing, not unpacking; now that the rollers had made the move, what difference did it make? "Yes, we need four." Jesse lectured him on the pillars of foam rollers: density, surface texture, shape, and size. This was knowledge that aging brought. He was surprised Norman didn't know—no wonder he was so uptight. Eventually Norman gave in and all four were pulled from an oversized box, Jesse agreeing they could throw out a weighted medicine ball (which was leaking sand) and those large rubber bands with differing tensions, an impulse buy during the early days of COVID when both of their gyms were closed.

"Does Joshua Tree even have a town gym?" Jesse asked as he sorted some of their workout gear for the garage.

To which Norman replied, "Joshua Tree is not a town."

Norman turned his attention to another box that wouldn't budge. "What's in here, weights?"

Jesse peeked and confirmed that was exactly what was inside. Norman protested again—they never even used weights at home and yet they'd paid to move them—before Jesse calmed his husband.

He grabbed Norman by the waist and they swayed like they were at a middle school dance, Jesse holding the medicine ball between them like a chaperone might place a balloon, until it leaked sand everywhere (at which point he set it aside carefully), whispering in his ear the whole time about a move being an opportunity for reinvention. "We can be anyone here."

Norman relented and spun Jesse around, dancing to music only they could hear. Jesse was right, the move was supposed to invigorate their relationship. "You know what I was thinking back in L.A.? As the moving van was all packed and pulling away?"

Jesse didn't.

"What if it just . . . exploded."

"*The van?*"

"Yeah."

"Then all our stuff would be gone."

"Exciting, right?"

Jesse thought about that for a moment, what a real fresh start would be like. What it would feel like to own no foam rollers, or clothes or books or dishes or memories, and then he said with all sincerity, "You're weird."

The glass and concrete house, from the right angles, disappeared completely into the arid landscape when the sun was at its most blinding. At dusk, it was a womb of warm light that glowed, the tamarisk trees muting the tall windmills that blighted the distant horizon. It made them feel like pioneers of sorts, and Norman an astronaut—indeed the dry land that stretched undeveloped to the distant mountains could easily be mistaken for Mars. The pergola out back provided shade for lunch, and when they needed a break from unpacking they ate takeout pizza from a place called Sky High Pie.

"From here, it looks like the earth could be flat," Norman mused as he reached for another slice.

"Maybe it is."

Norman gave his best *Oh, you think so* look. The pizza they chose, one of the restaurant's signature pies, was topped with a fried egg. Norman poked at the egg and the soft yolk jiggled. Jesse reached over to help, pulling a slice from underneath it.

"All conspiracy theories are at least eighty-five percent true. At least according to my mother."

Norman shook his head as he bit into his lunch. A kalamata olive rolled off the slice. "I wish it were flat, then it would be easy to push you off the edge."

Jesse laughed and rewarded Norman with a kiss, then tenderly wiped pizza sauce from his husband's face. Did other couples talk to one another like this? Maybe they were pioneers in that way, too. "Eat up. We still have to put the bed frame together before it gets dark."

Indeed it was pioneers—Mormon pioneers—who had trekked across the Colorado River to arrive where their house sat now, naming the sharp, Seussian trees that dotted the landscape after the biblical figure Joshua; the trees' short trunks and outstretched limbs cast shadows that reminded the settlers of worshippers dropped to their knees in supplication. Everyone who came to Joshua Tree arrived a little bit lost. Even today, the small, offbeat dirt roads, many of them unnamed, would short-circuit the average GPS.

"Do we really want to settle where Mormons did?" Jesse remembered asking after the first time they saw the house; they had shared smash burgers at a saloon called the Tiny Pony, flirting with the handsome waiter as they mulled over making an offer. ("What's good here?" they had asked, both about Joshua Tree and the Tiny

Pony; the waiter replied, "I am.") Granted, Jesse's knowledge of Mormons was limited to what he'd learned from the Broadway musical by the *South Park* guys and a distaste that lingered from the election of 2012. He didn't want the hand of god reaching down from the sky to bury golden plates anywhere near his yard—he'd just as soon be left out of it.

"Are you kidding?" Norman countered as he sipped his cocktail, the Big-Ass G&T. "Utah has some of the most spectacular land in the nation. It's home to five national parks!" The way he saw it, when it came to real estate, the Mormons knew what they were doing.

Jesse let it go, and when they left (with the waiter's phone number scrawled across the bottom of their check), they agreed that if their offer was accepted they would make the Tiny Pony their new local place, and come back for the chorizo breakfast tostadas, if not more.

After the Mormons arrived, the ranchers and miners soon followed, looking for their own bite at the promise of California. The Joshua trees provided homesteaders with abundant materials for their corrals, while miners found use for the wood as fuel for the steam engines used in processing ore. And a mere century later, the artists and homosexuals came.

Instead of a hard way of life, herding cattle or mining for silver or gold, Joshua Tree's two newest residents were determined to find tranquility here, a place where they could enjoy each other's company again away from the hardships and social pressures of city life that emboldened the worst versions of themselves.

"Come on, we'll only go for a bit," Norman would say of a party or gallery opening they felt obliged to attend in L.A. "We can do the Irish goodbye."

"I'm more a fan of the Irish hello." When Norman cocked his head, confused, Jesse clarified, "That's when we don't go at all."

But here, already their blood pressures were lower. They unpacked their most precious things from bubble paper and valued memories along with them: a ceramic plate from a fondly remembered trip to Croatia, a lacquered box from a special anniversary, a framed photo from their first New Year's together. They looked for new places to display these totems, Norman carefully editing the whole time. "Is this important?" he asked as he unwrapped a random tchotchke.

"Of course not," Jesse replied, wanting Norman to feel free to choose a home for it. He even held his tongue when the home Norman chose was the trash can. But he couldn't withhold a look.

"What. That was from West Elm, wasn't it?"

"Jonathan Adler, but go off."

Norman felt contrite and pulled the little figure out of the trash. "Okay, but this home is unique. It should have unique things."

"It has us," Jesse offered with a smile.

"It has us," Norman agreed, and Jesse swept the Jonathan Adler sculpture back into the garbage. They had agreed: nothing mass-produced.

After the bed was assembled, the two of them christened the house by having sex in the new rain shower, as it felt important to break routine, then ate cold pizza naked behind the house, since there were no neighbors to see. They fell asleep that first night listening to the sounds of the desert and the hum of their new home. Everything was new, but for one night at least they felt like their old selves, happy.

When they were settled, they developed new hobbies, playing elaborate board games like Wingspan, a card-driven engine-building game where you attract birds to one of three habitats in your growing bird sanctuary as you acquire food and lay eggs while learning interesting facts. *As a ground-nester, the killdeer will fake a broken wing to lure prey away from its young.* "That's like when you faked a sprained ankle to get out of gay skiing," Norman said.

Jesse shook his head. *Gay skiing.* It had indeed been a gay ski trip he had gotten them out of, a weekend in Big Bear called Ski Dazzle.

Soon they were watching the real-life birds that made a home of their property. Roadrunners and hummingbirds and shrikes. They became obsessed with a pair of nighthawks who appeared after dusk like clockwork, seining the air for insects, which in fact were technically not hawks at all, but a class of bird called goatsuckers, because long ago people thought they flew into barns to drink milk from the teat.

"Do you think it's weird how obsessed with birds we've become?"

Norman did not. "I suppose we're just at that age."

Norman read books and plotted projects for the yard that he would begin when the heat broke, vowing to only take on clients and jobs that interested him. Jesse wrote (or said he would write, procrastination being a big part of the task), while he enjoyed the home's modern amenities: the kitchen they redid with a dual-fuel stove that was perfect for both cooking *and* baking, and the bathrooms in bright turquoise and rose-colored tiles that felt like they could be found in luxury hotels. When one would go for a hike, the other would say, "Try not to die," a gentle reminder of their new home's unforgiving conditions and the rattlesnakes that made nests nearby. They prepared meals together to eat at a table, slowly while sharing a bottle of wine—something they had stopped doing in Los Angeles, each preferring to grab overpriced salads with trendy ingredients (Lebanese cucumbers, candied nuts, dried figs) from the place on Norman's commute home, eating over the sink or in front of the TV.

They debated the merits of calling the waiter but honestly felt too content. Each night they dozed off quickly and without struggle, the stresses of the day now fewer and no longer in need of processing; they once fell asleep holding hands. In short, their relocation from L.A. had been a success, both for themselves and for their relationship. In many regards they were like newlyweds, minus the *passion*.

"What do you like in bed?" Norman implored, as if they hadn't once been intimately familiar. He wrapped his arms around Jesse from behind; because Norman was shorter it looked like he was giving the Heimlich. "It's been a long time since we tried something new."

"You mean like the waiter?"

"Fuck the waiter."

Jesse laughed. "I think that's what he wants us to do."

"Come on," Norman urged. "I'm being serious."

"Seriously?" Jesse asked, but before Norman could say any more he replied, "Sleep." He wriggled free of his husband's grip, laughing in that way that meant *We're okay, aren't we?* On many days it felt more like they were agreeable roommates than spouses. But they were okay. Better than most, worse than some. What more could one reasonably expect after thirty years?

A shift happened when Norman downloaded the app, noticeable and all at once, like a change in the wind when the heat came that could suddenly blow the doors off a house. Jesse found Norman one night behind the house in the farthest of three new teak lounge chairs they'd just had delivered, one for them both and a guest. It was a cloudless night, the air just cool enough to suggest that an end to a brutal summer was in sight; Norman was holding his phone to the sky.

"What are you doing?"

"What does it look like I'm doing?"

Jesse frowned. This was reminiscent of their conversations when they lived in L.A., questions answered with questions, peppered with annoyance and a dash of frustration; he thought they'd left that behind. "If I could read your mind, I wouldn't have asked." He wondered how a spouse could be such a stranger.

"I'm sending signals," Norman said, relenting after a silence. He rubbed his elbow like it was sore, then wiped sweat from his brow. The desert could be cold at night much of the year, but it was surprising to them how it didn't seem to cool much at all in the longest of the summer months.

Signals that you're an idiot. Jesse wondered how long his arm had been raised like that; they'd finished dinner two hours prior.

"I downloaded an app."

Jesse bit his lip. In his life he'd maybe downloaded a handful of apps that did not already come loaded on his phone. *An app to do what?* "I once saw a photograph of a monk that kept his arm aloft for fifty years to prove his devotion to god." It was the kind of thing that Norman always responded to.

"Where?" he asked, taking the bait, and as he turned to his husband, so did the bright screen of his phone.

Jesse covered his eyes. "Online."

"No. Where was the monk?"

"Oh. In the Himalayas, I think. Or Bhutan."

"Bhutan is *in* the Himalayas. You just said two places that are the same." Jesse ignored this swipe, and Norman returned his phone upright so that the screen was facing the sky. He then repositioned his phone in his hand, holding it in his very fingertips as if the extra two inches were important. "What did it look like?"

"Bhutan?" Jesse struggled to remember. The photo had been taken just outside a monastery. He had expected to see mountains, but there wasn't much in the way of landscape he could recall.

"His *arm*." Once again they were talking past each other.

"Oh, right," Jesse said, even though the arm in the photo had been the monk's left. It had long atrophied, the fingers curled into the palm as if whispering for help. After five decades, the appendage was little more than weathered skin clinging to bones. "Mummified."

"Maybe I should try that," Norman said, and then, defiantly, he held his arm even higher.

"Try to make your arm look mummified?"

"No. Prove my devotion."

"Devotion to *what*, though?" Jesse asked, but he did not want an answer. Norman had been looking for meaning with increasing thirst, but if he should be devoted to anything, Jesse thought, it should be him, since they had both taken vows.

Fortunately, Norman just shrugged.

"Want to play Wingspan?" Jesse asked, figuring Norman wouldn't last fifty more minutes—let alone fifty years. "I could set up the game to give you more time." When Norman declined, Jesse went inside the house to watch an old episode of *Six Feet Under*, but lost interest after the episode's hallmark opening death. How could he focus on TV when his husband was sending signals into the sky? *Signals to whom?* It generally bothered Norman that much of humankind clung to the idea that nothing soared the skies above Earth beyond the ISS and humanity's imagination. But Jesse was not one of those. The universe was vast, bigger than anyone could imagine, so he was a firm believer in intelligent life. But he *also* believed that what made them intelligent was their determination to steer clear of here.

But Norman always wanted to know more.

And that was how it went for the next two weeks. After dinner Norman would quietly take to the yard, phone held aloft, and after an hour or so of this nonsense, Jesse would follow, offering blankets or snacks.

"Why do aliens avoid Earth?" Jesse asked one night. His go-to: a joke to lighten the mood. "The reviews are terrible. It only has one star."

"That's funny," Norman said without laughing.

"Maybe we should find a therapist here." He said it in as gentle a voice as he could muster. He hadn't loved the therapist they had in L.A., who had often taken Norman's side, but it did help them when things seemed darkest. And . . . *weirdest*.

"What do you mean? We're cured."

Jesse's mouth contorted into a pretzel. "We're not cured."

"We moved here, didn't we?"

"A *ham* is cured." The conversation didn't go any further, so Jesse retreated to watch TV.

One night he actually sat next to his husband, remaining silent for as long as he could. He spoke only when the silence became unbearable. "I don't hear anything." Despite nights of teasing, on this occasion he actually meant to sound helpful, supportive—perhaps the app wasn't working or Norman had the settings all wrong. Of course, it came out sounding critical.

"The signals are not for you."

I see, Jesse thought, even though he didn't. "Is there another app you could try?"

"I paid for this one," Norman said defiantly.

"I suppose you used our joint credit card." It was the perfect racket, Jesse thought. An app, an intangible thing made of code you couldn't see, sending signals no one could hear. Jesse wondered if the app even did anything, or if someone had just figured out how to charge dupes a subscription for a colorful widget to park on their home screen. "Does the app inform you if it receives anything back?" Jesse assumed if one couldn't hear the signal, they likewise might not hear the reply.

Norman looked at him, offended—he seemed to truly believe. Which, sure, on one hand, harmless enough. But the trouble with drinking the Kool-Aid, Jesse thought, is that you never know when it's the last glass.

"I'm trying," Jesse said. And honestly, he was.

Norman said that he was trying, too. Trying *what*, though, Jesse was not sure, and so he went back inside to watch another episode of *Six Feet Under*. The opening scene, which featured a woman who hit her husband over the head with a frying pan, killing him because "he was boring," proved especially satisfying.

Jesse approached Norman in his home office the following afternoon and whispered something filthy in his ear, something new he might genuinely enjoy in bed. Norman, for his part, looked startled. Hoping for an opportunity to connect in a way they hadn't in a while, Jesse reached around his husband and pulled up an Airbnb listing on Norman's iPad for a UFO-themed house nearby. It was copper in color and shaped like a saucer with strings of decorative lights, elevated off the ground with stairs that descended for landing. "Look, isn't this a trip? I thought maybe we could go for your birthday." He swiped through the photo gallery; the house had futuristic-looking furniture and was stocked with science fiction books and movies. It looked like a fun weekend getaway.

"Isn't this only a few miles from here? Not much of a trip."

Jesse's eyes pleaded, *Work with me here*. "It's shaped like a flying saucer!" He was doing his best to share in his husband's interests. Isn't that what good spouses do? But Norman barely glanced at the listing photos. Since once again he'd failed to get Norman's attention, he brought up something that would. "I was thinking we should get a dog."

"You're kidding," Norman said, even though this was well-traveled ground, the only surprise Jesse's chutzpah in raising it now.

"We could name him Saucer. Or Endeavor, like the space shuttle."

"Don't be ridiculous."

"Sit, Endeavor! Roll over, Dev."

"I'm begging you to stop."

"I once knew a dog named Rocket. Although I think he was named after arugula."

Norman dropped his head on his desk. His forehead left a little grease stain on the blueprints he was reviewing. Jesse usually knew when a cause was lost, but on his way out, he paused in the doorway and carefully knocked on the frame. He hesitated before speaking. "It's just, what if I'm not always here?"

Norman kept his eyes focused on his work. He then softened his tone. "Where are you going?"

"I applied to three residencies this winter to work on the book." Jesse traveled a fair bit for work; in the past he taught whole semesters out of state, and if he were to leave again he would feel better leaving Norman with a dog for company. Even with Jesse there, he was spending too much time alone. But Norman's argument against it was always the same: A dog required a fence and it was his belief that property should not have barriers. They had six and a half acres and he saw no need to divide them. And the land beyond theirs was undeveloped. He liked walking out their back door and seeing nothing but open ground all the way to the mountains. It was the same objection he had to swimming pools, another running disagreement between them.

"What if *I'm* not always here?" Norman asked gently; looking back, Jesse had to wonder if he'd known what was coming. But at the time, stinging from rejection, he had only a snappy comeback.

"Then I would get a dog." And a fence. And maybe a swimming pool.

Before summer was over, Norman was gone.

DAY TWENTY-FOUR

A shadowy figure stood outside his front door as Jesse pulled his Jeep up the drive and, with no delivery truck in sight, it sent a chill down his spine. Part of him had been expecting an unwanted visitor for weeks, but when none materialized his nerves slowly calmed, like he'd taken half a lorazepam, just enough to take the edge off, like someone starting to believe he might have gotten away with a crime.

As expected, he'd heard an earful from Randall Moss, the man who lived in the Airstream trailer on the vast property across the street. The morning after Norman's disappearance, he pounded on the door sharply at six, an hour when Jesse would not usually be awake, but he had been up all night when Norman had . . . *left*, and so coffee was on—a second pot.

"Randall," Jesse said wearily when he answered the door. "Coffee?" He thrust a mug into his neighbor's hand to play nice. Randall was older, in his late sixties, and just about the opposite shape of Jesse, a hair over five feet and rather rotund. It was almost hard to imagine them as the same species.

"You two and your renovation," Randall groused. "I thought the worst was behind you. But floodlights at two a.m.?"

Jesse was surprised it was the blinding lights more than the wind that rattled his neighbor, since Randall lived in what seemed to Jesse like a glorified tin can. But he had anticipated this encounter and had an answer at the ready. "Sorry, Randall. We're doing a bit of nightscaping." His heart raced at the lie. He went on to explain that nightscaping was simply landscaping done under the cover of night, and that the guy they'd hired was a real artist, except he pronounced it *ar-TEEST*, as he knew that would play to Randall's disdain for elites. "He might also be a wind shaman, if there is such a thing?"

Randall, to his credit, wasn't buying any of it. "Then what was with the klieg lights?"

This is what shock had done to Jesse, he already forgot this complaint was about lights. "Oh, he brought a few lights to make his way around, but I think mostly that was the moon."

Randall shook his head—*that was no moon*—and Jesse thought it best to change the subject.

The more he lied in the days that followed Norman's disappearance, the more he came to feel like he was overreacting. It was a cover-up so good he began to doubt the crime. Maybe he hadn't seen what he thought he had? Maybe it was as simple as Norman needing some space—not *going* to space—and that he was merely away on a build or overseas visiting his parents. But then night would come, and the loneliness would strike, and Jesse would remember anew that he'd been abandoned.

But even with the most perfect crime, there were always loose ends. Which is why Jesse both expected the shadowy figure at his door and why it was so unsettling. He slowed the Jeep to a crawl to get a better look at the front of his house, but his visitor was obscured in part by a ficus. He put the car in park and killed the engine and when he opened the door he was flustered, even though he told himself over and over again to remain calm as he approached his own house carrying a canvas bag of groceries like a shield.

And then recognition set in.

"Lally?" Jesse asked, nearly dropping his tote and pulling her into a tight hug, the ferocity of which surprised even him. "How long have you been standing here?" Norman's sister, Lally Alfano, was the thing he'd forgotten—lately, it was easy for Jesse to imagine himself the extent of his husband's relations. Norman's parents had retired back to Italy to renovate one of those grand *proprietà* the government was giving away for pennies on the dollar to those willing to restore them to glory. He had a brother, Robbie, who'd died when Norman was a teen, more than a decade before Norman and Jesse had met. And Lally, a flight attendant, flitted in and out of their lives as her busy flying schedule allowed. In fact, Jesse wasn't even certain he had her current phone number.

"Are you going to invite me in?" she asked, pushing her brother-in-law off her after a quick squeeze.

Until she asked, Jesse wasn't certain he was. But she furrowed her brows, thick like Norman's but more feminine, and pushed back the single gray streak in her dark hair to insinuate that *no* was not an answer she'd accept.

"Of course. It's just . . ."

She was still wearing her uniform, the clothes scratchy and vaguely outdated. He reached for her roller bag, which was surprisingly light; he exhaled in relief, she wasn't planning on staying.

"It's just *what*?" Lally challenged.

Jesse tried to remember what was behind the closed door as he fumbled for his keys. A can of frosting left open on the kitchen counter into which he dipped a spoon when the mood struck. (No cake, mind you. Baking required too much effort.) Drawn shades, leaving the house not dark exactly, but certainly not bright, either. Bags of burnt popcorn, because even though every microwave had a popcorn setting, every bag of popcorn apparently came with a dire warning not to use it. But this was Norman's sister; refusing her entry would ring more alarm bells than swallowing his shame and allowing her inside. Jesse mumbled something untrue about their nonexistent housekeeper recently quitting as he unlocked the door. Lally didn't seem all that surprised, as if it was common knowledge that Jesse and Norman were a nightmare to work for.

"Is that Norman's shirt?"

Jesse glanced down at what he was wearing. It was a T-shirt with a xenomorph from the movie *Alien* colored in red, white, and green that said *It-alien*. "This?" Lately he had taken to wearing Norman's clothes, thinking if he could get inside his husband he could just understand. Some of his shirts even still smelled like him. But they were clearly different sizes, and this particular shirt barely covered Jesse's midriff.

"I can't believe you go out in public like that."

Jesse tugged at the hem like a teenage girl going through an awkward growth spurt; until a few weeks ago, he wouldn't have believed it, either. He opened the door fully and stepped aside to, against his better judgment, allow company in.

"I texted Norman to tell him I was coming."

Jesse braced himself. "Did you get a response?"

Lally felt along the wall for a light switch until she found one. "Typical Norman, he did not text me back. So I took a Lyft from the airport."

Jesse hoped she wouldn't see her brother's phone abandoned on his nightstand, the battery now long dead. He would have to keep her clear of their bedroom.

Lally's eyes scanned her surroundings with both awe and disgust. "I can never tell if this cold, industrial thing is a look you two are going for, or if two men are naturally bad at keeping house."

"Oh, don't kid yourself. We work hard at it." Jesse turned a dying houseplant, so that its last few healthy leaves hid the worst of its rot.

"I can't believe you left the ocean for this. Are those windmills?" she asked, staring out the back of the house—the tips of the blades peered over the tamarisk trees. It was true it wasn't the ocean, but it was not without a view.

"Would you like to freshen up, Lally?" He pointed to the guest bath down the hall. Lally was one of those names that rich people swear is short for something perfectly benign, Elizabeth, perhaps, when the rest of the world would go with Liz or Betty. In this case it was a name their late brother Robbie called her when she was young, some butchering of *little sister* and her given name, Lauretta. The name used to strike Jesse as odd, but years on it rolled off the tongue.

"Do I *need* to freshen up?"

Jesse didn't see an upside in his answering that question honestly. "Of course not. I love that uniform. It really brings out the gray in your skin." Lally made a sour face; the playful rapport they used to have when they were young and saw much more of one another now bordered on rude. Still, she took his point without protest and hauled her roller bag down the hall, Jesse worrying about their concrete floors on Norman's behalf.

Once alone, he scrambled to close the cabinet doors beneath the island, while pushing a mostly empty pizza box into the trash, followed by a few dry bones of crust that sat by the sink. He looked at his house through a stranger's eyes. The décor was minimal, which made the mess maximal. But it wasn't the mess that Lally had scrutinized; if anything it made the home seem more lived in and therefore less unwelcoming. It was the aesthetic and architecture. The polished concrete floor, which ran seamlessly throughout, notwithstanding the few cracks that had appeared the night of Norman's disappearance; it felt lucky the house hadn't lifted cleanly from its slab foundation. The wood beams and the glass that made the place feel so open. The very modern chandeliers and the midcentury concrete-block walls, walls that made it very difficult to place art, save for the few pieces on top of the low bookcases that were propped up without wires or nails. A complicated macramé wall hanging of knotted rope did brighten one corner, but it looked as much like a net to ensnare prey as it did something crafty that might soften a home.

The kitchen island was long and narrow, the countertops an ivory marble with pencil-thin veining that ended at the refrigerator, a commercial-grade model that cost as much as a certified preowned car; Jesse had spent hours alone over the past weeks listening to the ice maker drop its two different-sized cubes, an event that was always both startling and comforting. In front of the island in place of barstools was a long planter dug right into the floor, filled with unwelcoming barrel cactuses planted in a sea of pea gravel. That impulse cooks had of wanting their kitchen to feel warm and for guests to pull up a stool while they cooked? This was the opposite feeling of that. It screamed *Don't look at me*, if not *Go away*, and perhaps for that reason Norman and Jesse had yet to host a dinner party. There was nowhere to enjoy a glass of wine and the pleasure of one's company while preparing a meal, inhaling the intoxicating scents of the evening's menu while trading in juicy secrets. At least the items Jesse was scrambling to tidy—a box of crackers in the entryway instead of the pantry; a basket of laundry, unfolded, Jesse uncertain anymore if it was on its way to or from the machine; pens, so many pens, scattered across the counter—were evidence that *someone* lived here. Any resident of this space seemed schizophrenic, something he felt Norman's designs were as much to blame for as his housekeeping. Still, at the last moment, Jesse hid the can of frosting in their dishwasher, which had the same facing as the cabinets and thus disappeared when he slammed it closed.

When Lally returned, the house was looking more or less presentable, save for his papers on the dining room table, and Jesse was putting away his groceries. She had changed into yoga pants and a top that fell off one shoulder, and she headed straight for the dual-zone wine fridge and selected herself a Sancerre. "Do you mind?" she asked after she had already found the corkscrew.

"Help yourself," Jesse said as he stashed the last few items from his bag in the cabinet. "A glass might calm your nerves before your audition for *Flashdance*."

Lally shook her head. "You're mean."

I'm mean? Jesse thought. *I'M SPIRALING!* He quickly gathered himself. "It's this new book I'm working on," he lied, hoping she would understand he was under a lot of pressure.

"No it's not." It was the first thing she said that he actually heard, and he felt it deep in his chest. He had been this way for a while. Is he the one that drove Norman away? Was he to blame for all of this? He didn't mean to be. He remembered emailing Norman a study that said partners who playfully insult one another are three hundred percent more honest and loyal. The subject line of his email? *You Odious Crone.* Norman never replied. What if he deleted the email without opening it? What if he never read the study or got the joke and thought Jesse was just being unkind?

Lally paused, narrowing her eyes. It was clear now she could see he was spiraling, and she hesitated, the corkscrew halfway deployed. "Maybe we should wait for Norman." She abandoned the wine and wandered over to the dining table, which was covered with legal notepads filled with Jesse's scribbles and piles of paper that only in the most generous interpretation could be described as stacks. Lally flipped through a few pages without asking permission. Jesse had scribbled his memories of that night as he often did with important events, perhaps to write about one day, perhaps to prove to himself that they actually happened. "Is this it? Is this the new book?" It wasn't exactly like she was Shelley Duvall discovering Jack Nicholson's gibberish, but there was nothing on the table he wanted her to see.

"Let's open that wine," he said, steering her back to the kitchen. He grabbed two long-stemmed glasses from the cabinet, admiring the varietal-specific bowls he and Norman had picked out to highlight the crisp whites they enjoyed on warm California evenings. Another lifetime, it seemed.

"*Should* we wait for Norman?" Lally repeated, this time phrasing it as a question.

Jesse struggled with the corkscrew, tearing a bit of cork. "I think we would be waiting a very long time."

Once he'd served them two generous pours, Jesse told Lally that Norman was in Minneapolis on one of his usual work trips. It was a story he had tried out on himself, and one that seemed most believable.

"Minneapolis."

"Or Cincinnati."

Lally nodded slowly, taking this information in. "What is it this time? An office building? Department store? They don't still build malls anymore, do they? Although I haven't been through Cincinnati in a while."

"Medical building," Jesse lied. It was the last thing he could remember Norman drafting, a project too industrial to satisfy his creative soul but one that always paid well. "People *need* medical buildings," Jesse had assured him one night when Norman seemed downhearted. "We have an aging society."

"People need *books*," Norman volleyed. Jesse assured him only to crush spiders.

Lally sipped her wine, then ran her hand down her neck like she was a dog being encouraged to swallow a pill. She approached the counter to set her glass down, stopping just in time to avoid stubbing her toe on one of the barrel cactuses. "That's welcoming," she muttered, bending down to see if they were real. "You know, it's just as well Norman's gone. You guys could benefit from some time apart."

Jesse rubbed his eyes until they hurt. "We could?"

"*You* could. What has it been, a decade since your last book? And he's designing buildings left and right? You let him take the lead when you should be spreading your wings."

Jesse looked puzzled. Could Norman be doing him a favor?

"Besides, I'm really here to see you."

"Me?" Jesse hid his face behind his wineglass like he was looking for something, sulfates or tannins, so that she wouldn't read the surprise on his face. It had been a long time since the two of them had been in the same room without Norman.

"Is that so hard to believe?"

It was, in certain regards. In the early days of his relationship, when he and Norman had that apartment in Venice Beach only a few hundred feet from the sand, Lally, a dozen years younger than Norman but only a handful of years younger than Jesse, used to be a regular fixture in their lives. She would drop in unannounced, behavior not as strange as it is today given that it was a time before cell phones and people were generally more difficult to reach. They would go for tacos at a hole-in-the-wall place on the water, one of the last few stands holding on as the bars and restaurants that made the beach unique fell one by one to chain places that made Venice feel like Santa Monica, or any other part of L.A. Jesse and Lally would grab extra tacos for Domingo, a homeless man with an easy gap-toothed smile who was the unofficial mayor of the surrounding blocks, which they referred to as "the village," then listen intently to his stories about how much better things had been in the seventies and his predictions for the future, like he was some sort of prophet.

Jesse suddenly had an overwhelming desire for tacos, not just any, but *those* soft tacos, made with tortillas warmed on a gas flame and with the perfect amount of diced raw onions and cilantro. And Norman's company then, when they were young, when they couldn't stand to be apart for even a day. He inhaled deeply, like if he tried hard enough he could transport himself back there. "I have an idea," he said, placing his wineglass down on the counter before he drank any more. And after she mounted only a mild protest, and Jesse agreed to change his shirt, he took her to the Tiny Pony, as they had the only kitchen open late for miles.

The Tiny Pony tavern was surprisingly busy, but Jesse was able to snag their usual table and they were quickly served drinks. It felt strange to dine in their spot with someone who was not his husband, but also better than sitting alone. At least it was homey; the warm light came from pendants that hung over the long wooden bar, and the tavern was filled with laughter. Ordinary people living their ordinary lives, none of them aware that they could be snatched at any time by light that was even warmer. While they were studying their menus, the floor shook, causing Jesse to grip the table, bracing for the worst. Thankfully, it was merely three enthusiastic women trying to demonstrate line dancing to their dates. Slowly, he eased into himself.

"It's been a long time since we've sat at a table like this."

Lally looked around and seemed equally enmeshed in the nostalgia. Without so much as a cell phone in sight, they could have easily been back in the 1990s. But instead of responding, Lally sat silently, head bowed, looking in the wine she had ordered. After a moment, she opened her mouth, then closed it, and did that again two or three times.

"What?" Jesse asked, suddenly concerned she had some news about Norman and was struggling to find a way to break it. The silence grew even more uncomfortable, an onion blooming before them, Jesse assigning horrific new meaning to each layer.

"You seem a bit . . . adrift," Lally confessed. The restaurant was loud, and they pulled their chairs in tighter to the table as a new party was seated behind them.

"Do I?" Jesse had thought the past few weeks were strange, but the way this visit was unfolding, it might be even stranger.

Lally exhaled like she was being unfairly pressed, even though she was the one who started it, the one who was lurking uninvited on Jesse's doorstep. "I'm not surprised. You're the passenger in your relationship, Jesse, always have been. You should use this time away from Norman." And then, as if she were worried she had been too harsh, she added, "I'm glad you're writing."

He spun his michelada in a circle. "If you can call it that."

"Your life needs some purpose, Jesse. Apart from Norman, I mean. That's true for both of us, if I'm being honest. I meant what I said earlier."

Jesse cocked his head. "Are you asking me to join Scientology?"

"I want the embryos."

Jesse sat very still, like one might in the presence of a bee or a T. rex, hoping to become invisible, then shook his head like a cartoon character that wasn't sure he'd heard something right. "You want the what?"

"Don't make me ask twice."

He replayed her words in his head. "I didn't hear you ask once."

"I would like the embryos, *please*."

Jesse suddenly wished he employed a stenographer so he could read her back the transcript. "Still not a question."

Their waiter approached. "I see you have drinks?" Jesse glanced up to find himself face-to-face with *the* waiter, the very one he and Norman would flirt with. "Oh, it's you. Where's the other one?"

"The other one?" Lally asked, catching up.

"The hot daddy," the waiter said with a smile.

"Okay," Jesse said, cutting him off. "Hot daddy's *sister* and I are going to need a moment to decide." The waiter took Jesse's hint and in a flash they were alone again. Jesse did his best to explain. "Norman and I come here a lot. We're maybe a little too familiar with some of the staff."

"Like the waiter, for instance?"

Jesse nodded. "Now I follow him on Instagram and he posts three shirtless stories a day, all in the same pose, and like—am I supposed to hit the fire emoji *every* time? When did his self-esteem become my full-time job?"

Lally stared at him like she was willing the clock to go back three minutes. "Not all of the embryos, mind you. Not necessarily. But some." She paused with a pained expression on her face.

"Oh my god, are we *still* talking about this?"

"May I have access to more than one but less than all of the embryos we created?" When he failed to respond, she held Jesse's gaze and challenged him. "Jesse."

"Lally."

"You're not doing anything with them!"

Jesse wondered how Lally could possibly know that, unless she had called the medical facility they were employing for cryopreservation, and he highly doubted they would give her that information. "This is really a conversation Norman should be a part of." It was, of course, a cowardly loophole; Norman might never again be part of this conversation. But it was, in the moment, something Jesse was willing to exploit.

"Should he?" Lally crossed her arms defensively. "You don't want to be parents anymore. And that's fine. You want to do unspeakable things to the waiter. I don't judge! But you shouldn't punish me because of it."

In one sense, she was right. (Although not about the waiter, as both he and Norman had become rather vanilla—they wanted to do regular *speakable* things.) But in regard to the embryos, should Norman have a say? The embryos in question were the product of an egg donation from Lally fertilized by Jesse's sperm thanks to the miracle of IVF, created before the pandemic, when Jesse and Norman thought after marriage what they should do next was have kids.

"What could you possibly want with the embryos?"

Lally put both hands on her hips and Jesse saw her as he had when they were younger, the kid sister he never had. "I thought I could put them in a jar like sea monkeys and keep them as pets."

Jesse responded flatly, "Oh, that's nice."

"I want to be a mother, Jesse."

"So, be a mother."

"Do you know how old I am? My eggs were borderline geriatric when we harvested them. Not to mention I'm single. C'mon. I have perfectly healthy embryos sitting in a freezer ripe for the taking. This may be my only chance. Don't make this more humiliating than it already is." Lally turned her wineglass three times on the table before picking it up to sip.

Jesse blanched at her phrasing. *I have.* Legally, Lally had nothing. She made them sound like a bowl of Halloween candy rich people leave unattended with a little note that says, *Help yourself.* "They're not 'ripe for the taking.'" Jesse made obnoxious air quotes to convey his disgust.

"These babies are my best option."

Jesse downed the last of his drink in one spicy sip and motioned to their waiter for another. *Babies.* They had all been specifically told not to think of the embryos that way so that it wouldn't be traumatic if they had the unused ones destroyed. If they needed proof, they were told babies would die in the freezing process, where embryos—embryos lived. "You have other options."

Lally shook her head no. "None as good as this one."

"You could adopt."

"As a single woman my age who travels? I'm not the most ideal candidate."

"What about one of those Romanian children that turns out to be an adult? You could adopt one of those." Lally didn't find that at all funny, but Jesse told her to think about it—she could have a spread in *People.* "I can't be the father of your child."

"Oh, but I could be the mother of yours?"

"You weren't going to be the mother of our child, you signed paperwork to that effect."

"Genetically. You know what I mean."

Jesse fished his phone out of his pocket and stared intently at his lock screen. A small part of him hoped that Norman would call at that moment; even if the caller ID said OUT OF AREA and it was most likely a telemarketer he would answer with the highest of hopes. Alas, his phone betrayed him and the silence in the room became deafening. On the jukebox someone played a song from Carole King's *Tapestry*; until this moment, it was an album that never failed to soothe him. Eventually he laughed. The timing of it all. The embryos had been in a freezer for seven years.

"Why is this funny?"

"It's not," Jesse admitted, and he signaled to their server for another round.

Lally glanced at Jesse's phone, which he'd set on the table. "What if we *call* Norman," she suggested.

"*Long distance?*" Jesse asked.

"You're right. It's late in Minneapolis." A frown spread across Lally's face. "Did you do something to him?"

Jesse's face turned red as his new michelada was placed in front of him. He buried his face in the menu to convey that they had yet to decide. "Do something? Like what?" It was the first time it occurred to him that he might be a suspect in Norman's disappearance.

"Relax, I'm kidding." Lally lowered the menu in front of her brother-in-law's face. "Unless you really *did* do something to him."

"What? *No.* Of course not."

They sat silently for a minute, listening to Carole move the earth under her feet while the sky came tumbling down, tumbling down. Jesse didn't know if he'd ever be able to hear that song the same way again. "Is this what you meant by my life needing meaning?" Oh, god. It was all sinking in. All Lally could do was shrug. "How long are you planning to stay?" he asked, hoping to change the subject.

"I have the jump seat on an early plane to L.A. Then I'm working a morning flight to Philadelphia."

"The City of Brotherly Love," he said, since Norman was her brother. And technically he was, too, by marriage and history, as they shared a lot between them, including nine embryos in a storage facility in Beverly Hills. They sipped their drinks and waited to order food, and Jesse listened to snippets of other conversations in the absence of their own.

"I'm not asking you to be a father. You know that, don't you?"

Jesse wasn't really sure what she was asking.

"I'm just saying because I know you have issues in that department. You and Norman are off the hook. This is something I want to do on my own. I can do this entirely without you."

Without you. The words bounced around inside his skull; he knew almost certainly they, more than the alcohol, would be the cause of his headache tomorrow. Jesse had been *without* his entire life, at least as far as a father was concerned. His mother, were she here, would cross her arms and scoff at the idea that he had been left without everything he needed, and she would certainly hate the idea of him in therapy, blaming her, no doubt, for what ailed him. But what Jesse felt he needed, particularly when he was younger (and if not needed, certainly *wanted* from time to time), was a male role model. Someone to teach him about masculinity. His mother had even wondered around the time of his coming out if that was what made him gay before Jesse adamantly squashed that offensive theory, explaining that was not how these things worked. But maybe it is what made him commit at such a young age to a man—an older one at that. His need for stability. His absolute fear of men leaving. "Please. Let's not talk about my father."

Lally tilted her head to the side, and her hair grazed her one bare shoulder. Jesse knew what she was thinking. That he and Norman had called off their plans for fatherhood because Jesse hadn't dealt emotionally with his own lack of one. This was not true, but Jesse felt no need to defend himself against her silent accusations. Lally opened her mouth to speak, and again Jesse said, "Don't." His annoyance then gave way to sympathy.

For his entire adult life Jesse had had a partner by his side, and he suddenly felt for Lally, who hadn't. Everything he accomplished, he accomplished *with* someone, never stopping to think about the value of simply being in a relationship, if that vaulted him forward or held him back. But now his eyes were open. Had he not had Norman, what might he have accomplished? How many books might he have written if he hadn't been so . . . *happy*? Conversely, what leaps had he taken without thinking because the safety net of Norman was there?

Until now. Maybe he did need this time on his own. Maybe he needed to become a man of action. But he wasn't going to let Lally entirely off the hook. "I can't believe you'd say that about us wanting to be parents. You know what we went through."

Lally's demeanor softened. She even reached out for his hand. "You're right. That was uncalled for. You didn't deserve what happened to you."

"And I don't want to do things with the waiter." Certainly not anymore. Unless "things" included schooling him in having a less irritating social media presence.

Lally studied him as he passed their table. "He's cute," she offered in a conciliatory tone.

Eventually they ordered dinner and Jesse got his tacos, the special that night. Someone killed the jukebox in favor of karaoke. They dared each other to sing, but neither did. They even had a laugh or two. It was good, Jesse thought, to feel connected to Norman, to have a laugh with someone who'd known him nearly as long as his husband had. "I'll talk to Norman," he said of the embryos at the end of their meal, and Lally thanked him. That was all she wanted him to do. Jesse needed to keep her on his good side. He didn't need anyone running around looking for Norman half-cocked. And with any luck, in a few days she would drop it. Lally was often that way with ideas.

Lally slept that night in his guest room, even though she protested and said she could Uber to an airport hotel.

"An Uber driver will never find you. Half the streets up here have no names."

"I found you, didn't I?" Lally protested. And Jesse had to admit that she had.

"Still. You'd better let me take you to the airport."

"At the crack of dawn?" Lally shook her head like she couldn't ask him to do that.

"I'm up early these days. Can't sleep." Eventually she relented.

But when Jesse woke the next morning, Lally was already gone. No note, bed made, barely any evidence that she'd even been there.

What is it, he thought, *with this family?*

DAY TWENTY-SIX

Jesse pulled into the COD parking lot two hours early and found his usual spot. *Take that, Lally,* he thought. The passenger in his own relationship? He was fully behind the wheel now. But he also knew his sister-in-law had a point, or days later the criticism would not still sting. Slowly, he made his way to the faculty lounge, where he hoped to do some work. The coffee was, as expected, terrible—somehow both bitter and weak, with a slightly fishy taste (but he may have just had COD on the brain). He reached for the sweetener only to graze the hand of another professor.

"Oh, sorry," he said before looking up to see the most handsome man, late twenties maybe, with a whisper of premature gray. He looked not unlike Norman when he was young.

"No problem," the man said with a smile. He had dark brown eyes, and perfect scruff that was just shy of a beard. "You go ahead." He gestured at Jesse's coffee. "You're going to need it." His own cup of coffee was from somewhere off campus.

"So that's the secret," Jesse said, pointing at the other man's cup. He then offered his free hand to shake. "Jesse."

"Orson," the man said, and held the handshake longer than Jesse might have expected. "And there are many secrets when it comes to survival," he said with a wry smile. Jesse caught himself staring at the ample chest hair visible behind the two open buttons of Orson's shirt.

"I think I'm learning," Jesse said.

Orson replied, "Ironic, since you're here to teach. But yeah, for starters you're going to want coffee from off campus." He then reached for the sweetener and added some to his cup. "Off to class. See you around, Jesse."

Jesse smiled and watched him go. As far as collisions went, it didn't have the same impact as his initial meeting with Norman. But it also was not nothing.

The lounge was blessedly quiet and he found an empty round table where he could work, offering polite nods to the room's few other occupants, not one of whom held a candle to the mysterious Orson. Faculty lounges were the same from campus to campus—at least at the schools where he taught—and he was comforted by familiarity. The exhausted looks of teachers, wearing clothes from whatever era they had felt most in their prime. The slight smell of wet, mimeographed exams, although no one understood why—technology like that had not been in use since he was in grammar school. Reams of paper stored on shelving that sagged in the middle under the weight. He held his paper coffee cup by the rim, as at least it was blessedly hot, and before he sat down he perused a few posts on a bulletin board. Someone was selling a Volkswagen Tiguan with only twenty thousand miles. There was a flyer for a poetry club with an illustration of cows, *moos* in place of *muse*. But what caught his eye most was the word MISSING in bold red lettering, above a photocopied image of a woman with blond streaks in her hair who looked like she played the tambourine.

"Sad story there," said a deep voice behind him. Jesse spun around to see a man who looked like Wallace Shawn. "She went hiking in the Monument and *poof,* disappeared. Never heard from again."

"Just disappeared?" Jesse asked, appalled.

The man waved to another faculty member he knew, then poured himself coffee. "It happens."

Shaken, Jesse wandered back to his table and sat down. These things didn't *just happen*. How could one be so cavalier? Or maybe they did. Maybe what happened to Norman (and thus to him) was not all that special? To vanquish the thought, he reached for an abandoned newspaper, an old copy of the *Desert Sun*. The hot topic was the new surface of the tennis courts at Indian Wells, home of the Paribas Open—Laykold over the previous brand Plexipave; the new surface was already in use at the US Open and the Miami Open, the other two largest tournaments in the United States, giving Laykold the triumvirate. Jesse doodled on his pad—*Sorry, Plexipave!*—before tearing off the page, crumpling it, and dropping it on the floor. He turned his attention to the assignment he'd given to his students—to write about a time when they felt abandoned—and after several false starts, and wads of crumpled yellow paper joining the one by his feet, he started to write in earnest.

I was six years old when my mother got me a dog, a rescue shepherd mix; at that point I had been begging her for a pet for months. I didn't have a father, and there were only so many things she wanted her son to miss out on. In that regard I was able to play her like a fiddle. At the pound I had picked out a cat, but my mother said cats killed too many things she was fond of like chipmunks and birds. That may have been a lie, as I heard her curse a bird once for flying into a window with a thud, making her drop her cigarette. She probably thought a canine would get her sensitive kid to toughen up—and a shepherd was a lot of dog. But my friend Petey had a pet tabby who brought home dead mice to lay at their doorstep—oftentimes just the heads—so who knows. I named the dog Snowball, which is what I was planning to name a cat.

"There he is! Our newest teacher, back in the saddle." It was Luisa Flores, his department chair, hovering over him, arms full as ever as she awkwardly tried to eat an apple. Her curls were not as pronounced today; her hair had more of a wave and it softened her face as a whole. She leaned forward to take a bite of her snack, stealing a look at Jesse's notepad. "A dog named Snowball," she observed. "What are you working on?"

Jesse self-consciously covered his work with his arms. "The assignment that's due today. I thought I would do it alongside the kids."

Luisa laughed. "Kids? Nathan is forty-five."

"Who's Nathan?" Jesse asked without thinking. Luisa set her books on the table and plunked herself down in a chair. "Oh, Nathan!" Jesse said, reading the look on her face. Nathan Treadwell. *Non-Trad.* "Yeah, I guess 'kids' isn't exactly the right word." And then, as if reading her thoughts, he glanced at his work and added, "I haven't arrived at the funny part yet. And, if you don't mind, I'd like to select any books for the syllabus."

Luisa shrugged. "It's your class." She went on to say the course was a late addition to the fall schedule and she was only trying to help.

"Say, speaking of new additions, do you know a faculty member named Orson? He was just in here. He looked on the young side, so I thought maybe he was new, too."

"You could try the faculty directory. How many Orsons could

there be?" She took another bite of her apple and returned her attention to Jesse's notepad. "What was the assignment? If you don't mind me asking."

"To write a humorous account of a time you felt abandoned."

Luisa raised a finger in the air and pointed at the sky. "Aliens," she said while gnawing an obnoxious piece of apple skin.

Jesse shuddered. "Excuse me?"

"Abandonment. When I asked about your summer, you said your husband was abducted by aliens."

Had he? Jesse supposed he could have let that slip in an attempt to be flippant; he was only now snapping out of a haze since Lally's visit. As Luisa still seemed to be charmed by the idea, he agreed. "Oh yes, my husband was abducted by aliens."

Luisa tossed her apple core into a nearby rubbish bin with surprising dexterity, and the resulting sound made the other faculty in the room flinch. She brushed her hands clean and then looked Jesse deep in the eyes. "I still say you're lucky. I would give anything if aliens just swooped down and took my husband. Honestly, they can have him!"

Jesse gritted his teeth and held up crossed fingers on both hands. *Here's hoping.* Since this was all a joke to Luisa, he took the opportunity to ask a serious question. "But how would you move on with your life? One day he's gone, and then what. What do you do with the next day?"

Luisa considered this, as if she, too, were completing the assignment. "Burn his Barcalounger?" she mused. A wistful smile made Jesse think she was imagining dragging it onto the lawn and doing just that. "Honestly, marriages were not supposed to last this long. The Pilgrims had the right idea dying at forty."

Jesse laughed politely. "Okay, but after you burn his chair. Do you have him declared . . . *dead*?"

Luisa's expression drooped; this from a man she had hired to teach humor. Jesse recognized the change in demeanor. He needed to keep this light.

"It's for something I'm writing," he lied. And then covered his work again. "Not this."

"Oh, well. I would divorce the bastard."

You're the passenger in your relationship. "Yeah, but how. He's *missing*."

Luisa chewed on this for a moment. Then she called to another professor reading a book over by the window. He had sort of Ben Franklin hair, a style Jesse had previously heard called a skullet. "Larry." Larry looked up from his book. Luisa pointed at the MISSING flyer on the wall. "What did Donna's husband do when she didn't come back. After a year, didn't he say he was initiating divorce?"

Larry chewed on his thumbnail while thinking. "Yes. I think he said as much at Charles's retirement thing. Her family refused to have her declared dead, so instead he pursued divorce."

"Did he say how he went about it? Given that she was . . . *you know*."

Larry did know. "He had to advertise for her in the paper."

Good lord. The *newspaper*? Jesse glanced at the discarded *Desert Sun* and immediately imagined someone seeing his ad and doodling, *Sorry, Jesse!* the way he had written, *Sorry, Plexipave!*

"You have to make a reasonable effort to serve a spouse with divorce papers," Larry continued. "If you don't know where to contact them, you have to advertise a month or two in a paper that's local to their last known address."

"Really?" Jesse asked, horrified. He couldn't imagine admitting such a thing to the entire Coachella Valley. *Help, I can't find my hus-*

band! In newsprint? He didn't know that many locals, or people who still read a newspaper, but his neighbor, Randall, would certainly see. What if his students did, too?

"There you go," Luisa said, somewhat triumphantly. "Personally, I'd take out a front-page ad."

"Or maybe there's a place to do it online. Facebook, or something. Either way, he had to request permission from the court to proceed this way. I remember that. But otherwise, I didn't press. We all wanted the focus to be on Charles and his retirement." Larry directed his next bit at Jesse. "Charles taught environmental horticulture here for forty-one years."

Luisa kicked her chair back under the table, and it made a horrible scraping sound. "I'll let you get back to work."

Jesse smiled politely and watched until he was sure she had gone, waved his thanks to Larry, mostly to make sure he understood their interaction was through, checked his phone for the time, and returned to writing.

After a few terrible months, Snowball and I negotiated a fragile peace given that we were both a bit scared of each other. We would snarl at times, but also collapse together when exhausted, a pile of limbs on a couch, too tired to care. I don't think Mom regretted her decision, she may even have thought her plan was working; there was something about Snowball, despite his name, that toughened me up.

But it's not possible to outrun irony, and one day Snowball came home carrying the neighbor kid's dead guinea pig, a white and tan ball of fluff named Licorice. Licorice didn't look a damn thing like his name, but that's something he and Snowball had in common. Licorice was filthy like he'd been dragged through the mud, but at least the corpse was intact. Thank goodness for small miracles. I panicked. If Snowball was in trouble with anyone, I wanted it to be me; by that point I couldn't live with the idea of him being taken away.

I yelled and waved my arms and generally carried on until Snowball thought I'd damn near lost my mind. He dropped Licorice in the driveway and moseyed on to the toys he knew he could chew without me flapping my wings like a sick egret. Well, I must have been someone even I didn't recognize, because I remained calm and went into crisis mode. I picked Licorice up and shampooed his tiny body in the laundry room sink with Woolite. I knew fur was not wool, but neither were Mom's delicates and that was all I'd seen her use Woolite for. And what was more delicate than the corpse of an old guinea pig? Carefully, I used Mom's blow-dryer with the diffuser attachment to make Licorice look fluffy and new; when I was done, even I had to admit he looked like he was sleeping. Then, when I knew the neighbors weren't home, I snuck into their barn using the window that didn't latch and returned Licorice to his cage, where he promptly keeled over. Good enough, *I thought, and got the hell out.*

Jesse stopped, cracked his knuckles, and took a sip of coffee, which tasted even more like fish as it cooled. Orson was right. This would be his last cup from the school.

It was early evening when I heard the scream, which in itself could wake the dead. Snowball and I stood side by side, each knowing our part in this horror, but both determined to feign innocence. As long as we stuck together, no one could break us. That is, until my mother approached. Snowball took off running, leaving me holding the bag.

"Goddammit, Snowball!" I screamed at the time, for which my mother threatened to wash my mouth out with not Woolite, but actual soap. Snowball hid himself well for two days.

You couldn't even see the neighbor's house—there was a strip of city property and a string of power lines between us, but it was clear where the scream came from and what the fuss was about. The neighbor kid had discovered his dead pet. Still, it seemed like an unholy amount of screaming over a rodent, and one that was old, at that. My mother found out later through the neighborhood grapevine that Licorice had actually died a day or two earlier of natural causes (or as natural as you could get for a guinea pig), and the neighbor family had buried him on the edge of their property under the shade of a tree. Old Snowball had been exploring the property line when his nose told him there was buried treasure nearby. I never told anyone what really happened, how the neighbor's pet returned from a dirt grave clean as new and with the gentle fragrance of laundry, inside its locked cage, and Snowball took the secret to his grave. He wasn't ever going to share a cell with me if I ever got found out. But at least he wasn't going to rat me out, either.

When Jesse finished, he reread his work and smiled. Not his best writing—it needed a copyedit—but perfectly acceptable for a class assignment, an introductory one at that. They could all have a laugh at Licorice's expense. It wasn't even in the top five times he felt abandoned (a more recent example had shot to number one with a bullet), and honestly it probably wouldn't make the top ten.

Comedy, after all, equaled tragedy plus time—something there had not yet been enough of in regard to current events. But it was funny and that was enough. He wasn't ready to be an open book with his students, and it would take a lot more than a liter of Mountain Dew for him to spill.

"Who here feels abandoned?" Jesse asked as he entered the absurdly large classroom and set his belongings on the desk; one by one they all raised their hands as he fished his own pages out of his messenger bag. *Good*, Jesse thought. It saved him the trouble of explaining why they should. Non-Trad aside, younger people had better feel abandoned—acknowledgment was the first step toward change. They'd been abandoned by the promise of everything: a living wage, affordable housing, a sustainable planet, happiness, cable TV, the concept of retirement, the ability to step foot in a classroom without the fear of getting shot, a world without measles, three-camera sitcoms, politicians who weren't Twitter trolls. What boomers weren't taking with them, the rest were fighting over for scraps. But telling them as much was no way to evoke a laugh, and this was, after all, a class on comedy writing.

"Good. Abandonment *should* be fun," Jesse snickered, but Snickers, who today would surely be renamed 3 Musketeers if nicknames weren't locked on day one, disagreed. "Okay, well not fun. But part of mining humor is finding it in unexpected places." He stopped as a faint echo rang in his ear. "Did this room get bigger?" The size of the classroom was one of those absurd details he would have dwelled on after his first class if Lally's visit hadn't derailed his week. The room was the same, but there was now a militia of chalkboards, enough to create a maze. Headphones looked around like he was only just noticing that they were but seven in an auditorium that was built for two hundred. "Who wants to share their story first?"

In that moment it was Jesse who was feeling abandoned, as no one, not even Unicorn, volunteered.

"Come on. I know you all did the assignment." It was usually a few weeks into a semester before excuses started rolling in. "No one?" He crossed back to the desk to grab his own feeble story, deciding to lead by example. "We're not looking for perfection, it's just the first assignment. Here. I'll read you mine. And you can see this is just meant to be an exercise."

Jesse wasn't sure what his students expected from an award-winning author, but after a quiet start they found the story delightfully lowbrow, and it gave them permission to laugh. It was one of the things he'd always prided himself on—knowing his audience, even if that audience was usually Norman. It was one of the many reasons he felt so adrift now, not just that he was missing his partner, he was missing that confidence in himself. And yet he plowed forward, finding his voice, and when he finished he asked the class to discuss the story and what made it funny.

"The absurdity of it," Snickers blurted. It was always young men who offered their opinions the loudest. But Jesse had to give him props, it definitely had an air of the absurd.

"The surprise ending," Mountain Dew proffered, firing on all cylinders, clearly having done the Dew. Jesse agreed and wondered if the story he was living might eventually have a similar twist he could mine for inspiration.

"Woolite," Non-Trad added.

"Yes, nostalgia. Plus, it's just a funny word."

Unicorn was the last to offer her thoughts, and when she did she did so without making eye contact with her classmates. "I found it had a surprising tenderness. From the softhearted way the boy treated the guinea pig's body to the obvious care he had for his neighbor's feelings."

"If he really cared," Backpack interjected, "wouldn't he have come clean about what really happened?"

"No," Unicorn disagreed. "He didn't want their last image of their beloved pet to be one filled with violence. He wanted them to picture their guinea pig gently drifting off to sleep. I was able to laugh precisely because the story was not mean, it was just a boy in over his head trying to do his best."

Jesse had to sit on the edge of his desk to catch his breath. He was still that little boy, nearly a half century on, now deeply in over his head and yet still trying his best. Jesse's field of vision started to narrow and he felt pinpricks on the back of his neck. "Yes, I think that's an important observation. Humor can be kind and still funny."

"Mr. Doctor, are you okay?" Headphones was already taking a few steps toward him; he must look like he was going to fall. Jesse grabbed the desk with both hands.

"Yeah, yeah, no," he said, which meant absolutely nothing, so he took a few deep breaths before adding, "I'm fine." Mountain Dew poured him a few sips and pushed her glass in his direction and for once he accepted, thinking maybe his blood sugar was off. He was loath to think she had a valid reason for drinking such slop, but he did feel better soon after he swallowed. "Wow, did you know this was actually good?" Mountain Dew beamed like she'd been given an A. Jesse gathered his thoughts and continued. "Further to Unicorn's point. Many, often straight male, comedians think comedy needs to be mean, or that it's impossible to be funny in politically correct times." Headphones and Snickers worked up a slight protest, but Jesse was thinking as much about himself and Lally's allegation that he had become mean. "But comedy can be gentle, or directed inward like I did with my story. But even then, I wanted to tread carefully, as I was writing about the emotional boy I was and not the empty shell of a man that stands before you today. See? That was directed inward. After we share all of our stories, we'll discuss some more examples."

Headphones kicked the party off with a rousing tale of feeling abandoned in a doctor's office restroom and his utter humiliation when he realized he'd spent his time in there producing the wrong specimen. This had the class both groaning in discomfort and squealing with delight as Headphones leaned into the awkwardness of the situation (and let's face it, without much in the way of privacy or inspiration, a feat of great derring-do) without ever crossing a line into something too vulgar, and Jesse made a mental note afterward to see what had actually been committed to paper and what had been embellished in the room; Headphones was a natural performer and maybe even belonged on the stage, but that was a different class. "It was the first time I had health insurance!" Headphones protested when he finished his story, as if that were a reasonable excuse for jerking off in a public space. The others didn't buy it and thought even if it was his first time seeing a doctor, he should have known the difference between what was requested from a fertility clinic versus a yearly physical.

Snickers and Backpack likewise acquitted themselves nicely, although Jesse knew instantly neither was in danger of becoming a world-class humorist; their stories were convivial more than comical. (That was fine, as they were easy and generous with a laugh—every comedian needs an audience.)

Mountain Dew wrote about a friend of hers from high school who had died of cancer. A few days after the friend passed, Mountain Dew received a package from the deceased, something she had arranged to be delivered after she was gone. Inside was a Ouija board along with a note that read *LET'S KEEP IN TOUCH!*; Mountain

Dew hated that her friend got the last laugh. Unicorn's story was about being dropped off at summer camp by a single mother who was clearly at the end of her rope. While it did not elicit the heartiest laughs from the group, it did most exemplify what humor could say about the human condition, and therefore Unicorn kept her title.

But it was Non-Trad who pulled the biggest surprise out of his briefcase. Jesse had expected a sad story of divorce, or being stood up at the altar; men who feel awkward around women often find themselves gravitating to comedy. His story took place in the wake of a breakup, yes, but it centered on something unexpected. Jesse could see that his story was handwritten, double-spaced on a legal pad, handwriting neat enough for a ransom note as penned by some meticulous thug.

"A what?" Jesse asked early in the story when Non-Trad uttered a word with which he was not familiar.

"I'm sorry?" Non-Trad asked in return, unsure why he was asked to stop; indeed, he was just picking up steam.

"What word are you saying?"

Non-Trad looked strained, like he was trying to shake off annoyance, like it hadn't been the very teacher standing in front of him that said comedy was building a rhythm, before smiling and saying, "You'll see," and repeating the word again.

Banorah.

A banorah, as it turned out, was a banana menorah, or rather a banana-shaped menorah (and not a menorah that burned bananas like candles, as Jesse first imagined). Non-Trad had discovered this treasure in the window of one of those paint-your-own-pottery places that were ubiquitous in the 1990s; casts of shows like *Friends* often used "fun" backdrops like this for their *People* magazine photo shoots. Non-Trad was young at the time (more trad than non) and had just initiated a difficult breakup with his high school girlfriend because he didn't think she understood his unique sense of humor. He wasn't sure what inspired him to head to a Color Me Mine, but what one had to remember (or understand if they were too young) is that there were a few years late in that decade where it felt like painting pottery to music by Toad the Wet Sprocket, say, or Third Eye Blind or Counting Crows, and then waiting for it to be glazed, was the cure for what ailed most people. On the day of Non-Trad's visit, the banorah was displayed prominently in the store's window alongside more professional-looking pieces, nine holes drilled along the banana's top edge. It was painted a garish yellow, with a bit of green along the neck and the crown. Was it amateurish? Absolutely. But it was also a stunning example of pop art, as if the ghost of Andy Warhol had donned a smock and glazed it himself. He inquired within about the surprising piece; someone had come in, painted it, left it to be glazed, and never returned to claim it when dry. It found a spot in the store window but, alas, was never the draw or conversation starter the store manager had hoped. People who did inquire replied, "Oh" when told it was a banorah, as if a banorah was a perfectly everyday item one might see, or they simply dismissed it as a banana with holes. Eventually it was forgotten. But our hero had taken an immediate shine to it, it matched his own sense of whimsy, and, *hey*—who among us had not lived up to potential?

Then-Trad begged to purchase the banorah. It was against store policy to sell items once they'd been painted by customers. Usually, if they were halfway decent they sat in the window until after ninety days they were tossed for a new crop. He asked when the banorah's ninety days were up, or where on the calendar it sat, like a hopeful boy wanting to adopt a puppy from the pound. Eventually the store manager, who was quitting later that week anyway for a job at Virgin Megastore, which paid fifty cents an hour more, took pity on him.

He'd been meaning to clean out the window anyway to let his replacement put her stamp on the display. He charged the same as a fruit bowl, because it was the only comp he could think of.

Trad prized the banorah and found premium placement for it on a shelf. Hanukkah came late that year, overlapping with Christmas, and he lit candles on the first night. Being Jewish was never something he gave much thought to; he was estranged from his parents, and even before that, his identity was always cultural more than religious. But there was something about the banorah that connected him to the memory of his grandfather, the other person he could think of who would be as charmed by this odd item as he was. The banorah wasn't exactly a rabbinic legend, but it ushered in its own season of miracles and lights.

At the outset, Jesse found it was a slight cheat on the assignment. Initiating his breakup as he did, Non-Trad wasn't abandoned so much as the banorah. But he used a banana, a long-standing symbol of, if not comedy, clowning, to tell the story of a man abandoned by family and faith to illustrate how it was never too late to find your way home. When he finished, Jesse was on the verge of tears, of laughter, yes, but also genuine weeping.

Upon seeing the stricken look on his professor's face, it seemed Non-Trad's immediate thought was that he'd misfired. "Sorry, it was meant to elicit laughter."

Jesse wiped his eyes, wishing momentarily to be invisible; he didn't want Non-Trad to feel sorry for even one second for having created something as beautiful as that. "Happy sad," Jesse explained. He then launched into Dolly Parton's line from *Steel Magnolias*. "Laughter through tears is my favorite emotion." No one had seen the film. Jesse held his composure and complimented Non-Trad again on using humor to captivate his audience and really having something to say.

"*My* story has something to say!" Headphones protested.

"Yes, it says you have a medical fetish." Jesse collected the stories from each of them. When class was over, he stayed behind in the cavern of a classroom and read Non-Trad's story a second time.

It was never too late to find your way home.

DAY FORTY-ONE

Jesse flinched in that way one does in a deep sleep, a reaction you think is unique to you but is apparently universal; he had no idea how long he'd been napping, or when he began to dream. It was a weekend afternoon on the bike path along Venice Beach. Jesse, on Rollerblades, lost his balance; how he'd come to flail in such an embarrassing way he never quite understood, he'd always been quite good on skates, but there were pockets of sand and trash on the paved pathway, not to mention idiots who stopped short to take a picture with a disposable camera, all of which was dangerous for bikers and bladers. Jesse careened into his future husband's bicycle heading the opposite way, knocking them both to the sand. Jesse took the brunt of the hit and, as he wasn't wearing a helmet, gave Norman, the handsome stranger on top of him, quite a scare. In Norman's recounting of their story, a meet-cute they told countless times over the years, embellishing it only slightly when they themselves got bored of the telling, Jesse's first stunned word to him was "Dad?" And given that Norman was older by a few years and already starting to gray at the temples, everyone always had a good laugh at that. Norman cleared his bicycle from the path and helped Jesse out of his Rollerblades and over to the nearby lifeguard station, where the guard on duty was built like he played collegiate sports and had a chest covered in hair that, drenched in sweat, glistened in the sun. He shined a light in Jesse's eyes to look for signs of a concussion, but the only light Jesse was interested in was the one in Norman's eyes. He was offered water as he recovered from his daze, and he and Norman sat and talked and laughed at their predicament.

"Don't you have someplace to be?" Norman finally asked.

"Where you go, I go," Jesse replied, using the dangling sleeve from the flannel tied around his waist to dab at his forehead and double-check that he was not bleeding. That became one of the sayings they repeated over the years, the first hit in the jukebox of their relationship.

Where you go, I go.

What a joke.

Jesse had been startled awake by his cell phone, his ringtone something called Departure, which he was now determined to change.

"Norman?" his voice croaked when he answered; he must have been asleep for some time.

"Mr. da Ruth?" an unfamiliar female voice replied. "Jesse?"

"Jesse *del* Ruth," Jesse corrected. It wasn't Norman, and now he wished he hadn't so hastily answered. "This is he."

"Mr. del Ruth. This is Jill from BHRC."

BHRC? The letters were vaguely familiar, but it took Jesse a moment to place them. Beverly Hills Reproductive Center. Or Clinic? The *C* was one of the two.

"Uh-huh."

"Mr. del Ruth, we're looking at your statement here, and we have yet to receive payment. Have you not been getting our bills?"

Jesse's eyes darted to the mountain of mail that sat on the kitchen counter unopened. Norman had set most of their bills to autopay, so he didn't feel pressured to open any of it. "I'm sorry, who is this again?"

"Jill from the BHRC? Your annual payment is past due."

"Payment for what?"

There was an awkward silence on the other end of the line. "Storage."

Storage.

"Sir, if there is a question about the increase in rates, the contract you signed does allow for price adjustments due to unforeseen circumstances, in this case an increase in security. Perhaps you heard about the recent car bombing in Orange County? It's quite a world we're living in."

"Right." It was all Jesse could think to say.

"I could take payment over the phone with a credit card."

Jesse lied and said he didn't have his wallet.

"Sir, if we don't receive payment by the end of the month, there will be additional late fees, per the contract." Jill went silent and Jesse heard the shuffling of paper. "The other contact listed is Norman Alfano. Perhaps we could speak to him?"

"He's . . ." Jesse didn't know what to say. "Unavailable."

"Of course, if storage is no longer desired, I can arrange for that."

Goddammit, Norman.

Jesse rushed Jill off the phone by promising to send payment. He felt the urge to throw his phone clear across the sofa, but instead he opened his camera roll and began scrolling through the more than fourteen thousand photos of his life with Norman, wondering where their relationship went. Trips, homes, friends, fads, years—where had they all gone? The photos were now documented memories, as the memories themselves seemed unreliable. As he scrolled through his album, there was a growing urge to yell, *Liar!* He began to doubt that any of them happened, and he felt so very alone.

As certain as he was that no one would understand if he dared share the truth of his situation, there was one person who actually might. Or, if not the reality of it, the *emotion* of it, and that was what he desperately needed. So he got in the car early the following morning and drove out of Joshua Tree, stopping for gas when he hit the 10.

The drive to Santa Barbara was an awkward one, which involved plowing through Los Angeles before merging with the Pacific Coast Highway and heading north; there was no more direct route. Even flying required a connection through San Francisco. Jesse tried music and then a true crime podcast, something he and Norman used to enjoy together, this one a profile of a serial killer from the 1950s who worked for a company contracted by Caltrans and was convicted of murdering at a minimum six children before disposing of the bodies under the Santa Ana and Ventura Freeways while they were being constructed. It gave him the creeps as he sat behind the wheel, and he felt deeply for the families of the victims. Families torn apart in the night never to be reunited. And yet their loved ones were most likely buried under the very freeways they used on their daily commutes, quite literally under their noses. Was Norman similarly close by, easily discoverable if Jesse knew just where to look? He turned off the podcast, settling eventually on silence and his thoughts, which was not any more healthy but had become the norm. He cycled through a catalog of grievances: the way Norman always dropped one Advil on the floor for Jesse to find; the way he would fall asleep on his back, one arm dramatically raised above his head, bent at the elbow, like he was a Victorian woman collapsed on a fainting couch and only smelling salts or convalescing in the open air would revive him; the way he ate peanut butter from the jar with a fork, leaving marks like a backhoe. His mental state brightened when the 10 freeway ended, and he emerged from the tunnel to see the sparkling ocean. The light reflecting on the water resembled stars.

He phoned his mother, Gail, when he started seeing signs for his destination.

"I'm in Santa Barbara," he said when she answered. He wasn't quite yet, but almost.

"Who is this?" his mother demanded in her most accusatory tone. She approached every call like it might be from a Nigerian prince tricking her out of her money.

"JJ." His mother, the only one left who knew Jesse Sr., was the sole person who still called him that. "Your son."

Jesse Sr. had been a Marine deployed in the messy final days of Vietnam. The last combat soldiers were being actively withdrawn (or, for many, redeployed to other countries throughout Europe and Asia) in the early months of 1973, but Jesse Sr., it seemed, had orders to stay on with some of the military command to protect U.S. installations. His mother, to hear her tell it, had breathed a sigh of relief, as the war officially was over. By then, it was hard to know which she hated more, the war or the anti-war movement. Both seemed a threat to the young man she loved, and threatening to the simple life she envisioned for herself and their baby when he returned. She thought him staying on would allow for frayed nerves to calm on the home front, she would eventually welcome him back and so would everyone else—she just had to wait a little longer for the national mood to brighten. She was pregnant the day she received the fateful knock; only the week before she had written to Jesse's father with the news. Within the span of a year she had traded the life of a single girl for life as a single mother. It happened so fast, she barely had time to breathe.

His mother made some noise like she was confused, and Jesse wondered if she could hear him over the rumbling of the freeway. He could picture her in the kitchen with a pencil in hand; she always held a pencil when on the phone, assuming there would be something to write down, information, perhaps, to pass along to the police. "Why?"

"Why am I your son? Well, when a man and a woman love each other very much, sometimes . . ."

"No, why are you in Santa Barbara?"

Jesse scrambled for an answer that wouldn't startle her or put her on the defensive. Only one sprang to mind. "I was in the mood for some ice cream." Ice cream was his mother's kryptonite. As Jesse parked the car, he wondered if he was here to talk about his father, or becoming a father—or neither or both. Maybe there were just times when even a grown man needed his mother.

Jesse had seen a therapist his junior year of high school, around the time he was becoming a man, and again when he and Norman began to discuss kids, as he had the same fears Lally tried to press upon him now. It didn't take Freud to see his anguish. How could a man be a good father when he himself never had one to hold up (for good or for bad) as an example? His therapist asked what made him certain he would be a bad father and not an overachiever in the parenting department, striving to give a child everything he'd missed out on and more. That had not really occurred to Jesse, and the simple profundity of the suggestion made his time in therapy short-lived. He'd had a question, his question was answered, and eventually he and Norman had embryos made. Yes, it was Norman's idea to ask Lally to donate the eggs. But Norman had also been the one to back away. It was confounding at the time; Norman had not been able to articulate any reason beyond the cliché. They weren't ready, the timing was off. There was, after all, a global pandemic looming. But now it all felt like one more clue that Norman had always had an eye on the door. He didn't want to be tied down, committed to a child, a family. He was always looking to the stars. But maybe this was something that Jesse could do without him. One area where he could be a man of action.

McConnell's Fine Ice Creams was a Santa Barbara institution and had been around as long as his mother had been alive, and the flagship store on State Street downtown was only a stone's throw from where the original location stood; mother and son had spent many a Saturday there when Jesse was a small child. The way his mother drove, Jesse knew he would arrive first, so he took his time cruising along the water with the windows down, taking in ocean air that was thick with salt and the scent of fried seafood from the string of restaurants along the shore. The air was cool and almost wet, two things it never was this time of year in the desert. Jesse inhaled deeply. It had been a long time since he'd called Santa Barbara home, but it reminded him of Venice Beach and his recent dream of first meeting Norman.

He lucked out with a parking spot and waited outside McConnell's until he saw Gail Wyler's hair (dyed chestnut as ever) bobbing in the crowd. He watched as she glanced in a storefront window to adjust her signature pearls, which she wore over a turtleneck; no one had seen her neck in more than a decade. She looked so much like every other wealthy woman in Santa Barbara, it was almost impossible to tell that her money was not generational, but new.

"Well, this is an unexpected surprise." Most mothers would say *pleasant*, or *wonderful*, but Jesse didn't make a fuss. They hugged each other, each using only one arm, as two would be too intimate. They exchanged pleasantries about the weather and books and the endless campaign Gail was waging to get her neighbors to remove their trash barrels from the street the same day they were emptied, before she thought to ask, "Where's Norman?"

"Oh," Jesse said, scratching his head while looking over his shoulder like Norman might have just ducked out of sight. The trip was such an impulse, it hadn't occurred to him that she might ask. "Abducted by aliens. Actually, I didn't see any aliens, but there was a bright light and—" Jesse made a sound like *shoop* and gestured something being sucked into the sky. He could have gone with the Minneapolis medical clinic line again, but there was no bullshitting his mother.

Gail pressed her tongue against the inside of one cheek and narrowed her eyes. But unlike Lally, his mother wasn't one to press.

"I'm serious."

"I believe you," Gail replied in her most indecipherable tone.

Once inside, they were immediately overcome with the smell of cream and freshly made sugar cones and it transported Jesse back to his childhood. Gail ordered her standard dish of Coffee, while Jesse opted to mix two flavors: Double Peanut Butter Chip with Sweet Cream Caramel Brownie. His mother made a disapproving face but said nothing. Instead, her ire was transferred to the poor kid who worked the counter when she went to pay and he flipped an iPad around for a tip.

"A tip for what?" Gail asked.

"For waiting on you," Jesse said in his loudest stage whisper.

"He didn't wait on me. I tapped my own credit card to the screen. If anything, he should tip me." She defiantly pressed NO TIP. When she saw Jesse's horrified look she relented and pulled two dollar bills from her wallet and made a production of dropping them into a jar. "If you're going to make such a big *deal*." She then pointed at the young woman who actually served the ice cream so that the cashier understood the tip was for her.

"Gracias!" the young scooper enthusiastically replied, and Gail's head nearly exploded. Jesse laughed. Intentional or not, it was perfect performance art.

When they were safely outside, Gail continued her rant. "A gratuity is a reward for service."

"They're just kids, Mother. They probably shopped at the Toybox not that long ago." Although Jesse had often joked to Norman that his mother ran the only toy store in the country with a NO KIDS ALLOWED sign, the truth was Gail *loved* kids. Until they committed the unforgivable sin of growing up. "Do you want to walk?" He pointed in the direction of the pier. The limited seating in McConnell's was always full, and a weekday afternoon was no exception. "The sun's out." His mother detested the desert for its hot-oven wind and the fine grit that seemed to coat everything, but sunshine itself was the way to her heart. Gail put on her sunglasses with her free hand and craned her neck at the sky, her face a solar battery recharging.

"Were you always this tall?" she asked while she was looking up.

For the first time in a while, Jesse felt self-conscious about his height. "I think I'm shrinking, actually." He hoped soon Norman's clothes might actually fit.

"That's your posture, it's always been bad. And what do you call those?" She pointed at his shoes.

"Moccasins."

"You drive in those things?"

"They're driving moccasins." She nodded, and Jesse did his best to keep his cool. "Oh, hey. Let's turn here. We could walk by the Box."

Families of soldiers like Jesse's father who are officially determined to be captive, missing, missing in action, a prisoner of war, interned in a foreign country, captured, or otherwise detained by a remote force on foreign soil were owed compensation. In Gail's case, her husband's full salary and benefits. She kept the name del Ruth long enough to complete the paperwork but didn't see turning over her identity the rest of her life to a man she'd known only briefly. Jesse Sr.'s salary allowed her to stay home with her son for a time, but it never really kept up with cost-of-living increases and the inflation of the Carter era, so eventually she took a job selling educational toys at Tupperware-like parties in people's homes. She was surprisingly good, becoming a top earner for the company, and young JJ was more than happy to demonstrate the toys in use. Eventually she didn't see why she needed to survive on commission while some unknown big shot gobbled the lion's share of the profits, and she rolled the dice on a toy shop of her own, the Toybox, which became a destination for children and families; several locations followed, and when she sold them to a conglomerate, she made a killing.

"Oh, god. Wait until you see what they did with the storefront." Gail stabbed her red plastic spoon into her scoop of ice cream so that it stood straight up. "Awful."

They turned anyhow, and Jesse marveled at how much had changed while remaining exactly the same.

"It's been a long time since I've heard from you. I saw on TV now it's trendy for liberals to cut family members out of their lives for having a difference of opinion."

"Just say 'Fox News.' You say 'TV' like they announced that on *Wheel of Fortune*." Jesse allowed his ice cream to melt on his tongue. He missed McConnell's; occasionally you'd find a pint in the grocery store, but never his favorite flavor, and it always cost as much as a tank of gas. "And I promise no one is cutting anyone out of their lives over a difference of opinion." *Morals, maybe.*

"Fine. I saw it on the news. It's our job to be informed."

"My job is to teach college. And occasionally write books."

"Very occasionally." Gail pulled her spoon out of her ice cream like she was the rightful king of England. "Thank god they still make plastic spoons. I thought the turtles would insist we use paper."

Whether she meant turtles as an insult for progressives, or turtles as in actual turtles, Jesse did not know, but he liked the idea of turtles gathered together to vote. "We could make spoons out of turtles," Jesse suggested. "Little baby turtles. Glue sticks to their hollowed-out shells. The rest we could use for soup." He hoped this registered as horrifying as he intended. "And you only cut people out of your life when their presence is more painful than their absence. I don't think we're there yet."

They paused under an awning so their ice cream wouldn't melt further, and he watched his mother trace one of the bricks in the sidewalk with her sandal, then stomp on it to make it level. His mother grew inconspicuously quiet; that was the thing about her media diet—she could talk a mile wide, but only an inch deep. "How's the brownie?" she finally asked.

"I bet the person who invented the brownie was trying to bake a cake and fucked up." He held up the dish for her to take a bite, and surprisingly, she did. She made a meal of chewing it, solid chunks befouling the smooth ice cream, but did not seem displeased when she eventually swallowed. After, they continued their stroll.

"So, while I'm here I wanted to ask you something about Dad."

"Not this barrel of fish."

It was hardly a topic they'd exhausted, especially given the enormity of his absence, so Jesse pressed. "What do you remember about him?"

"What do *you* remember?" she challenged.

"I don't remember anything. You may recall he disappeared before I was born."

In fact, Jesse could only recall hearing his mother speak about Jesse Sr. once. He'd been in high school at the time. He came home late from concert band practice, where he had been assigned to play the trombone, and his mother, two-thirds of the way through a bottle of syrupy wine, something she usually mixed with Fresca (which, from the grocery list stuck to the fridge, he could see they were out of) to make something she called her "little spritz," was not her usual self. She talked in circles about every which thing, the permission slip she signed for his spring trip and who was doing what at her store's team-building day—something she fought vehemently against despite her employees' insistence, but claimed was "not torture"—before running out of mindless things to say and breaking down: It was the anniversary of the day his father had disappeared. Or, rather, the day she was informed of his disappearance, as who the hell knows exactly the moment when someone *actually* disappears. (Until recently, Jesse had agreed with her on that front.) It had been seventeen years, the age she was when they were first introduced. She'd lived as much of her life without him as she had before they met. Or something like that. She was slurring her words and not entirely making sense and math was neither of their strong suits; he understood then why she usually cut her wine with Fresca. Anyhow, it was the only time she'd ever entertained questions about his dad. "You were a real fighter," she had told him at the time. "I don't know how you held on." Jesse didn't know, either, especially given his passive personality now. His mother had never remarried, even though she dated a man with one leg for some time, holding out hope that her first love might one day return. When the time came, she fought tooth and nail to keep Jesse from leaving for college, even though he was only going to UCLA; she, too, had a fear of abandonment.

"He didn't disappear, your father."

"Oh, I'm sorry. Do you have his current address? Maybe I could take him out for donuts next."

"Your father is *missing*. There's a difference." She waved her spoon about to punctuate her thought.

Was there?

"What do I remember? He had big hands. Long thin arms and big hands that looked like paddles. We went to an auction once, some silly thing his division put on, none of the items were worth very much money, it was sort of mostly for fun. But your father raised his hand to wave at a friend and accidentally bought a dinner for six at some fish shack."

Her annoyance at this detail all these years later made Jesse smile. He got his irritability from his mother, as much as he wished that weren't true. But Jesse got his lanky limbs from his father. Maybe he couldn't piece Norman together, but he could perhaps piece together himself.

"*Your* hands are not that big, thank god. Still, you should have stuck with the piano lessons I paid for."

His teacher didn't make much teaching piano; Jesse recalled whispers about his also being a masseur. (One way or another he was going to make money with those magic fingers.) "How did you deal with it when you found out he"—Jesse carefully rephrased—"went missing?"

"This is ancient history."

Ancient history? Jesse pushed his sunglasses up his nose with the top end of his spoon; he couldn't very well explain his predicament, why it was relevant or how history is always in danger of repeating itself. "He didn't disappear building the pyramids."

"I didn't dwell on it. There's your answer."

"You didn't *dwell* on it? You were pregnant and your husband disappeared, but you didn't dwell on it."

Gail frowned. *Disappear.* They had been over this. "Dwelling on a problem preserves the problem. I got on with my life."

"But you didn't, though."

"I raised you, didn't I? Although from the way you're behaving, not very well."

"Your only significant relationship was with a man with one leg."

"What does his having one leg have to do with anything?"

It was obvious, Jesse thought. "You picked a man who couldn't leave!"

"He could leave. He could leave at any time!"

"What was he going to do, hop away? HE ONLY HAD ONE LEG!"

"Don't be ableist," his mother replied with disgust, throwing her empty dish in a curbside trash can. Jesse wondered how a woman who thought even Jesus was too woke knew such a word. "Why all this nonsense about your father?"

Jesse insisted it wasn't nonsense but didn't say much else. He still had more ice cream to eat, since he had done the lion's share of the talking. He offered his mother another bite, but her spoon was already in the garbage, so she declined. He manically scraped the bottom of his dish for any last taste of ice cream; the spoon made a desperate, unpleasant scrape like rodents trying to escape a trap, and they continued on.

Gail was not exaggerating about the Toybox's new look. It was painted in bright circus colors and had an awning that looked like a big top. "Good lord. The city approved this?" Jesse asked. It was garish.

Gail just looked at him to say, *See?*

"Let's go in," Jesse said, and before Gail could stop him he was holding the door open for her. She only reluctantly entered.

It was the smell that was most familiar, as if Jesse's childhood had seeped into the paint and the carpeted floors. They were drawn into the long narrow space, past the toddler area, past games and puzzles and magic kits and rock polishers. Jesse had spent hours inside this store doing homework while his mother tallied the day's receipts. A woman with a young son whisked past them, and Jesse and Gail both stared into their past. The mother held the son's hand; neither of them could remember a moment so intimate.

"Oh my god, it's still here!" Jesse exclaimed when they came across the clawfoot tub at the back of the store. Near the books, it was filled with pillows for children to climb in and read. He opened his phone to the camera and handed it to his mother. "Take my picture."

"Oh, don't climb in there," Gail protested.

Jesse knew she was imagining the tub filled with germs. But he didn't care. There were so many photos of him in that tub when he was young, and he desperately wanted one more. He lowered himself in, which took more strength than he imagined, and his limbs draped comically over the side like enormous tentacles. "Why not?"

Gail sighed. "Because you can't go backward in time." Jesse had to admit she was right; as soon as he was wedged in, he didn't easily see a way out.

A manager approached to check if they needed any help. "I see you're here with your little one," she said with a laugh.

"Not so little," Gail said, but to her credit she smiled. "We're just browsing." Jesse could see she was embarrassed and hoping not to be recognized, which opened the door for some fun.

"This is Gail Wyler," he informed the manager.

His mother shot him a look while the manager tried her best to place the name. Then a lightbulb. "The former owner! We're delighted to have you back. Let me know if you need anything."

"Actually, we were wondering if you could take our picture." He instructed his mother to give the woman his phone. "Here, Mother. Sit on the edge."

Gail treated him to one of her famous death stares, but she sat for the photo, perhaps figuring it was the quickest way to end this misery. When the manager returned Jesse's phone and left to help a customer at the register, Gail asked, "How does Norman put up with you?"

Jesse returned to the lie. "Norman's in Milwaukee. Apparently, I'm easier to handle from there."

Gail scoffed.

"What? It's a real place."

"The alien thing was more believable."

Jesse saw his mother clearly. She accused everyone else of being a snob without any irony. "To dwell on a problem preserves the problem," he repeated.

Gail checked her watch, hidden under the sleeve of her turtleneck. "What about it?"

Jessie kicked his legs over the edge of the tub like oars. "I'm just trying to decide if there's actual merit in that or if it's the biggest line of bullshit ever spoken."

Gail blanched at such language in the Toybox. "Well, you asked."

With his long arms, Jesse reached for a book called *Thaddeus the Platypus*, flipped through its pages, and put it back. "Do you think if Dad knew he wasn't coming home, he still would want to be a father?"

Gail looked at him, confused.

"That, even if it was just for a moment, he was happy to know I existed?"

"What kind of questions are these?"

Jesse didn't know exactly. He'd always harbored some fear that he was the product of an immaculate rejection. That his father didn't want to be saddled with a kid, and decided a life in the jungle was better than a life changing diapers. He tried to explain as much to his mother.

"Your father flunked out of the Boy Scouts. He wouldn't last five minutes on the run." Gail pressed the back of her hand against her forehead like she was growing too warm. "Besides. We have no way of knowing if he ever got my letter. If he ever knew about you at all."

Jesse sighed. He wanted to know.

"You can't know everything. Now get up, before we receive any more looks."

Jesse extricated himself from the tub, lucky he didn't wrench his back doing it. "Then I wish I could know everything that will happen in the future and then I wouldn't worry about it now."

Gail checked her watch again. "Knowledge of the future is not helpful."

She said it so definitively, Jesse knew she was right. If he knew what was going to happen in the future, it would be *all* he would worry about. Especially if what was coming was not good. He just wished he could make peace with being abandoned. Something that was perhaps growing into a recurring theme.

When they left the Toybox, the skies threatened rain, and Jesse invited himself to stay at his mother's for the night. They ordered takeout in the downpour from a Mexican place they both liked, a favorite once upon a time of Julia Child's, and watched a show Gail said was good but wasn't. He slept soundly in his childhood bedroom, his limbs overhanging the twin bed like they did the tub in the store. When he woke up, Norman was pressed against him, the warmth of him both familiar and shocking. Jesse froze, inhaling the scent of Norman's hair, wondering how aliens had stocked the same shampoo Norman liked, the one that smelled like basil and rain. And then in a blink it wasn't Norman by his side, but his father sitting on the edge of the bed, watching tenderly as he slept. And then he woke up for real, shocked all over again to find himself alone. The smell of coffee brewing was only a mild comfort.

Jesse dressed and went downstairs to find the sun shining—the storm had rolled through, though he remained convinced something bigger was coming, something that wouldn't lift overnight.

THE EMBRYOS

The embryos had been fertilized with heartbreak.

When Jesse and Norman first decided children were something they wanted, they agreed on only one thing—adoption was the way to go. They disagreed on the number, the sex, the situations they might be open to, which continents they'd be willing to travel to (no penguin nestlings!), and how soon they could open their home. But some things were unarguable. The world was too hot, too hungry, too crowded to bring someone new into it, not when they could satisfy their desire to become dads and do some small amount of good by giving a loving home to a child in need of one. As it was, Jesse liked to take long, hot showers, and when Norman would challenge him on the wastefulness, he would say he was actually doing well by the environment by not procreating. He was using his water, his children's water, and maybe even his children's children's water, but that was it. After that, his existence would no longer be a drain. Adoption, as Jesse said, allowed him to retain both his penchant for long showers and the moral high ground.

They registered with an agency that was highly regarded, but not before Norman did his due diligence. They endured the paperwork and home visits, the supplemental forms needed to explain the wild discrepancies in Jesse's income in the three years of tax returns they provided. (*The life of an artist and academic!* they'd cheerfully say, because they couldn't decide which made them seem more desirable.) They redecorated a spare room, not as a nursery (they didn't want to appear *too* eager) but as a study someone could easily envision as a nursery, sat with social workers who picked apart their lives, and had friends and family members—including Lally—write glowing letters of recommendation that made them seem both stable and wildly unique. They assembled a booklet with photos of themselves cooking dinners in a kitchen that looked like it was ripped from a Nancy Meyers film. Walking barefoot along the beach during golden hour while laughing (at what, neither remembered). Tending to their backyard with pruners and shears and something called the Garden Weasel. Of course, absolutely none of this reflected their *actual* lives. The kitchen belonged to their friend Rani, a caterer who lived in Ojai. Norman loved the beach but detested the actual ocean and was deathly afraid of seaweed—he screamed whenever water would lap his toes. The Garden Weasel they had to borrow from their landscaper, Odie, who along with his brother Mando usually pruned and weaseled for them; Jesse didn't even know what it was for. Their booklet looked so professional it could have been published by Random House, and while they were warned that the average wait to be selected was eighteen months to two years, the receptionist at the agency let slip that sometimes gay male couples were chosen sooner, as it was of comfort to certain birth mothers to imagine themselves their child's only mom. When all the paperwork was completed, they agreed on dinner to celebrate.

"Waiting for Jesse," Norman said in perfect singsong as he stood by the door with car keys. It was a common refrain in their house.

"Hold on, I have to get my road Tums."

Norman knew he would regret asking but couldn't help himself. "What in god's name are road Tums?"

Jesse approached the door swinging his arms in a way that made it look like he was hurrying, but only from the waist up. "They're the Tums I take in the car on the way to the restaurant, different from the Tums I have after the meal when we get home."

Norman shook his head. He didn't like Jesse aging; if Jesse was old, then Norman was positively ancient, even though they were a mere six years apart and their age difference had flattened over time. The young men they were when they met would never have dreamed of conversations like this, but Jesse would say in his own defense that it's impossible to imagine something as simple as a cocktail or tomato sauce betraying your esophagus in such a way.

"Stop it. I have a good feeling." Jesse rubbed his hands together like a fly. "I think I'll have a martini." They had two, toasting each time for luck.

Their phone rang seven weeks later. They celebrated with more martinis (bookended with Tums) and got to work turning the study into that nursery. Jesse commissioned a mural of a cow jumping over a moon. Norman bought books about newborns.

But something seemed off from the start. The adoption was a late-breaking decision from a birth mother who was due in less than five weeks. She already had three children and carrying this pregnancy as long as she had before committing made it seem like she had made the decision on impulse. That should have been their first warning, but Jesse chalked it up to common sense. Three kids already ran the asylum, but *four*? Four would tear it down. So there was part of Jesse and Norman that understood. Although she looked exhausted, the birth mother, Valentina, was clearly stunning. Her family was from Peru, and that gave them pause, not for reasons of race but rather of religion—a creeping fear that her Catholic extended relatives might not approve of this baby being raised by two men. And although Valentina hinted otherwise, the father, whoever he might be, did not seem to be part of her decision.

Still, things progressed quickly and the shortened timeline allowed them to ignore the obvious warning signs, which were piling up like a bad freeway collision as the nursery progressed right along.

"Is that a yak?" Norman asked when the mural was done.

"It's a cow," Jesse replied defiantly. "A cow jumps over the moon." But when he tilted his head to one side he saw it. "Oh, yeah. That's a yak." He paid the artist to paint over it and try again.

Soon they flew to Scottsdale for the birth, bringing too many bags (it was unclear how long they would need to stay) and a pile of cash to cover the mother's living expenses for three months afterward as she recovered from the trauma, physical and emotional, of giving birth.

"This feels like a bribe," Norman worried as he counted the money, like a cop might have slipped an exploding ink pack into the bills.

"It's standard procedure," Jesse assured Norman, just as the agency had assured him.

They were there in the delivery room when the baby was born, a girl whom they planned to call Agnes after *Agnes of God*, the Jane Fonda film directed by Norman Jewison (they liked the name more than the film, but they both *loved* Jane Fonda). Each of them wore plastic bracelets that allowed them to come and go from the maternity ward—the kind that designated them as the parents; Jesse even cut the umbilical cord before passing out cold on the floor. When he came to, a bevy of confused Peruvian faces hovered over him, before tenderly helping him to his feet. That was the last moment of kindness extended their way.

Valentina's family loudly objected when Jesse wanted to bond with the girl skin-to-skin; that was a nonstarter with the birth mother's parents, who, while they didn't seem to be that involved in their daughter's life and helping raise the three kids she already had, had very strong opinions about their new granddaughter that they shared in Spanish with increasing urgency and alarm. Eventually Jesse and Norman were in the middle of a screaming match in a language that wasn't their first. They held their ground as best they could, Jesse, the tallest in the room by a mile, growing particularly red. The dream was alive; the baby, all six pounds, eight ounces of her, with a dusting of dark hair and a mighty grip, was here.

But when it became clear they were being accused of unsavory things, not the least of which implied racism and purchasing a brown baby, even the agency was forced to tell them the adoption was a lost cause. Of course, they'd been warned that this kind of thing happened, although rarely in as dramatic a fashion, that in all cases the mother could change her mind. Yet that didn't seem to be the case here; it was the mother's family that was blowing this to shit, and Jesse and Norman held in there as long as they did, as the family, as far as they understood it, were not the ones with legal standing to make the final decision—Valentina was. When Jesse unbuttoned his shirt, insisting there was a limited window in which to bond with his daughter, an accusation so hideous was hurled (the accusations by bigots and homophobes, Norman later observed, never changed no matter how many rights people gained, how many advances were made, or how many seasons of *Glee* had aired) that Jesse and Norman knew they would have to cut this most final cord.

It was dusk as they walked through the hospital's sliding doors and a blast of hot air hit their faces. They retreated to their tragic rental car—a model with a celebratory name like Fiesta, but not that—and cried to a Melissa Manchester CD that a previous traveler with Hertz Gold Plus Rewards had left behind as Norman squealed out of the hospital parking lot, Melissa instructing them the whole way not to *cry out loud*. At the first red light, they desperately clawed at the hospital bracelets to get them off. But the bracelets were made from some polymer that maddeningly would not break, and before they gave up, they inflicted scratches and wounds on their wrists that took weeks to heal, which was a lot faster than their emotional scars, which perhaps never fully scabbed.

"I need a drink," Norman confessed, and they drove in circles around a strange city until they found the only thing open, a health food store that didn't carry alcohol but had kombucha and a tea with St. John's wort. They drank them silently in the car, Jesse picking at the label on his tea as he read it.

"Imagine being John the Baptist and to honor you they lend your name to a wort."

Norman wiped kombucha from his lips as the fermentation tickled his stubble.

"I'd rather be forgotten than remembered for a wort."

"He's remembered for baptizing Jesus."

"I don't think so. At least not anymore. It's this wort."

"They were cousins, or something."

Norman's latent Catholicism surprised Jesse whenever it surfaced. Jesse didn't have any religion, but the church was very much part of Norman's Italian upbringing. "Cousins. One got an entire religion, the other a wort. Imagine the family reunions."

Their contact from the agency, who no doubt by this time had heard an earful from Valentina's family, called Jesse's phone to make sure they were safe. Jesse put the conversation on speaker, but only he spoke. She said there was still hope, that sometimes cooler heads prevail and emotions always ran highest during delivery. Hope? She hadn't been there; Jesse and Norman knew there was none, that this gorgeous, curious infant, who drank them in without blinking, was not to be their daughter, even though they had been the first to hold her when she was born.

"What does St. John's wort do, anyway?" Norman asked after the phone call was over. It was warm in the car, but neither would roll down his window. They somehow found safety in a sealed bubble, as if everything that had just happened could not touch them.

Jesse read further down the label. "Cures mild depression." He then handed the bottle to Norman in disgust, who chugged it until the bottle was dry. He wiped his mouth with the back of his hand.

"Another several crates of these and we might be in business." Jesse laughed, and then so did Norman. *Mild.* The whole thing, ridiculous. When the car was quiet again, Norman confessed, "I've been thinking maybe it *was* a cow."

"What was?"

"The mural."

Jesse face-palmed. *The mural.* "It had horns."

"Bulls have horns."

"It's not *the bull* jumped over the moon. It's *the cow.* Cows are female bovines."

"Okay, but aren't yaks just hairy cows?" Norman produced his phone. "Hey, Siri. Aren't yaks just hairy cows?" Siri informed them that yaks are not cattle; they have horselike tails and are sometimes referred to as grunting ox. *They're closely related to the water buffalo of Asia and Africa.*

"How much do you think we would have to pay the guy to paint over the whole thing before we get home?"

Norman shrugged. "Let's just sell the house."

"Where would we go?" Neither of them had discussed leaving L.A., not seriously anyhow. But perhaps it was time.

Tired of Melissa, Jesse punched the car stereo and the CD ejected, replaced by the radio, and while the song playing was immediately familiar, Jesse couldn't place it. When he did, he swung his arms like he was waving away a bee, no one having warned him that that one Richard Marx song they played at his high school prom would be a trigger for the rest of his life. He turned the radio off, and silence enveloped them. Until Norman laughed.

"What?" Jesse asked. Norman held up his bottle of kombucha, pointing at the label.

"You shouldn't drink this if you're pregnant." Norman laughed even harder this time, and then Jesse did, too, until neither knew if their tears were from laughing or the trauma they'd just been through. Norman wiped his eyes with the back of his hand so he could see the label more clearly. "But it may reduce the intensity of menstrual cramps."

Jesse flipped the radio back on because *why not* and Richard Marx was still right there waiting. Jesse could picture the video still clear as day from afternoons home alone watching VH1 once he'd outgrown tagging along to the Toybox. Richard bathed in a blue spotlight sitting at the piano looking plaintive, his stupid mullet gleaming. *Who just sits in a spotlight?* Norman offered his kombucha to Jesse, since he'd finished the tea, but Jesse refused and so Norman took one last sip before breaking their seal by lowering the window and spitting it out in a disgusting, fermented spray. "THIS SUCKS!" he screamed into the void of the parking lot, finding a napkin from a previous outing to Chipotle in the center console and using it to dab his mouth. He then threw the bottle out the window; it smashed against the concrete base of a streetlamp in the center of the parking lot. Jesse grabbed his own bottle, then opened the car door and likewise smashed it on the ground, shattering it in all directions. "I don't think I can do this again. We held her little body in our hands." Norman could still feel the way her tiny torso had radiated heat and life force, as if she had been his incubator.

Jesse had wiggled all ten of her toes, taking careful inventory before a nurse swaddled her in a blanket; they had teeny-tiny nails. "I'm not sure I can, either." He then peered out the door at the pavement; they'd really made a mess of the ground beneath them. Jesse switched the radio back to the CD and Melissa sang three more tracks before Jesse returned to the health food store and sheepishly asked for a dustpan and broom. If only all of their messes were cleaned up that easily.

"I have an idea," Norman said as they drove back to their Airbnb.

That night they called Lally.

DAY FIFTY-TWO

Solitude was driving Jesse mad. His eyes may have been opened by Lally's visit to the possibilities of what one might accomplish on one's own—outside of partnership—but it turned out, in his case, the answer was: *Not much*. The TV, which early on brought him comfort, made the house seem even more empty, and there was nothing he could watch that distracted him. His phone was worse, 256 GB of dread, underscoring the fatal intensity of living. After two more calls from the BHRC asking for payment, he stopped answering his phone altogether, ducking calls from even his gregarious literary agent, Brian Leung, someone who could be counted on for the juiciest industry gossip delivered with the joie de vivre of a bon vivant. Jesse had done some writing, to feel like his old self. But nothing that yet resembled a book, certainly not one that anyone would buy.

Instead he scrolled hours and hours of Instagram reels; when he ran through all the videos posted by the Dairy Queen woman, his feed populated with chiropractic back-cracking videos featuring startling sounds (each one more satisfying than the last, as if he were wringing Norman's neck) and successful contestants on *Family Feud*, a show he'd only watched as a child with flat ginger ale and saltines when he was sick. For a time, he played along, guessing the top answers on the board, but to what end? There was no bigger feud than the one in his family, one-sided though it may be.

The house made creaks and sounds that he didn't remember, and the light refracted differently through the windows as the season began to change, casting all kinds of new colors and shadows; it began to feel alive. He felt paranoid all the time, but it may have been the pot, something he was smoking too much of. When the house felt like it was closing in on him, he would stand in the driveway and look at the sky, which he was doing now.

"Evening." Jesse's neighbor, Randall, had ambled up the driveway; he waited until he was standing right next to Jesse to speak. "You aware there's been a man parked outside your house?"

Randall Moss was stout, with a penchant for short sleeves that cut off at the elbows, making him resemble a bowling ball, rounder than he actually was, and his military haircut and thick, black-framed glasses completed a look that Jesse could best describe as Apollo launch commander, or Oklahoma shop teacher in the midst of demonstrating the lathe. Randall was someone Jesse tried to avoid; not only did he inspire conversations any reasonable person would chew their own leg off to extricate themself from, but he was soaked in the kind of cheap drugstore aftershave that athletes like Pete Rose used to advertise in full-page magazine ads while wearing tighty-whities. Jesse had just spotted a single nighthawk, the first he had seen in weeks, and he was worried Randall would spook it.

"A man?" Jesse tore his gaze from the sky long enough to look beyond Randall's shoulder to see if this man was still there.

"Not now, but earlier."

Jesse shook his head. It was just like Randall to get him worked up about nothing.

"Been there for several days. Watching you, I think."

Jesse tensed. "Maybe he's watching *you*." It seemed far more likely someone would be surveilling Randall. He seemed much more like the type of person with secrets to crack.

"Nope, nope. Definitely you."

"Okay, now you're creeping me out."

"American car, I think. Silver. Dent on the rear passenger side."

"American, you *think*?" It was unlike Randall not to notice every detail, particularly about an out-of-place vehicle.

"American, a 2010 Chevy Impala with the LTZ trim package and the optional added spoiler. You're telling me you haven't noticed him?"

Except for the few times he deliberately left the house, Jesse's comings and goings were not what they used to be and were far from interesting. As paranoid as he'd been of late, he didn't see how he made much of a subject. Someone expressing an interest could almost be seen as welcome. Maybe this was the opportunity to make a new friend. Of course, that was as deluded as many of his recent thoughts; loneliness had a strange way of warping common sense. "Should I be worried?"

Randall blew air through his lips. "Odd to see him parked here three days in a row. If I see him again, I'll tell him to move it along."

"You do that," Jesse said, more encouraging than dismissive. He made a mental note to double-check the locks on all the doors and windows tonight before bed. "Is that what you came to tell me, Randall? That a man has been watching the house?" He bit his lip, thinking he had sounded unnecessarily rude; he was out of practice when it came to casual chitchat.

"No, I came with an invitation. Tomorrow night is going to be one of the best nights to see the Milky Way. I'm heading to the Monument to photograph it. Any interest? Thought you might enjoy tagging along."

Jesse was startled by this unexpected turn of events. "Well, Norman's traveling."

"I figured," came the reply, and Jesse had to wonder who had been watching whom. Randall held up his hands in his best *Say no more* gesture. Then Jesse surprised himself.

"You know what? The Milky Way *is* something I would like to see." Plus, he was curious if it would give him any perspective on where Norman might be in it.

"Okay, then," Randall said, clapping a few times in excitement, and Jesse hoped he wasn't being lured to his death. "I'll pick you up around nine."

Jesse nodded and returned his attention to the sky.

Randall ambled back down the drive before turning and offering a parting remark over his shoulder. "You're looking in the wrong direction, you know."

Jesse did not take kindly to his observation—how the hell did Randall know what he was looking at? Or for. "As a libertarian, you of all people should know we are free to look wherever we want." Randall had his own feelings about exactly how free people were in a country run by the billionaire class, and Jesse had certainly heard an earful about it. But Randall didn't quibble; despite Jesse and Norman's rather fancy house (compared to his own Airstream, at least), neither of them had the kind of wealth that perturbed him.

"Think about it," Randall chuckled. And then one last time. "You sure you don't know this guy in the car? Silver. In need of a good detailing."

"Oh, the silver Impala in need of detailing! Yes, we're having an affair." Jesse hoped Randall had a good meter for sarcasm.

Randall waved him off. "I'll get a plate number next time."

Randall drove like the devil, his car seat shoved so far forward he could steer with his knees, leaving his hands free to clean his glasses on his shirt, gesticulate during conversation, and open a pack of gum. It took them little more than fifteen minutes to get to the entrance of Joshua Tree National Park, something that should have taken closer to twenty-five.

"Jesus Christ," Jesse said when they blew through yet another stop sign. He glared at Randall, who paid him no mind.

"No traffic this time of night." And that was true. They'd only seen two other cars on the road since they left. *Still*, Jesse thought, and he looked back at the camera equipment in the bed of Randall's Ford pickup. A tarp covered most of it; Jesse hoped it was indeed a tripod and not a shovel. "Besides. We've got a ways to go and need to make good time."

Now Jesse worried he really was being kidnapped, as seemingly the only limit on their time was the sun coming up, unless Randall needed to be somewhere to create some sort of alibi. "You just missed the park entrance. Turn around."

Instead of slowing down, Randall sped up. "The *western* entrance."

"Why, where are we going?"

"The eastern one." Randall wiped his mouth with the back of his hand like he was salivating with anticipation. "It's the last pool of natural darkness."

"Anywhere?" Jesse asked, alarmed. We really were ruining the planet.

"No, of course not. In Southern California."

Jesse burst out laughing. *The Last Pool of Natural Darkness.* It would make an apt name for his autobiography.

"What?" Randall asked. He turned to Jesse and stared.

"Nothing," Jesse replied, motioning for Randall to keep his eyes on the road; who knew what might come bolting out of the dark. "I'm excited, is all."

They sped forward into the night.

After two hours, Randall pulled his truck to the side just before midnight, seemingly satisfied that they'd made it deep enough into the park, and sat wordlessly, his hand on the keys, frozen in thought.

"You okay?" Jesse asked. It was the kind of daze Jesse found himself in often of late. Randall chewed his lip as he turned off the engine; things fell eerily still. When he killed the headlights, things fell perfectly dark.

"Yeah, you?"

Jesse thought best how to answer. "Did you see those MISSING signs posted at the park entrance?" He'd just caught a glimpse of them in Randall's high beams.

"People go missing all the time in the desert. Hikers get lost. People don't bring enough water for the heat. Poor saps. You hear other things, too."

Jesse felt goose bumps. "Like what?"

"Maybe it's best not to discuss it in the dark." Randall fluttered his fingers all spooky-like and then exited the truck.

Jesse followed suit, holding on to the truck's open door, terrified that if he let go he would lose his last tether to a world blessed with light and the darkness would consume him whole. It's hard to understand just how dark darkness can be, so used to civilization we are. With his free hand, Jesse rubbed his eyes and slowly—ever so slowly—a new world revealed itself. He was blind, and then suddenly he could see.

Randall appeared beside him, but Jesse didn't even jump. Instead, he just whispered, "Incredible."

"You don't have to whisper. No one to hear us for miles." Randall nodded toward the truck's bed, and Jesse followed him to collect the equipment, aware as his fingers let go of the door.

They set up camp a few dozen feet from the truck, the night becoming brighter as they adjusted to the only light, emanating from the stars and the crescent moon. Jesse tried not to think about snakes and rodents and other nocturnal things that might be slithering around and hoped they had the good sense to be asleep. He took careful steps and studied Randall, his pupils dilated behind his thick glasses. It was now past the autumnal equinox, the time of year when the night was growing longer than the day and the air was noticeably cooler. Jesse zipped his hoodie up to his neck and shoved his hands in the pockets. And when Randall was satisfied he'd found the right rocks to anchor his tripod, Jesse took a moment to look up. The night sky exploded with not just stars but clouds of dust and gas in vibrant colors. His entire life, Jesse had looked at the sky; not once had he seen it like this.

"Whoa," he whispered. He wasn't sure if Randall heard him or not, but it didn't matter and he didn't care. Slowly appreciation dripped over him until he was soaked with understanding. Norman had made the right choice, the *only* choice. When the stars looked like this, the only logical response was to touch them. *I saw the world from the stars' point of view, and the world was much more intriguing.* It was a quote from somewhere, a book or a poem he'd read but couldn't recall. "Tell me everything," he said to the twinkling lights in the sky, wanting to know their secrets. This time Randall did hear him and began to detail both the equipment and his process in mind-numbing detail.

Randall explained about the tripod he chose, the Mach3, which he described as "a serious bit of kit." Jesse didn't know what that meant exactly, but he imagined it cost quite a bundle. In fact, Randall had three cameras with assorted lenses, and Jesse began to wonder if this was why he lived in an Airstream—maybe all his money went to this hobby. Randall urged him to step back when he placed the tripod, since the Mach3 had spiked feet. Jesse nearly tripped over a rock, impossible as it was to divert his gaze from the sky.

It was one of the last nights of the year to view the Milky Way, at least its core, which stood almost vertical. Soon the core would remain below the horizon and wouldn't show itself again until spring. Jesse's eyes watered, thinking this was his last chance to see Norman, who in a few weeks would totally disappear from view.

"You ever been married, Randall?"

Randall remained focused on his tripod, adjusting one of its legs until he was satisfied it was level. "Why do you ask?"

Jesse hesitated before stammering, "I wish Norman could see this." Was Randall someone to open up to? In the moment—or even of late—there was no one else. "We have different interests a lot of the time. But I think this is something we could appreciate together." He imagined them in the teak chairs in their backyard, taking all of it in, instead of Norman lost in his app. Often, Jesse thought they were too attached at the hip. But what could life have been if they shared even *more* with one another? In all this time, Jesse didn't think he'd ever missed Norman more.

Once he'd made one final adjustment, Randall indulged him in conversation. "My wife said to me once that every relationship has a thermostat setting. It was something she'd seen on one of those talk shows. You can adjust the thermostat a few degrees in either direction, but it will always revert back to the setting where it's most comfortable. You ever hear of anything like that?"

"No," Jesse replied, and then wondered what his setting with Norman would be. *Energy saver*, perhaps.

"She was never comfortable with our setting, always too cold, she'd say. Eventually she ran off with our tax guy, if you can believe that."

Jesse was appalled. Tax guys were not exactly known for running hot.

"Soon after, I bought the Airstream and moved out here to live a simpler life. And pay as little in taxes as I could." Jesse didn't press Randall, who returned to his camera bag to select just the right lens, further.

Begrudgingly, Jesse admired the precision with which Randall worked. It was funny to see a man who just a day ago seemed not to have a purpose other than to annoy him turn out to have a real talent and passion. Norman had read Jesse's books through different drafts, but that was Norman seeing the output of his labor—not the labor itself. If Randall had shown him a picture he took of the Milky Way, it wouldn't have the same impact as seeing him take it. Jesse was suddenly overcome with sadness that Norman had never sat in on one of his classes—he wanted Norman to know that side of him. The teacher, the one with knowledge to impart. And he desperately wanted to see not just Norman's blueprints, but his husband actually drafting. "You really know what you're doing."

Randall continued his setup without missing a beat. "I practice this at home in total darkness." The insinuation: blindfolded. It made Jesse nervous, the thought of Randall pointing a camera his way under the cover of night, especially with these intimidating lenses. What had he observed? What did he really know about the night Norman disappeared?

"What kind of photo are you going for?" Jesse asked, his voice reed-thin.

Randall simply pointed up, and Jesse wondered if he wasn't already regretting inviting a guest.

Jesse cleared his throat. "Like, do you just point and click at the sky? Or are you trying to frame something in the foreground?" That afternoon Jesse had googled images of the Milky Way to see what he was in for, and he had seen both kinds of shots.

"See that Joshua tree?" Randall asked. "The one that looks like it's in prayer."

To Jesse, it looked like the tree had its arms raised in surrender. "Yeah."

"I'm using that to frame my shot. Come see."

Jesse hadn't actually expected to be invited to look through the lens. Randall seemed strangely protective of his equipment and looked at Jesse's movements with some disdain like he was a wild bull or a klutz. He delicately approached the camera, careful to avoid kicking the tripod legs. When he looked at the digital screen on the back, he understood Randall in a new and profound way.

The Joshua tree grew by itself, whereas others seemed to take root in groves. Randall's tree, like Randall himself, was a loner, but instead of appearing sad it seemed strong. Resilient. And there was something remarkably human about not just its silhouette but its very presence. Life itself was a miracle, particularly *this* life, on this planet, under a blanket of endless stars. It was Randall, alone in an Airstream, on a vast plot of land. It was a Joshua tree, alone in the desert, standing against the galaxy. It was Jesse without Norman, the man who gave his whole adulthood context. Jesse suddenly mourned every night he had spent indoors or looking straight ahead instead of up, consumed with the drudgery of circadian life. How is it that night followed every day, and we hardly ever marveled? Once again, Norman and his stupid app had been right.

"There are more than two trillion galaxies in the observable universe, each with an unknowable number of stars."

"Trillion?" Jesse asked. "With a *t*?"

Randall went on to explain that there were more stars than there were grains of sand on the shores of all the lakes and oceans on Earth. The light from the stars we can see was emitted long before all of humankind. And it all started with a tiny particle of incredible density that expanded with the addition of heat. It was impossible not to think of his relationship with Norman in that context. Something so vast that began with such a small event, the collision of two people on a beach, igniting a spark that expanded their lives beyond either of their imaginations. In that moment, Jesse desperately didn't want his life to become small again. He didn't want to give up the house, he didn't want to live in a trailer. He didn't want to be a loner. He didn't want to be his mother. He didn't *want* to pay taxes, but he didn't want to live on the outskirts of society, either. He had to find a way to connect.

"Randall. What did you mean last night when you said I was looking in the wrong direction?"

"Excuse me?" His neighbor seemed confused, like he'd been expecting a compliment on his composition.

"Last night, in my driveway."

"Oh, that."

Yes, that.

Randall gently nudged Jesse away from the camera and looked through the lens one more time, then stepped back to study the digital screen, the corners of his mouth drooping ever so slightly as if he were witnessing two very different views of the sky. He didn't speak for a long time, taking a series of test photos with various exposures, stopping in between to fuss with the focus. Only when he seemed satisfied and ready to take what Jesse imagined to be a keeper did he reply. "You were looking for answers, no? I recognized that look on your face." Normally Jesse would find something absurd about the idea of Randall being a student of humanity, but tonight he was discovering his neighbor anew. "I used to be just like you. When people want answers, they look up. Always have, since the dawn of time. Since embers first flew from the earliest fires."

It was, in fact, exactly what they were doing right now.

"I think I know what you're going through."

Jesse felt nauseated. "You do?"

"I do," Randall confirmed. "But you all don't realize the answers to everything are not . . ." He pointed at the sky.

Some sort of desert dweller made a plaintive wail, and Jesse took an involuntary step closer to Randall. "So where are they? *Down?*"

"Underground. For regular folks, like us, anyway."

Jesse took issue with "like us," as he struggled to imagine any categorization that would group himself and Randall together. Even a neighborhood association, if they had one, would be hard-pressed to agree they belonged under the same banner, what with Jesse's life in his grand architectural marvel and Randall seemingly squatting on property, possession being nine-tenths of the law. But Randall was like a thresher shark that way, tail-slapping its prey with something benign to stun it into submission before going in for the kill.

"Have you heard of the third alternative?" And there it was. You can see someone in a new light, but lighting only changes a subject's appearance, not their molecular structure.

"The *third* alternative?"

"That's right."

"I've not heard of the first or second alternatives, so let's for the sake of argument say I haven't. Alternative to *what*?" He immediately hated himself for buying into the premise.

"Look, we've long agreed that overpopulation and environmental degradation will be the downfall of humanity."

Jesse once again wondered who the "we" was; it was hard to see much agreement in the world today. And while he didn't disagree, he looked at the land around them, free of people as far as they could see, and said, "Oh, we have, have we?"

Randall ignored him and pressed on, as if it were his experience that all people would understand if only he could educate them. "Soon the planet will be uninhabitable, or if not *uninhabitable*, unable to sustain human society as we know it. The ruling class knows it. The politicians know it. That's why they're building rockets. That's why they're colonizing Mars."

Jesse laughed and once again looked at the sky for the reddish dot he'd spotted earlier. "They're colonizing Mars," he repeated incredulously. Might Randall—*of all people*—hold the key to Norman's whereabouts? What if his husband wasn't abducted by aliens, but rather the government or some asshole billionaire who needed architects for their new colonies? While that seemed unlikely, nothing seemed implausible. Not anymore.

"Well, Mars is hard to get to, I'll grant you that. First they're building clandestine bases on the dark side of the moon. Which they can't do without Russia, which is why that lizard Elon is so involved. He has his head so far up Russia's ass. You ever notice his eyes are really far apart? If his eyes were any farther apart they'd be close together. If you gather my meaning."

"Rarely do I gather your meaning."

Jesse turned to face his neighbor for the first time in this conversation. Randall made a gesture about Elon's eyes being so far apart they were in danger of meeting on the back of his head.

"Randall, I've met maybe five truly crazy people in my lifetime and you're easily four of them."

If Randall was offended by this, he didn't allow himself to falter. In fact, Jesse was almost certain he detected a smile. "People thought Pythagoras was crazy. Isaac Newton, too. Visionaries are always challenged."

"Oh, now you're Isaac Newton?"

Randall outright laughed. "Maybe not Newton. But stop for a second. You honestly think the rich and powerful aren't working on ways to survive a climate disaster?" It was clear from the tone of his voice that he didn't think he was the crazy one. And in this regard, maybe he wasn't. But Norman did not leave because of a climate crisis.

"And that's the first alternative? Mars? Then what, Saturn and Jupiter?"

"No, no, no. The *first* alternative is a series of strategic nuclear detonations."

"Of course," Jesse said, even though that seemed more frightfully immediate, and not just because it was labeled the first. Depending on who was detonating these bombs, he could easily imagine New York destroyed, or perhaps Moscow or Beijing. "Where?" he asked in a way that made it clear he didn't necessarily want the answer. Before they had moved to the desert, Jesse had googled whether Joshua Tree was outside the blast radius if North Korea decided to take out L.A. (It was.)

"In the atmosphere."

This, for some reason, was a relief. "In the . . . *atmosphere*," he repeated slowly to make sure he understood.

"That's right."

"What did the atmosphere ever do to us?"

"Trapped in pollution and heat for one. Want me to go on?" When it came to Earth's atmosphere, Randall seemed to have a list of grievances.

"I'm probably going to regret asking, but what's the second alternative?"

"Ah. This is why I brought it up. The second alternative was put into place in the fifties and sixties, up until 1969, when we went to the moon. The second alternative is underground."

"Like the Underground Railroad."

"No, literally underground. I know it sounds silly now . . ."

Now.

". . . as enlightened eyes look beyond Earth. But in the 1950s we were building. Cities, freeways, there was just a lot of digging. You know how our dipshit president brags about being a builder? He hasn't built shit. We used to build everything. Eisenhower? *He* was a builder. So no one even batted an eye when the government was constructing huge subterranean habitats for the elite. People were so used to construction."

"The elite wanted to live underground."

"The elite wanted to *escape* underground. That's why there was so much food that wouldn't go bad. Spam. Canned vegetables. Aspics. If it didn't spoil, Betty Crocker had a recipe. I bet we're standing on top of a huge bunker right now."

This was starting to concern Jesse. The desert was exactly the kind of place you would build something you didn't want others to see, especially in the days before satellite surveillance. But wouldn't the desert's soft ground and dry sand collapse in on itself if one started digging too deep? Jesse stomped his foot three times as if some sort of sonar or echo might detect if any serious concrete lay underneath. "But now people are going to Mars."

His neighbor nodded.

"So why do you say answers for us lie underground? The second alternative, if you will."

Randall shrugged. They had no golden ticket. "We're not going to be invited to Mars. Unless you have some launchpad in your backyard that I don't know about." Jesse's mouth was instantly dry, and he struggled to swallow. But it might have been the most salient point Randall had ever made. The third alternative was never going to be available to them; they would be lucky to somehow access the second. But still, Jesse was not convinced the answers he sought were right beneath his feet.

"What if the answers I'm looking for are for questions that are . . ." Jesse didn't quite know how to finish that sentence. "Bigger."

"What if the pyramids are just the tip?"

"The tip of what?"

Randall looked at him like he finally understood. "*Exactly.*"

Jesse had heard it referred to as ontological shock, the state of distress people fall into upon the discovery of nonhuman intelligence and learning that humans may not be the apex predator. In some ways, Jesse had been experiencing this phenomenon since the night that Norman left. There was a clear delineation: before and after. And standing in the far reaches of a national park in the middle of the night Randall had somehow made it worse, exacerbated his need to question *everything*. Up was now down and so down was now up? The way he thought about everything would have to change.

He thought of a trip he and Norman had once taken to Pompeii. The city ruins, buried under ash and pumice in AD 79, were unearthed in the mid-eighteenth century in what became the start of modern archaeology. Now a monument to the people who died in the aftermath of the eruption of Mount Vesuvius, it drew visitors from all over, including two Americans on their honeymoon who were staying on the nearby coast. Jesse and Norman thought it would be eerily romantic, roaming the streets where lovers perished, their remains found clinging tightly to each other, embracing for eternity. Unfortunately it was the opposite; much of it in fact was quite grim. To cope, they traded in jokes that day, which caused the two of them to erupt in laughter at the back of their tour group. How was your visit? *A blast!* This heat is making me impatient. *Don't blow your top!* I'll bet Pompeii was a party town. How do you know? *The people are stoned!* Despite the fits of giggles that followed them all the way back to their hotel in Sorrento, it was a somber day. Most interesting, Jesse thought, was the fact that Pompeii, a thriving city of twenty thousand, was itself built on top of another, much older city, built substantially by the Greeks following the Battle of Cumae a few hundred years before Christ. Remembering that now made Jesse wonder what they were standing on top of. Maybe not government bunkers—Randall could not possibly be right about everything—but the ground held some secrets, the fossil fuels for instance that proved the dinosaurs once roamed. Indeed, what if the pyramids were just the tip?

"Randall, am I crazy now, or do you actually make sense?"

Randall shrugged and offered a wry smile, then invited Jesse to look at the digital screen at the photo he'd just taken. *Breathtaking.* A photo made up of questions. "I'll make you a copy," Randall offered, and Jesse offered his thanks. But he couldn't stomach the photo in his house if that's what it represented. Uncertainty. Longing. Confusion. No, the photo would have to represent this night. The beginning of a real search for answers. The end of his grief-stricken, half-hearted attempts and his efforts to merely *cope.* He could no longer bear the vastness of everything he did not know.

They drove home mostly in silence listening to a cassette Randall had of John Denver as the rattle of the uneven roads lulled Jesse to near sleep. *The radio reminds me, of my home far away.* John Denver, too, met his end in the sky. But Norman hadn't perished. Something drew that light to their yard that night; Norman wasn't targeted at random.

As sleep took him, he realized that Lally was right. He was a passenger. In his relationship, in life, and now in Randall's truck. But now Norman was a passenger, aboard god knows what and who knows where. That left Jesse to drive. There was a job that lay ahead of him. It would be strenuous, it would be weird. People wouldn't understand. But it needed to be done and he was the only one to do it. There were times when Jesse felt disconnected from his professorial self—the rational thinker, the reasonable actor, the imparter of wisdom—more and more as of late. He was becoming someone new. Norman looked to the skies. But did he find answers? He would have to take a different tack. There was something buried deep underground, and he needed to know what it was.

Jesse was going to dig.

DAY SIXTY-EIGHT

Jesse went to the Ace Hardware in Twentynine Palms after class and filled a cart with the kind of items that would cause any sane cashier to put him on some sort of watch list. A shovel, a pickax-looking thing called a mattock to break through stubborn roots (although he debated, he passed on an auger), work gloves, and lots of plastic tarps on which to place dirt. He tried an extra-friendly demeanor so as not to arouse suspicion, but overcorrected and came off as maniacal. No matter. It was almost closing and the cashier only cared about leaving. Still, he sped home with one eye on the rearview mirror, paranoid he was being followed. Randall had, after all, observed someone and Jesse's behavior since then had only grown more erratic, but today as far as he could tell he was in the clear. In the yard, he surveyed the ground for the perfect spot, ultimately deciding there was no place like the middle. And then he grabbed his new shovel, placed the tip in the dirt, and jumped on it with his full body weight. It didn't hit concrete, but he was just getting warmed up.

He tried to avoid all thoughts of the future as he dug, at least as they pertained to Norman. Would he advertise for his husband?

Officially have him declared missing? Or worse, *dead*? He could write a hell of a death notice, that was for sure. Really put the "bitch" in "obituary." *Norman Alfano of Joshua Tree (a census-designated place), architect, beloved son and brother, tolerated husband. Norman designed buildings for hip replacements or the treatment of varicose veins. A devoted fan of sushi even though he lived in the desert and there was nary an ocean in sight, he was also a regular presence in the kitchen with a passion for standing in front of the exact drawer you needed to open and somehow had invented the art of holding a coffee mug loudly.* No, Jesse couldn't imagine doing any of that, especially while digging a hole that resembled a grave. He had to speak to Norman, get a message to him (and hopefully, in turn, a reply), to know with some certainty if he was forever gone. He refused to end up like his mother, whose tolerance for the world and for others was rapidly shrinking, who didn't even care to talk about his dad.

After days of digging, and in a moment of marijuana-fueled clarity, he came up with an idea how to do exactly that—communicate with Norman. He surveyed the massive hole he'd obsessively dug, and the mounds of dirt piled on tarps, pulled off his gloves for the day, and treated himself to a long shower before heading out.

The Integratron loomed large in Joshua Tree lore, a cupola structure about forty feet high and painted a shocking white to stand out against the cobalt sky. It was built in 1959 by ufologist George Van Tassel, who claimed the plans were given to him explicitly by extraterrestrials from the planet Venus; Howard Hughes, an aviator himself, had provided funds for its construction. It was Norman who had first suggested they go, and Jesse was almost embarrassed by his former resistance to such New Agey things now that his eyes had been opened to their significance. Van Tassel died in 1978, and the structure languished in various states of disrepair until three sisters bought the property and refurbished it as an acoustically perfect construction and made it available for meditation and sound baths, reflection, and connection, accompanied by the tones from twenty-two quartz-crystal bowls. Why twenty-two and not twenty-one or twenty-three, Jesse did not know. But the twenty-two were advertised to create binaural beats for the purposes of rejuvenation, and Jesse was in no position to argue.

The drive from Joshua Tree was insignificant; Landers, home to the Integratron, was not far. But Jesse, heart racing with anticipation, felt like he'd run a marathon by the time he arrived. He turned off the radio to regulate his breathing, the way he would outside the doctor's office when he was worried his blood pressure would register too high. If he wished to be in tune with the earth and her secrets, he had to first be in tune with himself. How could one reasonably expect to sense the surging of magnetic fields over the drowning roar of one's own deafening pulse? He had to get ahold of himself. He didn't have the money or advance planning to arrange a private visit, so he steeled himself for whatever other weirdos might have booked time in his session. He imagined women in long skirts and jangly bracelets and men with angry yellowed toes in sandals, and perhaps a few lesser members of the Polyphonic Spree. The more he conjured images of his fellow sound bathers, the more his heart would race again, so instead he tried to recite the ingredients for the famous *New York Times* chocolate chip cookie recipe (*cake flour, bread flour, brown sugar, granulated sugar, eggs*), something he suddenly had an insatiable hunger for. Besides, this was supposed to be a journey inward. It was perfectly acceptable to shut everyone else out. He just prayed there would not be any children.

Since Jesse had arrived early, he walked the grounds minding his own business, in awe of how the structure itself looked both effortlessly integrated with the landscape and like a completely alien craft that didn't belong at all. As he circled the structure, he tried to be in tune to any vibrations the land might be emitting (surely the location of this thing, random as it seemed, was no accident). He even got down on his knees and laid one ear to the ground. Dogs had extrasensory detection. He'd read they were sensitive to Earth's magnetic field and would align along the north–south axis before relieving themselves. If animals were aware of small variations in magnetic fields, perhaps other beings were, too. Why would humans be the only species left out? Jesse immediately dismissed this as nonsense before realizing that's exactly why. Human beings were not open to these sorts of things, inventing religions and cults to explain away what was actually magnetic and spiritual. Alas, anything he thought he might be picking up could have just as easily been reverberations from the sound bath still in session. And the only thing he now had in common with dogs was that he, too, now had to pee. He found the restroom (with no idea of its axis alignment) and then waited outside, away from the vibrations, picking at the growing calluses on his hands until one began to bleed. When he heard the crunch of tires on gravel and car doors open then slam, he became self-conscious and slipped back inside.

Like everywhere now, the Integratron had a store, a small gift shop that carried T-shirts and mugs and candles, yes, but also crystals and pendants that promoted continued healing long after your session was over. Jesse asked the clerk for a bandage, which she happily provided, and then studied each item the shop carried like he was looking for just the right souvenir, but it was impossible not to blanch at the prices, the gross consumerism that couldn't leave even spiritualism untouched. When they were out of his size in the one T-shirt he found unoffensive, he bought a selenite palm stone, something he could squeeze in his hand to calm himself. He judged a small group of young white women, birthday revelers or bachelorettes, who oohed and aahed over the elaborate incense holders but only bought shot glasses and one Christmas tree ornament; he hoped they weren't going to be in his session. Others lingering seemed more palatable; he even caught the attention of a woman with long white hair who looked like she just wandered out of the fields of Woodstock, having no idea the era of free love was over. She seemed as wary of the young women as he was, and Jesse relaxed, knowing he had at least one kindred spirit.

Minutes seemed like hours as he waited to be called in for his sound bath, and Jesse knew inherently he was putting too much pressure on whatever was about to happen. Answers would come, or not come, and he tried to convince himself this had to be about the experience itself and he could not judge whether it was transcendent. Unfortunately, that was an impossible task. In better news, the bachelorettes left, but not before one put a fistful of dirt into her small purse, leaving behind several mints and an old ChapStick to make room for it. It was horrid behavior, littering and thieving combined, and Jesse was appalled. Fortunately, so was Woodstock, who had picked up the young woman's trash with a surprising grace before their car had even spun out of the parking lot. He turned to Norman to express his fondness for the woman, momentarily forgetting he was not also there. That had to be a good sign—he *felt* Norman's presence. Instead he mouthed, *Thank you* when he next caught her eye and she nodded, then poked around the building like she was looking for something (or someone), too.

When it was finally their time, Jesse and the other members of his group were gathered by Nancy, a woman dressed in loose-fitting clothes that made her resemble a high-fashion monk; it was a look Jesse could see himself adopting were he to continue down a path of either enlightenment or sloth. (He couldn't indulge in wearing Norman's clothes forever—even if cropped shirts for men were currently in, they were *not* in for men his age.) She led them to the Integratron's second level, up what Nancy called stairs but seemed much more akin to a ladder, and Jesse, always the tallest, had to duck so as not to hit his head on the opening. Once on the second floor, however, the room opened up, allowing him not just to stand but to properly stretch. There were mats laid out for everyone covered with clean sheets, and bathers stood frozen before choosing their spots, like they had been asked to pair up in gym class; Jesse hung close to Woodstock. The others in his session were mostly couples, save for one small cluster of friends who tittered with nervous excitement. As far as he could tell, the only other single person besides himself and his mat neighbor was an awkward straight man with a meaty build who wore a short-sleeved dress shirt and slacks. He stuck out like a sore thumb, as if he'd somehow walked out of his year-end performance review at an insurance company and in line to have his biological cells rewired. There was no place in the Integratron for middle management, so Jesse focused instead on Woodstock, who gathered her sheet around her like she was an animal making a nest. She fanned out her hair when she lay flat, and it looked like it was charged with static electricity.

Different sound baths were offered, designed, Jesse imagined, to encourage repeat visits, and today's was called Pathways, which would have seemed tailored to Jesse, as he was certainly looking to discover his own pathways (inward, yes, but also one that might lead him to Norman), if it didn't sound so perfectly like a rehab center for C-list celebrities and CFOs. *Your journey to sobriety begins at Pathways.* Pathways, Nancy explained, was designed to increase our neuroplasticity so we could find new paths within our own brains. Thoughts, emotions, stressors, pain—these were all merely electrical jumps between brain cells, and it was up to us to show them new ways, leading us to a new understanding of the world around us.

The fuck? Jesse thought, but he kept any doubt to himself.

"If you want to find the secrets of the universe, think in terms of energy, frequency, and vibration." It was a quote from Nikola Tesla, whose great name had been tarnished by electric cars that had a tendency to explode, but it was read to them by Nancy like his reputation was still unsullied. Sound travels more efficiently through water, she explained, and since the human body is more than seventy percent water, apparently they were in for quite a ride. Sound also traveled more efficiently through the Integratron, and Jesse heard every whisper, rustle, and cough as people settled onto their foam mats. It was like the theater; if anyone needed to unwrap a butterscotch, now was apparently the time. There were no secrets inside this structure, not from each other, anyhow—he even heard a man wonder in hushed tones if he might get hard from vibrations. He wished everyone would shut up. The only secrets, Jesse realized, were the ones he was after—the ones from those who lent humankind the plans for the Integratron, and the ones contained within him.

Once she was satisfied everyone knew what to expect, Nancy sprayed the room with rosemary oil and burned palo santo, some sort of natural wood incense, and indeed the scents had a calming effect on the room and people seemed to relax into the experience, the occasional whispering fading into a random cough or a sneeze and then silence. Jesse reclined on his mat and studied the wood ceiling above him; leglike joists met in the center of the dome around some sort of round light, forming what looked like an enormous spider, the type of alien creature that was so terrifying in Steven Spielberg's remake of *War of the Worlds*. That in itself was disquieting, the thought of being caught in a web. So he closed his eyes and focused on Nancy's voice as she began her narration for Pathways and slowly integrated bowl after bowl, like someone in

Greece spinning plates at a wedding, and the whole room began to hum. *Total body stimulation at the cellular level.* It did sound almost sexual, what she described. Stimulation. Vibration. Circulation. Exhalation. *Release.* Maybe the man who joked about getting an erection wasn't that far off base, and he raised his hips in a discreet effort to adjust himself. Jesse wasn't certain he wanted to share all of that with strangers, but he made a mental note to purchase a recording of Pathways, for him to try again in the privacy of his own home.

Sound as nutrition. It was something Jesse tried to swallow as he controlled his breathing and listened to the singing bowls take charge of the room. And *charge* was a perfect word, as more and more Jesse felt something electrical happen to his body. It started in his extremities, his toes, and his fingertips. It was like he could suddenly feel his finger*prints*, energy running through them like they were hedge mazes on the grounds of an elaborate palace like Versailles. From there he became aware of his limbs as they began to lift from the floor, a sensation he couldn't quite place. He was both floating and not, on his mat and hovering just above it, like he was adrift on a sea of dense salt water. He struggled to see Norman behind his closed eyes. If there was ever a moment he could glimpse wherever Norman was now, this was it. He even whispered, "Norman" on an exhale. Alas, all he saw were great landscapes of color racing against the canvas of his closed eyelids. Not only could he not see where Norman was, he couldn't see Norman himself. The number of days since his disappearance became harder to remember offhand, and each day his husband's face seemed a little less sharp. He fell into a dreamlike state where he could only see Norman when he was young, like they both were the day they had met. They were on the beach. The waves were crashing. Even though he was indoors now, he could feel the sun on his skin. The ambient sound of people around him worked its way into his dream. Someone rustling on their mat was a sunbather applying sunscreen. A gentle snoring was the rippling of a kite flying high in the sky. The hum from the bowls filled in everything else: the water, the waves, the wind, the gulls, the sounds of children laughing, crying, screaming, asking for ice cream. He was in such a perfect trance, until he heard the one thing that sent him plummeting back to the hard wooden floors of the dome.

"Norman isn't here."

It was said in the faintest whisper, but he heard it plain as goddamn day; the words crashed into his ears like a freight train. He bolted upright on his mat, startling Nancy, who nearly dropped whatever it was she was using to tickle the bowls. He whipped his head around to see who might have said such a thing and saw only the awkward man in the slacks, the one who seemed so out of place, lower his arm to his side. Nancy glared at Jesse until, properly shamed, he reclined on his mat again.

Norman isn't here. Sound carried in the Integratron, even in the midst of the sound bath. Someone or something had said it. Jesse's blood ran cold as those words stood in for the energy as the thing that was most coursing through him. He no longer felt light. Instead of floating above his mat, he was strapped to it, the room starting to spin like he was suffering an attack of vertigo, until he rolled onto his side and practiced lifting his head in the manner he saw in a YouTube video as a way to reset the stones in his inner ear. Afraid to return to his back, he curled into a fetal position, hugging his knees close into his chest.

The sound bath continued for another ten minutes, another half hour—it was impossible for him to tell. *Norman is not here.* He felt foolish thinking that rerouting energy was enough to make contact. And even if he did, what did he expect Norman to say? *Sorry?* Was it an apology he was seeking? An explanation? An invitation for Jesse to come with? Nothing he imagined seemed satisfactory. So what was really the point? He banged his head against his mat, a form of self-flagellation, as the bowls kept singing, and the sound kept traveling, and others kept breathing, and someone kept snoring, and harmony kept spreading, and wounds kept healing—for everyone, it seemed, but him. So he continued banging his head on the mat in a vain attempt to feel . . . *something.* And if Nancy was upset by this, she didn't scold him, but what could she do, really, chained as she was to twenty-two quartz bowls lest the bath stop bathing and everyone was cheated of balance. Eventually Jesse stopped, suddenly fearing his head-banging was adding percussion to this symphony, and he didn't want to be responsible for that.

When the sound bath ended, he quickly purchased his download in the gift shop and raced back to his car to study his fellow bathers as they exited the Integratron. *Norman is not here.* This wasn't *The Amityville Horror,* the structure itself could not speak. He didn't think much of religion, or mystical connection, or cults, or believe that there was any sort of spiritual harmony to the world—even after this experience. But someone had spoken those words aloud. Of that much he was certain. Someone else was searching for Norman.

Jesse had to be the one to find him first.

DAY EIGHTY-SEVEN

After his failure at the Integratron, Jesse redoubled his efforts, making great progress in his backyard dig (however one might define progress). The hole was getting deeper, that was for sure, wider, too, and he had to consider how close to the house was advisable to go. This was where having an architect would have come in handy. At night he slept deeply, physically exhausted, and dreamed of another reality, one where he and Norman only nearly collided at the beach, yelling, "Look out!" before whisking past one another, a simple warning the only words they ever exchanged. How many of these near misses do people experience in life? How close are we always to our futures going in different directions?

When he woke, Jesse brewed a pot of strong coffee as he studied his changing body in the mirror. It had been less than a month, but his digging already had a noticeable effect. Or maybe it was his diet. Working as hard as he was, his body craved fuel and not the garbage he'd been feeding himself in the first weeks after Norman's disappearance. The can of frosting went back in the pantry, as he no longer had a taste for it. He craved lean proteins and vegetables and rice and sweet potatoes for energy and, too busy to cook, he signed up for a meal plan. He bought fruit that was precut for convenience, even though it was exponentially more expensive. The neat squares felt orderly, a gift. And rather quickly, he grew tan. A body started to reappear that he hadn't seen in years. He'd yet to dig deep enough to hit water, but somehow he'd found a fountain of youth.

When he could dig no more, he moved inside to continue his work there. He scheduled their mortgage payment to be deducted from their joint account so he wouldn't forget; transferred the bills that were in Norman's name over to his (the regular business of marriage, he told the woman at Southern California Edison, no other reason than that); sent a card to Norman's mother, who had an upcoming birthday, so his parents wouldn't reach out to see if everything was all right. In each task, he kept a casual tone, something just shy of aloof—it was the key to not raising suspicion. In the days after Norman's disappearance, he thought of himself as a battlefield surgeon in the midst of a harrowing war—he had to triage what was right in front of him. At the time Norman hadn't been gone all *that* long, little more than an extended vacation, even if such vacations would be to Italy or Thailand and not the nearest extrasolar planet scientists reasonably think could support life, a floating rock they called Proxima b. (Jesse had googled it late one sleepless night.) Now that it was growing more clear that Norman was not coming back, he had to focus on making their home his own habitable zone.

He started by rearranging the furniture in the living room more to his liking, orienting it away from the window and better positioned to watch television. As an architect, Norman never believed an appliance should be the focal point in a room, but Jesse, perhaps for the first time in his life, really understood the comfort of TV, its almost magical ability to stave off the worst symptoms of loneliness.

The right program could bring the illusion of life to a house that might otherwise be painfully still. Norman wouldn't be thrilled with these changes, but on the off chance he did ever return, Jesse didn't want it to seem like he'd been staring out the window the whole time like a loyal golden retriever. He liked the idea of Norman thinking him unbothered while working through a list they'd once made together of Criterion films. ("Oh, sorry," he'd say when Norman caught him engrossed in a movie. "Did you intend for us to watch this Wim Wenders *together*?")

He took their wedding portrait down from a shelf and tucked it in a drawer for now; he barely recognized the two men in that photo anyhow, happy and at the beach. For the bedroom he ordered new sheets made of bamboo to help him sleep and an elastic band that fit around the circumference of their mattress, gripping the fitted sheet tight like a bra; he hated nothing more than the way the corner by his head came loose every few days, even when he slept, as he currently did every night, in the mattress's middle. Now that he was alone he could do something about it.

He drove to North Palm Springs to visit the Humane Society of the Desert. Dogs barked from their kennels when his car door shut, desperate cries, he supposed, for freedom. He was greeted by a man who seemed to be the manager carrying a bucket with a rattlesnake that he had trapped by one of the dog pens. The man promised that a volunteer would show him around as he hopped in a truck to relocate the snake down the road. And sure enough, a woman named Lydia appeared wearing a bright Humane Society T-shirt and gardening gloves looking like she'd just been yanking up weeds. She looked at Jesse and smiled, pulling back the oversized brim of her hat. Jesse wondered if since she was willing to volunteer here, she might also be willing to volunteer excavating his yard. Two people could make more progress than one, and she already had the right gloves.

"What kind of dog are you looking for?" Lydia asked, snapping him back to attention. He felt suddenly embarrassed, like he couldn't remember how he got there. The barking didn't help settle his mind, and he began to feel oncoming flop sweat. He looked down at his shoes; they were blindingly white against the fine grit of the surrounding dirt. He should have worn the shoes he'd been wearing for digging.

The truth was Jesse wasn't sure what kind of dog he was looking for; he figured he'd know the right animal when he saw it. Lydia showed him every dog in the place, even making the loop twice. He scheduled several more visits, playing with different dogs in the visitor's pen, until he bonded with a shepherd-husky mix with heterochromatic eyes—one brown, one blue—who seemed just as abandoned as him. He filled out the paperwork to bring her home and then left to buy the requisite supplies.

Randall brought him a copy of the photo he had taken of the Milky Way, knocking on his door one afternoon when he'd just finished digging for the day; the photograph was artfully framed and wrapped, the presentation surprisingly elegant for a straight man. "Randall, this is really lovely. How did you do all this so fast?"

Randall shoved his hands into his pockets until they cleanly disappeared at the wrist. He either wore the same white short-sleeved shirt again and again, or he had a closet full of them. "I have a rather large printer."

In the Airstream?

"And my wife used to manage a framing business, so I know what to ask for."

Jesse held the photo with both hands; it was already a prized possession. "Do you want to come in?"

Randall hesitated before saying, "No, no. I can see that you're busy."

Jesse was busy, this time organizing the kitchen to his liking, but it was nothing that couldn't wait.

"I know right where to put this. Do you want to see?"

"As long as it's not the garbage, I'm fine."

Jesse was reminded of Norman throwing the Jonathan Adler piece in the trash when they had first moved in. He hugged the photo tightly to his chest, his way of saying it was a keeper. "Thank you, Randall. For this, for the invitation. You've opened my eyes to a lot of things."

Visibly uncomfortable with sincerity, Randall retrieved one hand from his pocket and gave a hearty wave. Jesse closed the door and stared at the photo, his eyes falling on each and every visible star. Norman was in there somewhere, he was sure of it. It filled a prominent place on the shelf, the empty spot where their wedding photo had been.

With his new body, his interest in sex returned; he got hard like he did as a teenager, spontaneously and often. He found his copy of COD's faculty directory, and scanned it to look for Orson. They'd bumped into each other a few more times around campus, and while Orson was much too young for Jesse, he'd noticed Orson's eyes lingering on Jesse's newly lean torso. And he was impossibly good-looking—exactly Jesse's type. Or *young* Jesse's type. He didn't much know what he liked anymore, as far as all that was concerned. Fortunately, there was only one Orson, an Orson Bodner who taught Applied Sciences. Jesse imagined texting him, even drafting several messages, but somehow his fingers always froze before hitting send.

After a good deal of thought, he moved money over from their joint savings account and he paid the BHRC; the embryos would be safe for another year. He was still ducking Lally, and uncertain about her request. But he couldn't destroy them to punish Norman or because he was scared of facing his sister. There were valid reasons to end the contract, but those were not.

He dug and he ate and he rested and he taught and he graded and once or twice he even laughed. Inspired by his students, he began writing again, not just dabbling. His voice might have changed, after all, he had new things to say, but he found that the activity of it connected him to his old self. He brought his dog home as a foster. It wasn't that he was afraid to commit, it was the policy of the rescue—they required a two-month trial. *Foster to adopt.* Maybe an arrangement like that could work for Lally, but he knew better than to suggest it. He couldn't think of a name for the dog that fit, so he just called her Shep (short for shepsky, her breed) for the time being.

Shep would curl up by his feet as he composed more texts to his colleague Orson, thinking it wouldn't hurt to meet for coffee. Eventually it would be unavoidable—he would reenter the dating pool. But it still seemed way too early for that.

Which isn't to say that he *didn't* think of Norman. He thought about Norman all the time. It was impossible not to when he was still digging for answers. One night he even laid a towel on the bedroom floor, found his AirPods, and started his download of Pathways to listen to the sound bath again in private. He turned the volume up and down, trying to find the exact levels needed to recreate the vibrations in the dome and fidgeted until something told him to stop, and he concentrated on his breathing instead. Deep breath in through the nose, long exhale out through the mouth. And when that didn't work, he tried a deep breath through his mouth filling his lungs, and a long slow exhale through his nose. He went back and forth between these two techniques, trying to telepathically communicate with his husband, until he must have fallen asleep.

At night, Jesse made his own bedtime routine. Norman's tongue scraper had long ago hit the trash and he would floss over Norman's sink. He would walk through the house checking the lock on each door twice and turn off the lights one by one. He took melatonin, which Norman called garbage, and fixed himself a glass of water with ice, and a second tepid bowl for Shep in case she got thirsty in the night. Shep slept with her one blue eye open, not willing yet to fully trust him, even though she was generously fed and had full use of Norman's side of the bed. He allowed himself three classic music videos on YouTube before setting his phone aside for the night, even if the algorithm kept feeding him more. And yet, sometimes sleep would not come. On those nights, he surveyed the mess he'd made of the yard; there was no way he could ever explain it. But it called to him, this open crater, and so he would throw on some shorts and put on his shoes.

From the edge, it was a jump to get to the bottom, more and more so as his work continued, deepened. It was something he managed deliberately so as not to throw out his back, placing one hand on the dirt as he hopped in, careful not to get any under his nails. His body ached all the time, which made him feel alive, but he also chewed aspirin like there was an oncoming shortage. His shovel was right where he'd left it, and he held it still, unsure where to dig next. Like at the Integratron, he put his ear to the ground and listened. One night, Shep appeared at the edge above him, then circled the hole where it started to cave in and used the dirt that was filling in to scamper down.

Jesse may not have known where to focus his efforts, but Shep certainly did. She sniffed until she found the right spot, then looked up at Jesse before digging. And dig she did! While Jesse's enthusiasm for the task had diminished somewhat, this dog had been waiting for this assignment her whole life. She then barked at the ground beneath her as she started moving faster and faster. Dirt piled up behind her, more quickly than Jesse could remove it from the pit.

"What is it, girl?" Jesse asked as he ran to her side with his shovel. "Back, back, back," he said, a command he was working on so that she wouldn't bolt from the house when he opened the front door. It was the first time they felt like a team, a pack, but there was still a fight to see who was alpha. Even so, Shep eased up and took a step back, her eyes not wavering from the spot she chose. Jesse stepped in to take over and positioned his shovel, then used one leg to drive it deep into the earth. And about eight inches below the surface, the shovel hit . . . *something.* It wasn't his imagination. He moved the shovel a few inches and drove it into the ground again. This time he was certain. There was something beneath the dirt.

Jesse gasped. Even Shep dropped to the ground in a low crouch.

"Norman," he whispered. Shep cocked her head; she didn't know who this Norman character was, but Jesse could tell she understood this development was something profound.

He tossed his shovel aside, where it landed with a soft thud, dropped to his knees, and began digging frantically with his hands; Shep took that as a cue to join him. Side by side, man and dog dug in the glow of the moonlight until the soft dirt gave way to something else, something solid, something hard. Shep barked, sharp and determined. Jesse reached into the wet, cold dirt, nails be damned, until his fingers gripped a solid object.

And finally something was found.

I STILL HAVEN'T FOUND WHAT I'M LOOKING FOR

DAY THIRTY-THREE

American Airlines Flight 2758 was two hours in the air and another three to their destination when the galley phone rang, making the flight attendant jump. On this red-eye flight, most of the passengers were asleep. The call was from the cockpit.

"Connie?" the copilot asked.

"Lally."

"*Lally*," he corrected himself. Before she could ask if he needed Connie, he ordered her to look out the window. "Starboard side. Don't let the passengers see." Lally put her hand over the receiver and did as instructed, her heart rate increasing as she wondered if this was it, if this was the flight she'd be called upon to dispense more than pretzels and ginger ale. Up until that moment, her night had been routine other than a sticky wheel on the beverage cart that caused her to work up a bit of a sweat. Even if she was getting too old for overnight flights, she still volunteered for the schedule, as passengers—like children and puppies—were the most agreeable when sleeping. This flight was no different. Most on tonight's manifest had had their shades drawn since takeoff; there were only dotted lamps for reading, illuminating a select few heads like busts in a museum. Only one passenger, 12B, had given her any aggravation, asking for a pillow, then a blanket, then water, then wine, but even he seemed finally to settle, giving in to the lull of the sky.

Lally spotted them immediately from the galley window, three unidentifiable lights, maybe a thousand yards off the wing in triangle formation, an apex and two more back and to the sides forming the base. Every few seconds the lights would switch positions at random, so rapidly if you blinked you truly would miss it. "What the . . ." Lally said, mostly to herself, as she almost forgot she was holding a phone.

"Show Connie," the copilot, Mark Pinkstaff, instructed. He was new to the airline, young and single and fun to drink with on layovers and even seemed to have a thing for older women. Lally had to make it clear when they first met that she didn't date pilots and that included first officers. While that was a lie, it was mostly true lately and she didn't want to lead him on. It was clear from the outset that Mark was someone to keep clear of; you could spot the ones that became emotionally attached. Which isn't to say she and Connie didn't have a little fun with his name.

"*Pinkstaff*? Why not just Fleshdong," Connie had said over Vegas, sending Lally into uncharacteristic fits.

"First Officer Rosepecker," Lally joked in return, then held out her hand with bravado, the way Mark did when he first introduced himself to the crew.

"What are they?" Lally asked of the lights. She endured a long pause, static crackling on the line. There was only a steel door between them, but it might as well have been a mountain range.

"Boeing, Boeing, Boeing," Mark said, his doofy voice making onomatopoetic bouncy sounds.

Lally didn't laugh. She didn't know what to think, but she knew for certain those were not planes. Aircraft did not move like that, that smoothly, that quickly. She wished he would just tell her the truth. "You know what they say about bad airplane jokes."

"Yeah," Mark said, defeated. *They don't land.*

Lally waved her arm to get Connie's attention and motioned for her to come to the front of the plane. Connie nodded and stormed the aisle at the pace flight attendants have perfected, the one that said they were too busy to get you headsets but that there was no cause for alarm. Connie was older by a few years, but had only started up again with the airline recently after taking time off to raise kids when her husband left her for a woman who sold long-term-care insurance policies.

"Do you have any of the Sun Chips up here?" Connie asked as she surveyed the galley for any signs of trouble, like the coffee maker acting up. The Garden Salsa flavor was her favorite. Noticing the phone in Lally's hand, she pointed. *Who are you talking to?*

Lally shot her a look back. *Who do you think?*

Dickfingers? Connie mouthed.

Lally pointed at the formation out the window. "What do you make of this?"

Connie looked, and then looked closer, taking a full step toward the window.

"Watch," Lally encouraged her, and waited until she was certain Connie had seen the lights jump. Connie snatched the phone from Lally without saying a word.

"Pinkstaff, what the hell."

Lally observed Connie as she listened intently to their copilot, nodded, and finally hung up. "What did he say?" Lally asked as Connie started digging in a drawer for her favored Sun Chips, the ones in the little red bag.

Connie found her prize and stood upright, triumphant. "He said it was just one of those things."

"One of those things?" Lally placed her hands on her hips incredulously.

Connie opened the bag with a pop and offered Lally the first chip; she declined. "Don't tell me this is your first UAP."

On second thought, Lally took a chip. UAP sounded like some kind of gynecological exam.

"Unidentified aerial phenomenon." Connie pressed a chip against her tongue, turned it over and did the same again, then tossed the chip in the trash without eating it. When she clocked Lally's confused look, she said, "Oh, I just like the flavor crystals," like that was a perfectly normal thing to do, akin to a bump of coke in the eighties. "And I'm still trying to fit back into this uniform." She slapped a hand on her hip.

But that wasn't what Lally was reacting to, although it was disconcerting behavior at best. "Unidentified . . ."

"Wait," Connie said as she tossed another now-naked chip in the trash. "Anomalous phenomenon. The *A* stands for 'anomalous.' Connie denuded a third chip with her tongue.

Lally's jaw went slack. She'd heard stories from some of the other flight attendants she'd been scheduled with over the years—everyone has a story. She just assumed they were like ghost stories, maybe there was a *kernel* of truth, but exaggerated over the years if not outright made up. "You mean a UFO?"

Connie laughed. "'UFO' sounds so . . ." She trailed off without finishing her sentence, but made some spooky sound right out of a 1950s sci-fi TV show with little green men.

"And that's that?" Lally asked. She looked down the aisle and at the sleeping passengers. No small part of her was ready to leap into action, but to do *what* she wasn't sure. Just then, the cabin lights flickered and for the first time a look of concern spread across Connie's face.

"That's weird."

Lally swallowed hard, but the oxygen masks weren't dropping, they hadn't changed altitude as far as she could tell, and no one seemed all that bothered.

"Not *that* weird," Connie said. "Just the APU."

This one Lally knew. APU was auxiliary power unit. In fact, lights flickered on planes all the time when switching power sources. From the ground power to the power generated by a plane's engines upon takeoff. Switching to auxiliary power in the sky. If it hadn't been for the lights hovering off the starboard wing, Lally would not have given it a second thought. But right now, it felt like an unexpected knock on the door in a horror film after something else had gone bump in the night.

"Jumpy," Connie said, placing her hand on Lally's arm to calm her; it had the opposite effect. "Don't tell me you still cling to the idea that nothing soars the skies but us, a few satellites, and our own imagination."

Lally wasn't sure she'd ever given it that much thought. "Well, no."

A woman decked in head-to-toe Lululemon like she owned stock in the apparel company approached the galley with a sour expression; Lally preemptively handed her a bottle of water without so much as making eye contact. Fortunately, that was exactly what the woman was after, what most women who flew in yoga pants were after, and once she completed some obnoxious stretching in the aisle she quietly slipped back to her seat.

"We used to see these sorts of things all the time back when I first started. Nine times out of ten, they're nothing. Birds, clouds, toy balloons, weather balloons, research balloons, dust . . . birds."

"You said birds already."

"Lightning. Now we don't even notice them because we're so used to drones and satellites and all that. Pilots see these things and just roll their eyes."

"Dust?" Lally was replaying this list in her head.

"You know. Light refractions due to pollutants in the air. Harmless."

Lally remained unconvinced. "Mark didn't just roll his eyes. Mark picked up the phone and called me."

"Mark's bored. It's the middle of the night. We've got . . ." Connie checked her watch, which was small and gold like a grandmother's. "Roughly two and a half hours left in this flight. He's just pulling your leg."

Lally looked out the window again and, sure enough, the lights were still there. That might be true, but also true: This was no light refraction.

Connie peered into her snack bag as if counting the number of chips remaining. "Sometimes they're psychological manifestations."

Being called crazy didn't sit well with Lally, especially by another woman. She was beginning to think Mark and Connie were both putting her on. A hazing of sorts, even though they were the ones new to the route.

"Well, you know. I don't mean that as harsh as it sounds. They overwork us, we're tired. The short turnarounds. A bad night's sleep in an airport hotel. Different pillow every night. The altitude. Pressure in our heads. Not to mention . . ." Connie made a whistling sound as she leaned back and nodded up and down the aisle at the passengers. "It adds up. And it just gets harder as we age."

Lally was pretty sure she'd just been called crazy *and* old, and she still wasn't sure what to do. "So we just . . . forget we saw it?"

"Unless you want to start alarming passengers."

"Connie!"

But Connie was rummaging for the right zero-calorie beverage to pair with her flavor crystals and didn't take her protest seriously. "What do you want us to do, shoot them down? We're not exactly a fighter jet. You think Mark is some top gun? He had to have me help him download the American app on his phone. *Me!* Like I'm his mother." She finally gave up the ghost. "I'm going to head back to the rear. I think there's one apple juice left." She held her finger to her lips to keep Lally quiet, lest a passenger hear and request it before Connie could claim it. "Don't worry. I just take two sips, then spit it out." She patted her hips a second time.

"Connie, come back here."

As Connie left the galley she pointed one last time at the window and said, "Just you wait, in a few minutes they will be gone."

Lally did wait before checking once more, but the lights remained. She was then distracted by 12B, who was awake again; he didn't like his wine and wanted a beer. He gave her the little wine bottle back; since it was only half empty, she decided it was fine to serve him the beer, but her card reader was acting up (first the lights, now this), so she gave him his drink on the house in a rush to get back to her perch in the window; now they seemed farther away.

Moments like these always made her take stock of her life. Well, there were very few moments like *these*. But plenty lately when she felt anxious. Alone. It wasn't how she thought her life would go. Her brother Norman met someone with relative ease decades ago; they had quite literally bumped into each other. That was the way things were supposed to go. You go to school, get a job, meet someone, have kids. Her parents had done it that way, they met in school.

Norman and Jesse followed that path more or less, and they were two men! But life hadn't worked quite that way for Lally; things had always been harder for her.

It started, she supposed, when her brother Robbie died. And then later when she got braces and headgear; unlike her grief, which she became adept at making invisible, braces were an exterior physical awkwardness to match her inner emotional one. Everyone told her how lucky she was, as she was the first in her family to get them, when everyone else had to accept whatever grew out of their head. As soon as they came off she realized how grateful she'd been to have them, but for two years, her life was hell. It wasn't just braces, but this entire headgear contraption. Boys wouldn't look at her, girls wouldn't talk to her. Not to her face, anyway. Plenty was said behind her back. Kids were cruel, and she absorbed every word of it until she was cruel to herself, too. She was lost without Robbie, who had been her defender.

It got better for a time in college, but by then she was spending evenings and weekends with her brother and his new boyfriend, preferring their grown-up friends to her own. She was everyone's little sister, and the crowd that Norman and Jesse cultivated had a hard time looking at her as anything but. Even when she thought she might be open to having a lesbian affair (in college, such a cliché), the women she met never considered her a sexual being. The few straight men they encountered, waiters and bartenders and barbacks who flooded the Venice Beach scene, didn't seem to see her that way, either, and Norman, in an effort to comfort her, told her she was someone likely to blossom later.

And now it was later, too late even, if you asked most men, who always had their eye on someone younger, someone dumber, someone who giggled easily and would go along with the status quo.

Lally's one serious relationship had been with a gourd farmer, of all things. "A what now?" Norman and Jesse had teased. She had to tell them they heard her right. "You can't grow gourds in California," they protested. It seemed like such an East Coast thing. How did the Pilgrims have the first Thanksgiving if gourds were grown outside of L.A.?

"That's simply not true," Lally told them. She'd learned a lot about gourds. They preferred warm weather and ample sun and at least six hours of direct sunlight a day.

"Maybe *we're* gourds," Jesse had mused.

"Maybe," Lally retorted. "You're bumpy and unevenly shaped."

When the relationship ended, Norman and Jesse had gotten her drunk at a local bar. They sang karaoke to her, Elton John and Kiki Dee. *Don't gourd breaking my heart.* She hadn't dated much since.

Lally had little need for a man now, but she wanted a baby. That sometimes required a man, but she already had two: Norman and Jesse. Between them they had created nine viable embryos, three boys and six girls, currently taking up space in a freezer in the Mid-Wilshire district of Los Angeles. Not only did she deserve to become a mother, they deserved to become children, some of them at least. If Norman and Jesse had changed their mind about fatherhood (why, she didn't know), there was no reason for them not to agree to let her take custody—biologically, they were half hers, even if not legally. And, hey, if they later relented and did want to bring children into the world, their kids would be both cousins *and* siblings. How great! Hopefully they would grow up as connected as she felt to Robbie and Norman.

But where *was* Norman? Since she'd paid her visit to Jesse, her brother had not been answering his phone. At first she thought it was unusual perhaps, but not unheard of; he had a way of getting lost in a build. But it had been over a week and still no call back, despite repeated messages and texts. Something was not right.

So she wished upon the UAPs like stars. She wished to be a mother. She wished to find her brother to make that happen. She wished for more out of life. She wished for one bad crop of gourds, not enough to ruin a man, but enough to punish him just a bit. Then she unwished that wish, because there was enough negativity in the world. She wished for kindness and forgiveness. She wished for everything to be different.

Outside the window, the lights switched positions one last time and when Lally blinked they disappeared. She kept one eye open for them until the sunrise cracked the horizon and the day's first light appeared. Once they were gone, she actually missed them.

DAY THIRTY-SEVEN

Lally had never hired a private detective and didn't know anyone who had. In fact, it wasn't until she pulled out an old phone book, the last that had ever been delivered (even the white pages were now yellowed with age), that she even believed PIs were a real thing. Of course, Google might have been easier, but something printed felt more clandestine. Internet searches could be traced; flipping through the Yellow Pages could not. She felt like she should be drinking a dry martini, even smoking a cigarette.

Calling 911 had been her first instinct, calling a lawyer her second. But what was there really to say? Her brother wasn't returning her calls? Her brother-in-law wouldn't let her have access to embryos to which she had no legal claim? She'd heard the line enough in movies—*Ma'am, this line is for emergencies.* She had no desire to hear it from the police in real life. Nor did she want to pay exorbitant fees to be told she had no case. There was the option of changing her schedule, taking some time off to start an investigation herself, or trying to pick up an additional shift on a flight to Milwaukee to see if she could track down Norman there. The problem was, she was only ninety percent certain Jesse had said Milwaukee and not Minneapolis. Or maybe he'd said Minnesota in general. Or even simply the Midwest. She'd considered another surprise visit to see Jesse, but knew in her heart it wouldn't yield satisfying results. Yes, at the Tiny Pony he had seemed to warm toward her, but he would ultimately hide behind needing Norman's consent. The key to her happiness was finding her brother and finding him on her own—and *soon*.

She spoke to two people by phone, the first was a true old gumshoe, a man by the name of Wilford Ilsen, and *old* was being charitable. This guy had passed old sometime around the Carter administration. He talked about his "girl" being out that day and his inability to take notes without his glasses, and apparently only the girl knew their whereabouts. Lally had a clear picture of him as a withered corpse in a brown sports jacket, the lapels covered in soup. In short, he would not do.

Her second call proved more promising. A man named Harlan Faulkner answered the phone with confidence and panache; the literary nature of his name seemed like a sign. Faulkner was not Chandler, but it was close enough, and Harlan was a man she could imagine feeling safe with. He was not young, around Lally's age, but he was most certainly not old enough to have stormed Normandy. Also, his "girl" was a gay man named Lyle, which put her instantly at ease. Harlan assured her she was doing the right thing and discouraged her from feeling silly. She was right that the cops wouldn't care, but people who were missing were harder to find the longer they were gone—especially those who didn't want to be found. Weren't all private investigators former cops? Harlan said there was a reason they were *ex-*; he even made it sound reasonable, like they were unable to reform a broken system from within. She was ready to hire him over the phone. The only complication? He insisted they meet in person.

When she had three days off in L.A., they arranged to meet at his office on La Cienega Boulevard. La Cienega intersected Wilshire near where the embryos were stored, but she tried to keep that coincidence far from mind. None of that mattered if they could not locate Norman. Besides, Harlan's office was closer to the intersection with La Tijera—a road she knew well, as it led to the airport. The building was unimpressive from the outside, but surprisingly professional inside; instead of broken blinds, the windows had roman shades and the waiting area had a new-carpet smell.

Lyle asked if she wanted water while she waited for Harlan—he was just wrapping up a call—and when she said yes he gave her a clean drinking glass with water from a blue dispenser. Without asking, Lyle showed her his boss's license and proof of insurance. "A lot of people don't know to ask to see these, but Harlan thinks it's important that you do." Lally smiled and thanked him; he reminded her of her brother back in the nineties. Young, confident, and approachable with stylish glasses. She asked how he got into this line of work; he had a face for commercials. "Lady, please," he began. "I was made for this line of work. I can get a story out of *anyone*." Lally understood, as she was on the verge of spilling hers. Lyle didn't pry, but she made note to be careful what she shared with him in the future. She asked why Harlan insisted on meeting in person and Lyle said it was a comfort thing, and because oftentimes hiring a private investigator leads to them having to testify in civil or criminal court, and Harlan likes to show that he's a professional who comes across as such. It's only to her benefit. Hearing this reason was the first time Lally thought there could be something seriously amiss. Court? A trial? She masked her discomfort by drinking her water, asking no more questions until Harlan finished his call. It was not awkward—Lyle did plenty of talking. So much so, she began to think he had it backward. Literally anyone could get a story out of him.

"Lally?"

Harlan stood in the doorway, both more and less intimidating than she'd imagined. Something about him reminded her of Gene Hackman but sturdier, or someone of normal looks they used to let be a movie star before everyone on-screen was required to look the same. He was surprisingly muscular for a man of his age, which she imagined to be early fifties. He had kind eyes that reminded her of her father's, and he wore a similarly wide tie. "Yes."

"Come on in." He smiled, his teeth as white as sunshine. That was L.A. for you—even the private dicks had their teeth whitened. He gestured for her to join him in his office, and she placed her water glass on the corner of Lyle's desk with an apologetic smile. She took the nearer seat of two that sat across from his desk, wondering how he could conduct a stakeout unnoticed (that smile was like flashing high beams). The chair's ivory upholstery was somewhat stained, she imagined from years of nervous people sweating bullets in the very seat she sat in now. Since the carpet was new, maybe an updated chair was on order.

"You're here about your sister, yes?" He was soft-spoken and there was a hint of an accent, Chicago maybe. Or Boston.

"Brother, actually." Lally nodded politely as he flipped to a clean page in a legal pad to take notes.

"Brother. I'm sorry. When did you last see him?"

"*See* him, see him?" Lally asked; it had been a while. "He called me on my birthday and everything seemed fine. I think that's the last time we spoke."

"When was that?"

"June." And then because she thought it important to be precise added, "Thirty-first."

Harlan lifted his pen from his paper. "June only has thirty days."

"Twenty-first! Sorry." She looked over her shoulder to see if Lyle could bring her more water, but Harlan had closed the door behind them. She didn't think she would be this nervous. "Gemini. Or Cancer. Sometimes it depends on who you ask."

"Okay," he said with his kind eyes. "Just try and relax. No trick questions, I promise."

As Harlan made a quick note, Lally adjusted herself in her seat. If she couldn't quell her nerves, she could at least appear more comfortable, but in a moment of panic she forgot how people sat properly in meetings and draped one of her legs over the chair's arm before quickly undoing the pretzel she was making of herself.

"A lot of people only talk to their family on birthdays and holidays. But I take it this is unusual."

Lally did her best to explain everything that Norman was to her, their history and his role in her life still. He wasn't just some random relation; since their brother Robbie died and her parents had retired to Italy, he *was* her family—the entirety of it. An older brother, a wise uncle, a father figure. And on top of that a best friend, or at least he had been. "In short," she added after she'd gone long, "it's not the norm." *It's not Norman.*

She described how she'd dropped in on Jesse and found his behavior odd. Skittish. Unfocused. Jesse always told it to you straight, that had been the nature of their relationship since they first met. When she was twenty-two and in line to buy a top at Urban Outfitters, he would quietly substitute it with another. He would override her when ordering wine in restaurants or when she discussed possible vacation destinations. (Visiting Estonia? She should try Tallinn over Pärnu.) Recently when she hinted her eyes were looking tired and she might like a surgical refresh, he mentioned if he were her, he would start with her chin. It sounded awful in the recounting, but she had always appreciated his bluntness. Which was what made her certain he was hiding something now.

"How long have they been married?" Harlan asked when she went on about Jesse for too long.

"Since 2016."

"That's all?"

"It wasn't legal much before then. In California, at least. Except for a short time in 2008. They've been together since the nineties. Why?"

Harlan made notes. "When someone disappears it's prudent to take a look at the spouse."

"*Disappears?*" To Lally that seemed a bit strong. She simply wanted to know why her brother was not returning her calls.

"What word would you use?"

"I don't know. I hadn't really thought about it." She fished in her purse for Norman's business card. He'd shared one with her when he had the logo for his firm redesigned. "Jesse said he was in Milwaukee. I'm pretty sure that's it. I tried calling my brother's office to confirm, but no one is answering the phone. He recently opened his own firm. I'm not even sure he has an assistant."

Harlan squinted like he was recognizing a theme. He then read the card. "Your brother's an architect?"

"That's right."

"And he was in Milwaukee . . ."

"On a build, supposedly."

"Private home? Public building?"

"Medical building, I think." It had been a few weeks, but Lally was almost certain that was what Jesse had said. "Does that help?"

Harlan hummed. Lally wasn't sure if that meant yes or no. "We can check with the city for permits."

"All of this is of course according to Jesse."

Harlan nodded.

"But Jesse wouldn't harm him."

Harlan looked out his window into the back alley. The view was a tangle of telephone wires, and the sky was a dull pigeon gray. "You'd be surprised."

"I would be," Lally agreed. Jesse knew more than he was letting on, but she would bet almost anything that was where it ended.

"What kind of time frame are we working with here?"

"Time frame?"

"How quickly do you need to find him?"

Lally wasn't certain how to answer that one without sharing too much. "Do you have an expedited service?" She could only imagine what the rush fees on a job like this might be. Harlan laughed, and she forced a weak smile.

"No, no. I mean, is there a deadline that you're under. You're trying to locate him for a family reunion, or to sign documents by a certain date."

"Oh," Lally sighed. She imagined Harlan had any number of clients, as someone was paying for Lyle and this office space. She didn't want to be bumped down his list of priorities. "No exact date, but there is a pressing legal matter. So, something like the document thing." She hoped he wouldn't ask, as she didn't know how to explain to him the realities of her ticking biological clock. Fortunately he had no follow-up.

Harlan explained that the first step, should they move forward, was to see if Jesse was telling the truth. If he was, this could be more or less open and shut. But if Jesse wasn't telling the truth, that would be another matter entirely. "But I must warn you, there are limits to what we can do. I have a pretty good track record of finding missing persons, but we make no guarantees. Some mysteries have no answers. Or at least ones that we'll ever know. Like who really shot JFK."

"My father thinks a bird flew into him."

Harlan stared at her, trying his best not to laugh. Lally shrugged. If only he knew her father. "Well, that's a new one to me. I might have to look into that."

Lally held his gaze and pleaded with her eyes. "Please find my brother first."

She signed the agreement after Harlan went through it with her point by point; Lyle made a copy for her records before complimenting her shoes and she paid the agreed-upon retainer. She sat in her car when she left, surprised by her decisiveness, even if in the privacy of her rented Honda she was having second thoughts. Did people really do this, hire private investigators? Should she have called someone else? Isn't this what congresspeople or even senators were for? She didn't know. What she did know was what she wanted to avoid at all costs. Calling her parents in Italy to tell them their favorite child was missing. Especially since none of them had gotten over losing Robbie.

DAY SEVENTY

Lally went about her life the best she could for four long weeks, keeping her flight schedule, even taking on extra shifts to help the time pass. At every layover, each new city, she talked herself out of calling Harlan. He was doing his job, she hoped; he would call her with news. What were the rules? How much space did you give a private detective in order not to seem too anxious, too desperate, perhaps even suspicious yourself? It was worse than dating someone new.

And wouldn't she be so grateful if Harlan were the one to find Norman? She imagined it would be impossible not to throw herself into his arms when he brought her the news that Norman had returned safe from Minneapolis or wherever the fuck he was. Yes, she had gone to Harlan's office on business, but she was still a woman. She hadn't seen forearms on a man like that since childhood cartoons of Popeye, and, in her lonelier moments, she could all but feel them wrapped around her. Could she, she wondered idly somewhere over the Midwest, be falling for an actual sleuth? Ridiculous, the very thought! Private eyes fell for the femmes fatales that appeared in their offices in desperate need, not the other way around. Humphrey Bogart for Mary Astor. Jimmy Stewart for Kim Novak. Jack Nicholson for Faye Dunaway. Okay, so a missing brother wasn't exactly the Maltese Falcon, but it wasn't nothing, either. That day in his office, Harlan seemed moved to help, doing his best to remain rational and calm her emotions. And so every time she would land after a long flight she would immediately turn on her phone, living a grander and grander fantasy—Norman was found just in time to be the officiant at her wedding to Harlan, who had fallen madly in love with her over the course of the search—in the moments before her phone caught a signal and she realized there were no messages. Until one morning, in Columbus, there was.

Hello, Lally? It's Harlan calling about our little project. Give me a call when you can. I'd like to update you where we are.

She listened to the message three times. Where *we* are. That meant he hadn't found Norman; otherwise he would update her on where her brother was. But she did like the collaborative sound of "we" and "our." They were in this together.

Lally didn't know the protocol exactly, but when she landed at LAX she stopped in the terminal and bought a Starbucks card for Harlan's assistant, Lyle, before exiting the airport. Sometimes, on a cross-country flight, people left little gifts for the flight attendants. Often they were useless crafts, a nice thought, perhaps, but one more thing for her to carry (she never dared throw them out until the next city). Bookmarks were the only useful homemade gift. Starbucks cards were prized—they never failed to make her day. Easy to carry. Usable in any airport. Thoughtful. These gestures made her inclined to treat assistants well. A chatterbug like Lyle didn't exactly need to be hopped up on caffeine, in fact it might be a detriment to doing his job well, but that wasn't really her problem, and besides—it was the thought that counts.

She returned Harlan's call when she was clear of LAX, perhaps overcautious behavior, but Lally didn't want anyone she worked with to know her personal business, and she was always convinced that the government listened in on more calls in the vicinity of an airport. Lyle answered on the third ring and put her straight through; Harlan asked to meet for drinks. It was more than coffee, less than dinner, and while it might confuse someone else (was drinks a date?), she found it a thrilling invitation, fuel on the fire of her fantasy. No dame met her private dick at Chipotle. She quickly agreed but had another flight out early, and so she could not meet him until her next layover in two days. He said that would allow him time to make another trip to Joshua Tree to get the most recent lay of the land and warned her he might request another small retainer when they met. Which was fine. What was a little cash in the face of true love?

The bar he chose was located inside a restaurant with the word *Stagecoach* as part of its name, one of those out-of-date places with a revolving dessert case and dark wood paneling—the kind of joint that might still have a smoking section; in short, it was absolutely perfect. Harlan was sitting on a barstool when Lally entered wearing a wrap dress she had rescued from the back of her closet, a von Furstenberg knockoff, midi length, with two chest pockets that made it look both dated and timeless. Harlan wore a slightly different version of what he was wearing the last time they met—something men could get away with, but femmes fatales could not. He waved to her and she smiled, quietly longing to make him over, he could use a woman's touch, but she knew from experience it was almost impossible to ask a man to be other than he was and she was happy at least to see he had his sleeves rolled up, as if he knew the effect his forearms had on her. Of course, what made him so attractive was that he didn't. She pulled her hair down as she approached the bar, doing her best to play her part, and he asked what he could get her after they shook hands. (No wedding ring, she noticed, or tan line where one might be, making her feel equally the detective.) He was drinking a scotch, even though it appeared they were shy on single malts in favor of blended bottles with unfashionable labels like Cutty Sark.

"Pinot grigio," Lally said, not wanting to be too extravagant; she knew whatever she ordered stood a good chance of winding up on her tab. Harlan gestured for the bartender and in an instant a glass with a heavy pour was placed in front of her centered perfectly on a cocktail napkin. A Sheena Easton song was piped in through the speakers: "Almost Over You," even though when it came to Harlan, Lally was anything but. They were the only two at the bar.

"What is this place?" she asked with a grin. She offered her glass for a toast, and he raised his own to meet hers. They both sipped as Harlan looked around the bar as if taking it in for the first time.

"Oh, sorry. I like it because it's a little out of the way." It was like they were trading in state secrets.

"Are you kidding? No apologies necessary. A little overdone on the wagon wheel theme, but I am in love with the dessert case." She was already debating between a slice of coconut cake and the Boston cream pie. But honestly, why should she choose? The wine burned her throat, and she coughed once, as delicately as she could, which broke the spell of her fantasy. "Besides, we are here about Norman. I would go anywhere for news."

Harlan reached into his worn leather bag to produce three folded pages. He smoothed them out on the bar. In the corners they were torn like they'd once been taped. Across the top of each was written MISSING. "Are any of these Norman?"

Lally leaned in for a closer look. One of them was a woman.

"Not this one, obviously," he said sheepishly, removing the woman from the lineup. "I just wanted to show you a pattern. One is always upsetting, but people go missing. It's just one of those things. Two is disconcerting. *Three* missing people in a concentrated area is a sign that something's up."

Lally pulled the two remaining pages closer to her skeptically, not knowing whether to hope one would be Norman or not. They were aged, faded from the sun, and she did her best to iron them with her fist against the oak bar, but all of that was for show. As soon as she took even a sideways glance at them, it was clear neither of the men was her brother. If Harlan was hoping for a break in the case, sadly this wasn't it. She made her mouth really small, a look Norman had called the cat's anus when they were young.

"Ah, well. Nothing's ever that easy."

"Do these men have families?" Lally asked, not sure why her heart suddenly went out to them. "And this woman, too?" She was described as a teacher from the College of the Desert.

"Someone made the posters and hung them all over town. These were far from the only copies."

Lally shifted her weight, relieved that her search wasn't derailing anyone else's. "Should we be making one of these for Norman?" Was that what Harlan was suggesting? She struggled to remember if she had a recent photo, or imagine how she would get it to Kinko's. If there even were still Kinko's.

"That's your call, obviously. You'd have to tell me if he's lowercase missing or, you know." He tapped on the uppercase red lettering on one of the posters. "At this point, maybe it's not worth spooking your brother-in-law. If he starts seeing these with his husband's face plastered all over town . . ." Harlan shrugged. But Lally understood the implication. If Jesse had information she needed, she didn't want to unnerve him or drive him further underground.

She sipped her pinot grigio; the glass was thick and heavy in her hand, the only knock against this place—a crisp wine deserved a more elegant presentation. "Is that it? What you had to show me?" Lally asked, suddenly wondering if she was getting her money's worth.

"No, that was just . . ." He didn't finish the sentence. "I've been staking out your brother-in-law's house. He doesn't come and go much. Not a lot to see."

"He's a writer, he works mostly from home."

Harlan wiped a napkin across his forehead to dab at some sweat. It suited him; manly men perspired. "Yeah, I don't think he's doing a lot of writing."

Lally tilted her head, confused. "What is he doing, then?"

"He's made more than one trip to a local Dairy Queen, if you know what that's about."

Lally shook her head. "I don't. I guess he likes ice cream."

"Other than that, he's . . ."

Lally was not a fan of the dramatic pause.

Harlan looked her square in the eyes, like he was bracing her for what he was about to say. "*Digging.*"

"Digging?" Lally giggled. He said it like he was the Fonz. *Digging his time alone?* It was not at all what she thought he would say. She imagined Jesse perhaps having an affair, or something like that. Wasn't that what these investigations usually uncovered?

"Digging," Harlan repeated. "In the backyard."

"You mean, like a hole?" The thought of it was almost absurd. It wasn't really like Jesse to do physical labor. Was this a metaphor? What might someone dig up on her, if she had been assigned such a tail?

"It seems he started a few days ago, maybe a week. He's making pretty good progress." Harlan took her hand in his; they were meaty and warm. He looked at her, clearly hoping she could see where he was going with this. "I'm sorry."

Lally dipped her chin. *Sorry for what?* Whatever it was, Harlan had the wrong idea. "Jesse always wanted a pool. Maybe that's what he's doing. It was an ongoing discussion with Norman. They went back and forth on it, but Norman didn't want to put up the fence that zoning laws and insurance would require. It ruined the . . . fueng shoo."

"Feng shui," Harlan corrected, and she felt her face grow red. "Lally, you don't dig your own swimming pool. That's psychotic behavior. You hire a company with trucks and a backhoe."

"But maybe for just like a small one." Lally gestured with her wineglass, nearly sloshing her pinot over the side. "A plunge pool."

Harlan disagreed. "Not even a wading pool."

"Well, then what are you saying?"

Harlan's eyes looked pained. "Why else does a person dig?"

Lally knew what he was trying to say. She'd seen enough episodes of *Dateline* on late nights in hotel rooms. You dig to bury a body. But that just didn't sit right. First of all, Jesse was lazy, physically anyhow, had been as long as she'd known him. No, it had to be something else. On the other hand, he wouldn't be putting in a swimming pool unless he knew Norman was out of the picture. Even that explanation was damning.

"I need to arrange a way to meet him. Observe his demeanor up close. I'm not getting a lot sitting in my car with binoculars."

"Have you seen him go anywhere?" Lally asked. "Besides Dairy Queen, I mean."

"Oh!" Harlan reached into his breast pocket for his phone. "I followed him to the Integratron."

"The Integra-*what*?" He was making less sense by the minute.

"The Integratron. It's this strange UFO-like structure built in the desert. You go there for sound baths."

Lally pressed her palms against her eyes. Her head was spinning, either from this news, her crush (although in the moment, that was fading), or the cheap wine. "When?"

Harlan futzed with his phone. "Just the other day. Here. I recorded some of it." He played an audio file and a haunting noise unfurled out of the speaker, like coyotes wailing a plaintive cry. Lally leaned in—she couldn't not—and listened very carefully, aware she was falling into a trance. She wondered suddenly if she was in danger. If Harlan hadn't somehow roofied her in this strange, out-of-the-way bar.

"What is that noise?"

"Bowls," Harlan replied.

"Like for *soup*?"

Harlan laughed. "They're singing bowls. I think made out of quartz crystal. I can rewind the recording if you like. They gave us a whole tutorial at the beginning of the session."

"Are you supposed to record the sound bath?" Lally wondered aloud. Living in Venice Beach as she had, she'd brushed up against enough of this hippie-dippy nonsense to know that must be frowned upon. "I'm surprised they didn't confiscate people's phones."

"Oh, they do. That's why I always carry two." Harlan pulled a second phone out from his pants pocket and held them both up for her to see. "I've become rather adept at doing things on the sly."

Lally pushed her drink back a few inches on the bar, worried about the roofie anew. Then she heard the faintest whisper over the bowls.

"Norman is not here."

Startled, Lally sat up on her barstool. "Was that the bowls?" In addition to singing, did they also reveal secrets in a chorus of celestial hums?

Harlan laughed again. "No, no. That was me just making notes for myself to share with you. Jesse was clearly there on his own. I just wanted that on record for you to hear."

Lally understood, but it seemed like Harlan was not good sound bath people; she doubted you should be talking during the experience. She could only imagine his frustrated neighbors begging him to stay still. She hoped he hadn't interrupted anyone else's experience on her behalf. Then again, she could never date a *good* sound bath person. Knowing the protocol suggested a fastidiousness that she could not accept in a man. She wondered how Jesse behaved in the Integratron, and asked.

"Oh, perfectly normal from what I observed. As far as one can behave normally in such a place." Harlan saw Jesse purchase something in the gift shop, but most of the time they were lying on their backs.

Lally recoiled at the idea of a gift shop, which seemed surprisingly crass.

Harlan scratched his stubble. "I wish there was a better way to observe him. Someplace I could keep my eyes open."

Lally thought diligently, resting her chin on her hands as she did, even closing her eyes for a moment. When she opened them, Harlan was staring right at her. "Like what?"

"Oh, I don't know," he said sheepishly, collecting the MISSING flyers before offering them to her. Lally tried her best to read his awkward discomfort. Had he been staring at her?

"Jesse teaches college," she blurted. "Maybe you could audit his class?" It was meant to be helpful, her suggestion, but Harlan looked panic-stricken.

"Oh-kay," Harlan replied, stretching the word as far as he could without breaking it.

Lally looked down, allowing her hair to hide her eyes. "I mean, if you want."

Harlan hesitated. "School was not really something I enjoyed the first time around. But I suppose I could give it a go."

Lally placed a hand on his shoulder and said, "I'll bet you were a great student." It was the most outright flirtatious she'd been yet, and she just as quickly smoothed his shirt and retreated.

Harlan's face grew flush, but he didn't otherwise stumble. "My whole class read *To Kill a Mockingbird*, what is that, like eighth grade? And then the teacher let us watch the movie. A lot of the kids were upset when Atticus shot the mad dog, wondering why he did such a thing. The teacher turned the question back on the class, and I proudly raised my hand and said it was because the dog was infested with rabbis."

Lally tilted her head before a grin crept across her face, and then she couldn't help but laugh. "You said rabbis?"

"Yes. With unshakable confidence."

"Not rabies."

"There was only one Jewish kid in my class, the town optometrist's son, and everyone pointed at him and laughed, even though it was my idiot mistake. I guess because he'd just had his bar mitzvah, so his being Jewish was front of mind." Harlan took a long slow sip of his scotch. "I feel bad to this day, if I'm being honest. So classrooms were never my thing."

Lally cupped her hands over her mouth to keep from laughing further. She waved to the bartender and asked for menus. "I'm going to get something from the dessert case. The only problem is I can't decide between a slice of the coconut cake and the Boston cream pie."

Harlan didn't hesitate. "Could we get a slice of the coconut cake and the Boston cream pie? Two forks."

Lally smiled, instinctively covering her mouth with her hand.

"Don't do that," Harlan said, gently lowering her hand. "Hide, I mean. You have a beautiful smile."

Lally could feel herself blush. "Old habit. I had braces for years. Norman used to say I had summer teeth."

Harlan leaned forward and cocked his head in a way that made him look like a spaniel. "What are summer teeth?"

Lally did her best to sell the joke. "Som're here. Som're there." Harlan didn't laugh, so she pointed in opposite directions to drive the punch line home. Still, no laugh.

"Maybe we should let him stay missing just for that." Harlan eased back onto his barstool and exhaled. "I'm sorry. That was inappropriate. I have an older brother. He teased me mercilessly. I guess I'm a little sensitive." He then quickly added, "We will find him, your brother."

The desserts arrived along with two forks rolled in paper napkins; they wasted no time diving in.

"Thank you," Lally said as she took her first bite.

"For saying we'll find him? It's why you hired me."

Lally meant for standing up for her, but she couldn't say that outright. So she hid her smile a second time, this time for fear her teeth were smeared with Boston cream pie.

ROBBIE

Lally walked through coach slowly, discreetly collecting trash from those few still awake and empty cans on lowered trays from passengers whose eyes were shut tight. The flight had been smooth and the passengers remarkably quiet, a dream for her third flight in three days. So much so that Lally was looking forward to a few minutes to herself in the galley to close her own eyes. But three rows from the rear of the plane, she spotted a woman on the starboard aisle, head bowed, shoulders shaking. The woman was crying.

Flight attendants see this plenty. It might be something as simple as a book or a movie that sets a passenger off. She'd delivered many a complimentary drink to someone who'd just finished a book where the dog dies (always when the dog dies), or a movie with a protracted goodbye. But often it was more immediate, more personal. People flew for all kinds of reasons. To attend funerals, to spread ashes, to start a new life after a divorce or breakup. Oftentimes it was best to ignore someone quietly weeping. It was their own business and not everyone appreciated a stranger who pried.

But something caused Lally to stop, crouch down, and reach for the woman's hand—we were all going through something, we all had our private struggles; the woman gladly accepted.

They stayed like that for a good minute, just holding hands, only a single gentleman brushing past them on his way to the lavatory, before the woman reached for her napkin with her free hand and dabbed at the corners of her eyes. "I'm sorry," she apologized in little more than a whisper. They were about the only words she could form.

Lally assured her there was no need. We've all been there. We always feel silly, embarrassed even, for being human.

Eventually the woman managed, "My sister."

Lally judged the woman to be near her age, maybe a few years older, or maybe her eyes were just puffy from crying. Either way, she saw herself reflected back at her and she, too, began to cry. "My brother," she said. But it was more than that. It was two brothers. Her childhood. Her life turning out not at all how she wanted it to be. There was just so much to mourn. And then both women started to laugh, laughter just another release. In that moment she was grateful for a compatriot in grief. Lally squeezed the woman's hand twice before letting go. "I'll get us some napkins," she said. She returned with napkins and a little bottle of wine. And then Lally hid in the galley and thought about her brother.

Her *other* brother.

Robbie Alfano was a classic middle child, lacking Norman's golden firstborn sheen, denied the attention Lally courted as the baby. But Robbie was pure magic, at least to Lally, especially when she was young. The age difference with Norman was a bridge too far to cross, but Robbie, the span between them, never failed to engage with her in a way that connected them both. He was a boy's boy who moved without fear of consequence, jumped in piles of leaves like shoulders could not be dislocated, built a ramp for his

BMX bike like bones could not be broken; when anyone in the neighborhood put in a pool, he was the first kid to cannonball from the roof. How did he get on the roof? No one ever really knew, that was just Robbie. Turn your back for a second, and he was inside the giant display of rubber balls the grocery store assembled in spring. He climbed things like Spider-Man; Lally would walk through a doorway, and somehow he was propping himself up at the top, ready to scare her and set her off in fits of delight. Oh, how he made Lally laugh! No one was sillier, or more committed to a bit, willing to risk punishment from their exasperated parents just to evoke a response.

Norman always seemed mature, more serious, and not just because he was older. Whatever Norman wasn't, Robbie was. Whatever Robbie wasn't, Norman was. For a time, Lally thought it took both of them to equal a whole brother. One to take her sledding down the steepest hills, and one to read to her when she needed a quiet moment on the couch. It took her until she was eighteen to appreciate Norman for who he was, and after Robbie was gone, not blame him for who he wasn't. She regretted that, but grief is a strange and malleable thing, especially for children. Less than a year after Robbie died, Norman left for college. It wasn't meant to be an act of abandonment, it was simply what eighteen-year-olds did. Whatever grief he carried he packed in a footlocker with things he acquired for freshman year and took it with him. Lally had two brothers, and then in less than a year she had none.

Therapists warned her parents that Lally might regress, slide back into old behaviors or develop new fears or problems at school. But even at that young age, Lally seemed determined to defy expectations. She jumped from six to sixteen overnight, becoming irritable and moody, and over the following years she isolated herself save for a close group of friends. It was why she was somewhat of a loner even now. Home was whichever city she was in for the night, whatever

Courtyard Marriott put her up. The apartment she kept in Los Angeles was merely a place to store her things; L.A. was simply a city she moved to as soon as she was able to try to reconnect with Norman.

It was only much later that she understood that Norman had replaced Robbie with Jesse; Norman, of course, would deny this, but once she saw it, she could not unsee how the two were so much alike. The age difference was the same; like Robbie, Jesse fell halfway in age between Lally and Norman. He was likewise quick to laugh and would stick with a joke until it had been run into the ground—a trait that eventually won him an award. In his youth he had been up for almost anything; fear only set in with age. There were differences, sure. He was an only child and not a middle, but his father had died before he was born and like Robbie he longed for attention. As a couple they had an undeniable gravitational pull on Lally. It was her friend Stephanie who first pointed it out—after more than a decade without them, she had regained not one but *both* of her brothers. Much later, when they asked her to be their egg donor, there was only one answer to give: She would do anything for them.

"Everything all right back here?"

Lally spun around to see Connie staring at her as she was elbow-deep reorganizing the galley cabinets. Lally had been lost in thought counting coffee filters. She turned away to hide her wet eyes. "Fine, just . . . fidgety."

Connie understood. "The quiet flights make me nervous, too." She rummaged through the beverage cart to take stock of the cans that were left. Then she paused and glanced up. "Say, are you okay?"

Lally laughed and dragged the back of her hand over her eyes. "I'm fine. 34C, that's all. She lost her sister. It struck a little too close to home."

Connie found the can of tomato juice she was looking for and stood. "I didn't know you had a sister," she said.

"Brother," Lally corrected. "Robbie."

Connie nodded and patted her coworker on the arm. "Let me bring this to 14D and I'll come back and help. With this." She gestured at the mess Lally had made on the counter, having fully emptied two cabinets. Connie didn't return to help, and for once Lally was grateful.

Lally was five and Norman seventeen when it happened. The winter had been unseasonably cold with a record amount of snow. The kind of season that felt personal, a vendetta. Every time you thought it was over, it came roaring back. Their Easter portraits that year were taken in front of a snowbank that dwarfed all but their dad. She and Robbie had lost track of the number of snow days—there was so much school to make up, at this rate summer break would not come until July. So instead they counted actual feet of precipitation that accumulated on the ground. Robbie had been the one who taught her to count, starting with her index finger, never her thumb. Thumbs were for something else, sucking for Lally, a habit her parents were desperately trying to break her of, spraying them with bitter concoctions before bed, while Robbie employed his like a Roman emperor deciding a gladiator's fate. So Lally grew up grouping things in fours. No one, not even Norman himself, remembers his exact whereabouts that day, other than just out for a drive. By that point he had a license and his own car. He wasn't allowed to drive it in winter (his clunker had those headlights that popped up from the hood when you turned them on, and more often than not they were iced over or frozen shut), but technically it was spring. That left Robbie and Lally stuck at home with nothing to do, as their parents refused to get cable.

"Why don't you take your sister outside?" their mother suggested. It was April, after all, and despite the snow the sun was shining, and it was better than staying indoors. She even helped bundle Lally up; Robbie never stood still and would just remove whatever he didn't want to wear as soon as they were out of sight. "It's your grave," their mother used to say in defeat, but no one ever heard her use that phrase again after that day. Lally was instructed to keep every layer on and she did, not yet old enough to rebel.

It's funny how memory works. Lally had lived this story, had repeated it over and over again to herself. She'd been told the story, not by her parents, who refused to speak of it, but by well-meaning therapists hoping to help her confront it, even when it was torture to endure. Eventually telling became not a retelling of the event, but a retelling of the last time it was told, pulling Lally further and further away from what actually happened, further away from Robbie. Slight edits and polishes and changes, made perhaps with well-meaning intention to alleviate those closest to the event of the worst of their guilt. Whatever actually happened was long gone, edges dulled with time. Lally hated that. She longed for the sharp clarity of the truth, the pain of it, perhaps thinking that was what she deserved.

It was Robbie's idea to build the fort. Or it was Lally's. Those were the only two options. The plow had recently come. That was how much it had snowed. Had it been a lesser storm, Norman and Robbie would have been the ones to shovel the drive. The plow left enormous snowbanks, especially at the keystone of their arched drive, leaving them the raw materials needed to create a fort. To achieve their vision, they didn't need to build up, but rather tunnel down and possibly through. The snowbank was away from the house; occasionally their mother would open the door and yell for them and they would yell back, proof of life that seemed satisfactory. Otherwise they were totally left to their own imaginations. Robbie dug first, and then Lally when his arms would tire. She was no match for the towering bank, so she was quickly relegated to snow removal. It was an important job, Robbie assured her, the tunnels had to be cleared.

Robbie hollowed out the snowbank as best he could, and the structure more than held. But Lally wanted another entrance, something smaller, just for her, and Robbie dutifully obliged. He dug another tunnel, and they raced each other to the hollowed middle. Lally would laugh and laugh and they would back out of their respective entrances (there wasn't really enough room to turn around) and do it all over again. For hours they worked on improvements to their fortress, a window here, a retaining wall there—they pretended the whole thing was surrounded by a moat of ice that would break if any enemy, say Norman, attacked. Lally had never experienced such a perfect day, the numbness in her toes and her fingertips notwithstanding. Minor inconveniences, worthy sacrifices in service to the triumph of their castle. Her cheeks were red with cold, with delight, with inspiration. In an act of defiance, Lally removed her snow mittens and then the knitted ones underneath. On her fingers she counted the entrances and window, and came up with three. But there was still a finger left on her hand.

"What?" Robbie had asked. But he already knew what she was thinking. The fort needed something else to be complete. A grand doorway that even adults would look at with wonder, an architectural marvel that would be undeniable. "I'll be right back," Robbie said, and crawled through his tunnel deep inside.

Those were his final words.

Confused and frightened, Lally rang her own doorbell. Her mother answered to find her mittenless, misreading her shock for cold. She ushered Lally inside and took her tiny blue hands in her warm pink ones, rubbing them until sensation returned. It was a few minutes before she inquired about Robbie, even sticking her face out the door. "Robbie?" she called, but there was no reply. There was also no obvious reason to panic. The glory of the fort was a snowbank again, an afternoon of work erased with collapse. It was only when no reply came that Lally burst into primal tears, which sent their mother sprinting out of the house in her slippers. She saw Robbie's boot near the snowbank and was enraged that the boy had taken it off. She tugged at the boot, which appeared frozen to the ground.

Except it wasn't.

She tugged again and again until it came off in her hands, revealing the foot, which had still been inside it. A foot she once held to play peekaboo. A foot she would kiss gently after a bath to distract him while she put drops in his ears. A foot she had pressed in clay when he was still only a few weeks old, to preserve its imprint forever. By the time fire and rescue arrived, called by a quick-thinking neighbor, Robbie had long suffocated. There was nothing that anyone could do. An autopsy later revealed asphyxia as the cause of death; he'd suffered three broken ribs from the weight of the wet snow. Robbie's death was ruled an accident. His boot was only pried from his mother's arms by their father when the crowd of neighbors and first responders that had gathered had gone. For hours Lally took refuge in the coat closet just inside the front entry, refusing to come out. How could she not be at fault?

As soon as Lally was old enough, she followed Norman to California; she'd seen enough snow for a lifetime. Because she was the only one to witness the snowbank's collapse, adults worried there was a growing weight inside her that might also one day cave in, and they waited on edge for years for her to fall to pieces. Norman welcomed her to Venice with open arms. He didn't know if she needed saving, but he wasn't going to wait until it was too late. She stayed with him until he got serious with Jesse, and then he set her up in an apartment. He still included her in his life with his new boyfriend, who, as an only child, delighted in having a kid sister, and Norman introduced her to all of their friends. Lally gasped it all in like oxygen. Family at last. She had endured everything: survivor's guilt, deep remorse, a relationship with Robbie that she kept fervently alive within. She'd done it on her own, as her parents closed Robbie's bedroom door and it was years until they spoke about him again.

Norman did the opposite when she arrived in California. He wanted to talk about Robbie nonstop, as if Robbie's absence had been haunting him, too. He wanted to know what Lally remembered, and what she didn't he wanted to help her fill in. He was an ally in not *blaming* their parents per se, but in acknowledging that their emotional absence did Lally real harm. But eventually Norman's need to keep Robbie so present was its own form of torture and Lally took to the skies, hoping the life of a flight attendant—the constant departures and changing schedules—would help her outrun her grief. But now, all these years later, she was left to wonder if she hadn't abandoned Norman. Didn't he endure the same loss—more, even, as Robbie was his brother for eleven years, while Lally only had him for just shy of six?

"You're finished!" Connie said when she returned, feigning disappointment that everything had been put away neat and orderly.

Lally forced a smile, but that was the most she could do. She scooted past Connie, pausing at an open window into the night. She looked for the lights she had seen weeks earlier. She hadn't seen them again or since and tonight she almost missed them, as if they might have much-needed answers.

Something was not right with Norman's absence, and she would get to the bottom of it. Lally was done with her family shrinking. She wanted it to grow.

DAY EIGHTY-SIX

It was late in Newark when Lally made it to her hotel, a nondescript eyesore by the airport that looked like any of two dozen other airport hotels she regularly cycled through on her routes. She was so tired that she slid her ID across the check-in desk without so much as saying a word.

"One night?" the handsome young night clerk asked in a tone that Lally could almost mistake for a proposition. It was nearly eleven thanks to a mechanical delay and then weather, and she had already set an alarm for four thirty a.m.

"If that." Lally scanned the beige lobby until her eyes fell on an obnoxious floral display of plastic birds-of-paradise and a spark of recognition set in. "Oh, hey. Is Candice on duty tonight?" One of the perks of repeated stays in the same hotels was becoming friends with members of the staff. Candice was one of her favorites, a single mother with a brash mouth and flaming red hair to match who kept a stash of good hooch that she was always willing to share hidden among the cleaning products in housekeeping.

"Candice?" The kid drained of all color like a Victorian child who had seen a ghost. He returned Lally's ID across the counter.

"Red hair. Kind of bawdy." Lally wondered if she had suddenly misremembered her name. Could it have been something else? Cadence?

The young clerk was at a loss. "Candice is gone."

Gone? *Died?* Of course, that didn't seem right; Candice was a decade younger than Lally. And *gone* had another meaning of late. "What do you mean, gone?" Was it possible the people in her life were being erased one by one?

"Just a moment." The young man stepped back and disappeared into a door marked OFFICE, the door slowly closing and clicking behind him.

Lally was exhausted, but no—she was positive her friend's name had been Candice. Or maybe her name was Candice and this was the wrong hotel. She looked at the lobby again, its garish light too bright for this late hour. No, this was the right hotel. They had made fun of the wall sconces, which looked swollen like balloons.

The night clerk appeared with a manager, middle-aged, beard trimmed too neatly, dyed too dark. One year, Robbie had been a pirate for Halloween; their father had lit a wine cork and snuffed it out, drawing a beard on Robbie's face with the ash. The manager's face looked like that, fake, like he was wearing a costume or had endured a premature facelift. "You were asking about Candice?" He was holding back rage, poorly.

"I—I was just asking if she was on duty tonight," Lally stammered, worried she had poked a bear.

"And why do you want to know?"

Lally was confused by his tone. "Well, this may sound weird, but we had become . . ." Lally tried to think of an apt, but innocuous, word. "Friendly."

The night clerk pointed at the computer, where presumably Lally's name was still visible on the screen. The manager nodded like he was making a mental note before returning his attention to their guest. "Candice has been terminated."

The way he said *terminated* made it sound like she had been snuffed out by a hired assassin. Lally laughed, but mostly from exhaustion. "*Terminated.*"

"For running an OnlyFans from this hotel."

Puzzled, Lally had to stop and think what an OnlyFans was. It was some sort of social media platform or porn site or both?

The manager clicked the pen in his hand five times as an outlet for his rage. He must have read her confusion, because he immediately clarified the offense. "She was having sex with guests in vacant rooms, filming it, and putting it on the internet."

Lally blanched. That didn't sound like Facebook—OnlyFans must be porn. And then it hit her, the reason for the manager's scorn. She had just admitted that she and Candice were friendly, in hindsight not the best choice of words. "I see."

"So if you're looking to be friendly with a member of my staff, I might suggest another hotel. Because that is no longer happening here." The night clerk turned red; perhaps he had been in on it.

Lally couldn't believe her ears. She pushed up her sleeves, ready to throw down. Was this really what he thought of her? She was well into her forties. Her joints cracked when she bent down too far. There were spider veins on her legs from spending so much of her life on her feet, and small bags were growing under her eyes from her schedule. There was no way anyone would subscribe to some kind of platform to see her have sex, lesbian or otherwise. But of course, as much as she wanted to, she didn't say any of that, so she instead growled, "I think just the room will suffice." She snatched her key card from the young night clerk and dragged her suitcase to the elevator, afraid to even ask for the Wi-Fi passcode. It wasn't until she was safely in the elevator alone that she realized the manager's assumption could also be seen as a compliment. In the right lighting and with a generous partner, maybe she could still be an object of desire. She chose to view it that way.

Her room was on the ninth floor, small, and had a window that rewarded her with a view of an air shaft that ran down the center of the building like a brick esophagus. She desperately wanted a shower, but when she went to turn it on she discovered four inches of standing water in the tub, cloudy, cold, off-putting. She couldn't help but think she was placed in this room on purpose, punishment for guilt by association. The TV remote was in a plastic sleeve, something that made her feel safe during the pandemic but was now a turnoff, like this hotel was the last place that needed desperately to be disinfected. And maybe, thanks to Candice's extracurriculars, it did. At least the robe in the closet looked clean. In lieu of a shower she removed her uniform, the zipper on her skirt sticking as some sort of coup de grâce on this stale day, and draped herself in the robe; there were slippers, two left feet. The minibar had the hotel chardonnay she found least objectionable, but the fridge kept it shy of cold. She thought about filling an ice bucket, but she was already out of her clothes and didn't want to risk running into the manager while not fully dressed. So she drank from the bottle; it was syrupy, but after a few sips she felt the warmth even bad alcohol brings. She looked down at herself and took stock of her life. For the first time in her career, she thought maybe it was time to hang up her wings.

Lally flopped on the bed, her arms spread like a cross, and stared at the water-stained ceiling. She used to love the idea that she was the one missing, unreachable. Her schedule was private and constantly changing; on any given day she could be nowhere or everywhere at once. In the time before smartphones, she was a phantom in the night. On her days off she would use her travel perks, hopping flights to Hawaii or Mexico. But now, in the wake of Norman's disappearance, she realized how annoying it was, how inconvenient for others who wanted to reach her.

The Wi-Fi was easy to connect to without a password, and she was grateful to avoid a call to the front desk. There was an email from Harlan and she smiled in spite of herself. Once again it was Harlan to the rescue, standing up for her in her retelling of Norman's insult, now raising her spirits when the world seemed determined to bring her down. The email had a video file attached. In the body was a simple phrase: *Well, he's a piece of work.* She opened it, hesitant, afraid of what she might find. The video was a wobbly mess, difficult to watch without Dramamine. It took her a minute to orient herself; the phone must have been in Harlan's breast pocket with only the lens exposed. A woman with curly silver hair was leading him into a cavernous classroom, with only a few students seated down front. A man slowly came into view, tall, almost disconcertingly so.

Oh my god, this is Jesse's class.

The curly-haired woman spoke first. "This is Mr. . . ."

"Hancock," Harlan lied.

"Mr. Hancock, with the midsemester accreditation board. He's here to observe."

"Is this a joke?" Jesse asked. "You look familiar to me."

"No joke," she heard Harlan say, detecting a slight panic in his voice.

"Well, take a seat, MSAB. We're discussing humor writing for a visual medium. Do you like films?"

The camera bobbed as Harlan presumably nodded. "Baseball movies especially."

"What's the best baseball movie?" Jesse asked.

"I don't know," Harlan began. "*The Natural*? *Field of Dreams*."

"It's actually *Addams Family Values*. Have you seen it?" The class laughed. She squinted to see the students, but it was impossible from the camera angle to make out any faces. But Jesse seemed to have their rapt attention.

The camera turned left and then right, as if Harlan was looking for how to react. "I don't think that's a baseball movie. So I don't see how it could be the best."

Lally grew hot watching this scene unfold. She felt protective of Harlan and didn't like Jesse taking shots at him. It didn't matter that Harlan was there to spy. Her whole body tensed.

"*Addams Family Values* is the best movie of all time, so it stands to reason that it is also the best baseball movie. Deductive reasoning."

There was a pause on the recording, and then the curly-haired woman laughed hysterically. She leaned into Harlan, so close that Lally could no longer see her face on the recording. She demonstrated an uncomfortable familiarity. "It's a class on humor writing. He's just having fun with you. Not everyone gets his sense of humor, but I think it's great."

Lally closed the video file. Maybe she would return to watch the rest of it some other time, but that was enough for tonight. Instead, she opened her bag and retrieved the MISSING flyers she had taken from her meeting with Harlan, which she had neatly folded in half before placing them in a side pocket. She smoothed them on the duvet, which was itchy on her bare legs, hoping against hope that hers was not one of the rooms featured in her former friend's side hustle. She studied the three faces. Harlan was right. One person missing was sad, three (four including Norman) meant something was up.

She zeroed in on the poster with the kindest face, a young man with skin darker than hers. He had piercing brown eyes, and a smile that was perfect precisely because it was crooked. In the photo he looked . . . *happy*. Unlike someone Lally imagined would run away—he resembled Norman in that regard. The telephone number on the flyer was for the Riverside County Sheriff's Office. She did not want to involve the cops—she wasn't even certain anything was wrong. But underneath that, in faint pencil, a second number was handwritten. Lally glanced at the clock. It was just after eight in California, late, but not *too* late to call. But should she? Yes, she figured. Yes, perhaps she should. As always, it took a woman to get things done.

Lally checked the tub again, then ran the faucet for a minute to see if that would get the water to recede. She considered reaching her hand in to see if something was blocking the drain, but the thought of touching a wet clump of someone else's hair stopped her cold. She called the front desk but hung up before anyone could answer; really she just wanted to hide. There probably wasn't a maintenance person on call at this time of night anyway, the solution most likely meant switching rooms, and she couldn't bear to speak to the manager again, let alone get back in her clothes. She thought about calling Jesse directly, bypassing Harlan to see if there was additional news. Instead, she picked up her cell phone and slowly, carefully, deliberately dialed the number in pencil on the flyer.

Lally didn't expect anyone to actually answer; in fact, she was downright surprised when a woman did. Exhausted as she was, just the sound of an outgoing call was comforting and she would have been happy to listen to the soft purr of the telephone's ring until sleep ultimately came. Startled, she blurted that she didn't have any information about the person on the flyer—she didn't want to dish out false hope, but wondered if there was someone she could speak to about the man in the poster.

"You could speak to me," the voice replied; the woman sounded almost as tired as Lally felt. Given that the flyer was sun-faded and the paper weathered, the woman was more likely than not as surprised to hear Lally's voice as Lally was to hear hers, which was shaky, but with a certain resolve. Either her loved one had come home, or the case had long grown cold. Lally wondered how many cranks she had been forced to talk to when the poster was new, lookie-loos determined to pry.

"I'm so sorry to bother you, it's just I have no one to talk to. No one, that is, who would understand." Lally took a deep breath, needed her diaphragm to expel the words. "I think my brother is missing."

There was a long silence during which Lally regretted many things. Not waiting for the front desk to answer for instance, not being in a new room in a hot shower. A shuffling sound on the other end of the receiver got her attention. She hoped the woman wasn't about to hang up.

"Where does he live, dear?"

Relief. "My brother? Joshua Tree."

"My River lived in Twentynine Palms."

Lally wondered who counted the palms. (The same people who did Thousand Oaks? Certainly for an arborist that was a worse assignment.) And if there were indeed twenty-nine. What happened when one died, or a new one sprouted? Did the town reincorporate as Thirty Palms? Thirty-One? Of course, she couldn't say any of that without sounding like a lunatic, so instead she said simply, "That's close."

"How long has he been gone?"

Lally didn't know exactly. "Two months? Maybe more. Longer since the last time I heard from him."

There was an awkward moment of silence where Lally now was tempted to hang up. "You did the right thing calling me, dear."

Lally was so relieved she wasn't bothering this woman, she burst into tears. Or maybe it had nothing to do with this woman. Maybe she had been holding so much inside her, a simple act of kindness was all it took to make the dam burst. Instead of scaring the woman, it drew her in closer.

In barely a whisper Lally asked, "Would it be possible for us to meet?"

Once they had made concrete plans for a visit and said their good-nights, Lally surveyed the stagnant water in the tub one last time to assess her options for cleaning herself before bed; the prognosis was dim. There was no avoiding her uniform; she would have to put it back on to switch rooms. She lowered the robe in the hotel mirror and imagined how different her life would be if she were a mother, how different her body would be if she had carried a child. She had always been thin, something that was often thought of as desirable. But thin isn't strong, and she yearned for a body that was up for new hardships.

"Do you know what's going on?" Lally had asked the woman before they ended their call. She hinted at the other flyers that were posted in the vicinity. It was too much of a coincidence. There had to be some meaning behind it all.

The woman was firm. "No, dear, I do not."

It was a question she could ask again as she stared at herself in the mirror. "Do you know what's going on?" She was aging, for one. Bodies. So unremarkably mortal. She didn't mind getting older. She didn't much fear dying. You make peace with that when you choose a life in the sky. It would be different if she had a child, but now, on her own as she was, living forever seemed like a chore. She just wished she believed more strongly that she'd be reunited with Robbie.

Or Norman, if that was the case. There had to be more to life than running all the time from it.

When she crawled into bed she sent an email to her supervisor. Unwilling to give her notice just yet (nothing so final should be done on a whim or when this exhausted), she put in for a few days off to give her time to think and get her priorities straight. Only after she hit send did she realize it read *I hope this email finds you in a well.*

DAY EIGHTY-NINE

Twentynine Palms was an unremarkable town, dusty and not at all vibrant. If it weren't for the military training base, the largest in the entire Marine Corps, as well as some murals and public art, no one might ever have heard of it. The town center was small, folksy. Lally noted a few places she might stop that evening to grab a meal. Beyond the last traffic light—*nothing.* The Mojave Desert, which stretched into southern Nevada and the bottom of Utah. You wouldn't want to drive too far outside of town unprepared; you might never come back. And thus, Lally noticed the MISSING posters scattered downtown, beneath signs for the historic Route 66. She shuddered to think it was as simple as that—the desert was unforgiving.

The woman she'd called from Newark had agreed to meet her for coffee at an out-of-the-way café. Lally wore sunglasses and a scarf on her head, afraid she might run into Jesse or someone Jesse and Norman knew, although she was well aware of his frustrations with small-town life in Joshua Tree and couldn't imagine him going out of his way to spend so much as a minute somewhere even more remote. It was soon obvious she attracted more attention than she deflected, resembling the kind of horny widow in the market for an off-duty Marine that Diane Lane might play in a movie, so she decided to lose the scarf before she was even seated. Each time the bells on the diner door jangled, her heart leaped into her throat, but the new customer was always in fatigues. That was how it was in a military town, especially one that catered to America's endless thirst for desert warfare. She did her best to study the menu, her eyes returning to the tuna melt after every distraction. They'd agreed on coffee, but maybe she could eat. Would that be rude?

At noon on the dot the bells jingled again, and a woman with long white hair stood just inside the door. She was seventy, maybe older, and donned a navy tunic and matching pants in a loose fabric like linen. She wore her hair down in the way few older women do; it was the color of moonlight against the dark sky of her clothes. Jesse would assign her a hippie-ish nickname, Joan Baez perhaps, although Joan's white hair had been short for some time. No, not Joan Baez—*Woodstock* or *Grateful Dead*. Lally's feet were firmly planted, stuck to the floor beneath her booth from years of café grime or perhaps simply her own fear. But she stood just enough to catch the woman's attention, and when she approached Lally held out her hand.

"Hi, I'm Lally Alfano. I believe we spoke on the phone?"

"Yes," the woman said, and when she held out her hand a dozen silver bracelets slipped to her wrist, piling up like cars on a freeway. "Edith Marsay."

"Please," Lally said, gesturing for her guest to sit down. She motioned for the waitress, who held up a finger to signal she would get to them shortly.

"I hope this is all right," the woman said. She looked tentatively around the diner. "Not a lot of options. I would have offered to meet elsewhere, but I sold my car to help finance the search for my son." She explained how the police had only done so much, and then friends and volunteers picked up the slack for a time. The money had gone to a lawyer, who helped her keep pressure on local officials.

"It's fine," Lally assured her; she had her own mounting bills with Harlan.

"You're probably used to something fancier." The woman offered a weak smile. Her teeth were quite yellow next to her hair. If only she knew how often Lally ate on the run—she was not one to put on airs.

When the waitress made it over to their table Edith ordered hot tea with lemon, whatever they had, she wasn't fussy. Lally ordered tea as well, hers iced, but felt silly when it came to the tuna melt, yet she still needed food to settle her stomach, so she ordered toast.

"That's it?" the waitress asked. Lally indicated it was, but tried to say with her eyes that she'd tip well.

The waitress returned so immediately with their drinks it was almost unnerving. She served Lally her iced tea while gesturing to the sweetener already on the table, then set a teacup and saucer in front of Edith alongside a selection of tea bags before filling the cup with steaming hot water from a carafe. Lally added lemon to her drink as Edith selected her tea, Earl Grey.

When they had their beverages just so and Lally had fussed awkwardly with a packet of Sweet'N Low, she blurted out that she was sorry about Edith's son.

"River," Edith reminded her, and now that she was in front of her it seemed exactly like a name she would pick. "Do you have children?" Lally smiled, surprised to find her eyes growing wet. What was it with her recently? The woman recognized a struggle and cupped her hand over Lally's to console her before squeezing lemon into her own tea. "And I'm sorry about your brother. Tell me."

"About him?"

The woman nodded as she added honey.

"He was older. *Is* older." Lally hated that slip of verb tense. "He was like a father to me at times. Our father was, well, he was not always available to me. Emotionally."

"Most men of my generation aren't."

Lally smiled. It was a little more complicated than that.

"Was it just the two of you?"

Lally gently explained that she had another brother who died when she was young. Edith's eyes were pained, perhaps for her parents.

"River was my one and only," the woman explained, showing a photo of them on the home screen of her iPhone, a model more than a few generations behind. River towered over his mother and held an arm around her so tight Lally couldn't imagine him letting go. "It's unfathomable, the pain of losing two."

"That's just it." Lally leaned in so as not to be overheard. "*Did* we lose them?" It seemed odd to speak of them with such finality. Maybe they were but temporarily misplaced. "I suppose that's what I'm here to ask."

Edith strummed her fingers like that was the million-dollar question.

"He's very handsome," Lally finally said of River, extra careful this time to fudge the verb tense.

"That's his father in him. He died long ago." Lally thought of the embryos in the freezer and wondered whose genes were stronger, hers or Jesse's, and what those children might look like one day. She hoped to find out.

"It's not fair," Lally remarked.

"Fair?" Edith chuckled. "I'm not sure that's how life works, dear."

The waitress delivered Lally's toast alongside a jam caddy. She whispered her thanks, then offered a piece to Edith, who declined. When they were alone again, Lally confessed, "I hired a private investigator."

The woman cocked an eyebrow. She blew on her tea and steam encircled her face.

"He's based out of Los Angeles. I could give you his name."

Edith smiled grimly. Lally felt silly; certainly there was no money for that. "Did he find any clues?"

"He found your son's poster and a couple others. But other than that?" Lally bit her lip. *Nothing concrete yet.* "We're really just starting our search."

Edith looked down at her lap. "I'm not sure he's going to be of much help, dear. I don't want to see you waste your money. Some people don't want to be found."

She wouldn't allow herself to think Norman was one of those people. "You mentioned on the phone—" Lally began.

"Rumors," Edith interrupted.

"Rumors are about all I have to go on."

The woman lowered her gaze sympathetically, moving her phone from the center of the table off to one side. "Who was the last one to see your brother?"

"Before he went missing? That's hard to say. I would say probably his husband."

"Did he mention anything about the lights?"

"He didn't mention much of anything at all. He mentioned Norman was in Minneapolis." Then, at the woman's confused look, Lally added, "My brother is not in Minneapolis."

It was one of the first things Harlan had done. Checked with the City of Minneapolis for permits and that sort of thing. There were several medical buildings currently under construction, but Norman was not listed as the architect of record on any of them. None of the commercial buildings, either. Lally could have explained this, but fortunately the woman seemed to take her statement at face value.

"Before River disappeared, he talked nonstop about the lights. Strange lights that appeared from the sky."

"Had he . . . *seen* them?" Lally asked, remembering her own encounter with lights in the sky. Was she in danger of disappearing next? But maybe he hadn't seen them firsthand, maybe he'd just heard about them from a neighbor, say, and they became a topic of interest. She knew small towns and how rumors spread. Her family was the subject of many cruel ones after Robbie died. It wouldn't be that unlikely.

"Not when he first mentioned them. The first time I remember him talking about the lights, he was repeating what he'd heard secondhand. River was not the first to go missing, you know."

Lally didn't know, or at least not exactly, only that there were other posters and several more for cats and dogs (although that could have been the work of coyotes). Up until this moment, she hadn't thought about a chronology of disappearances.

"He was not the only one fascinated. There were whispers at the grocery store, talk around town. People hadn't seen the lights themselves, but everyone knew someone who had. The math on that doesn't add up. Not in a small town. Someone had to have seen them with their own eyes given the number of people who professed to know someone who had. But you know how word gets around."

"I don't understand. What kind of lights?" Lally imagined those lights they used at movie premieres, three beams that crossed in the sky. But the woman corrected her. This was a light from above shining down, like someone holding the brightest flashlight you'd ever seen from the sky.

"A *beam* of light," Lally clarified, and the woman agreed that was the right description. "And what does that have to do with the people gone missing?"

The woman furrowed her brow. "It's certainly odd." She held on to her teacup with both hands and challenged Lally to deny it. "Beyond that, I don't know."

It *was* odd, but so this date was becoming. Harlan had told her in one of their early meetings all the stories he'd heard, tall tales about strange occurrences in these parts. She'd listened with rapt delight, even forgetting Norman in the moment, a kid again at summer camp fawning over a counselor a few years older telling tall tales. He told her of the Yucca Man, a being at least eight feet tall who wandered in the night unseen, the only warning of his presence a foul stench that preceded him. He told stories of people gone missing in the mountains, Boy Scouts and Marines and experienced climbers. A famous actor, even. Some had been found, alive or dead, some merely a pile of bones. Some never at all. Eventually he heard himself and apologized, not sure why he was filling her head with such spooky nonsense when her brother was missing. It took her a minute to understand that her reaction should be one of discomfort, so lost was she in his eyes. But he hadn't mentioned anything about light; to Lally this idea was new.

"You must have a theory."

Edith surveyed their surroundings, so Lally did, too. Aside from the military contingent, there was a couple in their eighties, the man picking at a potpie. A young mother scrolling through TikTok on her phone, her child trying and failing to get her attention. Their waitress talking to a middle-aged man by the window who had opened an umbrella indoors and placed it upside down on the floor as if he were leaving it open to dry despite there being no signs of rain. No one was listening to them, but Edith leaned over her tea to whisper as if the whole diner was bugged. "The light calls to you. You step in it, and . . ." She snapped her fingers, but her creped skin didn't make much of a sound. It was eerie.

Lally rubbed her bare arms. The air-conditioning was strong enough that if a warm light shone down she would understand the urge to bathe in it. She could see goose bumps on her olive skin and hoped they were from the vent over their table blasting cold air and not this woman's uncanny behavior. Lally decided not to press on what amounted to hearsay. "You loved your son," she said. Edith nodded so subtly, if she hadn't been staring right at her, Lally would have missed the response. "Other than the light, can you think of any other reasons he might have gone missing?"

"His father was Black," she began when she finally spoke. Lally was confused by this statement, as it seemed very much beside the point. But she listened. "I loved my son very much, to me he was perfect. But I always forced myself to see him through the eyes of other people who thought him less so. Maybe that was overprotective, but that was my job as his mother, keeping him safe." This confession broke Lally's heart. "That will make sense when you're a mother."

"It makes sense now," Lally assured her, gently crunching some of the ice from her tea. She bit her cheek accidentally. Not hard, but she almost wished for sharp pain. "I'm not sure being a mother is in the cards for me," she said, almost swallowing her words instead of her drink; she didn't want to go off on that particular tangent. Fortunately, Edith didn't push.

"And your brother?"

"He's Italian," Lally blurted, confused by what Edith was asking. "We both are."

"I meant, does he have kids?"

Lally's cheeks grew warm. *Yes and no*, she wanted to say—it was one of the reasons she was so desperate to find him. But for clarity she said, "No."

"Mmmm." It was impossible to say where this woman's head was at. Was her son taken by something supernatural, or a victim of racists, the bright lights she warned of little more than the obnoxious headlamps of some pickup truck catching him at night on the side of a road, like Twentynine Palms was some sort of sundown town? For all she knew, maybe it was. Lally thought hard to remember the other posters; as far as she could tell, the others missing, like Norman, were white.

"Edith, are you all right?" It was a loaded question, given what they were there to discuss. She hoped the older woman knew what she meant.

But the only reply was a question. "Are you?"

Lally had to really think about the answer.

For so long she had thought of the embryos as her last chance at happiness, but that was only true (and perhaps only *mostly* true) because she had let other opportunities pass by. Her entire adult life she had run from commitment, afraid to love anyone fully after Robbie's death. She couldn't bear to imagine loss again in the way that Edith was facing it now, this woman across from her sipping tea with the quiet stoicism of having no regrets. Edith wouldn't go back in time and not have a child just to make her current life less painful. It would have been too high a price. Yet Lally had made that trade without thinking. Traded a life to avoid feeling heartbreak. "No," she admitted. "And I don't think I have been for some time."

Edith's eyes shone with recognition. "We all do the best we can."

Lally agreed. The travel, the flying, the running, the hiding. All of it could pass as healthy to someone not paying attention. But there weren't that many people who paid attention to Lally. Norman may have been the last one. In fact, this stranger was the only person who even asked her if she was okay lately and sincerely expected an answer. Not even Harlan did that, not explicitly anyway. Lally was operating under the assumption that everyone had it more or less together, that she somehow, chronically single, childless, lonely, was the only one in danger of spiraling. But sitting here in this diner in Twentynine Palms, with the woman missing her biracial son, the man with the upside-down umbrella on a day with nary a cloud in the sky, the woman ignoring her child in favor of a few minutes of peace, the waitress who thought that toast was not enough, Lally realized she had it all wrong. No one is okay, not a single one of us. The world had simply become too painful for anyone to feel unabashed joy. Maybe leaving, like Norman and this woman's son, was the only sane response to a world like the one they were in. There had to be a better place.

Again, Lally offered Edith some toast; this time she accepted, as if suddenly aware of a deep hunger that had been inside her for years. She even peeked through the jam caddy as if it contained some hidden delights.

"You will make an excellent mother," Edith said to Lally as she gnawed on her toast; Lally wished she felt as certain, and it must have shown. "I have a sense about these things. You'll see."

Despite Lally's increasingly pessimistic worldview, she was not really looking for a way out. She was looking for a way *in* before it was too late. She was looking to live her life, what was left of it anyway. So in that regard, come hell or high water, Edith's sense was right.

An excellent mother Lally was determined to be.

DAY NINETY-TWO

Lally peered at the house, seeing it perhaps for the very first time. On the few occasions she had visited before, it had been Norman and Jesse's, no other context was needed. All the house's details were blurred around the defining presence of them in it. Like visiting a childhood home as an adult. Were those power lines always there, so close to the bathroom window? Was my bedroom really this small? Did the roof always sag? It existed not as a collection of walls with defining characteristics of its own, although to the sister of an architect it probably should. It was its own little universe created only to house her family.

In truth, despite Norman's discourse on the subject, she was never that interested in the house itself and never much understood their move to the desert—who would leave the beach for sand with no ocean? What interested Lally was the feeling of home.

Staring at it through the windshield of Harlan's Impala, parked down the block so as not to be seen, and empty as it was of her brother, the place—architecturally marvelous though it was—looked rather desolate. Sad. Joshua Tree was so different from

Venice. The wind had kicked up enough grit and sand to mute the blue of the sky. Or maybe it was Harlan's car that was in desperate need of a wash, but both things could be true. She could understand why Jesse might want a pool, his sudden interest in digging. Was that why there was so much dirt in the air? Everything here felt so dry. Her contacts bothering her, Lally continually rubbed her eyes.

"What?" Harlan asked.

Lally turned to him, confused.

"You keep rubbing your eyes."

Why can't they just make windshields in my prescription? Lally pondered. That way she could ditch her lenses altogether. "It's my—" She stopped herself before saying contacts, as if imperfect eyesight made her less desirable. "Allergies. All of this wind isn't helping."

Harlan leaned over the steering wheel and looked up at the browning sky. "Unusual. It's not even the windy season." The Impala's windows were already sealed tight, but he closed the air vents so nothing agitating could get in. Only a real gentleman would think of that. "Does this make you nervous?"

You closing the vents? Lally wondered.

She must have made a face, because he sharpened his inquiry. "Being on stakeout. They put some clients on edge."

"I asked to come," Lally reminded him, and she had. In fact, she was beginning to wonder if her need to play spy had overtaken her need to find Norman. And she knew it wasn't that exactly. The work of a spy was considerably less glamorous than in old black-and-white movies. There was very little slinking around in dark corners, and she didn't even own a trench coat. (Although for the first time in her life she thought about buying one; she even stopped at the outlets in Cabazon.) It was that she was searching for a man, and here she had found one. It wasn't the one she was looking for—namely, her brother—but she had come to enjoy Harlan Faulkner's company. Eventually she would no longer be able to pay his retainer, but she could for a little bit longer and she was not ready to be left with no man at all.

"You're not nervous?"

"Instead of a nervous system, I have a super-chill system."

Harlan laughed. "I meant about what we might find."

Lally folded her hands in her lap, fidgeting a good while before answering. "I lost a brother once. I know what that feels like. This does not feel like that."

Harlan touched her arm, starting to speak twice before he managed actual words. "You lost a brother? *Another* brother? Is this something I should know about?"

Lally shook her head no before he could think of her as some sibling black widow.

Harlan must have felt her tense up. "Sorry. I didn't mean to pry. It's just recognizing patterns can be an important part of what I do."

"Childhood accident," Lally blurted, turning away from him so he could not witness any more pain. "I promise they're unrelated." That last statement might be a lie. Perhaps they *were* related. Grief has a funny way of finding you, announcing itself, even many years later when you think you've outrun it. She wasn't nervous that their investigation would result in their stumbling upon Norman's corpse. But she did worry that Norman was hurting. And that he was out there alone when he needn't be. But maybe she *should* be nervous. "I keep coming back to these missing people. You talk about patterns. What do they all have in common?" She imagined pain at the top of an imagined list.

Harlan narrowed his eyes, like he was supposed to get something that he clearly wasn't. She hadn't told him the degree to which she'd been playing detective on her own. And then it dawned on him. "They all went missing after Jesse moved to the desert. He's the common denominator."

Lally chewed on that, not wanting to believe what she thought he might be insinuating. "What are you saying?"

"What if Jesse is a serial killer?"

Lally snickered and then covered her mouth when it became clear Harlan was only half joking.

"Keep in mind, it's really difficult to be a serial killer these days. Cell phone data, DNA. It's not like it was in the heyday."

"The good old days of serial killing," Lally chuckled. "Well, Jesse has always excelled. If anyone could thrive in the current environment . . ."

Harlan smirked. "Of course, I'd be remiss not to point out that they all went missing after Norman moved to the desert, too. Maybe *he's* the serial killer."

"Are you forgetting he's also missing? He's a victim, if anything."

Harlan didn't see it as that open and shut. "Serial killers go on the run. Besides, it'd be a pretty good cover. A victim is also the killer."

Lally sighed; it was too much like the plot of an old dime novel, the kind people used to leave behind on airplanes. "I shouldn't have to point this out, but Norman is not the one currently digging a giant hole in his backyard."

Harlan had to concede this was true.

They were scraping the bottom of the barrel. Harlan had already checked Norman's cell records, thanks to a friend at Verizon. There'd been no calls since late August and his phone last pinged at the house. Lally didn't know his credit card numbers or even which bank her brother used. Bank statements would be harder to obtain without police involvement, Harlan had informed her, and Lally was adamant she was not yet ready for that yet. She worried about Harlan's interest waning, especially if she was going to keep his hands bound. What choice did she have *but* to imagine Jesse a serial killer?

"There he is! There he is! Look, look, look!" Lally dropped as low as she could, her head dangerously close to Harlan's lap. She yanked on his collar to pull him out of view, but he protested.

"It's fine. He's not looking."

"What if he comes this way?"

Harlan tracked Jesse's movements carefully before sounding the all clear. "He's just getting the mail."

Lally peered over the dash and sure enough, Jesse was elbow-deep in the mailbox. He was shirtless, dirty. Thinner than she remembered him being. Tanner, too. Although maybe that was the dirt. "He looks skinny," she said, concerned.

That, apparently, was not what Harlan was expecting her to say. "Skinny?"

"Like maybe he's not eating."

"His victims?"

Lally slapped Harlan's arm. "And, oh my god. Is that a dog?" A majestic shepherd-looking dog followed Jesse back up the drive. "When did he get a dog?"

Harlan shrugged. "I guess one of the days I was not here."

"It's so *big*," she marveled. Years ago, when they still lived in Venice, Jesse and Norman had discussed getting a pet, but she pictured them with a cat—or something small like a bichon frise.

As Lally resettled herself in the passenger seat she wondered how she could think him a deranged killer one moment and imagine him tenderly caring for a dog the next. "My heart is racing," she said, and she pushed her right fingers between the buttons of her blouse.

"Feel that." She used her free hand to place Harlan's on her chest. He indulged her before growing self-conscious and turning away.

"I thought you had a super-chill system?"

"I lied." Lally looked at him, concerned for his gullibility. "What if he saw us? That would really put a damper on his pool."

Harlan shook his head. Apparently he was also worried about hers.

"You have to trust me. He's digging a pool." Jesse had always been attracted to water. He was raised in Santa Barbara, for god's sake. It was the only explanation that made sense. Wherever Norman was, it was not rolled up in an old rug ready to be buried in the yard. "I'm telling you. Is it so hard to believe?"

"The Nutty Professor?" Harlan asked in disbelief. Lally hated herself for it, but she laughed, too. "It would take him a thousand years to dig a swimming pool."

Lally ran her fingers playfully through the hair on Harlan's forearm, scratching him gently with her nails. Almost instantly, something shifted between them. They locked eyes for what felt like an eternity; Jesse could have walked back and forth to the mailbox a dozen more times and neither of them would have noticed. She felt herself lean in, but Harlan did, too, or that was what she would tell herself later when she replayed the kiss in her head. They both initiated it, and perhaps they both did because it was pure passion and impulse and surprisingly hot—the kind of kiss that inspired teenagers to rip their clothes off in the back seats of cars. But they were not in the back seat of his Impala and their teenage years were very much in the rearview. They were adults who sat squarely up front, and bench seats were a thing of the past. But in the moment all of that was secondary to the kind of kiss Lally hadn't been blessed with in—she couldn't remember how long. And for a moment, even if it was just that, it was good to forget about everything—Norman, the embryos, the digging, Jesse's weight loss, her biological clock—and succumb to something so primal. And maybe it might have gone further, if—

They weren't interrupted by a sharp rap on the window. Lally screamed and recoiled, then buried her head in Harlan's shoulder, terrified Jesse was just on the other side of the glass. How would she ever explain herself? She peeked up at Harlan just long enough to register a placid expression (Harlan was always calm), which steadied her. With as much of her pride as she could muster, she swept the hair back from her face and straightened her blouse, which had somehow come untucked and somewhat unbuttoned. The mysterious knocker was on her side of the car. He had thick glasses and a flattop haircut Brylcreemed and shellacked and therefore unmussed by the wind; it made him look as out of place as they did. He said something the wind swallowed.

"What should I do?" she whispered to Harlan, covering her lips so the man could not see. Later she would remember this detail and admire her own instincts for this clandestine line of work.

"Roll down the window?" Harlan said it like it was obvious, but if people were disappearing around these parts left and right, she didn't think it was so clear. Especially for this guy, who, unlike Jesse, *looked* like he might pop up in a late-night Wikipedia serial killer rabbit hole, or on the walls of one's local post office. But wanting to maintain her stakeout cool, Lally lowered the window as naturally as she could manage, even though she only let it down a few inches. She was immediately rewarded with a fresh blast of sand to her eye.

"Good afternoon," the man said, looking from her to Harlan and back again.

"Can I help you?" Harlan asked. He was the definition of unflappable.

"I was about to ask you the same." The man placed one hand on the roof of their car and looked down the road a ways ahead of them. "I see this car parked here a lot lately."

Harlan shrugged. "No law against that."

"Nope, no law," the man agreed. "But it does arouse some suspicion." He was a white suit and pocket watch shy of looking like the sheriff of Hazzard County, setting spring-loaded speed traps to catch those pesky Duke boys.

"My wife and I were looking at property. Started by going to open houses, but now we were wondering if we should build."

The man cupped his hands around his eyeglasses like he was looking into their car with binoculars. Lally sat on her left hand to hide the lack of a ring, wanting to maintain this little fantasy, even though he was just as likely protecting his eyes from the wind. "Build."

Harlan rested his forearm over the steering wheel, making it look, to Lally's surprise, even bigger. "You know. A house. Is that your Airstream?"

The man looked back at the trailer behind him.

"That all depends who's asking."

"Well, I'm asking," Harlan said, and his befuddled tone made Lally smile. He held out his hand for the man to shake. "Kent McCoy."

"Randall." The man could only fit a few fingers through the open window and could only shake Harlan's fingertips. Lally was struck with a new fit of laughter; the daintiness of the handshake was too much, and she bit her lip to swallow the worst of it. Randall didn't seem like the type to enjoy being laughed at. Fortunately, Harlan continued undaunted.

"We thought maybe you had the right idea. That we should look for a stretch of land on this road and, well, build."

Lally admired Harlan's ability to both flatter and obfuscate, and, hopefully, defuse.

"There's no land for sale on this road."

Harlan nodded as if he were letting that sink in. "We just liked the view is all. You sure can see quite a distance. What about this house here?" He gestured at Jesse and Norman's place.

"That house isn't for sale," the man said definitively.

"No, I know that. It's just a big lot and I noticed there was a lot of digging happening on the property. I was wondering if it was for a foundation, or if a subdivision was going in."

The man didn't say anything else; they were now in a standoff. Lally and Harlan traded glances.

"Do you know the own—" Harlan began, but the man had had enough.

"I think it's time you move along."

Lally jumped in, hoping a woman's touch could de-escalate. "Oh, honey," she said, taking full advantage of the situation to playfully scratch Harlan's forearm again. "You said we could see the . . . Integratron, was it?" She turned to the man at her window. "Is that near here? Maybe we could grab a bite and see that."

The man did nothing but point to the cell phone on Harlan's dash. His meaning was clear: *You have GPS.* Lally was about to jump in with something about the reception out here, but the man decided their interaction was through. He tapped the car twice on the roof and turned to head back to his trailer. Lally quickly rolled up her window. She turned to Harlan and made a face akin to the gritted teeth emoji; he just rolled his eyes. When they looked down, they realized she was still holding on to his arm.

Harlan turned to Lally after they'd been driving for a few minutes in silence. "Can I ask you a question?"

"Is it related to the case?" She gestured for him to keep his eyes on the road.

Harlan checked the gas gauge before answering. "Yes and no."

"Well, there's no stopping you now."

"Why do you want to find your brother?"

Do people let their brothers stay missing? "*Why?*"

"Yeah." And then Harlan backpedaled. "Besides the obvious."

Lally was on the verge of regretting that kiss.

"In my office that first day, you said there was a pressing matter."

"Oh god," Lally said before she could stop herself.

Harlan turned to look at her quizzically.

Lally buried her head in her hands. This was the most unsexy thing to say. How could she put this in the least desperate way possible? "Do you have kids, Harlan?" The words came out muffled, but she thought maybe putting the attention back on him might help. And it was something she maybe should have known before now.

"No. Never had the chance. I was married once, but I think we knew early on it wasn't going to last. That kids would just make it more complicated."

Lally took a deep breath and began. She told him about the embryos. About how they were for Jesse and Norman and how she had been happy—honored, even—to play her part. And how over time their feelings about children had changed. About how they lost their resolve. (Not to mention lost Norman.) And about how the embryos themselves, half her genetic material, were just sitting there in cold storage, waiting to become, waiting to be loved, and how she could be the one to do that—love them—if only she could find her brother.

And about how there was only a limited window of time before all of this was no longer an option, before she wouldn't feel right about it. When she was finished, they clicked off a mile in silence. It could have freaked her out, but instead she felt that an enormous weight had been lifted from her shoulders. If bringing a baby into this world would cost her a romance with Harlan, then that would have to be the price she would pay. Still, she added, "But Norman didn't know any of this. So it can't have anything to do with his disappearance."

Harlan gripped the wheel with both hands. "Yes, but Jesse did."

He didn't need to say any more; the implication was clear. Norman could have been overseeing a build in Minneapolis or someplace, and after her visit with Jesse, he could have called Norman to warn him to stay away. To avoid her calls. To steer clear. If that was the case, Norman wasn't missing so much as hiding. But that didn't make sense with the other evidence—the cell phone data, for instance. Would he have purchased a new phone just to avoid her?

They'd driven for so long, Lally forgot where they were even going. But maybe it didn't matter. She didn't need a destination, other than away from how she felt deep inside, away from this mess. "I'm sorry. This is the worst kind of first-date talk. The crazy woman is baby-obsessed."

Harlan smiled and said, "Then it's a good thing this is not a first date."

Lally's heart raced anew. Instead of denying that this was a date, his tone implied this was more than their first. She yanked at her seat belt to give her some slack and then leaned her head on his shoulder, grateful for Harlan's confidence, for someone else to help shoulder the weight of her burden when it became too heavy to bear on her own. She could see how easily one could come to count on partnership.

And how unmooring it would be if it were suddenly, inexplicably, taken away.

DAY NINETY-THREE

It was nearing dusk when Lally pounded on Jesse's door with a ferocity that startled even her, the door solid in a way she wished she were, standing tall, absorbing each blow, the hard wood even seeming to push back against her clenched fist. The response was immediate, a loud barking that made her jump, but Jesse deserved a bit of a jolt and needed to know that this time she meant business. She glanced at her phone to make sure her text to Harlan went through; if Jesse was indeed a serial killer she needed someone who knew her last location. *At Jesse's*, it said. *Enough pussyfooting around.* If she and Harlan were to have any chance at a future, the search for Norman must end.

After what felt like an interminable pause, Jesse opened the door, looking bedraggled and covered in dirt. He strained to hold back the dog, which pulled against his grip on its collar; it seemed more excited than dangerous, smiling even, its tongue hanging limp out one side of its mouth. Jesse's hair was unkempt and in need of a cut, and his eyes appeared sunken and hollow. Whatever else he was up to (*drugs?* Lally feared), it was clear that he had been digging.

His hands looked calloused, and he wore bandages on several fingers. "What, are you trying to wake the dead?" he accused, peering behind her to see if anyone had registered the commotion; of course, there was no one to hear. Then he turned around and walked back into the house, leaving the door open for her to follow. "Hurry, so the dog doesn't get out." She hesitated before stepping inside and closing the door behind her, like this was her last chance to come to her senses. Once inside, Jesse gave the dog some sort of antler or bone and, satisfied the danger had passed, it trotted over to the shag rug to lie down and went about the business of chewing. Jesse barely made eye contact with Lally. "We've got to stop meeting like this."

The window blinds were mostly drawn and it was darker inside than out. The place was not as messy as she worried it might be, given that she'd never known Jesse to be one who thrived when left on his own. But from her quick scan it appeared he was managing; the house was even more organized and put together than the night they went to the Tiny Pony. The furniture had been rearranged, and inside had a more homey feel. It was outside where he'd made quite the mess. "Having fun in your sandbox?" she asked, turning on a lamp in the entry. Jesse stopped in his tracks.

"The entire desert is a sandbox. And it's not mine." He stayed perfectly still like he was considering how she knew to ask that, then said, "I suppose the man that's been parked outside my house is with you."

Lally's heart jumped at the idea of Harlan being *with* her; she wasn't sure where they stood after their kiss. But it just as quickly sank as she realized Jesse had said this was his house and not, as it should be, his and Norman's. She clenched her phone tightly, waiting for a reply from Harlan; so far one hadn't come. "And what if he were? With me, I mean?"

Jesse continued to avoid her gaze. "That come with dental?"

Lally tilted her head, confused.

"I mean, if the pay is good and it comes with benefits, maybe I should apply. Nobody can keep closer tabs on me than *me*."

Lally looked at her brother-in-law like she had many of her girlfriends when they were new mothers, wanting to do something for them when they were completely overwhelmed. There was no baby to watch, no obvious load of laundry to do, but she thought a conversation between them might be more productive if Jesse felt more like himself. "Go take a shower, Jesse. I'll stay here with the dog and brew us some hot coffee. It looks like you could use some."

"I only drink cold brew, of which I'm out," Jesse replied. "But I think I have Mountain Dew."

Mountain Dew was about the last thing she wanted to be offered, but in the interest of moving this along she agreed. "Fine. Go take a shower, and I'll pour us two tall glasses of, god help me, *Mountain Dew*."

Jesse laughed and she was grateful for that, grateful for any moment that made her feel like the old Jesse was still somewhere inside the husk of a man that stood before her. Finally meeting her eye, he placed both hands on her shoulders and said, "Thank you," in a way that was foreign and uncomfortably sincere.

When he retreated to the bedroom, Lally poked around as best she could without disturbing anything. Harlan would be proud, she hoped; how many hours had he spent outside the house trying to discern what was going on within, and here she was freely opening and closing kitchen cabinets. She found nothing incriminating, other than evidence of dietary confusion. Ketchup and mustard packets abandoned in a drawer looking like shriveled little pillows, alongside Chinese take-out menus stained with soy sauce; in the fridge there was indeed a two-liter of Mountain Dew, already a third of it gone, but also healthy dinners from an online meal service.

When she heard the sound of the shower, she moved deeper into the house; the dog eyed her suspiciously but remained blessedly quiet. Jesse's phone was on the coffee table. There might have been a time when she had known something as intimate as his password, but that time had long passed. Still, she picked it up, and there were no unanswered texts on the home screen. There were eyeglasses on the table, readers that she thought might be Norman's, although she struggled to remember either one of them sporting a pair. Several books were strewn on the couch, one with a dried baby carrot as a page marker. Nonfiction. A book about time travel or different space-time dimensions, and one about government and infrastructure in the 1950s. She whipped open the coat closet, wondering if she might find her brother crouched in there, and surprised herself by feeling relieved when he wasn't. She then looked for a basement door, but many houses in Southern California—including this one, apparently—were built on a concrete slab.

Out the back sliders was what Harlan had promised—an enormous hole. Mounds of dirt rose from all sides, making the excavation appear like a magic kingdom on the floor of a valley, protected from all who might advance on it by impassable hills. It was the work of a madman, and yet strangely also a poet. There was a beauty to the madness, even Lally reluctantly recognized it, the way some could see groundbreaking mathematics on a chalkboard when others just saw chaotic scribbles. The mounds were human anthills, magnificent in size compared to what created them and something to be studied. But Lally tore herself from the glass wall. There would be time to be mesmerized later. Afraid Jesse's shower would be short, she backed away.

Mail piled up on the console by the front door; some of Norman's was opened, much of his was not. Nothing *from* Norman and nothing personal that she could see, but that was not unusual—no one sent letters anymore. One open envelope was from the Beverly Hills Reproductive Center and she scrambled to pick it up. It was an invoice marked paid; the embryos would be stored safely for another year and she hugged the paper to her chest. She was surprised to see mail for them both from the AARP. Norman's was even offering a soft cooler if he renewed his membership, the kind of thing you would take to the Hollywood Bowl. She couldn't imagine either of them receiving these offers as anything but an insult.

"I've been thinking a lot lately of all the ways we are alien to each other, even the people we think we know best."

Lally spun around to see Jesse clad in a towel, his hair dripping wet. He pointed to the envelope from the AARP.

"I didn't know he was a member, either."

Lally, at a loss for words, set Norman's mail back down on the console. "You're not wearing your wedding ring," she observed. In truth, he wasn't wearing much of anything.

Jesse held his ring finger in his hand to disguise it. "It must have slipped off," he said sheepishly. "I'll go put on some clothes."

It was only when he turned around and shuffled away, the pads of his feet dragging across the floor, that Lally realized how muscled he looked. Digging obviously agreed with him. Perhaps the ring had innocently slipped off. But he was right. This Jesse *was* alien to her. Ripped and browned from the sun, spooky even, but not in any way she could put a finger on. *Haunted* might be a better word. She returned to the kitchen and poured them both Mountain Dew, surprised to find ice in the freezer. From the clerestory windows she could see the top of the distant mountains, and the blades of a few windmills that stood eerily still. She took a sip from her glass with great trepidation; the color was just awful. She was right to approach this potion with caution, it was like drinking antifreeze. It was all she could do not to dump hers in the sink, but she didn't want to be rude.

Her eyes were drawn to a ceramic banana. It had a handmade quality and she couldn't imagine Norman allowing it in the house and she held it up for Jesse when he returned, gripping the banana with both hands like it was Aladdin's lamp. He pushed his wet hair away from his eyes, cementing it against his head until it stayed parted to the side.

"That's a banorah," he said, as if it were an everyday word, and looked annoyed when she didn't get it. "Banana menorah."

"Hakuna matata," she replied before setting it back down carefully. "It's . . . *nice*," she said, although not all that convincingly. The banorah tipped on one side. "Since when do you celebrate Hanukkah?" She struggled to think if Hanukkah fell early or late this year; it was already almost Thanksgiving.

"I don't. One of my students gifted it to me after I gave him an A on the midterm exam."

"I hope it came with a gift receipt." Lally stood the banorah back upright as she had found it.

Jesse studied her carefully and Lally panicked, the way someone might if they were suddenly suspected of wearing a wire. "It was actually quite meaningful."

"And what about the dog? Was that a gift, too?"

Jesse shook his head. "I had one like her when I was a kid. She's a shepsky."

Banorah. Shepsky. These were all nonsense words. "Does she have a name?"

"I haven't come up with—"

Lally had had enough. "Can we just drop the pretense here?" Jesse had been the one to take a shower, but maybe this was her moment to come clean. "I'm worried about you. That's all. Well, no. That's not all. I'm also worried about Norman, and you may be the only person on earth who knows where he is."

"On earth," Jesse repeated, speaking cryptically, as was his default seemingly of late.

"Cut the shit, Jesse. Why did you dig up the yard?"

"Why did I— It's *my* yard. I pay taxes. What business is it of yours?"

"Your husband's disappearance has made it my business. Where is my brother?"

Jesse took his glass of Mountain Dew and drank half of it. "You think I dug up the yard to bury your brother? Is that what you're saying?"

Lally wanted to scream, *YES*, even though she remained convinced in her heart the answer was no. Then she noticed that the bandages on Jesse's hands were curling and coming loose.

"Is Norman in the backyard?"

"Have you seen the backyard?" Jesse led her over to the sliders. "I know Norman loomed large in your mind, but that's an awfully big hole just for him."

Instead of calming Lally, it made her furious. She thought of the MISSING posters she'd seen, and imagined more that she had maybe not. "You're burying *others*?"

Jesse laughed maniacally. "And there's still room for more!"

She shoved Jesse, hard, in the sternum, sloshing his Mountain Dew over the side of his glass. "That's not funny. You're scaring me!"

"GOOD. I don't like what I'm being accused of." He pushed his wet hair off his forehead and set his glass down. "I'm not burying anyone, okay? I'm not hiding your brother, either. If anything, I'm trying to find him."

"Underground?" It was at this point that Lally reached her limit. She was done thinking the best of people, she was done humoring men, she was over it all. "I want answers, Jesse. I swear to god. Or else." She prayed he didn't ask or else *what*, as, while the threat was far from empty, it was also not yet fully formed. "What do you know about the light?"

Jesse froze. That got his attention. "What do *you* know about the light?"

Lally kicked a chair in frustration. "That's it. I'm calling the cops." She walked over and picked up his phone, both to prove that she knew where it was and to keep him from calling the cops on her.

"Go ahead. You don't think I already thought of that? There's nothing the cops can do!"

Lally looked down at her hands and realized she was holding two phones, her own in her other hand. "The light, Jesse! Tell me."

For the first time Jesse looked scared, a trapped animal with nowhere to run and without the cunning nature to escape his predicament. His eyes darted around the room. "Okay. There was a light that night."

"What night?" Lally pressed.

"*That* night. The night Norman—" He covered his eyes at the memory. "Sometimes with light comes illumination. *Enlightenment*. A lightbulb going off. What Oprah calls 'the aha moment.' The light that danced on the apostles."

"The *who*?"

"Sometimes light is contact. The transmission of a message. Moses and the burning bush. A message from god? He thought so, a command to lead the Israelites out of Egypt."

"I hate professors," Lally muttered, barely under her breath.

"The light of angels bathed a thirteen-year-old French peasant girl—she led the French army in a momentous victory at Orléans."

Lally's jaw had gone slack around the mention of angels, and she was struggling to keep up. Jesse had clearly gone around the bend. No amount of sitting in a car with her crush outside his house would have prepared her for any of this. "Are you telling me Norman is Joan of Arc?"

"I am!" Jesse answered excitedly. He moved manically, his long limbs waving in Muppet-like fashion. "Or, the story of Joan of Arc at least. Because the light turned out to be real! Of course, she also met her end by a very different light, as she was burned alive at the stake, but let's not go there." He shuddered.

"JESSE!" She screamed it loud enough to break through the noise and get his attention. He walked toward her. She glanced at her phone, silently begging for Harlan to call. *Answer my text. Bang on the door. PLEASE.* Once more she needed this new man in her life to come through. Jesse grabbed Lally's shoulders and implored her to listen, his familiar face twisted in anguish.

"There was a light, the night that Norman left."

Lally was about to wriggle free, but there was something in the way he phrased it. "Left? You mean disappeared."

"No, I mean left. He left us, Lally." Jesse bit his lip, an attempt perhaps to figure out how he was going to make her understand. "Come here."

Jesse led her out into the yard, and they stood at the edge of his obsession. The evening air was cool, the sky a gauzy pink, the mountains in the distance reflecting light like a painting from the Romantic era. In short, the setting *was* almost religious. And as imposing as the piles of dirt looked from inside the house, it was impossible to get the real scope of what Jesse had done until you looked straight down into the ground. There was no other way to describe it—this wasn't just a hole, it was an excavation. This was the work of a true believer.

"What have you done?" It terrified Lally, the piles of dirt too much like the snowbanks that took Robbie.

Jesse stood and stared at his work with a look of both pride and sheer terror. He stood right on the edge, and when the soft ground began to give away under his feet, he stepped back only enough to avoid falling in. "The light. Is it religion, Lally? Is it prayer? Is it cosmic, is it divine? Is it ritual, is it some kind of collective unconscious? Is it from our dimension, from another? Is it from the present? The past? The future? I don't know. I go over and over it in my mind, and all I can come up with is this shit never happens in the cities. None of this would have happened if we had stayed in Los Angeles. This happened because of the desert. 'Come ye yourselves apart into a desert place and rest awhile.' Jesus said that to his disciples. I've read all the translations. Some say desolate place, some say deserted place, quiet place, isolated place. But it's *this* place. The desert. It happened here, Lally. There has to be a *reason*."

Lally shuddered, and it wasn't the November air. "Jesse, you're scaring me."

"I'm scaring me, too."

The dog ran outside with her bone, straight into the pit to bury it. Lally's eyes grew wide. Perhaps they were *both* serial killers.

"Norman wasn't scared," Jesse continued. "Why is that? The light came down and instead of running from it, he stepped directly into it."

Slowly, Lally reached out for Jesse's hand and held it, overcome all of a sudden with sympathy for someone who was not her adversary, not a serial killer, but someone she loved clearly in the throes of a full mental breakdown. "Jesse, I'm calling the police."

"WAIT. I found something." Jesse scrambled back toward the house and disappeared. He shouted from inside. "Not what I was hoping to, mind you, but it's something!"

Lally couldn't imagine what he was hoping to find, but if this was somehow impossibly a clue to Norman's whereabouts, she wanted to see it.

Jesse returned holding a box, small and wooden with ornate hinges. It was shy of a treasure chest, but more than a jewelry box, and he looked at her like he was wondering if she could be trusted. "Look."

"You found this, in *that* hole." It was comical, almost. A needle in a dirt stack.

They knelt on the ground like kids and opened the box carefully together; a small bit of debris fell from the cracks. The wood was dark and looked damp, evidence perhaps that it had indeed been long buried. Inside were paper letters, bundled together with a length of thick yarn. "They're from the architects whose names I could never remember, but now I do." At Lally's blank stare he added, "The architects who built this house."

"I thought Norman built this house."

"Norman *re*built this house." He pointed around at certain parts. "The glass ell, and the new master—sorry, *primary*—suite. He updated their design. But the bones of the house are still theirs. Eero and Judith Seidler. Love letters, some of them written right here." Jesse undid the yarn and pulled the top letter from the stack. "Do you want to read it?" he asked, offering it to Lally.

"Not particularly." Still, she took the letter and held it a safe distance from her face as if it might contain anthrax.

"It's okay, I read them. You don't have to."

"And?"

"They were all written on dates with odd numbers. Do you know there are no odd numbers without the letter *e*?"

With her free hand, Lally pinched the bridge of her nose. "So?"

"I just thought that could mean something."

"It doesn't, Jesse. What's in the letters?"

Jesse exhaled. "Everything." He flipped through the stack, pausing only to look at dates, which appeared to be in chronological order. "They were so in love, at first. You've never read anything like these. Deep, romantic love. Like, it was a miracle two such perfectly suited people found one another." Lally noticed his eyes grow wet. He wasn't just talking about the Seidlers. "And, then, over time, they weren't. Or maybe they were, but not in the same way. They took each other for granted. The letters became perfunctory. More business, less poetry. Angry even, a few of them. And then, one day, they just stopped."

Lally looked at the envelope in her hand; it suddenly seemed less foreboding. "I guess I'm not the expert here, but isn't that how relationships are? Isn't that true of you and Norman?"

Jesse seemed heartbroken. "Exactly. When you're in it, it doesn't really feel that way. But this is exactly the story of me and Norman. We built our love story on top of theirs, just like we built onto their house, just like they built Pompeii."

"The Seidlers built Pompeii?"

Jesse begged her with his eyes to keep up.

"But I was there at the beginning, don't forget. There was a time you and my brother couldn't take your eyes off each other. Not to mention your hands, despite my presence. It couldn't have gotten that bad."

Jesse shook his head sadly. "I couldn't see it. But Norman saw the light."

Lally finally understood, his heartbreak plain as day. He was as tall as any man she'd ever met, but here, kneeling on the ground clutching someone else's love letters, he looked like a small wounded child. "Call off your search, Lally. Norman left. We're not going to find him. Call off that man who watches my house."

Lally replied quietly. "You know I can't do that."

"I didn't hurt him." He pleaded with his eyes.

"We don't always know the ways in which we hurt people."

Jesse nodded, and a tear fell down his cheek. "You're right. I hurt him in so many ways. I didn't mean to. But I did."

Lally hung her head. Maybe what he needed was a priest. "I'm calling the police." She took out her phone, pressed 911, and hovered her finger over the call button. "We need to report him missing. It's time."

"Lally, wait."

"No, Jesse. No more stalling."

"WAIT!" Jesse screamed. He grabbed her arm harder than she was comfortable with, but without the intent to harm.

Lally hit call, put the phone on speaker, and held it up for Jesse to see. It rang twice.

"9-1-1, what's your emergency?"

"YOU CAN HAVE THE EMBRYOS," he blurted.

Lally's heart squeezed like a fist.

"9-1-1. Are you able to speak or should I send help?"

Lally remained frozen, eyes locked with Jesse.

"We're tracing your call. It looks like you're calling from . . . the street has no name, but we have your location. I'm dispatching the police now."

"No. There's no emergency. That won't be necessary."

"Ma'am, placing a false call to 9-1-1 is—"

"Butt dial. Sorry!" Lally ended the call, then dropped the phone like it was poison. She asked Jesse to repeat what he'd just said.

"You can have the embryos. One of them. Some of them. I don't know. Whatever you need."

The finality of his offer was a slap to the face. Both of her brothers were gone. "Norman's not coming back, is he."

Jesse shook his head slowly, like he was just accepting it, too. "Call off your search. Call off your search, and you can have the embryos. It's what Norman would want." He held out his hand and she took it. "More than that. It's what *I* want. But you have to promise me something. I won't be the father anymore, but when they're old enough to know, I want your child to know I didn't abandon them. I want them to know without a doubt that they are loved."

And that was when she knew. Yes, her brothers were both gone—but all was not lost. She opened her mouth and closed it, not knowing what to say. And then she saw it above them: Venus, the evening star. The brightest light in the sky. She made a wish, a wish to stop being afraid. To stop being alone. To stop living for other people. And then, without hesitating any longer, she looked back at Jesse and meekly said—

"Okay."

WITH OR WITHOUT YOU

THE RETURN

Norman took close inventory of his kitchen; he couldn't remember seeing it so bare. It hardly seemed like he lived here! There were eggs, eight left of the original dozen, balanced in the center of the carton the way his husband insisted (Jesse always took eggs from the outside working in), and some bread with the first signs of mold. He salvaged the heels for breakfast, artfully trimming the crust before dropping them in a toaster that seemed new; the buttons felt complicated and unfamiliar, but he might just be weak from hunger or, despite his earlier workout at the gym, not yet be fully awake. They were out of the olive oil spray he liked, so he had to use some EVOO from the bottle and when it began to smoke in the pan he cracked open an egg with one hand, immediately adding a second. As the eggs crackled and fried, he held his face over the toaster and felt a familiar warmth he couldn't quite place. He held it there until it was time to flip the eggs; Jesse liked them over easy. As he grabbed the spatula, he heard the shuffling of feet. Finally, Jesse was up, and perfect timing, too—breakfast was just about ready. Norman hoped his husband had slept better than he had.

"There you are, sleepyhead." He spun around to greet his husband.

Jesse screamed and dropped a water glass, which caused Norman to pierce a yolk in the pan. Jesse stood there in just his underwear, looking both ripped and tanned. *When did that happen?* Everything was both familiar and unfamiliar, like he was in a dream.

"There *I* am?" Jesse asked with recognizable disdain. Norman wasn't sure what he'd already done wrong so early in their day, but he felt a fight coming on. Sadly, that was not unusual.

"Yes, it's almost noon."

"There I am," Jesse repeated, somehow even more incredulous. Norman winced at Jesse's bare feet surrounded by glass.

"Don't move. I'll get the dustpan." Norman grabbed a nearby dish towel first, to soak up the water and scoop up the larger pieces.

Jesse stood perfectly still as a crouched Norman cleaned around him, still in his gym shoes.

"Oh, hey," Norman began. "Is it my turn to do the grocery shopping? We're out of a lot of stuff. And there's a jar of frosting in the pantry next to a spoon."

"Yeah, that's my frosting spoon."

Norman playfully bit Jesse's dick through his underwear, surprising them both. But he couldn't help himself! It looked even bigger now that Jesse's waist was smaller. Or maybe it had just been a while since they had been intimate. Either way, that must have been some workout. His testosterone was coursing. "Frosting spoon? Are you smoking pot again?" Norman felt Jesse respond, so he teased his husband further with his stubble.

"Okay, that's enough of that," Jesse said, pushing Norman away, then trying and failing to cover himself. The more Jesse protested, the more Norman persisted, crouched as he was right in front of him. Behind them a door slammed, this time startling Norman.

Is someone here? he mouthed, tucking the swelling in his own shorts under his waistband.

Lally, harried, hustled from the guest room cinching an old robe of Norman's around her middle, before cupping her breasts, which looked oddly big. "Oh god, Jesse!" she said when she saw a man kneeling before him. She made a display of shielding her eyes. "I heard someone scream, and the sound of glass breaking."

"Lally?" Norman popped out from behind Jesse, and now it was Lally's turn to shriek. "What is it with everyone this morning?" Norman crossed to the entryway mirror to see if he looked a fright. Quite the opposite; for not having showered yet, he looked pretty good. He turned back around to find his husband and his sister having a silent conversation with their eyes.

"Sorry," Lally apologized. "You were not who I was . . . expecting."

Norman held out his arms to hug his sister, but she remained glued in her spot. Perhaps she was afraid he hadn't gotten all of the broken glass. He glanced at Jesse, busy dressing himself in a T-shirt and sweats from a basket of laundry by the door. Who else had she been expecting in his house, kneeling in front of his husband?

As Jesse pulled the T-shirt over his head, he stopped and sniffed the air. "Do I smell toast? Oh my god, I'm having a stroke. LALLY, I'M HAVING A STROKE!"

Right then the toaster ejected two perfectly browned pieces of bread. Norman gestured as if to say *ta-da*. "I'm making us breakfast."

Unimpressed, Jesse replied, "Your eggs are burning." He nodded toward the stove, where indeed Norman's eggs were now over hard. Norman yanked the pan from the stove and set it in the sink. He flipped on the fan in the hood, feeling Jesse's and Lally's eyes on him the whole time.

"Wh-when did you get back?" Lally stammered.

"From the gym?"

"From Cincinnati."

"Minneapolis," Jesse corrected.

Norman's eyes darted between them, confused. "I was not in Minneapolis. I was at the gym."

"This *whole* time?" Lally turned to Jesse for confirmation. "I really overpaid Harlan."

What were they talking about? Who was Harlan? "Long enough to work back and biceps."

"Where were you *before* the gym, Norman?" Jesse asked slowly, so as to be understood.

Norman was now thoroughly confused. They were behaving as if *he'd* had a stroke. "I was in bed."

"*Our* bed," Jesse said with great skepticism.

"Who else's bed would I be in?"

Jesse ran back to their bedroom as if to check.

Lally unglued herself and lunged forward, throwing her arms around her brother in the tightest hug. "We were afraid we were never going to see you again!"

Jesse cried, "OH MY GOD!" from the bedroom, and it was followed by barking, and then pounding footsteps approached from the hall.

"Is that a dog?" Norman asked, but Lally only gripped her brother tighter.

"It's true," Jesse said when he returned. "Someone slept on his side of the bed."

As he gingerly hugged Lally back, Norman stared at Jesse over her shoulder. "Not well, mind you. You were taking up most of the middle. You're both being awfully dramatic. Does someone want to tell me what's going on?"

"You look incredible," Lally said when she broke their hug. She stepped back to look at this face. "So refreshed. I don't understand."

"I look incredible?" Norman studied the two of them. *Then why does everyone keep screaming?* "Jesse here is the one who's been hiding that body, which, I don't know how you did that. I feel like all I do is work out, and I don't get any results. And you . . ." He pinched Lally's chin. "You're positively glowing!"

Lally blushed and looked embarrassed and turned to Jesse, biting her lip.

"Are we going to talk about this?" Jesse asked. He took a step forward and then back, and then forward again, appearing uncertain if he should approach.

"Talk about what?" Norman leaned in to give his husband an awkward kiss before Jesse took one final step back. It was quite the pas de deux.

"Talk about *what*?" Jesse knocked a book off the counter in frustration, and it landed with a hard slap on the floor.

"Why do you keep repeating everything I say?"

"Why do you keep acting like everything is normal?"

"It is, isn't it?" And then Norman recognized a look of fear on both of their faces. "Wait a minute. What's wrong?" He turned to Lally. "Is it Mom?" Lally's presence suddenly made sense if something had happened to one of their parents. He'd worried about his mother in Italy, that contraption she used to get up the stairs. The wiring there was so old, he imagined her being hurled out a second-story window like that old bat in the movie *Gremlins*.

"It's not Mom," Lally assured him. "Or Dad. They're fine." She put her hands on her hips defiantly. "It's *you*."

Norman tucked his chin into his neck and narrowed his eyes. "Me? What's wrong with me?"

"YOU'VE BEEN MISSING."

Norman laughed. "Missing?"

"Where. Have. You. Been." Norman didn't appreciate Jesse's condescending tone. Of the three of them, he was the only one acting sane.

"I told you. I went to the gym."

"The *gym*."

"Well, I'm sorry. We can't all eat frosting from a tub and sleep until noon and look as good as you." Norman studied Jesse again and scratched his head. Even with his T-shirt on, his transformation didn't make sense. "Are you on Wegovy?"

Jesse pulled at his hair with both fists.

"Don't do that," he chided Jesse. "Lally will have to give you miles for one of those flights to Turkey for a hair transplant." Norman had read in the *Atlantic* that the country had become so synonymous with hair transplants that they referred to the national airline as *Turkish Hair.* He looked to Lally to shed some light on Jesse's behavior. She, too, was acting odd, but at least she seemed happier to see him. "Lally, honestly. Something is different about you." He dropped his voice to a whisper. "Did *you* have something done?" He pulled his face back to demonstrate.

"Oh my god." She crossed and stood behind Jesse as if she were in need of his protection.

"What is going on with you two?"

Jesse slowly stepped forward and grabbed Norman's face with one of his enormous hands. He squished open his mouth like a fish and looked inside. He then ran his free hand through Norman's hair and felt along the back of his skull. "It really is you?" Only after this thorough examination did he pull him into a hug.

It had been a long time since Jesse had held on to him so forcefully, and as confused as he was, and even with his sister present, for the second time that morning Norman was aroused. "Who else would I be?" It was difficult to form words in Jesse's forceful grip, and he melted in his radiant heat.

Jesse whispered in Norman's ear. "What story did I tell you on our first date?"

"You tow me awot o stowees."

Jesse tightened his grip, the hug now almost a threat. "Name one."

Norman's eyes bulged. "Soooooop." He then wriggled a hand under Jesse's arm to loosen his grip and pry himself free.

Lally thought she had misunderstood. "Did he say soup?"

Norman rubbed his jaw, more in shock than in pain. "Jesse's aunt and uncle had a cabin in Maine. They made him soup, chicken and . . ."

Stars, Jesse mouthed. His eyes grew moist, and he tried to blink it away.

"Stars," Norman repeated for Lally's benefit. "Whatever was left they would dump down the drain. Only, the drain was not connected to anything, so Jesse would race the stars and watch them spill out in the dirt." He then turned to Jesse. "You raced the stars," he whispered.

"I raced the stars and I won," Jesse replied, the tears in his eyes now obvious. "It *is* you." Now it was Norman who gripped Jesse, and for the first time Jesse stopped fighting and allowed himself to be held. Norman stood on his toes to press his cheek against his husband's.

"I love you," he said. "I don't tell you enough." Over Jesse's shoulder, he could just see Lally begin to cry, too, and when she reached up to wipe her tears, her robe fell open, revealing an old T-shirt of his that was too tight.

"Oh my god," Norman cried. "You're pregnant!"

Lally looked stricken.

"*Are you?*" Norman asked, excitement spreading across his face like a rash.

Lally blushed as she scrambled to close her robe. She then crossed her arms, not in defiance so much as to hide behind them.

"I didn't even know you were seeing anyone." He reached out one arm for Lally and welcomed her into the hug. He was now clinging tightly to them both, Norman, Jesse, and Lally smushed into one awkward embrace, Norman burying his face between them. "I'm so happy to have my two best people." And then he dropped the dreaded question. "Who's the father?"

Jesse was the first to push Norman away. "How about that breakfast?" he asked, seeming awfully quick to move on from good news. Lally likewise turned her head to one side, hiding her face. Norman picked up on their vibe immediately.

"What? What did I say? Did you break up?"

Lally started pacing. She shook her hands like they'd been asleep and she was trying to wake them. "Oh god."

Norman turned to Jesse for help; he'd really stepped in it, but *how*? Yet Jesse looked just as stricken, which was odd, because why would she confide in Jesse and not her own brother? She must truly be ashamed. "Lally, it's me. It's okay. Is there no father? Is that it? A one-night stand? I'm not here to judge you." Lally remained perfectly still. "Sperm bank?" She looked at Jesse, and that was enough for Norman to lose his cool. "Don't look at *him*, look at me! Who is the father, Lally?"

Jesse ever so subtly shook his head at Lally, encouraging her silence. In fact, it was so imperceptible that Norman might not have even noticed if Jesse's face hadn't also gone white.

"It's Jesse? JESSE!" He pushed Jesse forcefully with both hands.

"Ow, my sternum." Jesse motioned for Lally to step back before she was hit, too. "What do you want me to say? You were gone!"

Norman let out an incredulous gasp. "I was at the gym, so you fucked my sister?"

Jesse recoiled. "What? Don't be crass. I made *love* to your sis—" He couldn't even finish the joke. "I think I just threw up in my mouth." He looked at Lally apologetically. "No offense."

"None taken. You're not exactly my ideal roll in the hay."

"WILL SOMEONE PLEASE TELL ME WHAT'S GOING ON?"

"Calm down," Jesse pleaded. "The embryos. I let her have the embryos."

"*Our* embryos?" Norman was confused more than angry. "That's impossible. You would need my permission."

"Yeah, well. Turns out I got custody of them in our divorce."

"We're *divorced*?" Norman staggered and then slowly lowered himself to the floor. Maybe he *was* the one having a stroke. "I need to lie down." He lay flat on the floor in between them.

"Oh, I know." Jesse grabbed his phone and started streaming some celestial nonsense, something Enya might play to relax. "This should help soothe you. Have you ever had a sound bath? This one is called Pathways."

Norman writhed like a child protesting a nap. "I don't want to be soothed, I want to be the opposite of that. I want to be disturbed!"

"Well, you are that," Jesse agreed.

"You're not wearing your wedding ring," Norman observed. Everything was moving too fast.

Jesse rubbed his left ring finger, which was bare. "That I actually lost. Not unlike my husband, come to think of it."

"WE'RE DIVORCED?" Norman screamed. "AND YOU LOST YOUR RING?"

Jesse nodded, an embarrassed look on his face. "I might have reversed those things in order of importance, but yes."

"And *she's* pregnant. WITH *OUR* EMBRYOS?" He intended to point in the vicinity of Lally, but mostly his arm went straight up.

"Just one," Lally clarified. "The first couple didn't take. I'm not exactly a spring chicken. Which, in hindsight—*phew.* None of us wanted a litter. I mean, could you imagine?"

Norman could imagine none of this, so he pressed both of his temples as if he were keeping his skull from exploding. "How is any of this even possible?"

Lally jumped right in, babbling her nerves. "I did come to talk to you about it. But you weren't here, and Jesse was being all weird, so I hired a private detective. Or investigator. I forget what they like to be called."

"Not a very good one," Norman moaned.

"Dick!" Jesse offered, answering Lally's question with a joke. She stared at him. "Private dick," he explained, but no one was ready to lighten the mood.

"I WAS AT THE GYM!"

"You were most certainly *not* at the gym. Anyhow. When we started to suspect that Jesse was a serial killer, I was like, 'I can't have *his* baby.'"

Jesse snapped his head in her direction. "Hold on. You thought I was a serial killer? Like for real, for real?"

"Just for a short time. When you started tearing up the backyard."

Jesse cupped his hands over his face, embarrassed. "Oh, that was a phase." Jesse and Lally laughed like this was all a big inside joke. "Wait, but the night we agreed, you still thought I was a serial killer. You were going to have a serial killer's baby."

"I'm a woman over forty, Jesse. I'm not exactly swimming in options!"

Jesse pulled back a dining chair for Lally and encouraged her to sit. Norman looked on in horror, as if they were suddenly the loving couple and he was the third wheel. And then a large dog trotted into the kitchen and from the floor Norman did a triple take; the dog responded by licking his face.

"Norman, would you get Mafalda some water?"

"WHO?"

Jesse pointed at the dog, like, *Who do you think?*

"You named the dog after my grandmother?"

"I did, actually," Lally confessed. "She bears a striking resemblance to Nana, don't you think? I mean, other than being black."

"Oh, never mind. I'll do it." Jesse crossed to the kitchen and filled a bowl with water. Mafalda left Norman behind to lap loudly at the water as Jesse rescued the overcooked eggs from the pan in the sink and slid them into another bowl and hacked at them with a fork to cool. "Can the dog have these? At this point I don't think we're going to eat them."

Norman groaned and writhed on the floor, taking in more information per minute than perhaps anyone in the history of man. His eyes landed on the planter, which ran the length of the kitchen island. The barrel cactuses were gone, replaced with a softer plant. "Are these . . ." He almost couldn't bring himself to say it. "*Ferns?*"

"Cactuses are unsafe for a baby," Lally insisted.

"I'm sorry, do you LIVE HERE?"

"*Anyhow,*" Jesse continued, like he was trying to get Norman to focus. "I employed Harlan's services to advertise in the paper that I was looking for you to serve divorce papers. At this point we practically had him on a family retainer."

Norman pounded his fists on the floor. "Who the fuck is Harlan?"

"The private—"

Norman didn't wait for Jesse to say *dick*. "You announced that you wanted to divorce me in the papers? You got a dog? You dug up the yard?" He rocked himself on the floor, trying to self-soothe to the sound of Pathways. "This is a joke. You're joking. Lally has a pillow under her shirt, you're on some secret diet—and who knows where you got the dog, maybe it's an animatronic puppet. It's all just a practical joke."

"Not *that* practical," Jesse said to Lally, and indeed those were a lot of hoops to jump through for a laugh.

"I've never fully understood your sense of humor, even if I've always indulged it. But this is going too far."

Jesse put his hands on his hips. "I knew you didn't think I deserved that award!"

Norman sat up, propping himself with his hands. "I must have hit my head or something. This is a concussion, right? Or the lat pulls pinched a nerve to my brain. I'm going to go back to bed to sleep this off. You can make your own breakfast."

Lally stopped him. "You're not supposed to go to sleep if you have a concussion."

"He doesn't have a concussion," Jesse clarified.

Norman stood up slowly, stumbling when he felt woozy. "Then one of you check on me every few hours to make sure I'm not dead."

Jesse stopped him one last time, an inscrutable look across his face. "Norman." Jesse placed his hand on Norman's arm in a way that expressed genuine concern. "How long do you think you were gone?" And then he humored him by adding, "*At the gym.*"

Norman shrugged; he didn't know. "The usual. An hour? Ninety minutes?"

Jesse pulled back the curtains to the yard, which were still drawn to keep the house cool. Just outside was a sparkling blue swimming pool that shimmered in the late-morning sunlight. A deck and furniture surrounded it, and the landscaping was already growing in.

"What the—" Norman said, rubbing his eyes to make sure he wasn't seeing a mirage. He stepped closer, but cautiously, like the swimming pool might bite.

He'd been gone for exactly a year.

DAY TWO

On the day following Norman's return, Jesse and Lally insisted he go to the Hi-Desert Medical Center in Joshua Tree for proper medical tests. "I don't need to be prodded and poked," Norman protested. Jesse and Lally exchanged looks that were all too easy to decipher: Perhaps he had already been probed by whoever had taken him, an insinuation Norman didn't like one bit.

"Do it for the baby," Lally implored when Norman continued to balk. "Look, I won't even eat fish because of the mercury poisoning."

Norman recoiled. "You think I could give you *mercury poisoning*?"

"I don't know! That's why we need you to be tested."

"I'm not a tuna," Norman objected.

"Obviously," Jesse said. "But we're going to get you checked out to your albacore."

Norman didn't laugh. "It would be nice if you were on my side."

"We *are*," Lally assured him. "We are on your side."

"But we still need to look out for ourselves," Jesse added.

Eventually Norman had to agree that even astronauts were put into quarantine when they returned to Earth. But Norman felt less and less like he had come back to Earth than like he had landed in the Twilight Zone. "Okay, fine," he finally acquiesced. "I'll see a doctor." It was the only way to shut them up. He only hoped he wouldn't be fitted for a straitjacket.

Norman sat in the back seat as Jesse drove, as it was safer for Lally to sit up front where there were airbags. He felt very much on the outside. Only Mafalda had welcomed him into the pack without judgment, happy to no longer be the bottom rung on this ladder. He leaned his head against the cool glass window as he processed his grief. The divorce, the pregnancy he played no part in, Jesse being a suspected serial killer (!), his whereabouts for a year before he woke up in bed and went to the gym—in short, it was *a lot.* He shivered as the air-conditioning blew on full blast for Lally's benefit. The car had a familiar vibration, but there was a warmth he was missing but couldn't describe.

The medical center looked more like a strip mall than a proper hospital, but at least it had ample parking. And since Norman didn't really feel the need for actual medical care he didn't protest, except when Lally suggested they find a wheelchair to push him inside; he approached the hospital on his own two feet. It wasn't how he would have designed the building, but it was just one more thing on the list of thoughts he was keeping to himself.

"Is this an actual town hospital?" Lally asked with concerning skepticism, adding that it looked more like a post office than a place to get well.

To which Jesse and Norman replied together, "It's not a town, it's a CDP." For the first time since his return, Norman detected a hint of a smile on Jesse's face as they began to fall back in sync. He still couldn't explain where he'd been, but he felt a firmer grasp on where he was.

Together they walked through a door marked MAIN LOBBY/OUT-PATIENT REGISTRATION, and Lally was right—even the font they chose for the signage was evocative of the USPS. The lobby was like a lot of things in the desert, sand-colored and nondescript. Chairs were functional and gray and certainly not comfortable, even for the shortest of waits. Jesse and Norman argued over whose name to put on the admitting paperwork; Jesse was carrying a full teaching load this upcoming semester and therefore had new health insurance through COD, while Norman's insurance had lapsed. They took a seat and debated the pros and cons before ultimately deciding against committing insurance fraud.

"Let me get a picture of us," Lally said as she held up her phone for a selfie.

"In the waiting room?" Norman asked, not certain this was anything they would want to remember. But maybe Lally was right, maybe there was something seriously wrong with him and they'd want to capture the last minute before he was diagnosed. There were others scattered around the waiting room but no one directly behind them whose privacy they would invade, so he didn't further object. After she snapped a selfie, Lally handed him her phone to see.

"It's a good one," she said, almost like she was trying to stave off his criticism.

Norman zoomed in on himself, almost fascinated by his physical form. He had, after all, been *somewhere*. What damage might have been done? He was spending all of his time processing the mental, but what of the physical? How might his body have changed? "Have I always had these creases in my earlobes?" Norman looked up from Lally's phone for an answer. Jesse, checking over the last of the paperwork before returning it to the admitting desk, did this weird thing where he first furrowed, then raised his brows. Norman rubbed both of his earlobes. "At first I thought I just slept funny, but I can feel the crease on both sides."

"Maybe you should see a doctor," Jesse joked.

Norman pulled out his own phone and googled it. "It's either a natural sign of aging, or I have pretty serious heart disease."

"That's good!" Jesse said, but Norman didn't see how. Jesse explained they'd see him faster that way, heart issues always took precedent in the ER. "Anything else we should list?"

Norman couldn't think of anything, other than he hadn't taken a multivitamin in a year, and who knows what he'd done for nutrition. But before he could mention that, Lally blurted, "Government experiments."

"Government experiments?" Jesse repeated, confused.

Lally nodded. "See if they've done any. And have them check for radiation. Alpha, beta, gamma."

"I'm not sure they do that here," Jesse said with genuine disappointment. "But a complete mental examination is probably a good idea, he could have had a psychotic break."

Norman shook his head. "This is becoming less and less fun for me by the minute, and it wasn't all that fun to begin with."

Jesse actually seemed to sympathize with him, and reached for his hand across Lally's lap.

"Maybe we should see if I was unplugged from the Matrix."

Jesse turned to look directly at Norman, and Lally leaned back so as not to obstruct his view. "What is the last thing you remember?"

"Oh, that's good," Lally concurred, and they both looked at her for explanation. "Spending time with Harlan has taught me it's productive to focus on the concrete."

Concrete, Norman thought. The last thing he remembered was going to bed, annoyed by some scam email. From Union Bonk, no . . . *Bonk of America*. He was restless at first, he remembered that; sleep did not easily come. Norman watched as Lally turned to Jesse for confirmation, which was insulting. Why couldn't she just believe him?

"And then what?"

Norman couldn't remember. "And then I slept quite soundly, it felt like the best night's sleep of my life." He woke with a profound sense of gratitude, for Jesse, for his life. He'd dreamed of the moment they met, how perfect it was, the collision a chain reaction, hot and beautiful in ways that kept exploding. He wished that at least Jesse could see. And then he woke up and went to the gym.

"But you admit that's not *all* that happened." Jesse looked down on him with eyes up, wanting him to confirm.

Yes, he had come to acknowledge that. Too much had happened, too much had changed. He was surprisingly accepting of the pool—*who doesn't love a pool*—even if he thought that first evening that perhaps they were part of an ambush home makeover show for HGTV in which, under the cover of darkness, a crew redesigned a couple's yard in one night while they slept. But the dog? The pregnancy? "There's more that I want to remember," Norman finally admitted. "It all feels just out of grasp."

Jesse let go of Norman's hand, patting him twice on the knee. "Then let's get you checked out." He stood up and took the clipboard to the attendant at the front desk.

Norman liked this Jesse. Shock was giving way to genuine concern. He was happy to be at the doctor if instead of feeling contaminated he felt cared for. He smiled at Lally, who gave him a side hug. When he glanced up Jesse was deep in conversation with the admitting nurse.

"Oh, and he has a heart condition," Jesse finally said.

"Are you sure?" the nurse asked. At a casual glance Norman seemed fine.

"Yes," Jesse insisted. "Just take a look at his earlobes."

After hours of waiting and a barrage of tests from a team of doctors who seemed just as confused as he was, Norman was given the all clear; there was nothing wrong with him medically speaking—other than losing a year. He moved, he bled, he responded, he had excellent blood pressure, a good resting pulse, low cholesterol, and the reflexes of a man half his age. He wasn't radioactive, a clone, a cyborg, a pod person, some sort of Trojan horse, or anything likewise to be scared of. They offered to keep Norman for observation, but Jesse muttered something about not wanting to lose him again. Even Lally was impressed, and let her brother put his hand on her growing stomach. This was Norman, *their* Norman. To reward him for being such a good sport, they treated for dinner at the Tiny Pony.

"Hot daddy is back," their waiter said when he locked eyes with Norman. He grabbed three menus and showed them to an out-of-the-way table. He then leaned over to Jesse as he sat, and added, "Does this mean you're done with that cute otter you've been bringing around? Maybe you could give me his number." Norman stared at Jesse, who turned red.

"We'll see" was all he could stammer, clearly wanting the interaction done.

"Young *what*?" Norman asked.

The waiter continued undaunted, much to Jesse's obvious horror. "Otter. You know, young hairy guy. Oslo. Orion. What was his name?"

"Orson," Jesse said, looking at the floor like he hoped it would swallow him.

Norman made a note of the name Orson but decided not to press—*for now.*

"Congratulations," Jesse said when they had their drinks and he raised his michelada; Lally toasted with water.

"For what?" Norman asked.

Jesse sheepishly explained. Every boy of their generation had watched the 1983 miniseries *V*, in which carnivorous aliens wore synthetic skins, peeling back their human faces and revealing their true reptilian selves to feast on live, squirming rodents. Jesse didn't exactly think that Norman had somehow been replaced by an extraterrestrial, at least if you took him at his word. But there had been some lingering doubt.

"Congratulations on not being a reptile," Norman confirmed before picking up his menu. "Got it." Feasting on live rodents. *Preposterous.* And then he made a joke about inquiring to the chef about their roasted shrew.

After they ordered, Lally excused herself to the restroom. She waved at the bartenders, as apparently she and Jesse were regulars now. Once they were alone, Norman wasted no time. "Orson?" he asked, not meaning to.

"At least I didn't fuck the waiter."

"Oh, I'm so relieved," Norman said, trying to decide if that was true. But then he was genuinely curious. "I was gone. What stopped you?"

Jesse thought about it for a moment and said it didn't seem right. "He was ours to fuck together. It wouldn't have been any fun without you."

Norman forced a weak smile. "What a lovely sentiment."

"Norman."

"No, seriously, they should put that on a Hallmark card. 'I didn't fuck the waiter.'" Norman mimed opening a card. "'It would not have been as fun without you.'"

"You said it yourself. You were gone."

"I was taken."

Jesse challenged him with a look.

"Well, you certainly got over it."

Jesse feigned horror. "The best way to get over someone . . ."

. . . *was to get under someone else.* Norman was familiar. "Okay, clearly I don't remember what happened, so you tell me what *you* saw."

Jesse looked over his shoulder at the restrooms to look for signs of Lally. "I told you all this last night."

Norman was undaunted. "Tell me again."

Jesse told the full story in as much detail as he could recall. Norman listened intently, not breaking focus even when Lally reappeared; she saw them deep in conversation and continued outside to take a call. This time, he couldn't get over Jesse's description of the light. He didn't remember seeing it so much as feeling it. Enough to know there was some validity to what Jesse had seen. "And then you looked at me and stepped directly into it."

This was new information. In processing the story the night before, he understood the light had taken him. "I *stepped* into it."

"You stepped into it, Norman. What else do you want me to say? You chose it. You chose the light over me."

If that was truly how Jesse felt, that Norman chose to leave, he could understand his running hot and cold, and some of his decisions since Norman was gone. Depleting their savings on a pool? Maybe not that one so much, but this wasn't about the pool.

Lally returned to her seat at the table, awkwardly lowering herself into her chair. Norman sprang up to help, but Jesse was already there. He was on the outside still.

"Everything okay?" Norman asked.

Lally set her phone on the table. Norman couldn't believe she was worried about contamination from him but not from the germs her phone picked up in a restaurant. "Oh, yes. That was Harlan. I told him I had some big updates for him, which I guess is true." She looked at Norman and smiled. "You two don't need me around, so I thought I would go to L.A. to give you some space."

"*Space*," Jesse muttered.

"For a few days. I can see my ob-gyn. And some old flight attendant friends."

Norman wanted to know what Lally was doing for money, but he didn't need anyone else getting defensive. Instead he focused on this Harlan person. Norman didn't like having a character in their lives that he did not yet know. "What's he like?"

"Who," Lally asked. "Harlan?"

Harlan. What a name.

"Straight," Jesse answered, which sounded dismissive but made perfect sense. Norman had an immediate image of the kind of grizzled character from every cop movie, the one you suspected was soft on the inside.

"Now that I'm back, your case can be officially closed." Norman didn't know how these things worked exactly, maybe there was some paperwork needed to complete his file.

"Even if there's a new mystery before us?" Jesse speculated. He seemed to think there wasn't much to do until Norman's memory came back. If it ever did.

"Harlan's good with these things," Lally reminded them. "Maybe he can suggest a few tricks of the trade we might try."

Norman quietly agreed. There *were* things they could try: memory exercises, hypnosis, psychedelic mushrooms. And maybe it would come to that. Or maybe he should hire his own private eye. He'd find someone better than this Harlan character. "I stepped into the light?" he asked again, and Jesse nodded. "I don't know what I was thinking." Norman cupped his drink in both hands, even though it might warm the glass and melt the ice. But he did know what he was thinking, at least in the days and weeks before. "I was in a state. *We* were in a state."

"California," Jesse observed.

Stuck, Noman thought. "I don't know. You must have felt it, too. I thought the move to Joshua Tree would solve that, but it seemed to make it worse. I didn't want to divorce you, I didn't want to die. I didn't want to harm myself, but also I didn't want things to continue. I was tired. Oh god, was I tired. Tired of fighting, for us, for our rights, for the permits to redo the house. I was tired of America. Of people being so afraid of everything that's even a little different from them. I was tired of society failing the simplest of moral tests. I was tired of politics. I was tired of wealth disparity. Of a nation that chooses not to have nice things. I was tired of people telling others what bathrooms to use. I was tired of our tax system, our health care system, of everything being the dumbest way to do anything. Here's your insurance card, don't forget that eyeballs and teeth are add-ons! I was tired of everyone being so angry all the time. It used to be fun to be angry, remember? It used to be so productive! But now people are so *angry* when they get angry, and about the most innocuous things! I was tired of guns and reading about schoolchildren shot to death. I was tired of fights that had been settled fifty years ago being fought anew. I was tired of our rights being rolled back on purpose, by design. Remember when we came out? Men were dying. So many beautiful men. I never expected to be this old. Did you? I was *exhausted*. I think the light offered . . . *something else*. Something I thought moving here might hold. Meaning. Connection. It was warm. Even now, I can feel it on my skin. It was welcoming."

Jesse finally spoke. "Two things that I am not."

Lally placed a hand on his shoulder to calm him.

Norman smiled weakly. "Two things *the world* is not. I know you won't ever believe me, but the light was . . . home."

"Funny," Jesse said. "I used to think I was home."

"Norman, I'm so sorry," Lally said, ignoring Jesse to process this on her own terms.

Norman closed his eyes tight. He was reminded of the movie *Contact*; he and Jesse had once seen it together before Jodie Foster officially came out and before James Woods lost his goddamn mind. Jodie Foster traveled to space and experienced wondrous things, while on Earth it appeared she'd gone nowhere. Even though the circumstances were reversed, on Earth his absence was long, whereas he felt he was gone but a minute if at all; Carl Sagan knew what was up. When he opened his eyes, food was being placed on their table.

"Well, I can understand all that," Lally continued, trying to keep the peace. "I'm exhausted. And famished." She picked up the pickle spear from her wild boar sloppy joe and took a big bite.

Norman pointed to Jesse's dinner. "You're eating your smash patties without a bun?"

Jesse stared at his plate, confused. Was that not how he usually ate them?

"And you didn't get the fries? You always get the fries."

Jesse looked at him defiantly. "I think you'll find a lot of things have changed."

DAY SEVENTEEN

"Whose wedding is this again?" Norman asked as he handed the Laredo's keys to the valet in exchange for a ticket. He then reached into the back, where his Tom Ford suit jacket was neatly hanging.

"Non-Trad's. But they're already married, this is just the reception." Jesse smoothed his trousers with the palms of his hands.

"And Non-Trad is . . ."

"One of my students."

Norman straightened Jesse's tie before putting on his own jacket. "Do you know any of your students' actual names?"

"Of course I do. Nathan Treadwell. NT. Non-Trad." Jesse swatted Norman away as he continued to fuss, but this time playfully. Ever since his return, annoyance and lust had seesawed through them. They'd had passionate, all-consuming sex twice, which thrilled Norman, who felt starved for human touch, but Jesse was also just as likely to be withdrawn. "I don't know the name of his wife."

Norman shook his head. "Well, you look very handsome."

Jesse did not respond.

"And I look pretty good, too," Norman prompted.

"Yes, but you always look good," Jesse replied, as if it didn't ever need be acknowledged. Norman was the right size to fit most suits off the rack, whereas Norman knew from experience Jesse never felt more like a wheelbarrow of limbs than he did when they dressed up nice. Jesse headed up the few stairs into the restaurant, Norman trailing behind him.

The reception was at Le Vallauris, a premier French restaurant in Palm Springs on the grounds of the old Desert Inn, the storied hotel once owned by Marion Davies, perhaps best known as the mistress of William Randolph Hearst; the inn helped put Palm Springs on the map. In the late 1960s, most of the hotel was demolished to make way for a glitzy shopping mall, and it was a miracle the structure that housed the restaurant survived. The restaurant itself, once a favorite haunt of Frank Sinatra's, was now owned by the Soho House, which had put their spin on the menu but left the institution's character intact.

Cocktail hour was just reaching full swing on the patio, which was anchored by large ficus trees; at night they were decorated with twinkling white lights, making it feel like guests were dining under the stars. Or among the stars, as it was easy to imagine the entire Rat Pack, or Dinah Shore, or desert socialite Nelda Linsk, or any number of luminaries who graced this patio over the years. They held hands as they walked out into the courtyard. "I remember something," Norman blurted, feeling the warmth of Jesse's hand.

"From that night?" Jesse asked.

"I think," Norman said, although he needed time to process. "It'll come to me."

Tables were set for formal dining in the courtyard, white linens and their finest china, but were only sparsely populated, as most celebrants milled about. A bar was set up in the corner and each of them accepted a glass of champagne; Norman held his by the base of his flute. "Saluti," he said, *cheers* in Italian, to which Jesse replied, "A votre santé," because champagne was French.

A student Jesse called Headphones spotted them first; he was set up near the bar with speakers that were playing pop music in French and waved them over to say hello. He rivaled Jesse in height. Norman recognized a song by the band Pink Martini. "They have me DJ'ing this thing even though I don't understand a word of the lyrics."

"Quel dommage," Jesse said with a laugh.

Headphones brightened. "I know that one! Something cheese."

"Look at that, I *can* teach someone to be funny."

Norman cleared his throat.

"Headphones, Norman. Norman, Headphones. Headphones was one of my students last fall."

Norman held out his hand and they shook. "Jesse's husband," Norman stressed.

This kid Headphones seemed genuinely excited, and shook Norman's hand with gusto. "None of us would even be here if it weren't for this guy," Headphones explained, pointing to Jesse, and Norman turned to his husband, confused.

Jesse's face grew flush. "Non-Trad confessed that his girlfriend once said she couldn't imagine marrying someone who wasn't funny. It was one of the reasons he took my class. But I'd like to point out Nathan was already funny. I just . . . helped bring it out of him."

"And now look at them," Headphones exclaimed. Non-Trad and his wife were holding court under the largest ficus, posing for photos with guests. Headphones seemed legitimately happy for them, and Jesse commented that he was proud of the community his class had fostered. And that he was grateful to Headphones for making him feel less freakishly tall.

"Do you have any Mountain Dew?" The voice came from the bar behind them, followed by some heated words with the bartender. Jesse turned and smirked.

"Let me guess, another student?" Norman asked when he saw the look on Jesse's face.

Jesse nodded. "Mountain Dew." When Norman stared, Jesse acquiesced and offered her real name, "Melissa."

Mountain Dew spun around at the sound of her name. "JESSE?" She dropped her disagreement with the bartender and ran over to hug her former teacher. "You're not going to believe what they don't have at the bar."

"Outrageous," Jesse said before introducing Norman.

Norman extended a hand. "I suppose you're the one responsible for the green swill taking up a prime shelf in my fridge."

"And the student becomes the teacher." Mountain Dew laughed while taking a bow. "Now if only I could teach this bartender a lesson or two. Can you believe he told me he could make something akin to ginger ale by mixing Pepsi and Sprite? *SPRITE?* So now I have to slum it by drinking champagne." She took a sip and stuck her tongue out. "It's so dry."

"Not everything is made to quench thirst," Jesse commiserated. "But it's a celebration so we'll indulge them."

"They make Hard Mountain Dew, you know." She said it loudly and for the bartender's benefit, before excusing herself to ditch her half-full champagne flute on one of the tables. She then disappeared into the crowd.

"Who else am I going to meet tonight?" Norman asked when it was just the two of them. "Shoelaces? Fishsticks? I just want to be prepared."

"Fishsticks hates these things," Jesse said, playing along. "If she came it would be a real fluke." Norman groaned at the pun as Jesse pointed in the happy couple's direction. "Come on. Let's go wish them well."

Non-Trad greeted Jesse with a tight hug and whispered, "I owe it all to you." Jesse would hear none of it. This was all Nathan's doing. Over and over, Norman was introduced and squeezed and elbowed aside in favor of his husband—he couldn't ever remember Jesse being so popular. It was disconcerting. Had Jesse actually thrived in his absence?

"What?" Jesse asked at some point when he caught Norman staring.

"Nothing," Norman said sheepishly. "It's just, I realize I've never actually seen you teach. Apparently you're quite good."

"This is better than observing me in the classroom," Jesse replied. And Norman understood. He was seeing the *results* of Jesse's work, the building that came from the blueprints of his teaching.

Norman continued to observe his partner once they were seated for dinner. As the younger one, Jesse had long been expected to acknowledge the ways in which Norman had influenced his life—something Norman well realized. Norman had introduced Jesse to so many things. Friends. Fashion. Queer-coded books by Patricia Highsmith and Langston Hughes. The absolute culinary perfection of fried fish and chips served in newspaper before that became a thing of the past. But tonight it seemed Jesse was the one in command. His wit was unmatched, he was sparkling. Norman had the sense he'd never truly appreciated these qualities. Youth was finally a check in his favor, early fifties for a man, a certain sweet spot where looks, confidence, and success all commingled. How could one look at Jesse and ever not be delighted? He leaned in to kiss him on the cheek.

"You're quiet tonight," Jesse said when beet salads were deposited in front of them.

"Not particularly," Norman protested as he adjusted his chair and several leaves from the ficus tree fell like heavy snowflakes. "I had a nice chat with Charleston Chew."

"Snickers?" Jesse asked, confused.

"Ah, yes. I knew it was something with nougat."

"I like the alliteration, though."

Snickers, whose real name was Connor, was the last to join their table alongside his girlfriend, Mei, whom Jesse quickly dubbed Socks thanks to a colorful pair she was wearing that Snickers had custom-printed with images of their cat's face, whose name was, ironically, Mounds. (If he were nuts he'd be Almond Joy, Socks said to the feigned delight of anyone who would listen.) There was a seat for Headphones, too, who was here stag, but he kept jumping up to check on the music. Someone named Unicorn was MIA, but Jesse explained that was the way with unicorns—they were magical creatures you couldn't pin down. Mountain Dew had a glass filled with a liquid the color of nuclear waste. *Could it be?* She clocked Norman's look and confessed, "I had Postmates deliver six twenty-ounce bottles. I hid them in a topiary if you want some."

"A topiary?" Jesse asked, looking around the patio with delight.

Mountain Dew shrugged. "Ruining the tablescape seemed crass."

Jesse bowed his head. "It's impossible I ever worried the lot of you weren't funny."

Dinner was filet with a balsamic reduction, onion marmalade, haricots verts, and some sort of mash that might have been parsnips. Norman didn't realize how hungry he was until food hit the table, nor how much he'd had to drink to quell his nerves.

"Easy, tiger," Jesse said when Norman stabbed nearly all his green beans with his fork. His appetite had been ravenous since his return. Norman kissed Jesse again, since that was also the state of his libido, before shoving the forkful in his mouth. "Oh my god, these are incredible. Taste one." He stabbed the last few beans on his plate for Jesse to try, but Jesse waved him away.

"I have my own plate."

"Norman," Socks observed, "you act like you haven't been fed in months!"

Norman simply shrugged—there was a good chance he hadn't—then inspected one of the bottles of French pinot noir on the table. "What does Non-Trad do?" he whispered to Jesse. The label could not have been cheap.

"You know, I have no earthly idea." Jesse confessed that since this was his first time teaching at a community college, he wasn't used to his students having careers.

Norman caught Jesse's eye and held his gaze. "I feel very fortunate to be here with you." Their tablemates fussed over Norman, saying what a good partner he was, but his sincerity seemed to just make Jesse squirm.

"Don't encourage him," Jesse said, flagging down the waiter to order a Tito's. Then, apparently reading the social cues, he patted his husband appreciatively on the shoulder, a little too hard for Norman's liking.

"So, Norman," Headphones asked. "Are *you* funny?" Then off Jesse's appalled reaction, added, "What? It's a legitimate question. A funny person can be married to an unfunny one."

Norman jumped in. "We prefer 'serious' to 'unfunny.'"

Headphones unrolled his napkin to retrieve his silverware. "Whatever you want to call it."

Noticing Jesse's discomfort, Norman threw himself on the grenade. "First of all, I'm sure that Stilts, or whatever you guys call him, would be the first to tell you that humor is subjective."

"*Stilts!*" Mountain Dew laughed. And then she made some noise like *aaaaaaaah*, and Norman worried her drink might come out of her nose. "Because of his long legs." It was low-hanging fruit that had been there the whole time and yet none of them had seized it.

"Not helping," Jesse whispered.

"But am I funny? The answer you're looking for is: Lately? No. *Ever?* Also no, I'm afraid."

"That's not true," Jesse protested, although it partially was. "Norman's selling himself short. Besides, every comedian needs an appreciative audience." The waiter returned with Jesse's vodka.

"I know what you need with that," Mountain Dew said, and she scampered away after one of her hidden bottles. Immediately, a young man took her seat.

"There he is," the young man said, placing his hand on Jesse's shoulder in a way that was a little too familiar. Jesse looked panic-stricken and reached for his drink.

"Orson," he said, the vodka catching in his throat.

"Hey, Mr. B." Headphones waved and Orson smiled. Norman quickly deduced he must somehow be involved with the school.

"How's everyone over here? I had Nathan in Applied Sciences, but since I don't know a soul at my table I get the feeling I was a last-minute invite."

Jesse loosened his tie. "If he invited all his professors, I suddenly feel less special."

Norman stared. So this was the mysterious Orson. He was handsome. Younger than Norman had pictured, which was somewhat alarming; the top buttons of his shirt were undone and the body hair was as advertised.

"We were just debating with Jesse's husband, Norman, whether a mixed-humor marriage can work," Snickers said, bringing their new tablemate up to speed.

"Husband?" Orson repeated, clearly caught off guard. What Jesse had told him about their situation, Norman had no idea. Jesse didn't make eye contact with either of them, instead focusing on the ice in his glass.

"Well, to be perfectly honest, Norman is my *ex*-husband," Jesse finally said to a shocked Snickers. "So don't extrapolate too much from us."

Norman looked at Jesse, horrified. Then to the table he stated, "Because of a clerical error." He then extended a hand to this Orson, who shook it.

"We'll see," Jesse said, refusing to defuse the situation. Then, at Norman's horrified look, he added, "We have a few issues to work out."

"In the bedroom?" Headphones asked, not that it was any of his goddamn business.

"Ice balls?" Mountain Dew asked as she returned with her prize.

Norman threw his napkin down on the table and pushed his chair back. "Just to clarify, I do not have ice balls." Headphones was the only one who laughed.

Mountain Dew waved her hands. She tipped a wine bucket forward as it was chilling a bottle of white. Indeed, it was filled with ice pellets. "I was offering Jesse ice from this bucket." Mountain Dew took her newly folded napkin and draped it over her arm, then presented one of the bottles of soda as if it were the finest of wines. Jesse leaned in to "inspect" the label.

"Ah, that was an excellent year for Dews." They were both delighted by the bit, and she poured the soda into Jesse's vodka; he gave it a good stir with his finger and tossed it back in one gulp. The table cheered.

Norman had had enough of Jesse mugging for these kids, particularly Orson. "Don't be fooled by his childish behavior. He's squarely Gen X."

The Tito's, coupled with whatever's in Mountain Dew—Liquid Plumr, Windex, antifreeze, who knows—seemed to hit Jesse like a line of cocaine, and he slammed his glass on the table. "I may have been assigned Gen X at birth, but I identify as Gen Z."

Headphones whooped. "Yeah you do, Mr. Doctor!"

"There's no music playing," Norman informed Headphones, who jumped up and scrambled to his battle station. "I need some air," Norman added, and he turned to leave, even though it was an open-air patio.

Norman only got a few feet before Headphones's voice echoed through a microphone. "This one's for you, Non-Trad. Something for your generation. But not Mr. Doctor, because he identifies as GEN ZEEEEEEE!" Norman began to storm out. And then the first piano notes of Richard Marx's "Right Here Waiting" unspooled through the speakers.

Oceans apart, day after day, and I slowly go insane.

Norman froze. It was the same Richard Marx song that played in the random health food store parking lot in Scottsdale after the birth of the daughter they would never bring home. He turned back to the table and recognized the absolute panic spreading across Jesse's face; it was the same panic splashed across his. Norman reached for Jesse's hand. "A word?" Jesse nodded, stood, but didn't take his hand.

"You okay?" Norman asked when out of earshot of their table. He glanced at Headphones, who flashed them a smile and whooped his hands like he was encouraging them to dance.

"The song?" Jesse swallowed, even though his mouth was dry. "Don't be ridiculous. I'm fine." It was clear he was lying. "This is uncomfortable for you," Jesse muttered. "I should have brought Lally."

Jesse pulled them aside so that the chef could dish out dessert, some sort of sorbet the color of green tea.

"Why, so you could be alone with Orson?"

Jesse seemed almost impressed. "I've never known you to be this possessive."

"What is he, twenty-seven?" Norman asked.

Jesse widened his eyes. "Jealous?"

The thing is, Norman was.

"Tables have turned. I'm the older man now. To be honest with you, I kind of like it."

Norman couldn't believe his ears. "You're *twice* his age. You're not older so much as archaic."

"He doesn't seem to mind."

"And you just had to call me your *ex*-husband. Twist that knife."

Jesse seemed to think that was not fair. "It's what you are, isn't it?"

Norman couldn't believe his ears. He was so much more than that. "And what is he? Your *boyfriend*?"

"He's not anything. Calm down. We've only been on a few dates." Jesse looked around, perhaps nervous that people were starting to eavesdrop.

In the history of marital arguments, telling someone to calm down has only ever provoked the opposite effect. But Norman getting more worked up was not going to get them anywhere. He had no choice but to pivot. "I remember you underneath me, when I was in the light. You were standing underneath me. Waving a rolling pin. Could that be possible? And I recognize now you were fighting for us. And it may seem like I was giving up. But in my own way I was fighting for us, too."

Norman expected an objection, but Jesse seemed too stunned to speak. Maybe he was remembering the rolling pin, too.

"Do you remember anything else?"

"I remember that night. I was reading and had dozed off, I guess—I think you were already asleep." Norman glanced at Headphones. *How long is this song?* "I don't remember what woke me first, that awful racket and the blinding flashes of light, or just, you know."

Jesse shook his head. He didn't know.

"My general unhappiness with the world."

"You didn't think to wake me?"

"No," he replied, very matter-of-fact. He didn't recall thinking to, or on any of the previous nights his restlessness startled him awake, but he could see how that would have been the rational response to something that goes bump in the night. "The best way I can describe it is I felt this pull. Out of bed. Out of the house. Like I was in some sort of trance. I didn't think to wake you, because I wasn't thinking at all."

"It didn't feel like a pull to me," Jesse interrupted. "If anything, it felt like a push."

"I thought the light held the answers. I know it seemed like I chose to leave. But I only chose to know the truth. And the rest?" Norman shrugged helplessly.

"And what are the answers?" Jesse asked with an obnoxious defiance. "Where have you been this whole time?"

Norman's jaw dropped helplessly; he didn't have them—answers. At least not in that moment. At least not yet. The answer was that he wanted to be with Jesse. He just didn't know if Jesse still wanted to be with him. And he was too afraid to ask.

"That's what I thought."

Richard Marx ended his plaintive wailing. *I'll be right here waiting for you.* What did he know? Thank god Headphones had the good sense to follow it with something up-tempo. Bruno Mars, volume up. A woman screamed as she recognized "Uptown Funk" and leaped to her feet, almost knocking over a server balancing three bowls of sorbet. When they returned to their table, Orson was gone. And he couldn't tell if Jesse was sad or relieved by his absence.

After the dessert course had been cleared, some of the tables were pushed back to make more room for dancing, and Headphones announced he had a surprise for the bride and groom: a silent disco. Enormous over-ear headsets were handed out to each guest, much like the pair that earned Headphones his name. They were meant to provide a unique party experience that happened to work in perfect tandem with Palm Springs's strict noise ordinances. The high-quality audio picked up even the lowest bass line, meaning the party could go on well into the night without disrupting any of the restaurant's neighbors. The headsets lit up in three different colors—red, green, and blue—corresponding with three different channels. Everyone started out on the green channel, and then you could switch, and find others on the dance party with the same headset color and really throw down. Jesse and Norman, still in the midst of their fight, exchanged skeptical glances, Jesse even looking at his watch to see if they should leave. But Norman was game, determined to end the evening on a high note, and so they slipped their headsets on and were each instantly transported to their own, safe world.

And then everyone began to dance.

The music quality was so pristine and beat through the headphones with such a percussive engine, it was impossible not to move to it with the absolute confidence Norman and Jesse usually lacked.

Norman, self-conscious about his age and not knowing the latest trends; Jesse, too big for most wedding dance floors, his limbs too gangly to easily control. Jesse often kept his arms close to his body, always afraid he could accidentally strike someone, while Norman would bounce in place. But the headsets had a range of fifty or so yards, and so everyone could spread out, having individual experiences that were also somehow collective. In short it was absolute magic. Norman danced with Snickers and Socks. Mountain Dew waved Jesse over, and he danced with her; she was, of course, on the green channel. Eventually Norman sweated through his shirt and had to beg off for a glass of water.

Norman slipped his headphones around his neck as he rehydrated and was instantly struck by the absolute insanity that was unspooling before him. Like with his relationship, the second he was not a part of it, he was absolutely on the outside of it, and what was a party only seconds before was now just criminally insane people stomping and shuffling to no music at all. Everyone wanted to know where he'd been, but they had it all wrong. *They* were the extraterrestrials, complete with light-up ears, all moving and swaying and bending and grunting, some of them singing badly to songs that no one else could hear. Tonight they celebrated, they expressed love, they moved their bodies in time with music. But on other nights they were hurtful, even cruel to themselves and to others, hating their bodies, voting against their own self-interests, and lifting false prophets. Several would go home tonight and take drugs to soothe the unbearable pain of being human. Others might in the future die in floods or earthquakes because the planet was sick and turning against them and no one was doing anything to stop it. *My god*, Norman thought. *We are all of us aliens.*

He pounded a second glass of water, all of us also more than half this mystical blend of hydrogen and oxygen, and carefully slipped his headphones back on. Because he did not want to be a visitor in this strange and curious life. It no longer exhausted him like it once had.

He wanted desperately what attracted him to the light in the first place. He wanted to be part of a larger world.

DAY TWENTY-TWO

"Have you thought of any names?"

Norman was trying to be nice. Too nervous to drive himself, he had asked that Lally drive the Laredo; he didn't trust her aging car, and Jesse had refused to come. He couldn't remember the last time he and his sister had been alone together.

Lally adjusted his mirror to facilitate her rear view. "For the baby?"

"And no more naming things after our grandparents." Their other grandmother's name was Ersilla. Norman might not have fully accepted their situation, but he was not about to take his personal discomfort out on the child.

Lally bit her lip as she drove. "Can anyone be named Sigourney? Or just her."

"I think just her," Norman said before it dawned on him what she was implying. "It's a girl?"

She turned to look at him. Always the big brother, he gestured for her to keep her eyes on the road. "Just a feeling," she admitted. "But we can ask when we get there."

Norman scoffed at the very idea.

They drove for a time, passing a gas station and a fast-food restaurant he didn't know was out this way. "Do you need to stop?"

Lally assured him she was good, even if she did need a restroom more often than she cared to admit—the joys of a geriatric pregnancy.

"Where is this place, anyway?"

Lally pointed to his phone. They were using his GPS, since it paired with the Jeep. Norman saw that they would be there in four minutes.

"I'm nervous," he confessed.

Lally stayed focused on the road. "Jesse has a decision to make. I think it's in your best interest to give him room to make it."

Norman felt that in the pit of his stomach. But that's not what he meant in the moment. "I'm nervous about *this*."

"Oh." Lally nodded. "That makes sense. But you're the one who wanted answers."

"For Jesse." Norman nervously ran his fingers through his hair. "To be honest, I have all the answers I need. I want Jesse." It was the questions he was afraid of.

Like where on earth had he been?

SHE'S A PET PSYCHIC?" Norman roared when they pulled up to the house. On the front gate was a childlike sign painted with dogs and two cats that looked like they had some sort of palsy.

Lally pulled the Jeep to a stop and killed the ignition. "Calm down."

"Lally!"

"I told her your name was Mr. Whiskers and that you were a

Maine coon. So when you go in there, maybe you could meow and purr and lick your paw and stuff."

Lally released her seat belt, but Norman grabbed it and buckled her back in like they were not staying. "I'm going to kill you."

"I'm pregnant!" she protested.

Norman gritted his teeth.

"Calm down, you don't want her to hear you. Don't give her any ammunition. This only works if she knows nothing."

Norman stared at her, his anger not receding. In the moment, it felt like he knew nothing, too.

"Relax. It's just marketing," Lally explained of the sign. "She does people, too." And then, as an afterthought, she mumbled, "I'm almost sure of it."

The psychic's name was Julia and she lived only a few towns over from Joshua Tree. It wasn't Zelda, or Madame Truth, or Marigold, or anything that Norman found off-putting. Nor did she ask to be called the Oracle, or the Golden Woman of Wonder Valley. She was just *Julia*, and her appearance reflected exactly that. She looked comforting, matronly, not unlike someone who might publish a cookbook and then make one of the recipes on the *Today* show. The natural gray in her hair was left untouched, making her look older perhaps than she was; in fact, Norman wondered if she might be younger than him. Her eyes were kind but tired; they brightened only for a moment when she greeted her guests. She grabbed Norman's face like a grandmother might; the bracelets she wore on both arms rattled like snakes, but in a way that didn't startle him. "You're lost," she said like they'd wandered into the wrong house, and Norman could not agree more. Her sweater hung loosely under her chin, more cowl-necked than turtle; in fact, the only expected thing about her appearance was that she wore lots of rings.

"I'd like to be found," he confessed.

Julia worked out of her kitchen, which smelled like bouillon cubes; years of boiling cabbages and stews had steamed into the wallpaper (covered wagons and mills with waterwheels), causing it to peel at the seams. Norman was invited to sit at her table, where he nervously picked at the frayed edges of her tablecloth.

"Where should I sit?" Lally asked.

Julia looked at Lally less kindly than she had greeted Norman. "How about outside in your car."

Norman interceded on Lally's behalf, before it could become a thing. "I'd like my sister to stay. I feel like I could use a witness." He then gestured at her pregnant belly, hoping to foster some sympathy.

Julia held firm. "Too much interference."

"I'll be quiet, I promise."

She remained adamant. "Not that kind of interference."

"Oh," Lally said, understanding. She asked to use Julia's bathroom, where she sent Norman a text that read: *She'll probably tell you that you spent the year trying to lick your own balls.*

Under the table, he texted back. *Who says I didn't?*

Don't let her convince you that you have distemper.

"Phones off, please," Julia instructed.

He complied, but not before texting, *Unsubscribe.*

Norman heard Lally flush and she saw herself out, Julia waiting until she heard the sound of her front door close to speak.

"So, tell me what brings you here." Already Norman's hackles were up; not five minutes in and she was fishing for clues. It was exactly what Jesse had warned him about, and why he refused to come. This whole business was a sham, desperate people easy marks for the fleece, eagerly volunteering their questions without even realizing they were providing ammunition for their own stickup.

"*We're* desperate people," Norman had reminded Jesse.

"Not that desperate." But they both knew that was untrue.

Norman was determined to tell Julia only as much as she needed to hear. "There is a year of time I can't account for. Basically most everything from last August until now."

Julia appeared unsurprised, like that was a perfectly natural occurrence. "What is the last thing you remember before the time was lost?"

"Not much," Norman confessed. "It was night. I was in bed. There was a light outside the window. The shutters were drawn, but I could sense that much. The light grew, brighter, yes, but also warmer, if that makes any sense? I was drawn to it. I remember that. Wanting to be bathed in it. I do not remember getting out of bed. I do not remember going outside. I have a very hazy memory of Jesse. My husband. Beneath me."

"*Beneath* you."

"I know. It sounds hierarchal, or even sexual, but I don't mean it like that. I guess I was floating? In the light. Jesse was on the ground. Naked, which was not that unusual to be honest, holding a rolling pin, which was. Unusual." Norman flinched. He should have kept at least some of those details to himself. "And that's the last thing I remember."

Julia shimmied her shoulders like the Jackson 5 were playing on a frequency only she could hear. "I want you to remain quiet and try to stay perfectly still." Norman nodded and shifted in his seat to get comfortable, already disobeying one of her commands, but Julia had closed her eyes and didn't notice. And there she sat, as still as anyone Norman had seen. The woman didn't lock her elbows or grab the table, she didn't roll her head or pulse back and forth—nothing close to the dramatics that won Whoopi Goldberg her Oscar. She just closed her eyes and sat there in silence until Norman himself began to twitch. He ignored a single bead of sweat as it dripped down his forehead, even though it tickled something fierce. When he was just about to ask if everything was all right, she spoke. "*Fruit*."

Norman smirked—in some contexts *fruit* was a homophobic slur. "Fruit," he repeated. "You're seeing fruit?" Maybe a banana, since he had said Jesse was naked, perhaps a juicy peach.

Julia shushed him; it wasn't even worth opening her eyes. Instead, she doubled down. "Not fruit. Sweet." Her eyes fluttered behind her closed eyelids. "Not sweet. *Love*."

Norman chuckled to himself. They were off to a roaring start.

"If this is funny to you, it won't ever work." Her chiding did not break her concentration.

"Sorry," he whispered as if he'd been caught passing notes in school.

Julia was silent for a long time. So long, Norman was left wondering if that was it. But the thing is, she was not wrong. Love *was* exactly what Norman felt anytime he tried to remember. An overwhelming sense of it. And to Jesse's great horror, much of it was directed at him.

"You sound like a religious kook," Jesse groaned whenever Norman tried to describe it. "Like a five-year-old named Colton who writes a book about visiting heaven after swallowing too much water in a pool."

"Okay," Norman would say. "Your feelings are clear."

"Except you would spell *Colton* with a *K* and an *H* like the store. Kohlton. And you'd be invited on *All Things Considered*."

Norman was certain he hadn't been to heaven, but Jesse's making light of it was verging on hell.

He jumped in his seat when Julia spoke again. "I'm seeing letters. *F. L.* And *A.* Do they mean anything to you?"

Norman sat very still, wondering if the question was rhetorical or if it was okay to speak. "Florida?" he finally asked. God help him if he'd spent the year there.

"No, wait. I'm seeing them in a mirror or something shiny. A fender, perhaps. The letters are *A-L-F.*"

This time Norman didn't wait to speak. "My last name is Alfano. If that's what you're seeing, you're halfway there." It was a simple enough parlor trick, what she was doing; Lally had made the appointment, perhaps she had given Norman's name.

Julia soured, placing her palms down on the table, like she might use them to push herself out of her chair and walk away. Instead she arched a single eyebrow. "Are you so sure about that?"

Since the woman's eyes remained closed, Norman rolled his. He took stock of the room—the beaded curtain, the peeling wallpaper, the 1950s stove with two doors, one that read *Grillevator* (whatever a Grillevator does), and the tin ceiling, which seemed more New England than California dust bowl—before settling again on his chair, shifting his weight to balance himself and sit with a more rigid posture. The floor was sagging, that much he could tell. Soon she would need to hire a contractor to shore the foundation. "What else might it be?"

Julia ran her hands over the tablecloth as if she were smoothing it. Eventually she said, "That's not how this works. That's for you to tell me."

"Alien life-forms? Is that what you're seeing?"

"Is that what *you're* seeing?"

Norman knew what he should be seeing if that were the case; he'd sat through plenty of science fiction movies. But he had no recollection of being on board an alien craft, or otherwise being studied or (*gulp*) probed. Of course, *ALF* could mean other things. He and Lally had learned it also stood for *assisted-living facility* when they had discussed what might become of their parents. Maybe that was where he needed to be. Locked away. Perhaps that was better for him than being here. "I don't know what I'm seeing. I'm begging you, I need help."

Julia opened her eyes. Norman recognized her expression from his mother. Firm, but not unsympathetic. "Our thoughts don't communicate linearly, Mr. Alfano. Fractured is memory. I can only give you what I see."

"Norman," he corrected, wanting to steer her away from the ALF of it all, and also because he hoped it would humanize him, rally her to his side. "I've been somewhere for a year and I have no memory of where."

Julia nodded slowly, then shook her wrists to jangle her bracelets. "Perhaps it's not an issue of where. Perhaps it's an issue of when."

Norman placed his hands over his nose and mouth and exhaled.

"Not all thoughts are connected. Human beings have feelings, we can dream, we have memories, we can experience depression. We lead rich emotional lives. At least those of us fortunate enough do. But even with our advanced prefrontal cortical development we don't always know what we're participating in here. Extrasensory perception is off-putting to many people. Scary. I can only give you what you are giving me. I'm listening. It might do you good to do the same."

She was right. It calmed him somewhat, the idea of her as a participant and not a leader in this. A medium to conduct the message, not write it. They were in this together, he and Julia, a flimsy triangle with the unknown as a powerful apex. He might not leave here with the answers he desired, but he certainly wouldn't leave here knowing less than he did when he walked in, because it was impossible to know less than nothing.

"Okay." Norman glanced up at the tin ceiling, wondering if they would have more success outside. If the tin ceiling itself wasn't blocking crucial signals they needed. After all, some with a loose grip on reality wore tin foil hats. But he knew better than to suggest it, just as he knew what she would say. Too much psychic contamination in an open space. A plane passing by filled with anxious passengers. The mailman and his deepest thoughts. A squirrel running on a telephone wire overhead. God help him if she said *nuts* in place of *fruit*. "I'm ready this time. Let's go again."

Julia crinkled her forehead but didn't chastise him taking command. Instead, she reached out and placed her hands in his, and then all fell quiet again.

For what seemed like an eternity.

Norman cleared his head of everything but the warmth of the light. He tried not to think of it as love; she'd already picked up on that. But as something else equally enchanting. *Beginnings*, perhaps. A fresh start. Something had attracted him to it when it shone down in their yard that night; something had filled him with profound gratitude when it delivered him back. He sat in emotion rather than thought. And when he had been able to do all that, Julia spoke.

"The warmth. I feel it." She squeezed his hands tight, urging him not to move so much as a hair on his body. "There's a collision. No, an explosion. And then so many stars. Racing. And I don't know what this means, but maybe you do. *Father.*"

Norman felt a rush of cold air over his body that made his pores contract. If she was right, maybe he had been with god this whole time.

"Father?" Lally asked, gripping the steering wheel angrily with both hands. She was scanning the road for someplace with a restroom. "She just went there? And you paid her full fee?"

"And then some."

"You *tipped*?"

"Her fee structure is for, like, a Pomeranian," Norman argued. "I figure a human has to be more complicated."

Lally glanced at him skeptically. "A human, yes. *You*? No."

Norman rested his head against the passenger window. "I can't be in the doghouse forever. One of these days Jesse will have to forgive me."

Lally checked the Laredo's speedometer and said, "Okay, go over it again."

Norman closed his eyes and listened until he could hear Julia's voice. "Collision. Explosion. Then stars, so many stars. Racing across the sky. And then, father. But she didn't know what that meant."

Lally crinkled her face. "Did she know what *any* of it meant?"

"It's obvious, isn't it?"

They passed a gas station, but it had long since gone out of business. "*Is it?*"

Norman thought it was. "The big bang? Atoms colliding. An explosion. Stars, so many stars, racing across the sky. It's the origin of the universe."

"She said that. Across the sky."

"She simply said 'racing,'" Norman corrected himself. "But where else do stars race? And then father. I mean, it's god, right? Do you think I was shown the origins of *everything*?"

"Yeah, because you're so special. You're like every American who thinks Jesus is coming back in their lifetime because he just has to meet them. Been dead for two thousand years, but he just has to see Denise from Missouri."

"Perhaps I am god," Norman speculated. God comes down to Earth as a mortal to see what it's all about.

Lally slapped the steering wheel so hard it honked the horn. "Like that George Burns movie they played on cable when we were kids? Oh, you'd like that, wouldn't you."

"Maybe I created the universe."

"Yeah, if you did I have notes." Lally was definitely speeding now.

"I mean, I *am* an architect. It makes a certain amount of sense."

"Like zebras," Lally said. "Are they just gay horses?"

"Slow down."

"No, this is fun," Lally protested.

Norman pointed at the road. They were fast approaching a red light. "No, I mean *slow down*."

Lally stepped on the brakes, and they came to a stop just in time. "You'd think fifty-nine wouldn't be too fast for someone who'd traveled space and time to witness the big bang."

Norman scratched his chin and flipped down the visor to see in the mirror if he was developing a rash. It had been a few days since he'd shaved. He was surprised at how white his beard was. He couldn't have shaved while he was gone. How did he not return with a long white beard looking like Rip Van Winkle? A white beard would only make him more godlike, not less. And then it dawned on him.

"What?" Lally asked. "You have that look." The light turned green and slowly they picked up speed on the 62.

"There's another explanation, a much simpler one."

Lally turned to Norman, eager to hear it.

"It's also the story of me and Jesse."

DAY THIRTY-SEVEN

Norman spent the better part of two weeks at his desk on a desperate hunt for meaning. He was right in recognizing that the pet psychic's reading could have easily been the origin story of them as the origin story of everything. Collision, stars, father. It mirrored how they met on the beach, crashing into each other, Jesse's first word to him ("Dad"), and the story Jesse shared about racing the Chicken & Stars. But it was the *A-L-F* of it all that he fixated on. It had to be more than his name. It had to illuminate a part of this saga.

But what could it represent? A beginning? As the first letter in the alphabet it was certainly that. Alpha? From the Greek? Maybe she was seeing *alf* phonetically. *Alph.* For a long time Norman had been the alpha of their relationship, although it felt like a crown that had recently been passed. Aleph in the Hebrew alphabet often signaled oneness or unity, which he was hoping to find in his relationship, but it could also represent the beginning of creation, so that didn't clear anything up. In Old Norse, *álf* was *elf.* Given Jesse's height, Norman crossed that off his list as a nonstarter. But also *oaf*, at which Norman thought: *No comment.*

He tried his best to enlist Jesse's help with his research, but Jesse had already moved on, other than to say he should get his new crop of students to write a story about a pet psychic—plenty of humor to be mined in the prompt. He referenced a new kid named Slacks whose family bred chinchillas who he thought might relish the assignment.

Norman thought he might be able to foster closeness with Jesse more easily if they could just get away from the scene of his perceived crime. A romantic weekend was just what they needed. And so he planned the perfect getaway.

"Do you feel like you're being taken?" Norman asked. He glanced over at Jesse in the passenger seat of their Jeep, his eyes covered with the Tempur-Pedic sleep mask that for more than a year sat neglected on Norman's nightstand. Before Norman's departure they had traded it off and on during periods of restless insomnia; total darkness suited neither of them now.

"Where's Liam Neeson when you need him?"

Norman ignored the quip. "Just sit tight. We're almost there."

"What I do have is a very particular set of skills," Jesse mumbled in his best Irish brogue.

Jesse made jokes like this when he was uncomfortable. Norman knew it was not the first time his husband wondered if he hadn't come back quite right. It wasn't just the forced hospital visit or the barrage of medical tests. It was a strange look in the kitchen, or the way Jesse would monitor what he ate, or once in the night when he rolled over to find Jesse, eyes wide open, staring, the whites of his eyes all that could be seen in the dark. Even Norman himself continued to spend time in front of the mirror looking for signs that he might have been swapped for someone, or some*thing*, else. Alas, everything he saw was far too human—a body falling prey to age.

"What are you doing?" Norman asked when he saw Jesse adjust his mask.

"I'm counting the number of turns the Jeep makes in case I need to describe to the police where I am."

"Really?" Norman asked.

Jesse adjusted the mask again. "No, my nose just itches."

Their Jeep turned off the main road, crunching over gravel, before coming to a gentle stop on soft dirt. Norman killed the engine and everything fell quiet. "Okay, we're here."

Jesse swiveled his head to the side to look directly at Norman, who laughed. "I look like an idiot," Jesse complained.

"You look adorable," Norman corrected as he squeezed Jesse's thigh. The door opened and closed, and Jesse sat still as Norman ran around to his side. "This way," Norman said as he opened the passenger door and, not being able to see, Jesse had no choice but to take Norman's hand.

"This is just like *Phantom Thread*."

"*Star Wars*?" Norman asked. "I said no peeking."

Jesse groaned. "That's *Phantom Menace*. *Phantom Thread* is the Daniel Day-Lewis movie where he plays a tortured dressmaker. Vicky Krieps poisons him to keep him dependent on her, and therefore nicer."

"Vicky *who*?"

Jesse wriggled annoyingly as they took their last few steps over uneven ground. "Krieps! Sounds like *creeps*. HOW DO YOU NOT KNOW VICKY KRIEPS?" He shimmied, trying to shake the mask off. "We watched the Criterion Collection."

That all sounded vaguely familiar, but Norman was near his wit's end. "Okay, fine. Just remove the mask."

Jesse hesitated, suddenly afraid of what he might see.

"What's the matter?"

"I don't want to."

Norman growled and flipped the mask up on one side, exposing Jesse's left eye. At first Jesse stared straight ahead like he thought this must all be some sort of trick; there was no way he could actually be seeing what emerged from the ground.

He pulled the rest of the mask off like Sam Neill clumsily removing his sunglasses in *Jurassic Park*, blinked a few times to adjust to the sun, shook his head to make sure he wasn't dreaming, and sure enough, he wasn't. "Oh, you're a fountain of atrocious ideas."

But it wasn't Norman's idea, it was Jesse's, and so Norman didn't want to hear any of his contempt. Instead, he jumped up and down like a schoolkid, gazing in awe. "It looks even better than it did in the photos!"

The bright orange saucer was named the Area 55 Futuro House, one of fewer than a hundred Futuro houses constructed worldwide from the designs of Finnish architect Matti Suuronen, who in the late 1960s wanted a design that would commemorate humans conquering space; it looked not unlike a flat pumpkin. The structure was perfectly round with oval windows dotting the circumference and appeared to be levitating off the ground (but was supported by a metal infrastructure underneath that looked not unlike a child's jungle gym). Large boulders were neatly arranged around it, adding to the illusion that it had just landed. Behind it, nothing. The house sat on five acres of land. Norman ran up to the front and punched in a code on a hidden keypad, and stairs descended with a soft hydraulic hiss, attached to the back of the aerospace door. It looked so much like a UFO from a movie, it was a miracle steam didn't pour out, followed by little green men. *We come in peace.*

"Can you believe it?" Norman exclaimed. "Right here in our

own—" He stopped short of saying *backyard* to avoid the PTSD of it all. "Right here in Joshua Tree."

"Oh, I can believe it," Jesse replied, doing his best to mask his own personal horror. He approached the structure with caution, as if it might be hot from reentering the atmosphere, if not downright radioactive.

Norman ran back to Jesse, gripping him by the shoulders and shaking him. "You showed it to me some time"—Norman proceeded carefully—"*before*. And you were right. How fun! It's ours for the next two nights." Jesse looked stricken, and Norman feared he had horribly miscalculated, so he quickly explained his reasoning. "It's an olive branch, okay? You and me. I'm not going anywhere again without you."

"You don't get it," Jesse said, shaking his head sadly. "I don't want to be dragged aboard the mother ship while you go off on your next adventure. I want to have faith that you'll stay here with me."

Norman accepted Jesse's words as the uncomfortable truth, but childlike enthusiasm won out. "I am staying here with you. For two nights." Norman smiled, then sprinted for the door, bounding up the steps two at a time.

Inside, the house was even more bonkers. Where benches didn't line the curved walls, a round bed did, waiting for characters from an Austin Powers movie to shag. Chairs were placed throughout, decorated with colorful throw pillows, beaded with alien faces and one with a large eyeball. The whole thing was run off solar panels, and Jesse flicked each switch and tested the outlets half expecting them to be dead; instead, a soft pink light bathed the open room, and the coffee maker blinked twelve o'clock. The bathroom was outdoors, something he threatened to make Norman pay for, saying he couldn't imagine lowering the hydraulic door to descend the stairs into the night just to pee—he'd never be heard from again; they agreed to piss in the sink. There was no TV, but there were Bluetooth speakers and shelves with old books and games. He mused that this might be a trap, that maybe this *was* the mother ship and just as Norman lulled Jesse into a false sense of calm by making him a martini and promising to stay, the whole thing might whir to life. But once he rapped his knuckles on the wall and got a hollow response, at least that one worry was put at ease.

"They have Wingspan!" Norman exclaimed, pointing at a shelf. He peeled open the box and studied its contents. "The directions are gone." They both laughed, as anyone who tried to play this game without the directions was truly fucked. "And some of the wooden eggs are jelly beans. That's . . . *disgusting*." It had been six months since Easter.

Jesse agreed to play anyway, mumbling that a game seemed safer ground than any other activities Norman might have planned, especially given the way Norman was eyeing the round bed. "But I want credit for playing."

Norman cocked his head, confused. "What do you mean, credit?"

"I don't know what you're hoping to get out of this weekend, but I don't want to be blamed when it goes south."

Why would it go south? Norman desperately wanted to know, but he kept his mouth tightly shut.

They settled into their game with a bottle of wine, Roberta Flack singing contemplative lyrics in her warm voice through the speakers as they assembled their bird habitats. It was nice for a time, like they were immersed in their old lives. When there were only two turns left in this round, and Norman was taking forever to plot his next move, Jesse blurted, "How do you not know what you're going to do?" He was frustrated, he always knew his next four.

Norman understood Jesse was talking about the game, but his own concern was much bigger. He didn't know what Jesse's next move was going to be. Forgive him, leave him, punish him, ignore him—the options were overwhelming. One move he did know: Forcing Jesse to decide just because Norman hated living in limbo was not a winning strategy.

Jesse eventually stood from the table and wandered to the bookshelf to study its sparse collection. He pulled a copy of *Rabbit, Run* off the shelf. "John Updike once wrote that every marriage tends to have an aristocrat and a peasant. Do you think that's true?"

"A *pheasant*?" Norman asked, lost in his bird cards.

Jesse didn't respond; instead Norman observed him deep in the sentiment. Jesse was behaving like the aristocrat now, Norman the peasant, flailing trying to please his overlord. He even felt a little pathetic, hunched over the table as he was, pretending to decide whether to use his turn to get food or lay eggs, whether to play hard or to throw the game, which would result in a more pleasing weekend. Maybe that was the appeal with Orson, with someone younger. Jesse squarely fit in the aristocrat role he had grown into. Updike didn't say so explicitly, but maybe two aristocrats as a pair were disastrous.

"Your turn," Norman called, summoning him back to the table after securing two eggs and laying them on a bird with a stick nest.

"Ah, the old stick nest strategy," Jesse said like it was some sort of master chess move. He clung to the Updike book, like he might read it later in the hammock instead of using the time, as Norman hoped, to reconnect.

Roberta was singing "The First Time Ever I Saw Your Face,"

Norman's favorite. Norman sang along. "The first time ever I kissed your mouth, the earth moved in my hand."

Jesse bit his tongue, but it didn't stop him from speaking. "The last time you kissed me I felt resentment you didn't take out the garbage. But Roberta Flack doesn't sing about that."

Norman shook his head sadly. That had just been the previous night.

"Stop," Jesse instructed.

"Stop what?" Norman asked, trying his best to sound innocent.

"Looking so forlorn." Norman couldn't, and so Jesse lost his patience. "I'm still allowed to make jokes." He grabbed his wine and hit the button to lower the stairs.

Outside the sun was setting. Norman followed at a safe distance, like a puppy that had just been kicked. Jesse led him to the covered outdoor kitchen, where they sat on a bench facing the mountains. They sat for a time, not saying anything, until Jesse had finished his wine.

"I actually understand why you left."

Norman wanted to say he didn't leave, or rather he didn't know what he was doing was leaving, but thought better than to protest.

"You wanted more. The purpose of life is discovery. Exploration. It's why we're all here. To find meaning. To understand. In some ways *you* made the morally defendable choice."

"Thank you," Norman said, because it felt like an olive branch. The heavens had been a dream of humankind ever since the first cave dwellers looked up, dazzled by stars. He couldn't be faulted for that. That wasn't really why Norman went, that wasn't what attracted him to the light. But he knew enough not to say that on what could be the verge of reconciliation.

"But I actually liked all the mundane routines of our marriage. Making coffee. Going for walks. Laughing at movies we both enjoyed. Playing Wingspan. You know, life. Wanting that to continue, that's a valid choice, too."

Norman felt defensive and sat forward in his chair, nervously rubbing his wrists as if he'd just been freed of handcuffs. "I know, and that's what I want."

Jesse dipped his head. Norman always treated life like a sprint through each day, excited for the exhaustion of evening. Jesse was more tortoise than hare, stopping to enjoy life's pleasures. They would arrive together at the dinner table, often with little of interest to say. "So you say *now*."

Abruptly, Jesse stood and removed his shirt. He fired up the gas grill in the outdoor kitchen before unbuttoning his pants. He kicked them free of his feet and stepped off the platform where they had been sitting.

"Where are you going?" Norman asked. It looked like he was going to burn his clothes and walk into the desert, never to return.

"To cool off," Jesse replied, wandering in the direction of the outdoor shower. "You can explore something to make us for dinner." Norman watched him the whole way, unable to peel his eyes from Jesse's naked body.

Norman made two steaks and a balsamic reduction in a little pan, and asparagus he cooked on the grill in a foil pouch. They ate outdoors by candlelight as the sun set. Norman cranked up the speakers from inside the house, Nina Simone this time, no silent disco required—there was no one around for miles. Stars appeared in the sky one after the other in rapid succession; it was like watching celestial popcorn kernels explode. The steak was cooked exactly as Jesse liked, just a hair shy of medium. If he was looking for another reason to be mad at Norman, Norman took some pleasure in knowing he had come through. And eating outdoors always made food somehow taste better. Jesse was famished, that much was obvious; he was nearly done before Norman had cut his third bite.

"Good?" Norman asked, and Jesse nodded.

"Good." In that moment, he might have even been speaking of them.

Norman refilled Jesse's glass with the Spanish wine, a Tempranillo he'd selected. "It feels good to be present."

Jesse looked at him as he sipped his wine. "Interesting choice of words."

"You know what I mean." Lally was at home with Mafalda. It was just the two of them. No chores, no to-do list, no bills, no outside world. Just the two of them under the sky.

"Yeah, I do," Jesse agreed. For years in their relationship Jesse had failed to fully share his thoughts and curiosities. It was his work, Jesse would try to explain. "When you're writing a book you're living two lives." That made it difficult to be fully present in one. "That's the tragedy of love, isn't it?"

"What is?"

"That it always devolves into two people both wanting more than another person could reasonably give."

Norman sat with those words for a quiet moment. "Is that John Updike?"

"No," Jesse said. "That's me." He gently set his fork down on his plate. "Look. I know you want things to go back to how they were."

"But I don't," Norman protested. "I want to move forward someplace better."

"But maybe that's not together. Thirty years is a good run. Remember when we first came out? We didn't even know if we would live to *be* thirty, let alone be with someone for that long. We accomplished so much together. Perhaps it's time to see what we can do apart."

"Is that how you really feel?" Norman asked, trying to mask his heartbreak.

"I don't know how I feel," Jesse said, finishing his glass of wine. This time Norman didn't refill it. Jesse stared into his empty glass and asked, "Do you regret stepping into that light?"

Norman waited until he was certain he had Jesse's full attention. "I do not, because the light is what brought me back to you."

They sat in the uncomfortable sincerity until a coyote howled in the distance and Norman finally understood. This was not a choice between Norman and Orson, or Norman and someone new. For Jesse, this was a choice between Norman and himself.

Norman gathered the plates just as Jesse grabbed the rest of Norman's filet with a fork, nearly stabbing his hand in the process. Norman glared at him.

"Well, the coyotes can't have this."

Norman pointed to the wineglasses for Jesse to carry, and the bottle, which was not yet empty; the coyotes could not have that, either. "Are we going to finish this game?" he asked, referring to the Wingspan boards set up inside; they still had two more rounds.

A more loaded question had never been asked.

DAY FORTY-FIVE

It was time. Norman pushed back his chair and clinked his glass of champagne with a fork to get the party's attention. He stood and looked at the ragtag group he'd assembled around his dining table; as they quieted and looked his way, he placed one hand in his pocket to fiddle with the ring he'd stashed there. His heart racing, he knew it was now or never. "Jesse," he began.

In hindsight, throwing a dinner party was ill-advised. But it was something they had loved doing before their move to the desert, and Norman thought it might help them feel like their old selves. In Venice, they had prided themselves on curating their guest lists. A city councillor or state senator might be seated next to a poet. A local busker might play the guitar, while their accountant chopped parsley. Not everyone knew each other, but everyone had something to contribute to the symphony, and the resulting dinners would sing. After a hard sell, Jesse reluctantly agreed to Norman going ahead with his list. "But only if you invite the pet psychic. And if she can't guess the menu, she doesn't eat."

It turned out the actual guest list was much worse.

"You invited my *mother*?" Jesse screeched the night before the party. Norman was already hard at work on dessert, individual lemon poppy seed Bundt cakes he was preparing to put in the oven.

Norman held his ground. There was always a guest that made Jesse reluctant, a wild card who more often than not surprised them by making the night. Would that wild card this time be Gail? Probably not. But he was trying to foster a sense of family.

"Without telling me?"

"I'm telling you now. Also, I invited Randall."

"*Randall* Randall? Our neighbor Randall?"

"Actually, I think his last name is Moss."

"I know his last name is Moss. Why?"

Norman portioned the last of the batter into the little pans before offering Jesse the spoon to lick, which he declined. "Your mother needed a dinner partner."

"Dinner partner? What is this, the Gilded Age?"

"I would like a dinner partner," Lally stated, materializing out of thin air. Jesse jumped. She had taken to spending so much time in their guest room that they often forgot she was there. She gladly relieved her brother of the spoon, squealing when she tasted the batter.

"You're *growing* a dinner partner," Jesse sniped. Lally failed to verbalize a response given the spoon in her mouth, but she was not pleased. Suddenly, Norman snatched the spoon back.

"Ow!" Lally cradled her mouth. "I think you chipped a toof."

Norman apologized. "I don't think you're supposed to have raw batter in your condition."

Lally frowned. "My pregnancy is not a 'condition.'"

To placate her, Norman suggested she invite Harlan, even though he still wasn't entirely clear of their relationship status. Lally said she would think about it, which didn't clarify anything.

"Randall *and* my mother, really? What are you thinking, they might fall in love? Get married? She made her money in a toy box, so she can live in a toy house?"

"Why does it have to be anything other than maybe she'll have fun?" Norman dumped the mixing bowl in the sink with an annoyed *clang*. "Maybe we could *all* just have some fun."

"I could use some fun," Lally agreed, and she slunk back to her room to call Harlan.

"Is this going to be another gourd farmer situation?" Norman asked Jesse once they were alone. Lally had never really had much luck on the romance axis.

Jesse shrugged. "She seems quite taken with him." Norman was annoyed that he was not willing to engage more than that. The oven beeped and he slid his little cakes in.

By Saturday afternoon they were ready to entertain in fashion. Or, Norman was, as he had done the lion's share of the prep work. Jesse wore an overwrought expression while doing the bare minimum, his mouth slack as he folded cloth napkins.

"What's wrong?" Norman asked when he noticed Jesse grimacing. Jesse swore it was just a headache, and Norman gave him two Advil and told him to lie down. He noticed Jesse taking three Excedrin several hours later before showering; apparently the Advil hadn't done the trick. He dressed and plastered on a brave face to meet guests, but to Norman's trained eye, his expression was tortured and off, like an architectural rendering without any doors.

Luisa Flores, the English Department head at COD, was the first to arrive. She was perhaps an unlikely guest, but after the wedding, where Norman first fully appreciated Jesse's abilities as a teacher, he insisted Jesse invite someone from work. And Norman thought Jesse's return to the classroom was a good thing, something that had given his life structure while Norman was gone; he wanted to see it continue.

"My husband couldn't make it," she said when Jesse answered the door, handing her host a bottle of wine and pushing her way to the kitchen. She sniffed the air and found whatever was cooking to be agreeable. "That's a lie. He could have made it. I didn't want him to."

Norman was hard at work in the kitchen, where he'd spent much of the afternoon blanching and peeling tomatoes, smashing garlic, and pitting olives for his puttanesca. The simple act of sautéing chopped onion in olive oil was enough to transform the home. He'd even come around on the ferns in the planter and was looking forward to company joining him in the kitchen.

"Norman, I'd like you to meet Luisa, my boss."

"Luisa!" Norman exclaimed, wiping his hands on his apron before offering to shake. He shot Jesse a look. *Oh no. She's without a dinner partner.* Still, he welcomed her warmly with a glass of wine, and she volunteered to help cook.

"Where's Mafalda?" Luisa asked Jesse before turning to Norman. "You should see him in the faculty lounge. He talks about the dog all the time. He must have a thousand pictures on his phone." Norman wondered if Jesse ever spoke about him. And their only photo together of late was the one Lally took of the three of them in the Hi-Desert Medical Center waiting room.

Jesse informed her Mafalda was in the bedroom, but assured Luisa they would bring her out later to meet guests. He knew Norman too well, as he then whispered, "Don't be jealous of the dog."

Norman was saved by a knock at the door.

"Oh good, you're back," Gail said to Norman when he greeted her at the door. She tossed him the jacket draped over her arm. "How was your visit to Mars?"

Norman responded with half a hug. "It's good to see you, too, Gail."

Harlan was more polite when he finally showed, but a half step off the beat—something everyone realized when he brought the wrong wine. (It didn't bother Lally; she wasn't drinking.) He shook Norman's hand vigorously, giving him a skeptical glance up and down. "So you're the infamous Norman," he said, like Norman had been right under his nose the whole time. Norman wondered if he was one of those people who erroneously used *famous* and *infamous* interchangeably, but somehow didn't think so. Harlan then squinted as if waiting for an answer to the great mystery of Norman's whereabouts. Thanks to Randall, Harlan wasn't the only straight man in the mix, and Norman rushed to introduce them. Apparently, the two of them had started off on the wrong foot when his neighbor had caught Harlan red-handed spying on Jesse with Lally, and Randall seemed suspicious still. Jesse had to assure him it was water under the bridge. Randall called Harlan "Impala" all night, and Jesse smiled with recognition; he wasn't the only one who appreciated a good nickname.

Norman watched Randall pull Jesse aside. "I don't think we should welcome him into the fold," he said of Harlan.

Jesse, for his part, looked confused. "Are *you* in the fold?"

Norman stifled a laugh. At their old parties, Jesse would go out of his way to make everyone feel welcome, but tonight something was off. Jesse even seemed less spirited with Gail, and so Norman begged him away to the kitchen. "Are you all right?" Norman asked, and Jesse rubbed his temples like his headache persisted.

"Sorry. I don't feel like myself."

Norman poured him some water.

People gathered in the kitchen for bruschetta, which Norman served on slices of toasted baguette. Randall eyed the open planters in front of the island with suspicion. "Can you believe this?" Gail said, gesturing like it was a gaping hellmouth to the underworld. "And that one's supposed to be an architect."

"You should have seen it before," Jesse said, referring to the old cactuses. He kept the wine flowing, and it helped everything except maybe his headache. The doorbell rang one more time, and Jesse took a quick head count. Everyone they were expecting was here.

He answered the door reluctantly.

"Jesse del Ruth," the man said, and it took Jesse a moment to place the dashing Asian man on his doorstep as his literary agent, a man he hadn't seen in person in years.

"Brian Leung? What are you doing here?"

"YOU'RE BACK," Brian emphatically exclaimed. Norman looked up at the exclamation. He was the one who had been gone, but Brian seemed to be addressing Jesse.

Jesse seemed equally confused. "Excuse me?"

"Your new book! It's one hell of a barn burner."

For years, Jesse had been ducking his calls or making excuses, and he just assumed Brian had long since dropped him. "I sent it to you on a whim. I wasn't even sure you still represented me."

"Of course I still represent you. And I'm going to get you one hell of a deal."

"Brian?" Norman appeared over Jesse's shoulder, ushering the unexpected arrival inside. "What is this about a new book?"

"Jesse didn't tell you?"

Norman tried to mask the hurt on his face; Jesse looked down at his shoes. They would have to get into it later.

"Perfect timing. We have a dinner guest in need of a partner. Here. Have some bruschetta and wine."

Brian was confused by the chaos he was joining, but also

strangely delighted. Norman began to introduce him around, but Brian stopped him. "You don't need to do that." He was used to Manhattan's literary dinner parties and was more than capable of introducing himself. Jesse set an egg timer and put it on the counter next to Norman.

"What's that for?" Norman asked. He quickly counted the pots on the stove to see if he'd forgotten something.

"We have until the main course before I get the inevitable question." He didn't need to say what that was. Norman understood. *What are you working on next?*

After all eight of them were seated at the dining table, conversation zigzagged. Gail tortured Lally with horror stories about ill-behaved children who came into the Toybox, while Randall announced he was finally ready to break ground on a house, joking it was payback for the inconveniences Jesse and Norman's endless renovation had caused him. Brian discussed the success of Jesse's previous book with Luisa, who was excited to hear he might be publishing again, as she was thinking of retirement next year and she wanted to recommend that Jesse become department chair.

"The soup is incredible," Brian raved when there was a lull in conversation.

Norman beamed. Finally, appreciation from someone, even if only for minestrone. "It's amazing what one can do with a few simple ingredients."

"Is this Mom's recipe?" Lally asked. It was, although Norman had tweaked it with pasta and extra fennel. He told the table there were as many recipes for minestrone as there were Italian families.

"Lally is *your* sister?" Randall asked Norman, trying to keep everyone straight. Indeed there should have been an org chart.

"Jesse is an only child," Gail offered.

"Something he no doubt blames you for," Brian said with a wink.

Gail slurped her soup in agreement.

"On the bright side, at least I'm her *favorite* child." Jesse smiled at the others, thinking himself quite clever.

"Well, I wouldn't go that far," Gail replied.

"Excuse me. If I'm your only child, by default that makes me your favorite."

His mother fidgeted uncomfortably with the napkin in her lap. "By default, that also makes you my least favorite."

Norman and Randall laughed, but Lally, the mother-to-be, sank uncomfortably deeper into her chair.

"What is wrong with you? Just say I'm your favorite."

"I can't do that."

Jesse dropped his spoon and it clattered in his bowl, sending drops of soup over the side.

"I can't! I don't play favorites. You know that." Gail dabbed at the tablecloth with her napkin where Jesse had spilled, making him further seethe. "Norman. Okay? Norman is also my child. And *he* can cook."

"Not anymore! Norman and I are divorced," Jesse announced to shocked looks from the table. Luisa, however, ever mindful of her own marital woes, clapped.

"On paper," Norman was quick to clarify.

"What do you think divorce is?" Jesse asked. "Marriage is paper, divorce is paper."

"Ah, a romantic," Harlan said.

"A book is paper," Brian inserted, perhaps already counting the commission he would make on a large new publishing deal. And then he whispered to Harlan, "It's a good thing he doesn't write romance."

"Be that as it may," Gail continued. "I don't want to pick between you two."

Norman's heart raced, and he pushed back his chair and pulled a bottle of champagne from a bucket. He poured eight glasses and handed them out, including to Lally. He then clinked his glass with a fork and stood. It was now or never. "Well, Jesse. You're *my* favorite. And I have something I'd like to say before we have our main course." He shoved one hand in his pocket to feel for the ring. "Jesse. From the moment we first collided I knew you were the one for me."

"Oh god," Jesse muttered, and he pressed his temples again. Not the response Norman had been hoping for, but he forged ahead.

"In fact, it seemed we were on a collision course our whole lives. Destined in some way. I don't want some midlife crisis to overshadow the fact that we were meant to spend our lives together." He pulled the ring out of his pocket and dropped down to one knee.

"Is that my wedding ring?" Jesse gave an incredulous gasp.

"Yes. Yes, it is."

He took it from Norman and held it up to a candle to see. "Where did you find it?"

"What difference does that make, where I found it? I'm kind of in the middle of something here."

"I tore this house apart looking for it!"

Norman could see that this was a huge lapse in judgment, but since he was already down on one knee he really had no choice but to press on. Lally took pity on her brother and gave a supportive nod, while Luisa buried her hands in her curls. He took a deep breath and then asked, "Will you marry me . . . *again*?"

"I don't believe this." Jesse looked around the table to see if others were hearing this, too. "Is that what this last year was, a midlife crisis?"

Using his eyes, Norman pleaded with Jesse to remain calm. "We don't need to get bogged down in the details in front of company."

"YOU LEFT!" Jesse shouted. He looked around the table at everyone, who seemed genuinely surprised by his outburst, except for his mother, who was never one for grand romantic gestures of this sort and seemed put out to have witnessed it. "Oh my god. That's what this whole dinner was about?"

"I thought since we had those closest to us here . . ."

"Oh, you mean the conspiracy theorist from across the street and the private detective that was hired to find you?"

Harlan cleared his throat. "That seems a little rude."

"I agree with Impala," Randall echoed.

Jesse glared. "I'm sorry. Friendly fire."

Gail finally interjected. "Just take him back so we can have puttanesca." She looked at her watch as if she had someplace better to be. "You know you're going to."

Jesse threw his napkin onto the table. "No. No, I don't know that. And neither do you!"

Gail for once backed down. "Well, I suppose that's true."

"Are we allowed to drink this?" Luisa asked Brian, lifting her champagne.

Norman scrambled to find an ally or convert someone to his cause. "Gail, if Jesse's father were here, you'd take him back." As Norman spoke, he realized he was still down on one knee.

Jesse's mother gestured at the motley assortment of guests seated around the table. "I'm surprised he isn't!"

"Mom, that's enough."

Gail made a sour face and turned to Norman to answer his question. "No, of course I would not take him back. He'd be so *old*."

"YOU'RE OLD!" Jesse gripped the side of the table so hard Norman worried he might break it. Randall and Lally, meanwhile, shifted in their seats like they did not appreciate hearing a mother spoken to like that, Lally looking particularly aghast. It was always uncomfortable to witness another family's complicated dynamic. Lally reached for her champagne.

"I got old over time. Slowly, like a normal person. Your father would be old all at once. That's a totally different situation. Besides. We only knew each other for two years, and he was overseas for most of that. What would we have in common?"

"ME!" Jesse clenched his teeth like his headache was now overwhelming.

Gail threw her hands up, absolving herself from this tantrum. Lally managed a sip of champagne before Harlan gently relieved her of the glass.

"Oh, let her have some," Gail said, observing this interaction. "Alcohol won't harm the child. Vaccines, maybe."

"Mother."

"What? He's being an overprotective father. She doesn't need that. And both of you should do your own research."

Harlan interjected. "Oh, I'm not the father."

"I'm sorry. I thought you were together." Gail scrutinized him, perhaps wondering why he was here if they weren't together.

Lally made a gesture to indicate they were together-*ish*.

"Then who is the father?" Gail looked around the table, while Lally shot a panicked look in Jesse's direction. When Gail clocked this, she turned to Jesse, then to Lally, then back to Jesse again. "*Jesse?*"

Jesse pressed his palms hard against his eyes.

"*My* Jesse?"

Jesse mumbled, "I can explain."

Luisa turned to Brian, who likewise seemed to be playing catch-up. "Is this why they're divorced?"

Gail was incensed. "I'M GOING TO BE A GRANDMOTHER?" Instead of excitement, there was pure rage.

"Didn't you own a toy store?" Lally asked, uncertain how anyone could welcome this as bad news.

"Norman, get up." Gail instructed him to stand with a wild gesture. He was still down on one knee. "You're making us all uncomfortable."

Norman clutched his chest. "*I'm* making *you* uncomfortable?" But he did as he was told and slipped back into his seat.

Randall, who was used to peace and quiet, did not know what to make of the situation. "So. When did you decide to put in a pool?"

"Oh, yes," Luisa said, looking out the glass wall. The pool lights had come on and the shimmering blue was calming. "The pool is lovely."

"*When?*" Jesse retorted, his ire moving across the table. "When you told me to dig up the yard!"

"I told you to dig up your yard?" Randall was clearly confused.

"Yes, when we were at Joshua Tree looking at the Milky Way." Norman looked at Jesse. When did they do *that*? "You were going on and on about the survival of humankind. The second suggestion. The second *option*. Something like that. I came home and started digging. And there's no refilling a hole of that size, so I had to put in a pool!"

"The second alternative?"

"Yes!"

Norman looked back and forth between Jesse and Randall, waiting for someone to explain.

"Friend, I was looking to help you with your relationship."

"*My* relationship?" Jesse was appalled. Randall would be the last person he would turn to for relationship advice. "Randall, no offense, but you're divorced and live in a tin can."

Randall, to his credit, seemed to take none. "It looked from the outside like you guys were having trouble."

Norman jumped in before Jesse could say something even more offensive. "What is the second alternative? What is the first alternative, for that matter?"

Harlan looked up, his interest suddenly piqued.

Jesse, however, didn't see the need to get bogged down in the details; he was still stuck on Randall playing couples counselor. "It has to do with the planet, or something."

Randall shook his head. "That's an oversimplification, but yes. It's a theory that a cabal of the world's most rich and powerful already know that Earth will soon become uninhabitable due to global warming and overpopulation and that something needs to be done to prepare for that day."

"That's all a myth," Gail informed them, pouring herself a second glass of champagne. "And those windmills? They're killing the birds and the whales."

Brian cocked his head. "The whales?" They were at least a hundred miles inland.

Randall continued, undaunted. "The first alternative is fixing the planet we currently inhabit, which, you know—good luck with that. Man's excesses are well past the point of redemption. But think detonating nukes in space to let heat and pollution dissipate."

Gail rolled her eyes.

"The second alternative is to go under the surface, build vast subterranean civilizations. The third alternative is leaving the planet to start anew. Colonize Mars. Jesse, you may have heard *dig deep*, but I meant within yourself."

"WHAT?" Jesse barked, not believing his ears.

"It was a metaphor, friend. The first alternative would have been to work on what you had together, let off some steam and see what could be salvaged. It didn't seem like Norman was around all that much, so that left the second alternative and that meant you dig deep inside yourself to see why."

Norman could not believe his ears. "And the third alternative is we break up?"

Randall shrugged. *If the shoe fits.* He looked rather pleased with himself, the metaphor nearly perfect.

Gail, now tipsy on champagne, seemed delighted. "You told him to dig deep in himself, and he took that to mean dig in the yard?"

"It seems that way," Randall confessed.

"And the only way to cover up this folly was to put in a pool?" Gail clapped her hands at the delight of it all. "Oh, that's too rich."

"I apologize if that wasn't clear." Randall turned to Brian for backup. "I thought writers were good with metaphor." But Brian was looking over his shoulder in the direction of the kitchen to see if that puttanesca might be coming.

"And what's after that?" Norman asked.

Gail was confused. "You mean, like put in a hot tub?"

"No. What comes after the third?"

Randall ran his fingers over his flattop. "Then you're out of alternatives, I'm afraid. You just have to stare down what's coming."

Norman felt defeated. To him that meant waiting to see what Jesse decided, if not just his marriage but his relationship was indeed over.

"Look on the bright side," Jesse began. "Thanks to me, at least you can sit by a pool while you do."

Norman grew red with anger. "I'll bet that sounded cuter in your head."

Jesse pushed himself back from the table and stormed outside to cool off. The rest of the party listened awkwardly as the sliding door to the yard opened and then closed. No one really knew what to say.

Except Gail, who said, "Maybe he's going for a swim."

"Should someone go after him?" Lally asked Norman. But Norman was in no mood.

"I'll go," Randall volunteered, and he politely excused himself. Another opening and closing of the sliding glass doors.

"Well," Lally said after more tense silence. "I've lost my appetite." Harlan took her hand and squeezed it. Gail reached again for the champagne and killed the bottle by pouring what was left into her glass. She downed it in a single gulp, and it was very clear it was not in celebration.

Just then, the egg timer dinged. "Say," Brian said, changing the subject. "Does anyone here know what Jesse's working on next?"

Norman cleared the soup course and retreated to the kitchen to salvage his puttanesca. As he braced himself at the sink, replaying what had just transpired, he remembered the security cameras in the backyard. He pulled the feed up on the iPad they kept on the counter. Randall and Jesse stood still as statues by the pool's edge, hands stuffed into their pockets. They were awash in blue ripples made by the pool water as it circulated over the submerged pool light. Norman fidgeted with the audio, but when he took the cameras off mute there was no sound. Randall was not a man uncomfortable in silence.

Eventually Jesse spoke first. "You were really instructing me to look inside myself?"

"You tell me."

On-screen, the blue light rippling across his face made Randall look not unlike the Force ghost of a Jedi master. "You know, I never really had a father," Jesse confessed. This caused Norman to lean in closer, listening.

"I heard."

"So I'm not really sure how these pep-talk things are supposed to go."

Randall's face softened as if he were taking pity on the younger man. "No pep talk. Sometimes things can have more than one meaning. That's all. But you know that."

Jesse stared into the pool. "Part of the appeal of Norman, at least when we met, was that he was older. He was stability personified. I would have vehemently denied it then, and probably every day until now, but I think not having a father—or specifically not ever knowing what happened to him, afraid the other people in my life might *disappear* into thin air—fucked me up more than I realized."

Randall stood on his toes to put one hand on Jesse's shoulder. "I think it fucked your mother up, too. You might want to go easy on her."

Jesse said something in return, but the audio was garbled.

"Can you guess the common denominator for all the world's problems?"

"Is it people?"

"Human beings," Randall confirmed. "And you know, gay, straight, young, old, left, right, at the heart we're not all that different. We all have the same root problems."

Randall removed his hand from Jesse's shoulder. The audio crackled again, before Randall replied, "I bet it'd feel good to tell him that and not me."

Jesse looked up at the sky and pointed. "Oh, look. The nighthawks are back."

Norman quickly closed the security camera's app and stood

there overcome with emotion. *The nighthawks are back.* And Jesse noticed. One of the last things he remembered was telling Jesse that mating season was over. Perhaps their return symbolized renewal. The start of a new season for them. Norman wiped the tears from his eyes when he heard footsteps behind him. It was Brian Leung.

"Give you a hand with dinner?"

"Sure thing," Norman said, because he was too embarrassed to say anything else. He started plating the puttanesca and sent Brian to the table with two servings. When he returned for more plates to serve, Norman thanked him. "I'm sorry you had to witness all this."

Brian laughed. "You should see my family. This is nothing."

Just then, from the dining room, they heard Gail cry, "YOU THOUGHT HE WAS A SERIAL KILLER?"

Norman raced to the table in time to see Jesse whisk his mother away. "A word, woman." He pulled her by the arm toward their bedroom.

Norman encouraged everyone to eat while their food was hot. "If you'll excuse me, I should just . . ." But he didn't say what *just* was. He then followed Jesse and Gail down the hall, watching as she entered the bedroom cautiously, as if she were afraid of what she might find.

"Problem?" he heard Jesse ask.

Norman snuck up to the open bedroom door and stood guard. He could just make them out in the mirror that rested atop their dresser, positioning himself just so until he was almost certain they could not see him. He promised himself he wouldn't eavesdrop on their *entire* conversation, but he wanted to be ready to intervene if needed, or throw himself on a grenade.

"I've never been in a gay man's bedroom. I was afraid it might be filled with apparatuses and lubricants. Or erotic art."

"You're not in a gay man's bedroom. You're in your *son's* bedroom. Can you just be cool with that?"

"Oh my god, there's a *wolf* in here."

Norman had forgotten about Mafalda in her crate, she'd been so well-behaved.

"Mother, that's enough."

Gail fell quiet as she focused on the crate. "She reminds me of Snowball. Do you remember that dog? That was a good dog."

"This is a good dog, too."

That seemed to put Gail somewhat at ease. "Remember your bedroom when you were a boy? You were so into fire trucks. I brought so many home from the store." Norman held his breath as Gail paused.

"Why do you keep me at such a distance? Why is it so difficult for you to just love me?" It was a question Norman could have easily asked him.

Gail sat on the edge of his bed, and Norman watched in the mirror as she stoically ironed her pants with her hands. "You're the one having a child and keeping it secret."

"I'm not having a child, Lally is having a child. I just happen to be . . ." Jesse joined her on the bed's edge as if he no longer had the strength to stand. What a mess. He sounded completely depleted. "I don't know what I happen to be. Life is not going as planned."

Gail reached over and placed a hand on his leg. "It never does."

They sat quietly, side by side, as intimate a moment as Norman had observed between them. They were quiet for so long, he almost crept away.

"Why is there a rolling pin on the floor? Or don't I want to know."

"It's for my feet."

"Your *feet*?"

"My feet. Any more questions?"

Then he heard what he assumed was Gail moving it with her toes until she was able to rest her own feet on the pin.

"Bad things happen to people, kiddo. That's just the way it is. I don't see any benefit in milking the situation. You need to understand that if you're having a child."

"I'm not having a chi—"

Gail cut him off. "It's because you remind me so much of him." And there it was, Norman thought. Jesse had spent so much of his life searching for his father, in his mother, in Norman, and once again all he had to do was look within. "Happy?" Gail asked.

"Yes, actually I am," Jesse admitted. From the hallway, Norman knew why. It was so much better than the alternatives. "That Randall is really something."

"Which one is Randall?"

"It doesn't matter." Norman watched as Jesse took his mother's hand. "Thank you."

"For what?"

"Being honest with me for once."

"I'm always honest with you," she said with a wry smile.

They fell quiet, and Norman did his damnedest to stifle a sneeze.

"Do you think Dad would have been happy being a father?"

"You asked me that before."

"You didn't answer me before."

This felt too private. Norman wanted to back away, but was frozen, terrified to move.

"There's really no way of knowing." Gail sighed. "But honestly? I think he would have been thrilled."

Norman watched as Jesse's whole face relaxed. The pinched expression he'd been wearing for twenty-four hours softened, and he lowered his shoulders, which had been raised almost since Norman's return.

Then, sincerity not her strong suit, Gail mumbled, "I don't know what this is supposed to be doing for my feet."

Jesse demonstrated rolling his feet back and forth and she tried it. She was not sold.

"Fix things with Norman," she said.

Norman's heart raced at the mention of his name.

"It's not that simple."

Gail shook her head. "It is that simple. Your husband came back."

It knocked the wind out of Norman; he could only hope it did Jesse, too. Despite her posturing, Gail was unfailingly human. A woman whose anger masked disappointment and a long-broken heart. He tried to read Jesse in the mirror. Indeed, he looked as if he were seeing his mother completely, maybe for the first time in his life. "Yeah," he agreed. Norman hoped more than anything that this was the yes he had been longing for.

It was enough to unfreeze his legs, and he backed away from the door. He returned to the table and took his seat, followed a moment later by Jesse and Gail. No one said a word, but they were all of them eating, appetites suddenly ravenous. And while he was pleased with the sense of family he got from his table, found though it may be, the evening didn't give him what he still desired most: A husband. Specifically his. Back.

BULLET THE BLUE SKY

DAY FORTY-SIX

Jesse sat bolt upright in bed, awakened by the strangest sense of déjà vu. He glanced over to see Norman sound asleep, having taken a sedative after their company left, leaving Jesse with a huge mess to clean in the kitchen after their disastrous night, not to mention an emotional quagmire to contend with, too. At least the cleaning had proved cathartic; he packed leftovers in perfect glass containers and stacked them in the fridge, the dishes fit almost mathematically in the dishwasher, and the largest pots he washed by hand. He thought sleep might come from pure exhaustion, and maybe it did for a time. Jesse's head still pounded and he wondered how many Excedrin was too many to take in one twenty-four-hour period. He removed the novel splayed open across Norman's chest; it went from the mundane to an apt metaphor, the Norman of late an open book. Mafalda was at the foot of the bed, between their feet, eyes open, and she raised a single brow with curiosity.

Harlan had fortuitously rented a hotel room for himself and Lally in Palm Springs so they could spend some needed time alone, and after dinner and more awkward chitchat they had left with his mother after calling to confirm that the hotel had an available room. Luisa confessed she was having second thoughts about retirement, and with the school's accreditation up for renewal maybe now was not the best time for a new chair. Brian gave Jesse clear marching orders to write exactly what had transpired that night—he'd never experienced a better family saga, on the page or off, and he didn't want to see Jesse wait another decade between books. No one said it, but it was agreed what Jesse and Norman needed most was space, and they all said rushed goodbyes before the dessert course. Jesse sent Randall home with six of the Bundt cakes and he seemed delighted to have them, asking if they would freeze. Now the house was eerily still.

Jesse reached for the water glass he usually kept bedside only to discover it wasn't there. Annoyed, he pulled back the covers and placed his feet on the floor, toying with the rolling pin before standing. Quietly, so as not to wake Norman, he made his way to the kitchen guided by moonlight, wearing nothing but Norman's old It-alien T-shirt—while it was still short, it fit him much better now; Mafalda followed behind him, her feet making a gentle *pat pat pat* on the concrete floors. Instead of water, he opened the freezer and went straight for the lemon gelato they never got the chance to serve. The first bite melted on his tongue, earthy and sweet. All those tubs of frosting, and he should have been eating this.

Since he was awake and the sugar was hitting, Jesse thought he should at least make use of the quiet by preparing a lesson; no doubt after tonight's performance, Luisa would certainly be auditing his next class. He was once again teaching humor writing alongside a full course load, which required careful juggling. Maybe if he finished the semester strong, he would still have a chance at department head; second thoughts or not, she could only warm the seat for so long. He went to the closet, where he'd stashed a messy pile of his work papers to clear the table for company, and was surprised to find a book wedged between a box and the wall. Even with his long arms, he could just graze it with his fingertips, and when he leaned farther his head pressed against the door and he heard a disconcerting pop in his neck and felt heat run down his side. But he was still able to wrestle the book free and was shocked to see what it was: *How to Be Funny in Eight Steps* by Peter Killjoy, the book Luisa had tried to assign his first class.

How did that get in here? Jesse wondered. He thought he'd thrown it away. Still, he picked it up, amused, both by how ugly the cover was and that it, like Norman, had made its return. He took it to the kitchen to read as he ate the rest of the gelato.

Jesse flipped open the book to chapter seven, which was enthusiastically titled *Use a Character Switch!* The man loved an unnecessary exclamation mark. Peter Killjoy began by saying in almost any given story there were multiple characters, usually with distinct points of view. The three little pigs are the vulnerable ones as they try to protect their houses. The Big Bad Wolf, however, is the aggressor, the menace.

No shit. Jesse looked for a logo on the spine to see who published such drivel. He felt inspired to write a strongly worded letter of complaint, even if he knew Brian would advise him against it. Why antagonize publishers when you're so close to publishing again? Still, Killjoy was living up to his name.

Jesse read on. Killjoy posited, what if in telling the story, the pigs were the assholes and the wolf the poor victim? Wouldn't there be humor to be found in that? Jesse rage-ate more gelato and massaged his sore neck. He closed the book, looking around for a place to put it. The junk drawer seemed apt, but he didn't want to see it every time he needed a Post-it or battery. As much contempt as he held for the book, he just couldn't see throwing it away. It was still, after all, a *book*. He tucked it aside to deal with later and opened his phone to make a note on his calendar app to bring some books to Goodwill. The logo next to the notes app was for the app Norman had used now more than a year ago to send signals into the sky. Looking back, he had a vague recollection of downloading it in the early days of Norman's disappearance and logging in on his phone—Norman had used their joint credit card and his password was not hard to guess. In his desperation, he thought maybe it would be a way to reach Norman, to send a few signals of his own; nothing much happened at the time. Tonight he opened it with great hesitation, even though he was far from a believer. He felt a slight tingle in his index finger as soon as he touched the widget, a sensation decidedly not radiating from his neck.

Mafalda growled, low and guttural; Jesse shushed her so that she wouldn't wake Norman. Then, after a moment of halting silence, he felt it, too, a violent jolt, and the whole house shook. Jesse grabbed the counter to keep from falling, the plastic lid to the gelato clattering onto the floor. Outside, sudden winds whipped through the remaining tamarisk trees, the branches of one hitting the side of the house with a steady and growing drumbeat, and water from the pool sloshed over the side. *Earthquake*, Jesse thought, and mentally scouted the nearest doorframes. But the house didn't have many doorframes. He reached for Mafalda, who darted under the table, and as he pursued her, he saw the light.

The light was soft and flattering, not blinding as he'd remembered, but there was no mistaking what it was. Almost as confirmation, it grew brighter, at first imperceptibly, as if someone were raising a dimmer switch with the gentlest touch. Jesse was at the sliding door to the yard, unaware of how he had arrived from the kitchen; the gelato spoon still dangling from his mouth was pushed sideways as he pressed his face against the glass.

A Character Switch. Peter Killjoy, you son of a bitch. Perhaps you know whereof you speak. Jesse thought he might have to revise his entire curriculum because there *was* something funny about this. Poetic even. Jesse pulled the spoon from between his gritted teeth and slid open the doors.

He was instantly bathed in the most perfect warmth. The comfort a lizard feels sunning himself on a rock. The tingling sizzle of a tanning bed. The heat he used to feel as the object of Norman's desire. The safety he once upon a time got from his mother. The feeling he used to get when he would imagine playing catch with his dad. Pool water evaporated into a fine mist, creating a fog that equaled the one in his head, but at long last his headache was gone. He felt total, embracing peace. Somehow he heard Richard Attenborough narrating the scene.

The specimen of Homo sapiens, *remarkable only for its unusual height, walks slowly into the light, unaware that its fate has already been sealed. The tousled bedhead and worn fabric covering his upper torso might to some feel part of a mating display, but in this mammal's case broadcasts a deep laziness. The watering hole would seem like a natural place for mammals to gather, but this representative of his species seems almost embarrassed by it, taking great steps to walk around it. He freezes in his tracks, sensing something watching him.*

The narration stopped abruptly as Jesse turned back to the house to see Norman standing just inside the door with an expression only he could recognize; it was the same expression that must have been plastered across his own face the night that Norman left. Pained. Shocked. He knew how this played out. Norman shook his head and mouthed, *Don't*. Mafalda, standing next to him, barked her own warning.

Jesse didn't know how to explain it, it was a just a feeling deep in his soul. *Fix things with Norman,* he heard his mother say. And it was true, Norman had found his way home. But now it was his turn. He felt the draw Norman had that first night. "I WANT WHAT YOU HAVE!" he shouted. He wanted trust. He wanted passion. He wanted to want profoundly everything he already had. He wanted to say yes to Norman's proposal. He wanted what used to be. He wanted to feel love again.

He wanted certainty. And if it was meant to be, he would find his way back.

Norman understood. He had to. But great sadness fell across his face, like this was an unnecessary exercise, one they might both regret. And there *was* a sadness to it, like cheating on someone as revenge for being cheated on yourself. No good could come from that. But how could it be a mistake? Norman himself said that it was the light that led him back to Jesse. And now it would lead Jesse back to him.

He hoped.

Jesse's eyes welled with tears as he stood at the very edge of the light, which kissed and tickled his skin. Every hair on his body stood on end. "I love you," Jesse whispered.

Not hearing him, Norman cupped his ear.

"I LOVE YOU!" Jesse cried. They were the last words he spoke before he felt his toes leave the ground. Norman darted from the house, Mafalda on his heels, but they were no match for the light, which pulled Jesse higher and held him tighter. *I should have brought pants,* he thought, bracing himself for certain embarrassment. No matter. *We begin our time here naked, we can finish it that way, too.* He looked down quickly one last time. Their house was a thing of beauty, a real oasis in the desert—the pool only added to its majesty; together they had built something remarkable. Why could he never have seen it like this before?

Then where his headache had been he heard an echo.

The faintest whisper.

Dad.

And then just as quickly as the light appeared, everything went dark.

Jesse flailed, his arms windmill blades desperately trying to keep him upright, but the battle was already lost. He was going to fall—and hard; on his skates he approached seven feet. He made a split-second decision to throw himself across the bike path as the beach looked softer on that side. The man coming straight at him swerved his bicycle, and might have just missed him if the front wheel hadn't skidded on a wisp of sand that sparkled in the blinding sun. A crash now inevitable, they both took the impact and fell onto the beach in a tangle of sweaty limbs.

Stunned, Jesse slowly opened his eyes, first one and then the other. Above him, the sun. Below him, warm sand that itched and scratched. On top of him, a stranger's perfect body weight protecting him like that lead apron at the dentist. Slowly the man propped himself up, his head alien and blocking the sun, until Jesse's eyes adjusted and he registered the most handsome smile, surrounded by a halo of golden sunlight.

The stranger was older by a half dozen years. Handsome in the way men are when they are no longer boys. His aviator sunglasses were bent but not broken. Dazed, Jesse couldn't help himself. "*Dad*," he said. The word just spilled out of his mouth.

The man laughed and took Jesse's face in his warm hands, looking for obvious scrapes. His skin smelled like bananas and coconuts. Jesse was suddenly very aware this stranger was straddling him. "Are you okay?"

Jesse was beet red and not from sunburn. "I don't know why I said that," Jesse confessed, still confused, but with a sense of strong déjà vu. *Dad? Really?* "Where am I?"

"Okay," the man said, helping Jesse to sit up. "We're going to get you to that lifeguard station and have them check you out. Think you can make it?"

They were at the beach, Jesse remembered, when he braced himself with both hands; he let rough sand fall through his fingers, as well as an unfortunate cigarette butt. He tilted his head to the sky and let the sun's rays warm his skin where the man's hands had just been. In the distance he could see surfers dotting the velvet blue of the sea. *This.* This was why he Rollerbladed at the beach. The perfect feeling of sunshine. On San Vicente he'd already have been smushed by a sedan or a coupe. "I'm fine. Really."

"Oh yeah?" the stranger asked with a flirtatious smile. He helped him to his feet and when Jesse stood to his full height the man uttered, "*Jesus.*"

He held a finger up to Jesse's eyes and moved it from left to right. Jesse asked what he was doing and the man copped to not knowing—it was something he'd seen Noah Wyle do on *ER*. He then asked Jesse what day it was, and he seemed unsure, so he asked Jesse to tell him something he was sure of.

"I like Thousand Island dressing on burgers, but not on salads."

The older man laughed, throwing his head back. "Can you walk in those things?" he asked, glancing down at Jesse's Rollerblades.

Jesse shook his head no. "Here. Hold on to my shoulders." He leaned down and unlaced Jesse's size fourteen blades. Jesse did as instructed and grabbed onto the stranger's traps, which were surprisingly meaty in his hands. "I saw you coming down the path," the man said as he pulled off the first Rollerblade. "You have really good form."

Usually, accepting a compliment for Jesse was like a soda machine trying to take a crumpled dollar that had been through the wash—it never quite took and eventually all parties abandoned the transaction unsatisfied. But in the moment he just felt embarrassed.

"Until I fell."

The other blade was now off and the man held it in his hands and studied it front to back; for Jesse, the sensation of wearing socks felt strange in the sand. "You can just say thank you."

"Thank you," Jesse repeated.

"Thank you, *Norman*." Norman leaned Jesse's blades against his bike. "C'mon," he said, gesturing in the direction of the lifeguard.

"C'mon, *Jesse*," Jesse said with his most adorable smirk.

They walked hand in hand toward the lifeguard station, Jesse wondering the whole way if his tenuous balance was the result of the collision or walking on sand or being vulnerable in front of a handsome stranger; he was happy to have Norman to hang on to.

The lifeguard gave Jesse a bottle of cold water, which he pressed to his forehead like a compress before chugging half. He then instructed them to sit in the shade of the blue lifeguard tower for observation.

They made small talk, and when Jesse felt woozy he placed his head on Norman's meaty shoulder. "Easy," Norman said, and he leaned his cheek against the top of Jesse's head, and they sat like that, quiet and connected, until Norman asked him if he saw stars.

JOSHUA
TREE

The flashes popped with light so blinding, Jesse half expected old glass flashbulbs to shatter at the photographer's feet, and he worried about Mafalda's paws.

"Closer together," the photographer urged as she attempted to perfectly capture two grooms in their stunning Joshua Tree backyard, the love between them obvious to anyone who cared to look. After a casual cocktail hour, Norman and Jesse would be remarried. Lally would officiate, ordained with a certificate she'd obtained online. Gail was present, too, although in a less official capacity; since she'd ditched her signature turtleneck for the occasion she refused to take part in pictures of the wedding party, and mingled off to the side with a mysterious man roughly her age whom she'd brought as a date.

"Who is that?" Norman whispered, looking skeptically at the late addition.

"The fuck if I know," Jesse replied before turning to strike another pose. He hated the thought of losing control of the day, but lately he had been learning to let go.

They both fussed over Robbie Jay, the flower girl, as she joined them for a photo; she was already almost one. Roberta Jesse, they had named her, after Robbie Alfano and Jesse del Ruth Sr., two loved ones who were there with them only in spirit. She had dark hair like Norman and Lally, accompanied by surprisingly full brows for her age, and was in the highest percentile for height—in short, perfect. Mafalda followed guests around, waiting for them to spill, or to be rewarded with nibbles from weak-willed friends. And from Randall, who was short enough that his plate was always within reach.

"Hey!" their neighbor screamed as Mafalda grabbed yet another morsel from his plate, running under the trees to hide. Norman stepped in to intercede, leading Randall back to the charcuterie as they talked business; Randall had hired Norman to design a new build on his land, and they were about to break ground any day. "You can do the foundation," he'd joked to Jesse earlier. "My wedding gift to you. I know how much you like to dig."

"I don't get a plus-one to my own son's wedding?" Gail protested when Jesse pressed her on bringing a guest.

"I just . . ." Jesse began. He didn't understand. "Who *is* he?"

"Travis?" Gail called, beckoning her date away from his conversation with Harlan. Jesse stood agog as the man, lean with gray hair and a neatly trimmed beard to match, approached. "Travis Funt, I want you to meet Jesse del Ruth."

The man hesitated before extending his hand. *Great*, Jesse thought. His mother had invited a homophobe to his wedding. But when they did finally shake the man's eyes watered and he pulled Jesse into a tight hug. Jesse looked over the man's shoulder at his mother, who just looked annoyed once again that men couldn't keep their emotions in check.

"Now that's a name I haven't heard in a long time. Not since

1974 in Saigon." Travis loosened his grip but still held on to Jesse by his arms. "Let me get a good look at you. You're the spitting image of him."

"Of who?" Jesse asked, confused.

Travis Funt cocked his head to one side. "Your father."

Jesse looked around to see if he was being pranked. "I don't understand," he began. "You knew my father?"

Travis nodded. "I served with him on his last assignment."

Jesse started sweating, and he stuck two fingers under his collar in an attempt to loosen it. "Do you know what happened?"

Travis let go and looked down sorrowfully at his feet. "I'm afraid I don't, son."

Jesse forced a deep breath from his body. *Of course not.* That would be too easy.

Travis looked at Gail, and then back at Jesse. "But I do know he was excited about you. Boy was he ever. The last night I saw him, you were all he could talk about."

Jesse began to cry. *How?* he mouthed to his mother.

Gail looked away so as not to make a big deal. "I came across some old letters from your father and they mentioned Travis by name. From there, I found him on Facebook. It wasn't that hard."

Jesse couldn't wait to torture Harlan with this information. When she wanted to locate someone, his mother had done so in minutes.

"Everything okay over here?" Norman asked, sensing an energy that was different from the rest of the crowd. "Gail, who's your guest?"

It was Jesse who answered. "I don't think he's a guest so much as a gift."

"Oh, speaking of gifts," Norman said, and excused himself to dash off into the house. Jesse shook Travis's hand again. There was much more he wanted to say.

"This is a lot more fun than your last party," Luisa laughed in passing, her silver curls piled on top of her head. She was holding two plates of food, the second for her husband, who didn't seem nearly as awful as she'd always made him out to be, and who had Harlan deep in conversation about the Firebirds, the Coachella Valley's ice hockey franchise, an AHL expansion team. Luisa had put off retirement for another two years, giving Jesse a real shot at department chair.

"Let me help you with that," Travis offered as she struggled to also carry two drinks.

"Can you believe she brought him?" Jesse asked his mother about Luisa's husband once she was out of earshot. They both watched as Robbie Jay toddled over to join Mafalda at the tree line.

"Don't be so judgmental," Gail replied.

"Don't judge judgment," Jesse scoffed. "Judgment is all I have." Yet Luisa fed her husband a bite of crudité in a surprisingly tender display as they introduced themselves to Travis.

Gail looked around the lush backyard, family and friends dressed in their best milling about the pool. "Oh, I think you have a lot more than that." She downed the last of her champagne and added, "I wish your father was here to see this."

"Thanks to you, he is," Jesse replied, tapping his heart.

Gail fanned herself with a napkin. "It's always so hot. What is it with this town?"

"It's not a town," Jesse corrected. "It's a census-designated place."

Gail shook her head. On some level she would never understand her son.

Lally stepped forward with a fresh glass of champagne to offer his mother, under strict instructions from Jesse to keep them coming. They watched as Harlan joined Robbie Jay and Mafalda in the shade, lowering himself to the ground with surprising dexterity.

"He's such a good dad," Lally observed, and it made Jesse happy. But when he didn't reply she shot him a threatening look. "You're uncharacteristically quiet. Don't tell me you have cold feet."

"In this heat?" Jesse laughed. But then added sincerely, "Not even a little bit."

Norman reappeared by their side. "Did I hear something about cold feet? In that case, you'd better try these on." He handed Jesse an oversized box. When Jesse took the gift, he found it surprisingly heavy and struggled to keep from dropping it.

"What's this?" he asked, already judging that it wasn't wrapped.

"Open it," Norman instructed. "I found them in the garage when you were gone."

Gone. Jesse peeled the lid off the box, revealing his old Rollerblades. "Oh my god. I can't believe we moved these to the desert." Norman had been right to be critical of his packing.

Norman beamed, but while touched, Jesse was a tad confused.

"Why are you giving these to me now?"

"Look at the brand."

Jesse squinted under the sun, and turned to hold the box in the shade so he could see. They were something called the Macroblade in neutral and gray, a four-wheel inline skate manufactured by a company called Alpha. "So?" Jesse asked, still missing the point.

Norman slapped his forehead. "The psychic? Julia? She saw the letters *ALF*."

Jesse frowned. "'Alpha' is spelled with a *ph*."

Norman grabbed one of the skates. "But look." The curl of the *P* was partially worn so that it resembled the letter *F*. Norman smiled, obviously pleased with himself.

Jesse still thought it was a stretch, but he wasn't going to let anything ruin this day. "You're right," he said, and only Lally saw him gently roll his eyes before he kissed Norman on the cheek.

The truth of the matter is that it was a miracle they met, that any two people destined for each other do. They should have done everything they could to stay together, fought tooth and nail in ways big and small, before drastic measures were taken. They would never make the same mistakes again. *No,* Norman delighted. *All our mistakes will be new.*

"I didn't get you anything," Jesse fretted. Norman relieved Jesse of the box, setting it aside for later.

"I like myself better when I'm with you. That's a tremendous gift in itself." He put his hand on the small of Jesse's back. "I'm sorry I had forgotten."

Jesse was sorry, too.

"That's marriage, isn't it?" Lally observed, eyes suddenly trained on Harlan. Maybe it would be their turn next. "Two people who see the best of themselves in each other."

Jesse liked the way that sounded. "Are you ready?" he asked, turning to face Norman.

"I'll get the flower girl." Lally headed over to fetch Robbie Jay so the ceremony could properly begin. Harlan was whispering in the girl's ear, and she threw her head back and laughed. When she saw her mother all dressed up, she stopped laughing and clapped.

"Robbie Jay," Norman whispered.

"Can you believe all this we've built together?" *What a trip.*

Norman agreed. "And all we still have yet to build."

Jesse took Norman's hand, eager to be his husband again. "Where you go, I go."

Norman's eyes grew wet. "Where you go, I go," he repeated.

I promise it will be an adventure.

ACKNOWLEDGMENTS

Justice Anthony Kennedy, in writing for the majority in *Obergefell v. Hodges*, the Supreme Court decision that decided marriage equality, said that "marriage responds to the universal fear that a lonely person might call out only to find no one there." Not a bad jumping-off point for a novel.

Like Norman and Jesse, I came of age at a time when marriage equality seemed like an impossible dream. As a young man, I never imagined myself married, let alone writing a book about marriage and relationships, and so I owe an incredible debt of gratitude to the many incredible pioneers who gave so much of themselves to pave the way for this most basic civil right. While marriage equality is now the law of the land, we must always be aware that newfound rights and freedoms are fragile, and to those who continue the fight for equality, I thank you, too.

For many years I was not just a lonely person calling out to find no one there, but a lonely *writer,* and so I am fortunate now to have a true creative partner in Rob Weisbach, my agent of more than a decade. I don't know how he does it, but he delivers even bad news with such warmth that it leaves us both laughing and turning the page. This would be no fun without you.

I'm also indebted to my editor, Kate Dresser, who was so generous with her own bright light, championing this book from pitch through final pass, always reminding me that this was a book about our very human need for connection. Our yearning for it, our complacency with it, the tragedy in falling short of it. I'm grateful you connected so deeply with this idea.

Take Me with You is my sixth book with G. P. Putnam's Sons, and I'm grateful to work with some of the best in the business. Ivan Held, Lindsay Sagnette, Alexis Welby, Ashley McClay, Molly Pieper, Jazmin Miller, and especially Katie McKee and Tarini Sipahimalani, who always go above and beyond, I'm lucky to have you not only as teammates but as friends. Additionally, I'm eternally thankful for the great Sally Kim and the opportunities she gave me. Many readers stop me to rave about my covers and this may be my favorite yet. I have the incredibly talented Tal Goretsky to thank.

This marks ten years since my debut novel was published. Ten years, seven adult titles, one children's book, and countless new friends in a tough business that often feels like it's built on rejection. I am blessed to have this career, and it's because of readers like you. I'm grateful for everyone who has read, bought, borrowed, recommended, reviewed, shared, or otherwise posted about one of my books. What an honor it is to have you on this journey with me.

Finally, one additional quote from Justice Kennedy. "The nature of marriage is that, through its enduring bond, two persons together can find other freedoms, such as expression, intimacy, and spirituality." And so to my husband Byron Lane, my family, my reason for everything, I say this: I'm so damn lucky that not only are we somehow, improbably, *impossibly* even, on this strange blue marble at the same time but that our two pathways collided forming one road we now walk together. We have built a life of creative expression, startling intimacy, and great exploration. While this book is not about our marriage, one thing holds true—where you go, I go. *Always.*

Photograph of the author © Afonso Salcedo

Steven Rowley is the *New York Times* bestselling author of six novels, including *Lily and the Octopus*, a *Washington Post* Notable Book; *The Editor*, an NPR Best Book of the Year; *The Guncle*, winner of the Thurber Prize for American Humor; and *The Celebrants*, a *Today* show Read with Jenna book club pick. His fiction has been translated into twenty languages. He resides in Palm Springs, California.

stevenrowley.com
MrStevenRowley